M000018767

Mooncallers
Stars Wake

Edited by Kat Powell and Leda C. Muir.
Proofread by Kat Powell and Jeff Walden.

Fonts created by Peter Rempel and Manfred Klein.
Cover illustration by Theodore Tryon.
Back cover illustration by Leda C. Muir.
Chapter illustrations by Leda C. Muir.
Maps by Leda C. Muir.
Book design by Leda C. Muir.

ISBN 978-0-692-09372-6

To my mom, the cultivator of my world.
To my dad, who taught me that creativity needs no degree.
To Kat, my best friend and real life Oliver Kross.
And to loneliness — the reason it all began.

MY WORDS TO YOU

THERE'S A world in every head, in every heart. We visit them in dreams, in memories, and in nightmares. Because of that world, all of us, at some period in all of our lives, experience a feeling.

"I want to go home."

That is from whence Amniven came. A yearning for escape that grew so real that it now exists for at least one person. This is a plane in which souls from any walk of life are welcome.

On this journey, you may meet friends, lovers, guardians, and enemies. Believe it if you will, every inhabitant of Amniven is as alive as you or I. They live within me, and my greatest wish is for them to live within you too. That being said, do not expect this land to be any kinder than the one in which you currently live. I will not promise you a safe haven, for only you can provide that for yourself.

Amongst these pages, you might discover hope, humor, joy, insight, strength, and perhaps even love. You might also discover poverty, inequality, hierarchy, war, hatred, judgment, and all else that is universally feared. Just like the world of humankind, this world suffers, its people suffer, and while reading, you may suffer too.

But without pain, this story never would have come to be.

Tel Ashir
Capital of Tzapodia

L'ARNETH

NAYFAR
OCEAN

BULLDEEP
SEA

SKYWAY SEA

ICENAILS

RELLING'S
STEAD

ORPINTON

REDNUT

LITTLE
BEAR

GONDOUTH

THE
ONESHELLS

TARHELEN

THE GREAT BRIDGE

FROSTEETH

BIG
BEAR

TREESHELTER

WARRELWICK

DIGGINS

WHULF
CRESCENT

CORAL
INHALE

STONEHALL

SNOWSCALES

MORDRINK

NORTHREACH

SEALEAP
BUNCH

COVE
OF TAR

THE GREY

DOLMEER

SELFWASTE

CATHNIR'S
MOUNT

LIRDSWITH

GOOSE

SH'TARR'S
IRIS

ROCKBLEED

FINGERS OF
THE HIGHLAND

RISE OF
REFLECTION

CADLESPEAK

GUT
LEAK

HARPY
PASS

WITCHWATER
BAY

NEXA
POINTS

SPIRIT BEND
STRAND

ISTENHEIM

ELDER'S
EXPANSE

SKREECH'S
RAKE

SNOWDANE

CASTGRAVE

CASTERLY
GREEN

STORMY
PLAINS

THREE
TOES

SEER'S
FOLLY

CROSSPEARS

FILANNIA

BARKBREATH
TAIGA

YUPPIN

TIMBERTON

ETERNITY'S
OCEAN

SHADEGIVERS

RAMENNE

GEST

NEVERSPEARS

BLUE
FINGERS

OUROS
ANGLE

LANDHEART

CONES
OF SALT

RILENITE

MAGDELEN

AVI
YEROMIN

SYL'VAR

THE
WOODMOUTHS

THE SALTSPIT

OWLSWOOD

THE
SPINE

GOOSE
RIBS

THE SWALLOW

WESTERN
WOODS

ERANNOR

TEEP
MUNTS

BLANK
SPIRAL

SELNILAR

LOR'TISANIN

THE
ARROWWOOD

DARKRACH

NAV'AMANI
FOREST

CAL'AM
RAWIN

STRAIT OF
THE CRYSTAL
SHIRE

PREMENOUS
SHOAL

VAULT
OF REINAN

ORCHIRIS

BOAL

A'MARU
MOUNTAINS

THIRSTING
COAST

AVI
TULANI

ROCKLUNG
CANYONS

QUARTEAN

THE
FIREBELT

TRIHOUL

TEL ASHIR

FORSEMEET

LITTLE
OF NIRATZ

ZAM
SAKAL

TZAPODIA

SAMSAMET'S
ROOST

THE CRUMBS

LINNA

THE
UNDERCRY

PASHNAN

ARATOIA
DESERT

JADA
JUNGLE

THE
BLIGHTWATER

EMBERTON

OMOROL

OUR
BLOOD

MINDALIA

OLD NARANIV

PSYCOVE

HEEPS

ISLE
OF VARNN

THE LONG
WAKE

KAH'TUA
EACTADII

KATEUR

NAN
JAAMI

TUME

STAIN OF
MOUNTAIN'S
FALL

TALAMINE
BREAK

BAS'DADA

NARANIV'S
ARMOR

SAINT'S
EYES

UNDERCROWN
OCEAN

KEY

🌙 CAPITOL CITIES

☾ CITIES

◇ TOWNS

ANUNARU

ETERNITY'S
REFUGE

The Great Bridge, Tarhelen

BIGHT OF
TEMPTATIONS

THE
STIGMA

Hildic
The Golden Ship

The
Flow

Contention
of Wadosia

Dulcinus

Timeless
Mountains

GOLDENRISE

BOOT TIP

Soursun

Nonatria

Pulvitae

SIN DE
AMARUS

Mirror
of Narosciun

Amberus

Snake's
Head

Witchsleep
Apparition

Passinon

Northern
Hoof

Woodsworos

Gooddeal

Hook's
Cliffs

ETERNITY'S
OCEAN

THE
WRAITHS

Ocaranth's
Tear

Meeoren

BURNING
TOWERS

She Devil's
Knot

Horizon
The Hanged

Anathema

Devil's
Tail

THE
WATERWEAVE

LACRYMA

The
Dumping Jne

Clowered
Eyes

Devil's
Nose

The
Shread

Tin
Shiela

Loom of
The Daughters

Orion of
Mirrors

TAROT

The
Wands

Bay
of Oil

The
Shining Crag

ANATATRI'S
REACH

Owinoung
Tagna

Ab'binon

Scythe of
The Beast

Scythe
of Alatos

Dunes
of Duhar

Unhibord

Maitab

Lukti
Tuteeu

Nomad's
Steppe

The Delta
of Hadinol

Sandblood

The
Phoenix
Gate

Hulsemet
The Sandstone
Spire

Xikaui
Muugtaisiii

Clakur

The Long
Mean

Ralumen's
Favor

Titan's
Barrow

TAMEDUCA
DESERT

XENEOA

Farnioan
Parti

Cradae

AGANUTA
DEPTHS

Hand
of Oag

Daetri's
Braid

ANK'TATRA

Tiger
Stripe

Utad

Lukti
Tuyuit

Qa

Bulabn

THE
DRIPSEA

REMNANTS
of Tunghaei

Oasis of
Black Wines

Pondsop
Nastantet

The Longing
of Hadio

Su
Evas

Ouyane

MINYAE'S
COVE

Halzanar

Row of
Blossoms

STRAIT OF
MANY EYES

SALTWOOD

Peaks
of Sunna

ORENUIT

CURVE
OF YAYUN

Hukong

Coudon
Bowl

Mount
Wuirdt

Wasuka

LANOMILR

Soulsplit
Streams

TABLE OF CONTENTS

EYES WIDE OPEN
2.VENOMSNARE.24.OSC.3

TWO YOUNG sages trudged through Nav Amani Forest, cursing and swinging buckets at their sides. It had been their day off, but here they were, harvesting riverroot for the head sage instead.

"I'd like to see Mollah do all this work for once," complained Lali.

"Sending us out today of all days," said Hanalea. "I love Mother, don't get me wrong, but she's the craziest bat I've ever met."

"Don't say that 'round her," chortled Lali. "Once swatted me with that broom she keeps in her bunk 'cause I called her slippers ugly."

The woods thinned out into a meadow. Hanalea and Lali patted the moisture off their cheeks as they neared Tal Am T'Navin River. Riverroot poked up through the fissures in the shallows, but most tufts were sad excuses. It wasn't a rare sort of greenery, but the bulk of it germinated in unlit crevices and was inconvenient to reap.

Hanalea bundled up her gown and knelt on the bank. She fished around, and her fingers brushed a slimy leaf. She tugged, and it came loose right away. The edges were brittle, but it would do.

Nearby, Lali popped a cigarette into her mouth and hit it with a match. As she puffed, she tucked her skirt into her waistband and shimmied her bloomers up over her hips.

Hanalea caught a whiff of the cigarette. "Where'd you get that, Lali? Mollah'll kill you for smoking!"

"Sounds like a fine way to die," cackled Lali. "I bought a pouch of roseleaf off a Trihoul spiv I met in Traplane. He smuggled it from The Grey, n' I tell you, Hana, it tastes like royalty."

"Can I try it?" asked Hanalea, smacking her lips.

"I paid good coin for this. Get your own," said Lali, trekking into the rapids. Belly-deep, she began to scavenge. "There's a load of riverroot over here. My bucket'll be fat while you get all the scraps Mollah ain't askin' for. By the time you . . . aahhh!"

"What's the matter?" asked Hanalea, dropping her pickings.

"D-dead —" Lali tripped and surfaced again with her cigarette drooping from her lips, "— there's a dead person!"

Hanalea saw Lali's bucket in the water. The runaway container clacked on protruding rocks as it was carried off. A feminine body was bobbing around beside it. Hanalea molted her cloak and dove into the river. A minute later, she broke through the surface and sputtered, "Go back to Tel Ashir and send for somebody! She might be alive!"

Lali turned tail for the greenwood without untucking her skirt.

Hanalea was yanked under as the river clutched at her ankles. Her vision was obscured by the algae around her, but she saw white hair up ahead. She gripped the drowned woman's arm, and her loafers slipped along the river bottom as she clambered back onto the shoreline.

The drowned woman's lips were blue, and she wasn't breathing. Hanalea implored, "No, please wake up!"

Hanalea compressed the woman's chest and pinched her chilly nose to offer her air. The woman coughed. She was alive but wavering in consciousness. Her eyelids fluttered and fell closed again.

In little more than twenty minutes, reptilian feet pattered out of Nav Amani Forest. Four rangers from Tel Ashir led by Lieutenant Claymore scurried into the meadow. Their saddled dracas hissed and dawdled about.

"Miss Moots!" called out Claymore.

"Lieutenant, thank you for coming!" exclaimed Hanalea. "Lali found this woman, and she needs medical attention! I couldn't take her to the infirmary myself."

"Leave this to us," insisted Claymore. He motioned to his rangers. "Vishera, you ride the quickest. Take the wounded."

A seroden elf in a tweedy scarf, Avari Vishera, scooped up the drowned woman. Avari was three-quarters her size but carried her with no struggle at all. She hoisted the woman onto her dracas' saddle, climbed up behind her, and flashed a Tzapodian salute. At her behest, her dracas, Elthevir, spat, and they rode out of view.

Claymore turned to Hanalea. "If you'd like transportation back to the city, I'll offer it."

"How kind, sir," said Hanalea, red as a cherry.

In the city of Tel Ashir, Elthevir shot through Riverpass, down the Trest Hillocks, and across Yula Montier to the Kingslane. All along the ride, city-folk dipped out of the way to avoid being trampled.

The dracas skittered up the Steps of Sevinus and barreled into a flock of castle keepers who were skulking in the Porranim Courtyard. The keepers glared at Avari. She mouthed, *'sorry.'*

Avari didn't want to wet her uniform by touching the drowned woman again, but duty called. Stretched onto her tiptoes, she slung the woman over her shoulder. She spanked Elthevir's flank and grunted, "Piss off, chubby. I'll be at the stables later — but don't crap in the trough again. I got in big trouble for that last time."

Venturing inside of Castle Lavrenthea excited Avari regardless if it was to drop off a victim for the healers. As she neared the infirmary, she bounced onto one foot and kicked in the door, bursting inside like a teensy battering ram.

"Afternoon, sages. We've got an emergency!" she broadcasted.

"There are patients sleeping!" hissed a wizened woman named Mother Mollah. She was the head sage and as stubborn as she was old.

"We've got new blood to save. I'm no professional, but I don't think she's supposed to be this floppy," said Avari, jostling the body.

"Don't go wigglin' her," said Mollah, hobbling off. "And don't track mud on the tiles. You'll make more work for my girls and me."

Avari lowered the drowned woman into the cot that Mollah chose. Mollah rested her dark, wrinkly fingertips on the woman's cheeks. "She's like a corpse. It's a wonder she's got any life in her. We'd best change her. These clothes are soakin' her to the bone."

Avari started popping open the buttons on the woman's gown, but it was stuck to her like a second skin. Mollah worked the dripping fabric out from under her, huffed, and tossed it into a wicker bin.

"Where was she found?" asked Mollah.

"Tal Am T'Navin River, 'bout an hour ago. Two of your girls spotted her. Littler one ran to Claymore with her pants in a bunch, screaming about a dead person," said Avari airily. "I wonder where this broad came from. Selnilar, maybe? She has to be l'arian elvish. She's got the pointy ears, and I ain't seen snowmen with whiter skin. Bit bizarre-looking."

Bizarre was one way to label the woman. Her features were alien, and her skin was pale to the point of translucence save for the lilac blush in her cheeks. Complementing her white eyebrows and lashes was a mass of wavy, white hair that framed her heart-shaped face.

"She's l'arian, no doubt," said Mollah confidently. "It wouldn't surprise me if she's from Selnilar. The l'arian elves don't tend to stray. Not many itchin' for change. Come to think of it, this is the first time I've seen a l'arian elf since last I sojourned Lor'thanin."

"I've only seen 'em in Lor'thanin too," said Avari, fitting a sleeve onto the woman's arm. "Her family's probably worried sick, don't you think? Or no — maybe she has a pooch or a kitty at home! What if it has nobody to take care of it? Mollah, we've got to track down —"

"Her pets will be fine, dear," tittered Mollah. Avari, however, was tormented by the image of a puppy sitting alone in a window. Mollah sighed, "I'm sure whoever's lookin' for her will find her. The l'arian population isn't high, so when one goes missing, they —"

"What's that on her neck?" asked Avari, baring her ratlike teeth.

Electric blue runes were inked into the right side of the woman's neck, a tattoo. The line-weight varied, and some strokes looked like they'd been executed in a rush. As far as Avari and Mollah were aware, it was in an unknown language.

"Haven't seen anything like this before. Don't find many girls with inked skin. Looks like she's had it for a long time. She must've gotten it when she was little," said Avari studiously. "Mollah, got any theories on why she's half-dead? Not often that I get to play the rescue game."

"I'm no detective, but we can take a look," huffed Mollah.

Mollah cupped the woman's cheeks and tipped her head. There were no distinguishing features aside from her neck tattoo. No scars or discolorations except for a few moles. As for wounds, Mollah found nothing at all. Apart from unconsciousness, she was healthy.

"Interesting. She isn't injured. No lesions, swelling, and her belly doesn't need to purge," said Mollah, peeking into the woman's mouth.

"So she's sleeping? Hells, maybe I'll pretend to be asleep if it gets me out of work for a few days," puffed Avari, suddenly bored. "I've been training dracas hatchlings nonstop. Lieutenant Claymore's been working my arse like a latrine."

"Sorry to hear. But nothin' good comes right away. If you've got to train some lizards in order to move up in the world, that's how it should be," said Mollah, pouring water into a cup.

"I could use some sympathy!" said Avari, cracking her finger like a whip. "I slave nonstop to teach those flatheads some common sense. Do they thank me? No. Does anyone thank me? Especially no."

"Hush," said Mollah, clinking a spoon to the lip of the teacup. "I won't keep you, but tell the fellas in the barracks to stop by if they're feeling puny. Now go train those dracas! It's what you do best."

" 'Course it is — till one eats my arm off," whined Avari.

"I'll be here to stitch you up," said Mollah sweetly.

Avari giggled and pulled her scarf up over her nose. With a fond wave, she left. The door slammed and startled a few sages.

Mollah leaned back in a padded chair and lifted the steeper in and out of the tea until the water was black. She set the piping cup on a dish to cool and fixed her cloudy eyes onto the woman from the river.

Two days passed. After watching the drowned woman constantly, old age was catching up with Mollah. Nasally honks came from her mouth, and her frazzled bun bounced every time her head swiveled.

". . . thnagh — huh? Ha!" Mollah's snoring got so loud that she woke herself up. The sages nearby laughed at her.

"You've got a bear stuck in your throat," chaffed one.

"Mother, you'll wake your patient early!" jested another.

Little did Mollah's joking employees expect to be right.

The drowned woman suddenly exhibited signs of consciousness. Three sages scuttled to the bedside, a freckled girl, a thickset woman with bushy eyebrows, and one with a face like a baby's.

The drowned woman nestled her head into the pillow like a child having a nightmare. Her white eyelashes trembled, and she blinked vertiginously. It was liberating for her to see again. For a time, she'd been stuck in darkness with no feeling at all.

The woman lolled her head to the right and saw ogee-arched windows with sheer curtains. Shelves lined the spaces between them with glass jars and twisty plants upon them. Sunlight glowed through an open doorway, and it made her eyes ache.

The woman peered up and met the blurry faces of four sages. Her eyes opened all the way. The sages' mouths sagged in awe.

"Her eyes . . . look at them!" said Freckles.

"I see them," said Bushy-brow.

"Mother, what's wrong with 'em? Is she blind?" asked Baby-face.

To test, Mollah waved her hand. The woman's eyes followed. "No, she can see just fine."

The woman was uncomfortable with so many strangers staring at her. Mollah swatted her sages with a rag and said, "Scat!" She smiled at the woman. "I'm delighted to see you up and at 'em. My name's Mollah, but you can call me Mother Mollah. Do you speak common?"

The woman breathed, "Yes. You said . . . my eyes?"

"I hope I didn't offend you. I've only never seen any eyes like yours, and I've seen a good few in my day," said Mollah spryly.

The woman crossed her eyes. "What's wrong with them?"

"Nothing's wrong, they're just — what, you don't know your own eyes?" asked Mollah lightly. The woman shook her head at once.

Mollah rummaged through the nightstand drawer and revealed a hand mirror. The woman focused past the blotches in the glass, and her eyes locked with the ones peering back. All things were abstruse, but she was most unsure how to perceive her own reflection.

Concealing her pupils was a universe of starlight like one might see lying face-up on the clearest eve of sunrae, or the constellations past the eye of a telescope. They held everything that the night sky did: novas of no exact color, fluidic hues of blues, blacks, yellows, greens, and violets. She even spotted silvery falling stars.

Beyond their cosmic design was an inverted feeling. Parts seemed out of place like she'd been rearranged. She felt the controlled temperature of the air, counted the wrinkles in Mollah's cheeks, heard the clinking glassware, and tasted her cottony tastebuds, but she was given the impression that she was intruding. She felt with someone else's skin, viewed through someone else's eyes, listened by someone else's ear, and tasted on someone else's tongue.

Should encountering oneself be such an external experience?

The woman then realized that she had not the slightest idea where she was. "What is this place?" she asked.

"I should've told you when you came to," said Mollah shamefully. "You're in Tel Ashir, child. You were found in Tal Am T'Navin River a few days back. Do you know how you got there?"

Tel Ashir, Tal Am T'Navin River, and how she'd gotten there? The woman's head was crowded with new information, and that's what alarmed her the most — all of it was *new* information.

The woman turned back in retrospect. She found bits and pieces of the past, but the rest had been carried someplace far away. One was a view of the twilight sky through black tree branches that wound into springy coils. The next was an echo of a man who sounded angry at her. Another was a sweet taste, but it was too hot to drink. There was the spice of the forest, parched like it hadn't rained for a while.

All else was missing, handprints upon a glass that she couldn't break. The woman tried to feel anything at all, but it was impossible. She was astray in a maze of veins and cramped in a cage of bones.

Her starry eyes pulsed to grey. "Who am I?"

"You can't remember?"

"No."

Mollah's face drooped. She'd uncovered no head trauma, so if this woman was suffering amnesia with no injury tied to it, there was no saying how or when she would get her memories back.

"Oh, we'll find out who you are," said Mollah consolingly. "This must be frightening, but stay calm. Losing your head won't help you find it again."

Mollah's words were more comprehensible to the woman than her own thoughts. What other action could she have taken? Forcing her memories into place was no option because there were none as it was. She ferreted for a reason to distrust Mollah, but she came up empty-handed. Surrendering to vanished selfhood, she made herself comfortable.

"I'll take care of you till you've recovered. We'll take small steps. One thing at a time," whistled Mollah. "How about I make you tea? Sleepthistle, perhaps? Gentle on the senses!"

As Mollah brewed a pot of tea, the woman fiddled with the buttons on her gown and stared at the window over her head. Shafts of light seeped through the glass and tinted the walls poppy red. She couldn't see through it, but she could tell that the day was dying.

The setting of the sun, the Tehrastar, felt familiar but not close. No faces, no names, no home, but she knew sunsets, and that was enough for now.

All that the woman could do then was let healing run its course. She would be grateful to recover who she once was, but if she failed to, she would have no remorse.

It was comforting like a bad habit.

If she couldn't remember, she couldn't feel guilty for forgetting.

Siren
7.Venomsnare.24.Osc.3

With a wealth of tea and cheese inside her belly, the woman's recuperative process moved swiftly. She and Mollah had broken down the silence barrier and found that they got along well.

There were few activities in which to partake while confined to a cot, so Mollah suggested that the woman assist her in organizing her belongings. They rifled through a wraithwood crate overstuffed with dried flowers and keepsakes that Mollah had collected. The woman worked out a sheet of paper from under a tangle of chains. None of them had charms attached, but Mollah had to have been hoarding them for something.

On the page was a graphite sketch of a forest and a rivulet. The light of the Tehrastar was daubed across the mountaintops in white pigment. Upon the hill at the bottom front sat a figure in a sunhat. Their face was smudged, but she could tell they were smiling.

"This is pretty, Mother," said the woman admiringly.

"Been a while since I've seen that old thing," gasped Mollah. "My lover drew it for me. This is one of, oh, hundreds of his pieces. Take your eyes off 'im for a second, and he'd draw ya! Sketched this on our seventh year together. See that at the bottom? That's yours truly."

The woman should've known. Mollah smiled just like the person in the drawing. "How did you two meet?" she asked.

"Well, believe it or not, all the men in Tzapodia wanted a thick slice of Miss Mollah. I was quite a catch back then," sang Mollah.

"Back then?" asked the woman kittenishly.

"What a suck," said Mollah, batting the woman's arm. The woman grinned. "But out of all the fine lads, I found the one I wanted. I was buying roots in the bazaar when he said to me: *'madam, I'd like to paint you.'* Wasn't long till he asked me to be his wife. Willem Felloen's his name. He's gone, but I'm still mad for that old fool."

"Gone whe — oh." The woman frowned. "I'm sorry, I —"

"Don't be sorry," said Mollah, adjusting her thick-rimmed glasses even though they were already straight. "My Willem went helpin' someone who needed it, and he didn't regret it. I'll be with him again when my time comes . . . right on top of that hill."

The woman thought that Mollah was the toughest person alive. She reviewed the sketch, and the lines seemed more distinct now. She lamented over the man that Mollah loved who lay on a hill under a bed of wildflowers.

Death, thought the woman. She imagined what it would feel like if Mother Mollah went away and never came back again. Her chest ached at the prospect. They'd only just met, but that old woman was all she knew.

"I'm sorry you lost him, Mollah," sniffled the woman.

Mollah gave her a toad-like smile. "Death is a part of the course life follows, Starlight. When that course comes to an end, we rise to Eletheon, a realm of pure love and no more hurt. I tell ya, one day when Oscerin carries me there, my legs won't be stiff no more!"

The woman was then stricken by an emotion that she hadn't yet felt: fear. She sank through words of love and drowned in the notion that death gave you a new home, but what about her? The world was right outside, but she had no place in it. She knew that the sages couldn't shelter her forever. When she healed, she would be deserted to waste away into dust.

"Mother, where will I go from here?" entreated the woman. "I can't take up space in your infirmary for much longer, but I really don't have anywhere else."

"You're certainly right, but I've thought about this already," said Mollah, squeezing the woman's hand. "This world can be a cruel one without a roof over your head, and I would never put a girl like you on the streets alone. I have an idea that might solve your problem, and I think you'll fancy it."

Mollah was acquainted with a ranger in the Tel Ashian military named Avari Vishera who needed an apprentice. She was dinky in size but tough as nails with an energy like a toddler who had eaten a pinch too much sugar.

The woman didn't know what requirements had to be met to be a ranger, and she was unsure of her caliber of physical endurance, but she didn't wish to face life without a place to live. The woman agreed to a meeting the next day.

As they waited, the woman and Mollah assembled a snack platter with squares of tuma bread and slices of marbled cheese. This was a run-of-the-mill brunch in the infirmary. The woman glanced at Mollah, who stood over a head shorter. As she sliced and sliced, she wondered if perhaps there was an inordinate supply of grain and dairy in Tel Ashir, or if Mollah simply relished eating the same two things every day.

"Be careful with that knife," said Mollah, adjusting the woman's fingers into a safer position. "If you curl them like this, you won't get 'em caught by the blade. Remember that, won't you?"

"Sorry. I'll remember," said the woman, cutting as instructed.

"Good girl. You'll be a chef in no time," said Mollah buoyantly.

"You're flattering me, Mother. These look like mountaintops to me," said the woman, dangling two pieces of bread in front of her.

The infirmary door nearly flew off of its hinges. A brain-rattling voice announced, "Mother Mollah! I came as fast as I could!"

Across the way was a ranger, wee and blonde at the head with pointy ears sprouting from her explosively curly hair. It looked as though it had been a day or five since she'd bathed. Unlike the girls employed in the infirmary with ankle skirts and collared throats, she sported constricting leggings, dagger holsters, and a green scarf that buried half of her face. The woman struggled to imagine how loud she would be without fabric muffling her mouth.

"There you are, Avari. I was hoping you'd show up soon and not go hollering, but we can't have everything we ask for," said Mollah, grumbling the second half of her greeting.

From over a foot lower, Avari eyeballed the woman. "You finally got up. Good. Great. What's your name, girly?"

Mollah brought her palm to her face. Of course, the initial question that Avari had was one that the woman was incapable of answering.

"I'm not sure," said the woman with an insouciant shrug.

"Ha? You don't know?" wheezed Avari.

"No, she doesn't," confirmed Mollah. "That's why I called you here, Avari. I wanted to ask you if —"

"Is that cheese?" asked Avari with a hankering for the snacks.

"I — *yes,* it is," said Mollah, stepping in front of the platter. "But you don't get a single slice till you cool your broilers and listen."

"Sorry," murmured Avari. The woman took a mental note that cheese seemed to be a compelling incentive for Avari Vishera.

"Thank you," puffed Mollah. "Yes, she has no recollection of who she was, and hereat, she doesn't got a place to go. We can't have her wandering 'round Tel Ashir, so I thought you could take her in."

"She tells you she doesn't have memories, and your first thought is: *'I should fetch Avari?'* " laughed Avari.

Mollah sternly gestured to the cot. Avari flopped onto the mattress. The woman helped Mollah into her seat, and Avari was impressed by her inclination to assist. Then she caught a glimpse of her starry eyes.

"Woah!" screamed Avari, nearly rocketing off of the cot. She pointed at the woman's face, and she went crosseyed. "Those are stars! What are they doing?"

"Avari, it's rude to point," said Mollah reprovingly.

"But —"

"No buts," said Mollah, rock hard.

"Fine, fine," moaned Avari. She reached for a cheese slice, but Mollah swatted her hand. "Ouch — hey! But you said —"

"*After* you get to know her," said Mollah crossly.

"Damn it all," said Avari, nettled. She audited the woman. "Okay, so you're feeling well enough, but you don't have anywhere to go because you can't tell a horse from your own left hand?"

The woman stared at her left hand. "Er, yes, but I *can* —"

"If there were room amongst the sages, I'd offer her a position, but we're full. She's bright, great at taking directions, and a wonder at slicing bread too!" cheeped Mollah. The woman shook her head to warn Avari that she was, in fact, no good at cutting anything.

Avari pinched her chin and meditated on the proposal. It was beneficial to both parties; the woman would have a home, and Avari would have aid with the grueling work of a ranger. Her only concerns were minor. She prayed that the woman wouldn't turn out to be lazy, incompetent, or worse — *a pervert.*

Worries aside, Avari entertained the idea. An apprentice might be like a younger sibling, a personal assistant, or a pet. She could train the woman how to light a fire, pitch knives, and fillet a fish. They could go riding on missions and bunk in the barracks. Avari waded through a sea of revelries and finally said, "I'll take her."

"You will?" asked the woman, stars turning yellow. "Avari, I don't know how to be a ranger, but I promise I'll do my best to —"

"You're precious," tittered Avari. "You'd help me in the field and do deliveries is all. You're tall and heavy in the legs, so you won't be all that sneaky." The woman frowned at her thighs. "But I'll teach you whatever else I know about combat and all that ranger-y nonsense."

"It'd be a gainful opportunity to work with Avari, Starlight," said Mollah positively. "Avari is the second-in-command to a member of the Speaker's Mooncaller Council. That's not an easy rank to achieve. Also, Avari, you can have cheese now."

"Yes," hissed Avari.

The woman watched as Avari vacuumed cheese into her mouth. She didn't come across as conscientious, but she carried herself boldly, and the woman was delighted by that. She nibbled on a cheese wedge of her own.

"So what's the Speaker and the Mooncallers?" she asked.

Avari stopped chewing. "Mollah, you —" she hacked, swallowed, and tried again, "— you didn't tell her about the Mooncallers or the Speaker? She's been loafing in His Highness' castle all this time!"

"She still doesn't even know her own name. Tellin' her about Ares and the Mooncallers might be too much to handle," said Mollah.

Eyes on the woman, Avari puffed up like a puppy who thought it was bigger than other dogs. "Since Mollah doesn't want to do it, I'll brief you on how things work around Tel Ashir. All right, kiddo? If you're my apprentice, you'll be in the Tzapodian military which means you'll also be a member of the Mooncallers under the jurisdiction of the Prince of Tzapodia — also known as the Speaker — Ares Lavrenthea. That too complicated?"

The woman's stars bounced from thought to thought. "What I've gathered is: Tel Ashir is, I'm guessing, the capital of Tzapodia. I would be operating under you, a ranger, as part of the army of Tzapodia. The job would deem me a Mooncaller, and the Mooncallers heed to the authority of the Speaker and Prince Ares Lavrenthea. Is that correct?"

"Are you a sponge?" wheezed Avari.

"Got that scholarly air about you all of a sudden," said Mollah, offering the woman a slice of bread as a reward.

Avari approved of her apprentice's astute mind. "Smarty-Marty. But everything you repeated is right. Next, the Mooncallers are an organization that fights in the name of Oscerin the Moon Goddess."

"You really think a goddess exists?" asked the woman skeptically.

"Firstly, there are ten goddesses, not one," said Avari as she licked cheese and dirt from her fingers. "Why do we follow the Goddess of the Moon, and how do we know She exists? That's where the Speaker comes in. Ares Lavrenthea can hear Oscerin's voice. She talks to him, warns him about things, and tells him what to do or not do."

"See, Oscerin is one of the three *greater* divines who holds power over the other gods and goddesses. That's why it blew the world away when Ares came out as Her prophet. No one that Amniven knows of has ever had a direct link to one of the greater divines. So we follow Ares, Ares follows Oscerin, and you're in Castle Lavrenthea right now. This is Ares' infirmary, his city, his kingdom, and we're his Mooncallers."

Avari devoured the last few pieces and went on, "I've seen the Speaker once or twice since living here, and all that Oscerin tells him is extraordinary. I've heard His Highness is a big, ol' prick, but it's worth sitting through his addresses to find out what Oscerin's saying."

"Don't dirty Ares! You'd be pissy too if you had to keep your eyes on a country, Avari," scolded Mollah. "He just likes to watch folks squirm every now and then, but Tzapodia is in good hands. I've known Ares for decades. Under that thorny attitude is a sweetheart."

Avari coughed cheese onto the bedsheets. " *'A sweetheart.'* And I built *Thali ou Tirima,"* she laughed.

As Avari and Mollah squabbled about the Speaker's personality traits, the woman got bored and stacked bread into the shape of a house on the plate. When she was done, they were *still* bickering. The woman flicked her bread house, and it collapsed.

"I think I understand," she said, pulling her wavy hair over her shoulder. "Apart from all that, thank you both for —"

"Oh, right! What's that on your neck?" asked Avari, pointing like Mollah had said not to.

"My neck?" gulped the woman.

"I forgot about that," said Mollah, collecting her hand mirror.

"What's on my neck?" asked the woman again, panicking a bit.

Mollah handed the woman the mirror. She positioned it to reflect the tattoo. She saw two dark blue markings curled like letters. The stars in her eyes went still, and her mind was cloudy but crystal clear.

There was a memory.

14.SOFTSTEP.9.OSC.3

It had been three hours. She wished she'd brought her coat. The door opened. A faceless figure entered with papers in their hands. They slid out the top page and slapped it onto the table.

"Forgive the wait," said the faceless man. "Print your first and last name here, and we can begin."

"Do I have to?" she whimpered. Her voice was small, a child's.

"Yes, you have to."

Her teeth chattered as she dipped the feather quill into the ink pot. It saturated a little, but she didn't want to get it wetter perchance it bled. She scribbled her first and last name in the blank.

The faceless man handed the form to a second figure. "Her name's here. Dark blue. Her neck should be suitable."

She felt gloves brush her nape as they batted away her hair. She strained not to move, but it was difficult under the needle pokes. Her knuckles turned white, and she became dark blue.

The woman touched the ink, reliving every stab that had brought it to life. She hadn't wanted it then, but now it granted her a gift she'd thought she would never have again.

"This says my name," whispered the woman.

"Are you sure? Oh, that's wonderful!" gasped Mollah.

"You have your name tattooed on you?" snorted Avari. "Better than having an old flame's name in your neck. What language is that?"

"I'm not sure, I can't read it. I signed my name on a release form and recognize it enough to know what it says," answered the woman.

"Mysterious," said Avari. "Well, now we'll have something to call you by in the barracks, and we can search you up in the registries too. The Speaker's keepers've got up-to-date records on everybody in L'arneth."

Avari gleamed at the woman. "So what's your name?"

The stars twinkled green. She wished to keep it a secret so that she wouldn't lose it again, but she was also too excited to stay quiet.

"My name is Luxea Siren."

Beginner's Luck
10.Kingsreign.24.Osc.3

It had been upwards of forty days since Luxea Siren had woken up. After learning her name, Avari had requested records on women named *'Luxea Siren'* in L'arneth, but nowhere in Tzapodia's legal offices was there any information. Three women were on file with the name *'Luxea.'* Two were in Selnilar and had been accounted for, and one had lived on the outskirts of Harpy Pass, but it had been noted that she and her family had migrated to The Grey two years ago.

Luxea was not hurt by this. A part of her had sensed that there'd be nil. If someone was looking for her, they would find her, but until then, there was nothing to be done. She wondered from time to time who she'd been before the river, but she was learning to let go.

Avari found joy in teaching tips and tricks on stealth and combat tactics, but such a physically demanding job was not Luxea's forte. She made every effort to adapt to the rambunctious barracks lifestyle, but it felt like cramming a circle into a square.

"Morning, Siren!" said a man from the barracks hearth.

"Morning, sir!" said Luxea, heaving a crate of uniforms inside. Greeting her was the Chief of Border Patrol, Lorian Demartiet. He'd been remarkably helpful in Luxea's enrollment and taught her to feel accepted. As a felenoe, he had a build like a puma. His tawny eyebrows climbed past the line of his sienna hair to his floppy ears.

"How's your day?" asked Demartiet, catching his coat on a hook.

"Tiring," said Luxea, prying off the lid of the crate. "I think I'll have to start getting to bed earlier if I'm ever going to — uh oh."

Demartiet's whiskers prickled. "What is it?" he asked.

"The tailors messed up the seams again. They're supposed to be silver, aren't they?" asked Luxea, unveiling a uniform.

"Damned coots! This is the third time. Who did we hire to stitch these uniforms? Goats?" growled Demartiet.

"They'd look worse if goats were in the picture, sir," said Luxea, folding the jerkin again. "In any case, can I help you with anything, Chief? Paperwork? Errands? Preferably paperwork."

Demartiet scoured through his immigration forms and vacantly plucked a rogue hair out of his ear. "There's a task I have on my to-do list if you can stop by the Sapphire Bazaar," he said, stamping the top page. "I'd appreciate it if you'd take care of the disturbance."

"Disturbance?" parroted Luxea. "Sir, I don't think I'm qualified to fight off vandals or slap anyone into irons."

"It isn't that sort of emergency," said Demartiet with a fanged grin. "Elder Meyama at the fruit stand has been reporting that somebody's mixing her brineberries into the Emeraldei apple bin."

"Oh. How exhilarating," said Luxea remotely.

Demartiet frowned. "What do the Mooncallers stand for, Siren?"

Luxea boosted her shoulders. "As the Mooncallers, we must always offer our help to those in need, sir!" she recited.

"That's my girl! Get on out there and pick through some apples and berries," said Demartiet, curling his tail around his chair.

"Yes, sir!" beeped Luxea.

The Sapphire Bazaar inhaled coin and exhaled goods. It was a circus of food, tapestries, baskets, jewelry, rugs, perfumes, lamps, and all else one could imagine. The awnings varied in color and design. Some tents presented the name of the store or the items that they sold, but others were blank. Customers found those more tempting because they gave them nothing to expect.

Luxea wove through the quilted streets like a needle and dodged sales pitches. A woman in a red tent tried to splash her with wildflower extracts from the Western Woods. A man who had enough scarves on his head to warm a whole family nearly stabbed her with a skewer of sugar melon. One gentleman lectured her on Tzapodia's real estate and promised to alleviate the pain of her assumed outstanding mortgage.

The zoo of materialistic revelry got busier the deeper that Luxea traveled. Musicians competed to play their tunes the loudest, poets yowled in various tongues, and illusionists awed bystanders with parlor tricks. A sorcerer pulled flowers out of his sleeve and distributed them to passing maidens.

"Amma! Salma, a'falani! Flowers!" squealed a little boy.

"Vith. I see them, *Lalen,"* said his mother.

Luxea slipped into the crowd to observe. The sorcerer was tall with an even taller black hat, and grey hair puffed out from the brim like dirty cotton. He plucked a falscreamer out of his hat and grinned dazzlingly. The falscreamer, of course, screamed as he paraded it around, and it continued to do so when he released it into the air.

His onlookers were inspired, but Luxea's spirits were dampened. She wished that she could give people happiness like that. Taking a last look at the cheering little boy, she ducked out of the crowd.

Ten paces, twenty, and there was Elder Meyama's fruit stand. It was an orange and red striped tent with white bunting that appeared to have had a life longer than Luxea's. Meyama was crooked over a table with two bronzes and a sterling in her palm.

"Welcome! Are ye here for fruits, miss?" asked Meyama, sounding like the scent of fallen leaves.

"No, ma'am. I'm here to help with your misplaced berries," said Luxea formally. "Do you know who might be moving them around?"

"Mayhap one of them grease-lovin' seroden folk. Always sneakin' around, those ones," said Meyama as she dug through her apple bin.

Several apples spilled and rolled to Luxea's toes, but Elder Meyama didn't notice. Luxea, a public servant, packed the apples into her arms, bending again and again as more fruit poured over the edge of the bin.

"Here's one of them squishy buggers," said Meyama, scowling at a single brineberry between her fingers. Then she scowled at Luxea instead. "Where'd you get them apples? Was you stealin' my apples?"

"What — ? No, of course, not!" shrieked Luxea.

"It ain't the serodens Tzapodia's got to worry about, it's you thievin' l'arians!" screeched Meyama.

A crowd gathered around the tent, and allegations of what people thought was a heist were pitched at Luxea like tomatoes — or apples.

"Rapscallion!"

"She's a criminal!"

"Drajn nil baksha!"

Luxea was sure that she would be expelled from the military or maybe be put to death. Just as her nerves hit their breaking point, a tingling sensation shot down her arms, and — *POP! POP!*

Every apple in Luxea's arms exploded. Pulp was everywhere, clinging to the breast of her uniform and hanging from her hair. All she knew was apple.

Meyama was varnished in a moist layer of juice, and her face was as red as the brineberry in her hand. She obliterated the berry, whisked a cane off of the ground, and yowled, "Git! Git! Somebody, help me!"

Luxea shielded herself as Meyama battered her with the walking stick. When she was about to run, a man shouted, "Move out, please!"

An armored hand clutched the walking stick. It was Chief Lorian Demartiet. "Meyama, we just received an anonymous tip that *you* are the one who has been putting the brineberries into the apple bin. I'll hear no more accusations on Miss Siren's behalf."

"She was doing it herself?" gasped Luxea.

She left with Chief Demartiet. At the barracks door, he turned her to face him. He looked stern at first, but then he softened and drummed his catlike fingers on top of her head.

"Take the rest of the afternoon off and get clean," he instructed. "It was an accident, so don't beat yourself up. Go on."

Luxea went inside. Men and women of all shapes and races lounged around tables chatting over ales. Luxea tried not to draw attention to herself, but everybody was wondering what in this good world had happened to her.

Luxea fell into a walk of shame to the baths. Just then, Avari rounded a corner and smacked right into her. "Gah — oh, it's you!" Avari sniffed the air. "Get caught in the crossfire of a food fight?"

"No," drawled Luxea. "Some apples exploded."

"You sure you didn't go hog-wild on your lunch break? Your appetite gets scary sometimes, kiddo," said Avari flippantly.

"Stop. I just want to forget about it," sighed Luxea.

"Go and shower off. Hurry! I've got lots to tell you about my day with the lizards," said Avari, peeling a shred of apple from Luxea's sticky back and eating it.

Several soldiers cackled as Luxea left. Avari threw a knife at them.

Fifteen minutes later, Luxea exited the baths dressed in a fresh set of linens. She was pleased to see that the soldiers were ignoring her. As she ambled to the bunks, she heard a shout.

"THAT'S A FOUL!"

Avari was using her *'winner's voice'* and leaning over a Dragon Stones setup. Dragon Stones was a game with six circles etched into the board, and a groove with a dragon's eye painted in the center. The objective was to toss bloodstones into the middle. Serious participants engaged in *Extreme* Dragon Stones, where the bloodstones were heated over a fire beforehand. Only drunkards or those who weren't afraid of first-degree burns ever played it that way.

"That's nowhere near the second ring, you failure," scoffed Avari.

"Look here, that *is* the second ring!" shouted her competitor, a man named Yaani. "C'mon, I wagered all my earnings on this toss."

"Maybe you should have better aim," taunted Avari.

"I need a second opinion!" yowled Yaani. His bloodshot eyes caught onto Luxea. "Siren, tell your sore mentor that this is over the second ring."

"She'll give you the same answer: f-o-w-l," snarked Avari.

"It's *'f-o-u-l.'* Fowls are chickens," stated Luxea. "Fine. I'll look."

"Thank ye, apple girl," said Yaani snidely.

Luxea prayed that nickname wouldn't stick. Seven bloodstones were splayed across the board. Each belonged to a different soldier. None had landed their piece in the center, so the pile of bronzes, sterlings, and a few golds was sizable.

"Which one is yours, Yaani?" inquired Luxea.

Yaani tapped the board to show her. His bloodstone rumbled a bit.

"You moved it! Bamboozler!" screamed Avari.

"Yer the bamboozler!" howled Yaani.

Luxea was smack in the middle of two adult children. "Goodness. Well, Yaani, it isn't over the second ring," she said factually.

"See? Second ring my fat arse. F-o-u-l!" laughed Avari.

"If yer so great, show us what ye've got, Siren," challenged Yaani.

Luxea's feet shuffled. "I'm not sure if I should be —"

"Deal. We'll team up and blow you losers sky-high," said Avari.

"Avari?!" squalled Luxea.

A warrior named Felitia took an incandescent pan of bloodstones out of the fire. One steaming bloodstone tumbled out and plopped into Avari's palm. Avari hissed and made her toss. The bloodstone twirled to a disappointing halt in the fourth ring.

"Vishera's outta the game!" said Yaani haughtily.

"Luxie and I are partners, you gigantic brat. We can still win if she lands her rock in the right place," said Avari competitively.

Felitia finished heating the next bloodstone, and Luxea extended her hand. When she caught the stone, a moment passed without feeling. Then her stomach wrenched, and her muscles tensed.

Shocked, a rush of energy flew down Luxea's arm. There was a crackling sound, and the room went quiet.

Luxea's face untwisted. The pain was . . . gone?

She opened one eye and looked down. Her hand was coated in blue ice. It whistled and emanated a silvery smoke that blanketed the table. The soldiers were flummoxed. There were no mentions in the Extreme Dragon Stones guidebook of such a trick.

"What's that, Luxie?" asked Avari, lip twitching.

"I don't know!" shrieked Luxea. She tipped her hand, but the ice was crusted to her fingers. "Avari, it won't come off!"

"How'd you do that, Siren?" asked Felitia, fascinated.

Luxea shook her hand violently and cried, "I didn't — !"

The ice broke, and the bloodstone became airborne. It clinked on a rafter, spiraled back down, and the ice shattered when it smacked the board. The stone spun on an axis and *clicked* into the dragon's eye.

Avari rattled Luxea like a rag-doll. "That's my Luxie! You won! Good game, ladies and gents. Better luck next time."

"Cheater! I call a rematch," said Yaani out of an open frown.

"Siren went above and beyond the standards for this game," said Felitia as she helped Avari shovel the winnings into a sack. "That wasn't cheating, she crushed us in a single blow."

"What was that, Siren? How'd you do it?" griped Yaani.

"Beginner's luck?" guessed Luxea.

Avari tied her bag closed. "We're rich, Luxie! We could buy Castle Lavrenthea if we wanted to! We'll be eating like queens. Tomorrow let's get frozen larenda cups — o-or plumberry jelly rolls!"

"Okay," said Luxea, rubbing her fingers together.

That night, Avari hopped into the upper bunk and stuffed their winnings under her mattress; anyone might've been out to pilfer it. In the lower bunk, Luxea replayed the day through.

"Avari?" she whispered.

"Mm? What's wrong?" asked Avari, peeking over the ledge.

"I can't stop thinking about today," said Luxea, green stars shining in the dark. "Those apples popped, and that ice appeared out of thin air. How do those things happen?"

"Pretty spooky. Ooh, what if you're a sorceress?" laughed Avari.

"A sorceress?" echoed Luxea.

"I was joking," said Avari. "My apprentice, a sorceress? It would explain why you're so awful at heavy lifting. The chances are scarce though. Almost nobody's dabbled in sorcery for a long time."

"But I saw a sorcerer in the Sapphire Bazaar today," stated Luxea.

"Those fellas with hankies in their sleeves are just normal folks who're good at being sneaky. If you saw a real sorcerer, you'd know. If you want to test it out, we should go to the castle library. They've got arcana volumes in that dust-closet somewhere."

"Avari, can we, please? If I am, I could do tricks and — !"

"Don't get ahead of yourself. You might just be a weirdo."

The next day, flowers woke up from their slumber, and the early birds of Tel Ashir kissed each other good morning. But Avari hit Luxea with a much less pleasant wake-up call.

"Get out of bed!" she shouted, yanking the blankets away.

"No . . . too ear . . . ly," said Luxea, curling up like a caterpillar.

"No more sleep. The library gets busy fast. We've got to go before all the keepers hit the books. Page-turning losers," said Avari, prying Luxea off of the bed.

"Stop it — *uff,*" said Luxea, melting into Avari's lap.

"Look how cute you are," tittered Avari. She bopped Luxea on the nose and spilled her onto the floor. "But you're terrible at waking up."

Luxea and Avari wound out of the military quarter and down Yula Montier to Kingslane. There was nothing else like ascending the Steps of Sevinus. The sandiness of each stair glittered like a light on the water, and tasseled banners of navy blue and silver flapped in the warm, dry wind.

The library could only be reached through the vestibule. Soldiers weren't permitted to pass the sentinels without a writ from an officer, but Avari had received authorization from Chief Demartiet.

The air inside of the castle carried a spice like sandalwood but a sweetness like jasmine. The interior was pieced together by slate masonry, silver dripped down the walls like mercury, and stairwells spiraled up into destinations unknown. Luxea brushed her thumb along a pillar whose swirling, embossed patterns had been carved so close together that she couldn't even fit a fingernail in the cracks.

Castle Lavrenthea reminded Luxea of the night sky.

On the domed ceiling were murals that hardly held pigment anymore. To the left was a man with a crown in his hand, and to the right was the same man with horns growing from his skull. In tandem were other horned men cupping red goblets.

At the furthest curve were four dragons: black, emerald, bronze, and crimson. The black dragon soared over mountains, wings blotting out the daylight. The emerald dragon perched on a cliff over the sea, claw outstretched. The bronze dragon had a broadsword in its heart, reeling as death took over. The crimson dragon roared over a burning city, eyes blazing with unbridled hatred.

Luxea stopped walking. "Avari, who are those men?"

"They're the Lavrentheas," said Avari as if it was obvious. "See? The Lavrenthea bloodline starts over here with King Graed. He was the King when the people of Tzapodia were afflicted."

"Afflicted?"

"I told you about that before, didn't I?"

"No."

Avari huffed. "I'm no history professor, but Tzapodia belonged to the dragons around the middle of Era Two. When humans from Northreach and The Grey moved south, they killed them off. Over a few decades, all of the dragons were dead except for Samsamet."

Avari pointed at the bronze dragon.

"Is that Samsamet?" asked Luxea sadly.

"That's right," verified Avari. "She had a roost by the sea. Her eggs would've brought a new generation of dragons, but King Graed ordered his men to slay Samsamet and crush her babies because he wanted to build a kingdom in this territory — this kingdom."

"Want is no excuse to kill," said Luxea bitterly.

"Not everyone's as morally sound as you are," said Avari with an elbow to Luxea's ribs. "But Samsamet didn't let those fellas off easy. In her last breaths, she put a curse on King Graed and his men called *'draconism.'* Horns sprouted from the King's head, and he and every man who partook in the slaughter of the last dragons were doomed from then on to suffer as half-human, half-dragon. And their children, and their children's children too."

"But couldn't that be advantageous?" asked Luxea inventively.

"Sure, but the benefits don't come cheap," said Avari cryptically. "The more they rely on dragon blood, the further they fall into madness. When the affliction reaches full circle, they become a dragon for good. Control over power is paid with control over themselves. Ares Lavrenthea is the last pureblooded member of Samsamet's cursed children. I'm not looking forward to the day he has to go through that, but it won't be for a long time if he avoids using dragon blood."

Luxea gulped audibly. "So those other dragons . . . they were —"

"— once the Kings of Tzapodia," finished Avari.

Luxea had never guessed that her home had such a lamentable history. She reviewed the dragons' slitted, violet eyes and arrived at a new question.

"Which one of these paintings is of the Speaker?"

"None of them," replied Avari. Luxea made a *'huh'* noise. "Ares Lavrenthea isn't the King. He's the sole successor to the throne and does everything he would do as a king, but nobody knows why there wasn't ever a coronation. That's why some folks call Tzapodia a principality, but it's still a kingdom. As interesting as curses are, we've got a time crunch. Let's get this magick shindig out of the way before I go to the stables. Come with me today! Little Velesari loves you."

The sentinels guarding the stairwell gave Luxea and Avari no trouble when Avari flashed Chief Demartiet's writ of authorization.

At the middle of the winding flight of stairs, Luxea's eyes gravitated to a statue of a woman erected within the wall. It was several stories tall and shimmered like snow in the daytime. She had a downturned crescent moon set behind her head and looked like she was resting, but also secretive like she'd been weeping. Luxea felt the statue watching her through eyes fused shut.

In the library, scholars hung off of ladders and strained to reach one book out of the hundreds that lined the shelves. Four floors were connected by a maze of staircases, and tomes and antiquated registries were piled onto tables.

"I never get on right with books," grunted Avari.

"Books are marvelous. Someone put their heart into each one. The spirit of every writer is here with us," said Luxea admiringly.

"All right, Miss Philosopher. Let's find you a spellbook to play 'round with," said Avari, clapping her hands preparedly.

"Shhh!" hissed a librarian with peanut-shaped glasses.

Luxea and Avari sidled into a corridor, but they were unsure where to begin. They searched the bookcases for over thirty minutes. There were volumes on every subject except for magick. Luxea thought to ask the librarian but avoided him after the stink-eye he'd given them.

Luxea scanned up the bookshelf to her left where there were records on the beasts of Amniven and how to cook them. To her right were novels without titles, but low to the ground was a grimoire wedged askew with a white cover and blanched golden lettering. She tried to read its binding, but it was in a different language.

It could have been full of nonsense, but something about that white grimoire drew Luxea immediately. She reached out to grab it.

"Ashiishiaishi. . . ."

It whispered in a tongue forgotten by time. Luxea hesitated for a moment but forced herself to slide it from the shelf.

"Hashihia . . . !" echoed the grimoire.

"What was that?" wheezed Avari. "Luxie, what if you were right about books? Did you release the author's soul? Crapper. You don't think we just haunted the castle, do you?"

"Maybe it's a friendly ghost," joked Luxea. Avari took it seriously.

Luxea flipped open the white grimoire to a random page and ran her fingers over the paper. Air exhaled from between the sheets.

Avari stood on her tiptoes to peek over Luxea's shoulders. She pointed at a line and asked, "What's this — gah!" The book sparked and sent a paralyzing jolt up her arm. "That hurt! What's its problem? Why can you hold it? It won't even let me touch it! Old bastard!"

"I'm not sure. Maybe only certain people can touch spellbooks? There's no doubt that this is one. Words like *'arcana'* and *'incantation'* are written all over," muttered Luxea.

Avari was in a snit, but she supported Luxea more than she hated the grimoire. "Fine. Let's see if you're a sorceress."

Luxea focused, inhaled briskly, and spat an incantation.

"Nav'in ei th'luneth!"

A wave of ghostly, blue light flared out of her fingertips. It gathered at the conical ceiling, and white dust flittered onto the floor. It crashed like a tidal wave through the aisles, tearing books from the shelves and tossing them into the air. Avari's frizzy bun bounced like a tumbleweed as it flew past her.

When Luxea closed her fingers into her palm, the wave of magick glittered out into nothingness. Luxea stared open-mouthed at the white grimoire. Avari hadn't been breathing, but then she let loose a bark of laughter like an elvish trumpet.

"Hells, you're a sorceress!" yelled Avari, burying her face into Luxea's shoulder. "My apprentice is a sorceress! Wait till we tell the boys back at the barracks. Their blocky heads'll spin!"

"It felt so natural. Why aren't there more sorcerers?" asked Luxea.

"Because not everyone can do what you just did," said Avari matter-of-factly. "You were *born* with magick — all sorcerers are — and that's what makes them so uncommon. This is huge, Luxie. You might be one of ten or twelve in L'arneth. Damn, His Highness'll be ecstatic to hear that he has you in his ranks."

"In that case, can I focus more on magick than agility training? I don't think being a ranger is my strong suit," coughed Luxea.

"I could tell it wasn't your niche the second I laid eyes on you, Noodle-arms," said Avari playfully. "But magick or not, you can't skip out on your training. What if one of your spells fails? You'd be toast. My teachings will be there to save your flimsy arse."

Luxea's eyes lidded halfway. "Yes, I figured," she said.

Avari shook Luxea. "You can practice magick in the evening, but daytime is Avari-time. Demartiet and Claymore will let you use the training area if you ask. The Chief likes sparkly things. But don't light our beds on fire or fill the armory with ice. General Skythoan wouldn't be too happy about that. He'd sit on you until you stopped moving. But let's hurry up. It's 'round breakfast time for the hatchlings, and I promised I'd bring 'em root veggies."

The two maneuvered through keepers and scholars and found a librarian who agreed to help them, but he seemed frightened of Luxea after witnessing her display of magick.

Luxea left the library with the grimoire and a newfound talent.

LUCIEM SALAH
15.BLACKOMEN.25.OSC.3

MORE THAN a year passed. There wasn't a word that Luxea was being searched for or that she was missing. Time came and went, and she accepted that she would never know more than her name.

When she stepped out into Tel Ashir each morning, she was greeted by a rush of air that grew more addicting by the breath. There was no way not to fall in love with the crashing of waves and scents of desert wildflowers.

What became Luxea's favorite feature was the view of Sirah the Crystal Spire that loomed over the cobalt trees of Nav Amani Forest. It was a reaches-wide mass of translucent stone, an earthen storm molded by the hands of time.

Luxea also found friendships inside the musty walls of the barracks. The soldiers' love for ales and armwrestling were staples in her life. Her comrades ceased referring to her as *'apple girl'* and *'whelp,'* amongst other labels, and called her by first name or *'friend.'*

In sunrae, her division threw her a lifeday celebration. She was warmhearted, which had to mean she was a sunrae child. Luxea suspected that it was an excuse for the soldiers to imbibe, but she was happy they'd chosen to honor her.

It was a blazing hot afternoon, and Luxea and Avari were out in the corrals. In the past few years, some dracas had died due to drops in temperature during redrift, so it was requested by the Mooncaller Council that they are given pens with better insulation. The project required hammering nails, sanding wood, and patience — all in which Luxea and Avari had little aptitude.

"Move it to the right and bring 'er down slow. It should sit clean n' pretty between those boards," said Avari, leafing over blueprints.

Luxea swished her fingers. The plank of wood levitated to the right and clacked into place. She closed her fingers to sever the arcanan tie.

"Perfect. You're not bad with construction. Maybe we should get you into architecture. You could build us a cottage," giggled Avari.

"Nice to know magick is good for something," sighed Luxea.

"But the higher-ups'll be so happy with you after this!" squealed Avari. "Keep this up, maybe they'll promote you to *'Magister Siren.'*"

"Magisters don't become magisters by building dracas pens."

"Nothing good comes right away," said Avari thoughtfully. "If you've got to build dracas pens to move up in the world, that's how it should be."

Luxea's brows crawled up. "That was awfully wise of you."

"Vishera, Siren," said Lieutenant Claymore, approaching with a stack of papers in hand. His posture was painfully straight as always.

Avari saluted. "We're almost done with this pen, sir —"

"Leave it to the others to finish," interrupted Claymore. "Vishera, I need you to deliver goods to Lor'thanin. You'll depart posthaste."

"In Selnilar? Why me?" bleated Avari. "Aren't there folks in charge of deliveries? 'Scuse my language, but I'm a *damned* ranger, sir, not a —"

"The man who was meant to deliver these goods has taken ill, so today, you're a courier," said Claymore, as hard as a diamond effigy.

An idea sprouted in Luxea's head.

According to Mollah and Avari, it was likely that Luxea had come from Lor'thanin. The chances of her having fallen into Tal Am T'Navin from there were high; the river flowed right through it. If she was from Lor'thanin, maybe seeing it would help her to remember.

"May I accompany her, sir?" asked Luxea enthusiastically. "I'm more than prepared to make a delivery, and perhaps I can uncover some information about myself if I go."

"Luxie . . ." said Avari dejectedly.

Lieutenant Claymore hemmed, "I'm sure your loss of recollection must obstruct your willingness to attain your fullest potential, so I should like you to find closure. You may join her, Siren."

"Yes, sir!" said Luxea, saluting.

"Yes, sir," said Avari, giving a much weaker salute.

The moment that Claymore was out of earshot, Avari sighed and dragged her feet to the old dracas stables with not a word to Luxea.

The goods consisted of agricultural stock for a plantation in Lor'thanin. After Luxea and Avari strapped them to Elthevir, there was no room on the saddle for a second passenger.

Avari retrieved a mount for Luxea, but rather than a dracas, she brought her an old mule. The mule's name was Pudd. Luxea feared that its legs would snap if she sat on it.

Luxea scooted onto the oat-scented saddle and dangled the reins like she was holding a hankie. "Will I need these? Pudd looks like she'll die any minute," she whispered.

"You'll need them," said Avari, steering Elthevir to Moonpass.

In seconds, Pudd passed Avari and Elthevir, and Luxea nearly flew off of the saddle. Pudd's black eyes bulged out of her skull as she broke the sound barrier. That mule was pure adrenaline.

The red afternoon transitioned into a blue evening. The trees in Nav Amani Forest thickened, and their springy offshoots uncurled. Luxea and Avari stopped to cook supper on the outskirts of Lor'thanin.

"Here. I brought a few rabbits along," said Avari, tossing a skinned rabbit carcass onto Luxea's lap. "Just poke it with the spit and set it over the fire as I taught you."

The spit slid from its place with a *shink,* and Luxea pierced the end into the rabbit's mouth. She sat on a log with Avari and watched her strike a blade with a whetstone for a few minutes.

"So what's the matter? Did Elthevir bite you again?" asked Luxea.

"No," said Avari curtly. She motioned to the fire. "Turn the spit. We've got to eat soon. Inns in Lor'thanin only stay open so late."

Luxea rotated the spit with magick. The rabbit crackled. "Will you talk to me? You're never this quiet. I wasn't aware you could go this long without opening your mouth," she said, kicking a pebble.

Avari strode to the fire and prodded their meal with a stick. "I just worry about you going to Selnilar," she said sullenly.

"Why?" wondered Luxea.

Avari slipped the rabbit off of the spit. "You're probably from Lor'thanin. What if we get there, and you recognize it?" she asked, ripping off a leg.

Luxea took the other piece but waited to eat it. "But don't you want me to find out where I came from?" she questioned.

"Of course, I do," said Avari, staring at her meat with droopy eyes. "But what if you end up not coming back to Tzapodia? You had a life before this, and if you remember who you were, you might forget about me."

Luxea bit into the rabbit leg. "Even if I remembered, Tel Ashir is where I belong. I made a new life there, and calling anywhere but there home would feel wrong. I'd miss it — and I'd miss *you.* You're unforgettable," she said through a mouthful. "Precious that you got so riled up by the idea of me abandoning you. I nearly shed a tear."

"You're all I've got!" said Avari, pitching a bare bone into the fire. "I was fluffed as a pillow working alone before you came along, but you're my best friend, Luxie."

"And you're mine. I wouldn't know how to live if it weren't for you pelting me with directions all the time," laughed Luxea.

Avari relaxed without realizing. "My crap emotions aside, thanks for coming with me," she said, finishing her second serving.

"Of course. I've been trained for this," joked Luxea.

Once the two had stuffed their guts and kicked dirt to the fire, they left for Lor'thanin. The dusty heat of Tzapodia washed away with the frosty air of Selnilar, and the overcast sky reflected the lamplight from far below. The Crystal Spire came into view, erupting past the scudding clouds and transforming the A'maru Mountains into anthills.

At a straightaway, Pudd seized the opportunity to flaunt her unfathomable velocity. Avari struggled to keep up as Luxea held onto the reins for dear life. In minutes, they arrived at the white gates of Lor'thanin.

They dismounted, and Pudd urinated for a long time. Luxea and Avari decided it would be best to enter the city on foot. Elthevir took up the entire stable space on the road, so Luxea tied Pudd to a shrub near the gate and prayed that she wouldn't uproot it in her absence.

Avari ambled to the guard's post. "Be prepared. The security in this place can be pissy 'bout outsiders. They'll ask pointless questions, make us sign release forms and declare personal belongings, yadda."

Avari peered into the guard's window. "What? No one's here?" She leaned farther inside. "Hello? Is anyone there?"

"I thought security was harsh on foreigners?"

"It is."

Luxea meandered to the gate and gave it a nudge. "Avari? The gate is unbarred," she said uneasily.

"What?" Avari jogged to her. "Luxie, we should go inside. I want to know what's going on. We'll ask around, and in the worst case scenario, I'll flash the letter Claymore gave. That always works with official malarkey."

Avari squeezed through the opening before Luxea could protest.

Lor'thanin looked like the way a harp sounded. White flowers overgrew walls, and tents were fastened to the ground by robust ivy vines. The Sirah Temple wasn't far off. It was carved into the base of the Crystal Spire with arches of chalcedony shaping each sect. One could hear spring water spilling from the grottos beneath the spire.

They crept down the pyrite roads, peeked around corners, and popped their heads through tavern doors, but there was no one whatsoever in Lor'thanin. There were no flutes from lodges, no clinking plates in cafes, no chatter of city-folk, no guards, no lovers, no children, and no white horses. It was like they'd never existed.

"Where is everyone?" asked Luxea apprehensively.

"Quiet," demanded Avari. She motioned northwest to the Sirah Temple. "Look over there. See how the Spire is glowing orange? Our best bet for finding an answer is that way."

"I don't know about this," said Luxea unwillingly.

Avari hooded her head. "We've got to find out what's going on."

"But what if something bad happened?" asked Luxea.

"If that were the case, there'd be evidence of it. But there's nothing, Luxie," said Avari sassily.

"I —" Luxea gulped. "Okay."

Sticking to the shadows, they followed the road signs to Sirah Temple. The haunting stillness only grew. It was as if Lor'thanin had lost all memory of itself too. They crossed a street adjacent to the city center, and Avari waved Luxea under an awning.

"Now I'm starting to worry," said Avari, scanning the street. "I need you to stay here. I'll see if I can find anything up ahead."

"Have you lost it? You're not going alone!" squealed Luxea.

"If something goes wrong, I want you to be safe so you can get back to Tel Ashir," spat Avari. "Whatever's going on here isn't —"

The ground rumbled, and the ominous scrape of feet stole Avari's voice. She pushed Luxea behind her. Luxea clapped her palm over her mouth to maintain silence. Just then, a gigantic leg crashed down in front of them and dented the road. It had the circumference of a support column, and its flesh festered. With each blister that burst, another bubbled through the pus. Luxea and Avari were stiff as boards until the giant's footsteps faded with distance.

Luxea shook Avari. "What the hells was that? I haven't been trained for something like this!"

"Neither have I," said Avari. "Hurry, we're going up."

"Up?"

"The rooftop across the street. Go!"

Down an alleyway, Avari hoisted Luxea by the waist and hooked herself onto the ledge. Luxea grabbed her wrists and helped her up. The two low-crawled to the far end of the slanted rooftop.

Sirah Temple Plaza had been reputed to be a dreamscape, but it was a nightmare. The ground pulsed with black roots, and the base of the Crystal Spire crumbled like ashes in snow.

L'arian elves were barred into iron cages. They wept for faith, but none was left for them. Luxea had never seen others of her kind, but if these people had once looked anything like her, their nature had been sapped from them. They were skeletons with grey skin shrunken to their bones. They'd been merchants, warriors, teachers, mothers, fathers, sisters, brothers, and children — but now they were ghosts.

A hideous mutant lumbered past. It wasn't the same one that they'd encountered earlier; there were tens more. They were towering and oafish. Pedipalps erupted from their faces, a mess of eyes cluttered their brows, and spiny, twitching hairs coated their arms, legs, and lumpy paunches. Luxea thought they looked quite like tarantulas.

The abominations swung bodies over their shoulders like bouquets of wilted flowers and cast them into piles. The one just below the roofline heaped corpses together, tidying the area.

There was little time to ponder amidst the chaos, but one question was prominent: how did this happen without anybody noticing? If Lor'thanin's defenses couldn't prevent this, warnings had to be passed on to the Speaker. Tzapodia could be next.

"We should leave," said Avari timidly.

"What about them?" asked Luxea, motioning to the cages.

"We can't do anything for them!" said Avari regretfully. "They had the *Leitha'maen* here to protect them, five-thousand men, and that failed. How many are there of us? Two. We need to get out of here."

Avari shuffled away. As Luxea followed, a figure descended the steps of Sirah Temple. She blurted out, "Avari, wait! Who's that man?"

The person standing on Sirah Temple's staircase was a cleric adorned in Selnilarian regalia. Atop his braided hair was a pointed, silver headdress. Unlike the other l'arian elves, this man was healthy and smiling with contentment.

"What? It can't be him . . . *Luciem Salah,*" said Avari tremblingly.

"Luciem Salah? 'Light Seeker?'" translated Luxea.

"He's one of The Six like the Speaker, a guardian of the Joined Hands. Val'noren Paah is to Selnilar what Ares Lavrenthea is to Tzapodia," said Avari choppily.

"Then what's he doing?" asked Luxea feverishly.

"Simani t'leveloh lucier!" shouted *Luciem Salah*.

"What's he saying?" asked Avari. "I can't speak l'arian. Hurry!"

Luxea's mental wheels spun. "'Children of eternal purity.'"

"Una th'luxea'te llun ivis imen a'ansil hil tel niel amniva!"

"'Your deaths are for the one who carries us to a new world.'"

"Ithan e'nunavul, ei simani! Una anshah raixa te'bithe."

"'She commands it, my children. Your final judgment is here.'"

Luciem Salah opened his arms before him. A mutant plunged its bristly fist into a cage. It lifted a handful of prisoners and held them lower. *Luciem Salah's* thumb traced the lineament of one gaunt cheek.

"Hil'te fini senth Allath! Lucanin thith felua!"

"'We are all a part of the Brood. The Widow will reign.'"

The mutant's grip tightened. Bones snapped, flesh tore at the seams, and bodies popped like grapes. The mutant wrung out their lifeblood, and *Luciem Salah* stepped up a stair to not dirty his slippers.

Luxea was in a trance. Those were the first deaths she'd witnessed. Avari snapped her away from the image, stuttering, "W-we need to go, Luxie! We have to tell the Speaker!"

They slid down the rooftop and sprinted with fear biting their heels. They reached the white gates. Now they knew that past their promise of safety was a heart fueled by slaughter.

Luxea tailed Avari but ran right into her. Avari was as still as a rabbit at the head of an arrow. Luxea's stars turned dark violet.

Lumbering at the guard's post was a mutant the height of a tree, chewing on an animal corpse. Pudd's rope had been snapped, and she was gone. The mutant noticed Luxea and Avari's presence. Its squashed head turned fast, its twisted pedipalps clacked, and strings of saliva stitched together its broken fangs.

"Scale the wall to the right, and I'll distract it. On three, get ready to run," enjoined Avari. "One, two . . . three!"

They split apart. The mutant set its sights on Avari, but it moved quicker than she'd anticipated. It blocked her path. She scoped out a route, but it was risky.

"If I can't get by, run, Luxea!" shouted Avari.

"No!" shrieked Luxea. "I'm not leaving y — !"

The mutant swatted Avari like a fly against the gate. She touched the back of her head, and her fingers were red. She rolled onto her feet and barreled to the stables. The mutant surged after her.

Luxea threw out her hands. *"Amal luciem!"*

Light projected onto the mutant's face. As it yowled and scratched its crusted eyes, it blindly swished. Its curved fingernails caught Luxea's lower back. Stunned by pain, she tumbled into the dirt.

Avari bolted to help her, but the mutant squinted through the light and snatched her up with one craggy hand. Avari felt something crack inside of her waist. She dizzily unsheathed a saber from the scabbard on her back, embedded it into its knuckle, and clambered up its shoulder. The mutant slapped its neck and crushed her arm.

Avari fell to the ground. "Luxea, get out of here! Tell the Speaker not to trust the Light Seeker! Don't send anyone — they'll die!"

As she bled, Luxea grabbed Avari and yelled, *"Tashetha'hil!"*

Both of them vanished. The mutant roared and stamped about cluelessly. Luxea's concealment shroud wouldn't last, so she slipped her hand under Avari's neck and dragged her away.

"Stay awake. Don't close your eyes," said Luxea quietly.

"Luxie . . . I'm . . . sho . . . tired . . ." slurred Avari.

They neared the stables where Elthevir had been fastened, but he'd gnawed through his ties. As Luxea's magick wore off, she yanked Avari into the shadow of the forest. The mutant didn't see them, so she had a moment to catch her breath. The blood seeping from her back made her vision bleary, but she could see that the mutant was trudging in the opposite direction.

"Fala bithe, Elthevir!" panted Luxea.

The dracas prowled closer. Luxea unfastened the deliveries. They clattered to the ground and spilled fruits and little shovels. Elthevir folded his legs under him, and Luxea secured Avari and herself onto the saddle.

Without a sound, Elthevir bolted into Nav Amani Forest.

The Parallel
16.Blackomen.25.Osc.3

ELTHEVIR BROKE through Moonpass, and pedestrians cleared a path for him and his injured riders. Luxea saw Castle Lavrenthea dead ahead. She would do all that she could to reach the Speaker, but she had no clue where to find him.

In the Porranim Courtyard, Elthevir toppled and slid across the gravel. Luxea tipped off of the saddle. A nearby keeper flung his tablet and rushed to catch her on his satin robe.

The physical contact startled Luxea awake. The world pulsed white, and her back burned like hot coals, but she was coherent. She scrambled out of the keeper's arms.

"Take her to Mollah!" said Luxea, pointing at Avari. "Where is the Speaker? Please, I need to talk to His Highness — now!"

The keeper stared at his empty hands where his tablet usually was. It was in a bush somewhere, so he guessed, "It's the afternoon, so perhaps he's in the Ruby Bureau?"

"Where is that?" asked Luxea, staggering backward.

"It's in the Ruby Wing, at the back of the castle," said the keeper, hoisting Avari off of the saddle. "But it's in the royal sect, miss, so you won't be able to access —"

Luxea was already gone.

Drenched in sweat and blood, Luxea dashed through the vestibule. A sentinel watched over the western stairwell, and Luxea knew that he wouldn't let her through without a writ or a high-ranking officer present. Taking a leap of faith, she sprinted for the stairs.

The sentinel caught her arm. "Where do you think you're going? This is a private residence. Do you have authorization from a — ?"

"I need to see the Speaker!" yelled Luxea.

"I can't let you go on," said the sentinel, flexing his ropy neck muscles. "His Highness is a busy man. The offices in the Amber Wing can schedule for a courier to pass along your message to —"

"I'm so sorry, sir, but — *vastal'han ma!*"

Magick blew the sentinel back onto the stairs, and he was pinned down by his shield. Luxea ran past him and up the staircase.

"What is this?!" yowled the sentinel. He hurdled after her. "This is an offense! Intrusion! Intrusion!"

On the second floor, Luxea swung to the right. Two more sentinels were after her, flailing their gauntleted hands.

"Protect His Highness at all costs!"

"Catch that cadet!"

Luxea ripped to the left where a circle of Ashi priests knelt on a rug. She jumped over one priest and spilled their mortar of smoking herbs. The sentinels trampled by after her, and their sabatons stamped out the embers. Luxea tripped out of the room with an Ashi priest's veil stuck to her foot. She kicked it off and proceeded onward.

Luxea didn't know where she was going, but she thought that she was on the right track because her surroundings were becoming more regal. Every doorway looked as if it led to a treasure hoard.

As the three sentinels gained on her, she rounded a corner. She instantly collided with somebody much huskier than herself. The cup they were holding splashed tea everywhere. Luxea heard papers flying and a deep, agitated grunt.

The impact sent her down. She slid face-first across a rug. When she flipped supine to plead her innocence, she forgot how to talk. A very tall man stood before her, doused in hot tea and staring at a splay of paperwork on the ground. He had ridged, black horns curled at the sides of his head, and his left hand was clawed and coated in scales.

It was the Speaker.

Past his hip-length, black hair, Ares Lavrenthea read Luxea like a fortune. He was remarkably younger than she'd expected. She'd imagined a wrinkly man with many decades under his belt, but Ares was handsome and clean-shaven in the face. Had she not been bleeding on his floor, she might have asked for his star sign.

A drop of tea *plopped* from the silver ring in the division of his nostrils. A sentinel yelled, "Fetch His Highness a towel!"

A pack of eavesdropping serving girls hidden behind a bookcase squealed and scampered to the linens chamber.

"Your Highness, step away from this cadet! She is guilty of violent assault," said the sentinel Luxea had blown onto the stairs.

As Ares wiped tea off of his neck, he examined the absence of muscles in Luxea's arms. "I'm sorry — *violent?"* he asked cynically. His voice was as scarlet as the velvet of rose petals yet as black as ink.

The sentinel clapped shackles onto Luxea's wrists. Then she realized that she was in a worse predicament than when she'd returned to Tel Ashir.

"Wait!" belted out Luxea. "Call me guilty, but I need to speak with you, Your Highness! My name is Luxea Siren. I'm in Lieutenant Claymore's division. I'm here to tell you that — !"

"Quiet, scoundrel!" yelled the sentinel, shaking her. "As a prisoner of Tzapodia, I hereby prohibit you from speaking to our — !"

"Stop interrupting!" screamed Luxea. "Lor'thanin is — !"

"Silence!" shouted the sentinel, dragging her away.

"Back down," ordered Ares to the sentinel. "You. Siren, was it?" Luxea blinked back her lightheadedness and nodded. "Miss Siren, I doubt that you would go so far just to lie, so I'll give you a chance to explain your . . ." his honey-brown skin went white, ". . . eyes. What happened to your eyes?"

"I'll tell you about them, Your Highness, but listen first," pleaded Luxea. "I left with my mentor, Avari Vishera, to Lor'thanin yesterday, but it was under attack. The city is empty, there are only perhaps a hundred people left trapped in cages! Dammit, isn't some goddess supposed to tell you about things like this beforehand?"

Ares was offended. "If Oscerin doesn't reach out to me — which She hasn't — it's likely that She doesn't find it critical. If Selnilar were in any danger, they would send for aid from Tzapodia. I've heard no calls of distress."

"That's why *I'm* the one telling you!" wailed Luxea. "You're a guardian of the Joined Hands, aren't you? So do something! But, please, don't trust a word that comes from Selnilar. A man named *Luciem Salah* is behind the massacre, and —"

"The Light Seeker?" asked Ares with an edge. "That's a severe accusation, Miss Siren. Val'noren Paah is a member of The Six and avowed to peace. He would never . . ."

Ares tapered off and glanced at a pendant inside of his shirt. Incriminating one of The Six for mass murder was a wild allegation, but truth seeped from this woman's pale lips and pooled at his feet. He whispered a curse and whisked his claw at the sentinels.

"Have a troop dispatched to Lor'thanin. If there's an assault, we must redeem survivors. Go!" he said waspishly.

"No, don't send them! They'll die, Your Highness!" cried Luxea.

"You wanted me to do something, didn't you? Then be quiet," said Ares priggishly. Two of the three sentinels exited the hall.

"Please, don't let them!" yelled Luxea, wrenching free.

Ares hooked a talon under the cincture on her uniform. "Stop it! This isn't your decision!" He tossed her back to the sentinel. "Take her to the cells until further notice. Thank you."

The sentinel shoved Luxea, and her blood soaked his hands. He looked down and stammered, "I — er — she's wounded, Your Highness. Should I — ?"

Luxea's head flopped, and she toppled. The world blew away.

At Ares' behest, Luxea was taken to the infirmary, but she was to be tried for assault the moment that she woke up. That same day, eight men and a member of the Mooncaller Council departed for Lor'thanin.

It was the second morning since Luxea had broken into Castle Lavrenthea. Pale green eyes swollen from sleep, Ares pulled a snowy white tunic over his head and flattened his lank hair above his horns. As he reached for the tie, there were three knocks at the door.

"A moment," said Ares, lacing his tunic.

Ares unlatched the door, and his fingers went numb. Three men stood at his doorstep. Two were sentinels, and the third was an archer beaten beyond recognition. His teeth had been picked from his gums, his right eye bulged, and his left shoulder dangled from his tendons.

Ares towed him into his bedchamber. "Come in, both of you! What's his name, and why wasn't he taken to Mollah? These injuries will kill him if they aren't treated!"

"Rylin O'sara, Your Highness. He rode in this morning," said a sentinel, helping Ares lower the archer onto the bed. "Overseer Lovelle tried to bring him to the healers, but he insisted that he be taken directly to you."

The second sentinel muttered, "Your Highness, O'sara is one of the men you sent to Lor'thanin. He was the only one to make it out alive."

Emptiness filled Ares. All that he could hear were the echoes of Luxea's pleas. The price for his ignorance had been paid by the souls of eight brave men — and maybe nine.

Ares held Rylin's hand. "You're safe. Nothing can touch you."

"You're wrong! None of us are safe, Your Highness, not a single one of us!" said Rylin toothlessly.

"If you can, tell me what happened," said Ares quietly.

Ruby tears seeped from Rylin's one functioning eye. "We — we found no enemies at the perimeter, so we breached the gates. Nothing seemed out of place . . . until the temple. They took us right away! They watched us all along! The chief . . . they pulled him asunder. I can still hear him. This blood is his, and theirs! They held a blade to my neck, they were ready to kill me too, but the Light Seeker —"

"You're sure the Light Seeker is behind this?" interrupted Ares.

"Yes, but his will is not his own! She planted a seed inside his head . . . he drinks Her ichor like wine," gurgled Rylin. "Val'noren sent me to you as a warning, to impart that you are powerless . . . then he . . ."

Rylin fumbled with his uniform. Ares rolled back the collar, and torn flesh was stuck to the fabric. His waist stung in secondary anguish. Rylin's skin was ripped without a single clean slice. It had been etched into a symbol that Ares had never seen before.

"We will fall, Y-Your Highness," cried Rylin. "My faith wanes, and I know not where to turn. She is omnipotent. She is coming!"

"Who is coming?" asked Ares briskly.

"The spider — *the Widow!*" wept Rylin, tapping his chest. "She is the Brood Mother, the trihells themselves — !" His throat convulsed. "Let Oscerin carry me . . . I long for Her light. Beg Her to save me . . . save us . . ."

A death rattle leaked free. Ares shut Rylin's eyes out of respect and then his own out of guilt. *"Samnia in. Forgive me,"* he mouthed.

Ares had genuinely surmised that those men would prevail, but he'd tucked them into their deathbeds. Their blood was on his hands, and he stared at that evidence. He stumbled across the room to collect a change of clothing, disoriented from shock.

"Pass word to the families of their losses. I'll arrange a ceremony to honor their bravery and write my condolences. Take his body to Mollah before he's returned to his loved ones," said Ares vacantly.

Ares unlaced his shirt with glassy eyes. When the sentinels left the bedchamber with Rylin, he tipped backward against his wardrobe. The mirror judged him. His conscience had been made as red as the clothes on his chest. He should've listened.

A day went by. Ares wrote the last of the names onto a consolation letter, and then the feather quill dropped and splattered ink. His fingers slid up his hairline, and he flipped through the pages inside of his head. He cursed the most recent chapter, but when he settled on the blank spaces before time, something dawned on him. He hadn't yet visited the two survivors of this Widow's terror.

Ares slipped off to the infirmary and stopped at the side door. Inside, the majority of the cots were unoccupied, and sages were chatting at their leisure. Ares spied an employee with brown hair and a round belly who was organizing herbs.

"Em," hemmed Ares. "May I have your name?"

Eyes buggy, the sage squeaked, "Hanalea Moots, Your Highness!"

"Hanalea, would you fetch Mollah?" asked Ares collectedly.

"Right away, Your Highness!" said Hanalea, scooping a hand underneath her belly as she skittered off.

Ares slumped his head, and his horns *clacked* on the doorpost. Seconds later, the scrape of slippers echoed throughout the infirmary. Mother Mollah ripped around the corner like a boulder rolling down a mountain. She seized Ares' collar and yanked him down.

"What's the matter, boy? Have you got a fever?" She tried to touch his forehead; she could only reach his chin.

"Nothing's wrong with me. I'm a visitor," reassured Ares.

"A visitor? Who are you here to see?" croaked Mollah.

Ares hoped he had their names right. "Avari and Luxea."

Mollah scowled. "You want to see Miss Siren, do ya? Then mayhap you can take those ploughin' manacles off her while you're here," she said, tugging Ares by the flap of his coat. "The girls are resting up. Luxea's case isn't as serious. I had to give her a bunch o' stitches, but she'll be walking in a few days. As for Avari, that'll take some time."

Ares was led to a cot by the door to the ramparts. He took one glance at Avari, and guilt stole his eyes away. She was swathed in bandages, and black and blue bruises overwrote her yellow spirit.

"She'll recover, but it'll take patience," huffed Mollah. "The girl's a Nall like I am. Tough as the Mammoth and stubborn as Him too."

"Good," said Ares unfeelingly. He collapsed onto a chair and dragged his hands down his face. "I'm so lost, Mollah. Selnilar has fallen, Val'noren spills the blood of his people for a new divine, and I sent nine men to their deaths. It's all divided."

Mollah petted Ares' hair. "You know how many times you've come to me sayin' you don't know where to turn, boy?" she said supportively. "You can lament, but the burden of their deaths isn't yours to carry. Those men fell because they fought for you, and they fought for you because they held faith in you . . . yet you hold so little in the Ares that *we* see. It pains me."

"Faith in oneself is the hardest to grasp," said Ares. "Val'noren Paah is no fool and no man who sways easily, yet he swears that Widow is divine and declares the rest of us as his enemies. I worry that more will walk in his footsteps if bonds amongst The Six aren't repaired. Without those ties . . ."

"Yes, The Six are in trouble," sighed Mollah. "Have you spoken to the Lady Peyamo about this? She's always got smart things to say."

"I haven't had the opportunity," said Ares aloofly. He sulked. "But what if this is beyond us? Before he died, one of my soldiers spoke of the Widow with more fear than I've beheld in the eyes of any man. After all that I've given to help these people feel safe, Widow robbed it from him in a night. Maybe there was no hope to begin with."

Mollah *thwacked* Ares' head. "I've got no time for a pity party. Nothin' good'll come if you live in a damned storm cloud all the time. Have you forgotten, Ares? Oscerin is on your side!"

"I know that Oscerin is with me . . . but I could use you swatting me in the head every now and then," said Ares, dimpling at Mollah.

"I've always got time for that! All this aside, we've got to work on your stress management. Care for the mind is as essential as care for the body. And no, smokin' that roseleaf crap won't fix it. Don't think that I don't smell it on you! I'll fetch a bundle of sleepthistle to calm you," said Mollah as she hobbled to the shelves and picked dried leaves off of a stem. "We got this shipment yesterday. It's potent, so steep less than you normally do."

"I wouldn't want to relax too much," said Ares, following her.

"Hehe, *well —*" Mollah popped off the lid of a jar with a *thoonk,* "— for you, that might not be such a bad thing. You're always so tense! Makes me depressed just lookin' at ya."

"Oh, thank you," grumbled Ares.

A glint of silver caught Ares' eye. He looked, and it was a pair of shackles hooked to one of the bedposts. The wrist clamped by the other end belonged to Luxea.

In the instant that Ares' eyes rested upon her face, they rolled back, and his vision switched off like a light. His weight slammed the cabinet against the wall, and glass containers toppled from the shelves.

Oscerin spoke.

KEEP HER SAFE! THE STARS CANNOT DIE OUT!

Oscerin's howling ceased, and Ares' sight was gifted back to him. What the Moon Mother had given him wasn't guidance, it was a demand. Ares felt scared. He'd never heard Her like this.

Ares searched his chest in a cold sweat. When his fingers brushed his pendant, the presence of everybody in the room disappeared except for Luxea's. His legs were weak from walking two planes of existence, but he made it across the hall. An assembly of sages gossiped about their leader's behavior, and Mollah shooed them away with the sleepthistle.

Ares unhooked a ring of keys from his belt and shakily unlatched the cuff around Luxea's wrist. As loudly as he could, he yelled, "I need Miss Siren prepared for relocation to the Amber Wing!"

The sages hurried to Luxea and lifted her onto a stretcher. Mollah waddled to Ares, heedful not to tread upon the broken glass. "Why the sudden transfer?"

"Oscerin doesn't want her far from me. She knows something about this woman that I don't, and I can't overlook it," mused Ares.

"If Oscerin wills it . . . Watch over her, child. I can't tell you the state her mind is in after all that she went through. Be gentle, and don't give her none of your catty nonsense, got it?"

"No nonsense," said Ares inattentively. "I'll send for someone to clean up this glass, but I should go. Thank you, Mollah. As always."

Ares kissed Mollah's ratty, grey hair and turned out the door. The old sage's lips scrunched up into a smile, and then she gasped, "Your sleepthistle!"

Mollah chased after Ares.

The next day, Luxea opened her eyes. Her skull felt like it was packed with bread dough. She thought she'd had a nightmare. She could remember mayhem, Avari begging her to save herself, pulling them to safety, careening through Castle Lavrenthea, and warning the Speaker about Selnilar and *Luciem Salah.* Then she'd woken up.

Sunlight shafted into the room. Luxea thought someone must've opened the window. She stretched out her body and yelped. Her fingers snaked up her back and grazed thick stitches in her side. She shot upright. It hadn't been a nightmare, it had all happened.

This room wasn't in the infirmary or the barracks. Those places reeked of ointment and sweaty boots, but this one had an aroma of jasmine and sandalwood. Silver ribbons laced the walls, and the curtains had so many minuscule details in their stitchings that Luxea's eyes felt larger just by looking at them. Luxea's Tel Ashian uniform had been replaced with royal blue robes that smelled like sugarcane. She was sinking into an over-feathered mattress, and pillows fluffed into the small of her back like clouds on a day without rain or wind.

Luxea slid her legs out from under the airy duvet. The heat that radiated from the smoky quartz tile tickled her feet. Her toes wiggled.

Just then, the arched bedchamber door opened. The face of none other than the Speaker showed through the crack. An uncomfortable moment of eye contact passed before he leaned out of view.

"I didn't know you were awake. May I come in?" hemmed Ares.

Luxea debated if her attire was appropriate for company. "Um, yes, Your Highness. You may," she said, covering herself.

Ares inched inside with two mugs in his large hands. His silky, black hair was tucked into a bun behind his horns, and a red-beaded earring swung from his right ear. Seeing her leader in such a casual manner made Luxea feel off.

Ares bumped the door shut with the tip of his boot. "I hope you aren't startled. I happened to be passing by, so I brought you tea," he said, motioning to one teacup with his eyes. "It's sleepthistle. I don't know if you enjoy that sort, but I wanted to leave it for you. Try not to splash it on me."

"Thank you. I won't spill it," said Luxea. Steam dewed her cheeks as she sipped. "It's delicious. Sleepthistle is my favorite."

"Is that so? Mollah gave me far too much, so you may have the rest," said Ares, tugging the tea string. "How are you feeling?"

"Sore," said Luxea, rubbing her arm. "How long was I asleep?"

"Four days," answered Ares. "You were taken to Mollah, and you needed stitching, but all else is well. Also, you had probable cause for breaching security, so your trial has been canceled."

"Thank you for that. And for lending me a bed, Your Highness. I hope I haven't inconvenienced you," said Luxea, bowing.

"You did nothing of the sort," said Ares. He hardened. "Please, address me by my first name. Is it all right to call you 'Luxea?'"

Hearing her name from the Speaker's mouth gave Luxea a shiver. "I, er, yes — Luxea is fine," she stammered. Ares just stared at her as she noisily slurped her tea. "I hope this isn't rude to ask, but why am I in your castle?"

"Not rude, perfectly understandable," said Ares offhandedly. "Two days ago, Oscerin spoke to me . . . about you."

"Me? That's — but I've — what did She say?" asked Luxea, feeling as minute as a speck of dust.

"'Keep her safe. The stars cannot die out,'" quoted Ares.

Luxea rubbed her eyes to erase the night sky from them. "You're certain She was talking about me?" she asked unbelievingly.

Ares was a hair away from making a sarcastic remark, but Mollah had instructed him to keep his attitude in check. "I'm fairly confident that She was referring to you," he said flatly. "That leads me to the next step. I recognize that this is sudden, but I'd like for you to stay."

Luxea nearly screamed, "In the castle?!"

"Yes," said Ares, smacking his lips quietly. "I would never make you go where you don't wish to be, but if Oscerin wants you near me, I do too."

"But why me? And why you?" asked Luxea, vacuuming up the rest of her tea. "Don't take it the wrong way, I don't mean to sound like I don't want to be here, but — !"

"Gods — calm down," said Ares acerbically. "Not everything Oscerin tells me holds clarity, so forgive my failure to provide you with answers. I don't know why you or why me, but whatever Oscerin's reasoning is, I can't question it. If it comforts you, I'll have a bedchamber arranged for Avari too when she's discharged."

Joy tricked the corners of Luxea's lips into curling up, and Ares saw it. She took in his face longer than she'd yet let herself. First, she noticed that his eyebrows were twice as thick as hers and also twice as neat. She tried to cover hers. Then she observed that he didn't look poised like she'd expected him to, but more despondent. It dawned on her that anything Oscerin said to him must have meant the world. He might worry himself to pieces if Luxea rejected.

"Okay. I will," she said finally.

"That's alleviating to hear," breathed Ares.

He had a meeting with the Tzapodian secretary of justice within the hour, but there was another topic to cover with Luxea.

"I don't mean to overstay my welcome, but may I sit?" he asked.

"Go ahead. This is your castle," said Luxea casually.

"This is your bedchamber," said Ares, resting his elbow on the back of the sofa. "This isn't something I want to say, but you deserve to know. I must tell you thank you . . . and that I'm sorry."

"Sorry for what?" asked Luxea in an undertone.

Ares slid his finger along his bottom lip; it was his nervous habit. "You advised me against sending reinforcements, but I doubted the severity of your claims. It's an extermination. The Light Seeker destroyed Lor'thanin, his soul sworn to *'the Widow.'*"

"So Val'noren Paah killed the l'arians because Widow asked him to? But leaders are meant to protect other people," said Luxea blackly.

"Indeed they are, but one member of The Six found a reason to follow Widow, and that troubles me," said Ares, vacillating between talking and whispering. "I don't know what power the Brood Mother holds or how She swayed Val'noren's hand, but I underestimated how catastrophic this is. Lastly, I should've listened to you. Nine men were dispatched, but only one returned. He died shortly after."

Heartsickness burrowed into Luxea's chest, and the faces of every soldier that she knew flashed in her mind like a reel. She slunk down onto the sofa beside Ares and chewed her fingers. A part of her yearned for ignorance, but curiosity was a tempting force.

"Who were they?" asked Luxea with her thumb in her mouth.

Every name of the soldiers was forever burned into the space behind Ares' eyes. He listed, "Rylin O'sara, Petre Kane, Danis D'liara, Doc Navia, Eaia N'manya, Naji Komaar, Yaani Belaj, Gregory Stile, Lorian Demartiet."

The vibrancy of the room was blanched. Luxea tried to dam the flood of emotion, but woe filled her heart. "Chief? But he is — was — he always — and Yaani and Petre — I can't believe they're —"

Ares covered his eyes. "I'm sorry."

Luxea closed up like a flower into its petals and sobbed. "I want to forget this. I never want to see death again — to hear it. I wish none of it happened. All of those people, Avari, Lorian, and that stupid mule too! I didn't mourn for those in Lor'thanin. It's so selfish of me to cry only because I knew them. What's wrong with me?"

"You cannot lament every death, but no tear that you shed is insignificant," said Ares. "If you'd like time to yourself, I'll —"

"No. I don't want to be alone — I'm sorry," cut in Luxea.

Ares would have to make up for the appointment he was missing, but providing Luxea with company felt like an obligation of greater substance.

"I'll stay," said Ares faintly.

"Thank you, Ares," whimpered Luxea.

Luxea had mispronounced Ares' name, but he didn't correct her. They were quiet for a long time. Every once in a while, Ares stole glances at the stars as they wept for lives that were too late to save.

MAGELAS
2.KINGSREIGN.25.OSC.3

LUXEA HADN'T spoken with Ares since the day he'd waited through her tears. She'd seen him, but he'd always looked like he had something gnawing at his mind.

Avari was still unconscious, so Luxea visited her in the infirmary multiple times daily. Avari had bloodied her favorite scarf, but she couldn't live without her safety blanket, so Luxea ventured to the bazaar and purchased a new one with all of the coin she had. The last scarf was green whereas this one was purple. With Mollah's consent, she laid it over Avari's bandaged head.

Whenever Luxea wasn't with Avari, she focused on magick. Living in the castle gave her access to the library, so she'd collected an ample amount of books. Studying distracted her from the loss of her comrades. She thought that she should permit herself to grieve, but it was easier to forget.

The day was sunny and dry as it always was in Tel Ashir. Luxea dropped her stack of tomes on the table in the Amber Lounge, a part of the Amber Wing on the top floor of Castle Lavrenthea that overlooked the city.

An hour passed. Luxea closed a book and strained to reach for a red volume titled: *'A Brief History of Eastern Conjuration by Blacketh Benigh.'* She lifted it and wheezed; the history of the East was heavy.

Luxea tossed a few cushions out of the way, spun upside-down, and bent her legs over the sofa's back. If she held her neck right, she could still read. She delved headfirst — or feet-first — into the text.

A way down the hall, Ares emerged from the Ruby Bureau after a conference with a city planner from Trihoul. With some time off, he thought that a glass of wine or four or five were needed.

He licked his finger, sifting through codes and blueprints, but stalled at the periphery of the Amber Lounge. His leafy green eyes zipped to two pale legs bouncing without rhythm over the edge of his sofa.

Ares scowled. All of his cushions were on the floor, and there were about thirty books on his table. He tilted his head. *'Magick Sanctuary by Drisor Poppit,' 'A Series of Arcanan Blunders by Magistress Asla S.,' 'Sorcerer's Workbook Vol. 61 by the Children of the Spirits Association,' 'Illusory Foundations by T. Venwick Lageet.'* Ares lacked the focus to read every title, but now questions tugged on his tongue.

"Interesting subject matter . . . and way to sit," he spoke up.

Luxea dropped the clunky book onto her face and grunted. She tipped her head back, and their stares met topsy-turvy. She scooted herself upright with one hand at her skirts to stop them from riding up.

"Ares, hello. Good afternoon," said Luxea, setting the book down.

"Likewise, but my name is *Ah-raze,* not *Air-eez,*" he said stiffly.

"O-oh, *Ah-raze.* I'm sorry," gulped Luxea. "Er, yes, the books. I've been studying the arcana for over a year now. I — um — I'll clean the mess later."

Ares sank onto the opposite sofa and retrieved an ewer from the side table. "I would appreciate that. Wine?" he asked, pouring himself a glass.

Luxea's cheeks flushed. Avari always scolded her for imbibing. Surrendering to temptation, she said, "Yes, I'd love some."

Ares filled a second chalice. When the wine tickled the brim, he held it out for her. A drink in his hand and Luxea for company might calm his nerves, he thought, and he didn't know a thing about her, but he wanted to.

"You've been researching magick. Aside from the general history, I haven't looked into it. What pushed you to explore it?" asked Ares.

Red filled Luxea's mouth. "Well, I need to learn how to use it."

Ares' pupils grew and shrank. "You're a sorceress?" he asked.

"Did nobody tell you? Avari said you'd be ecstatic," replied Luxea.

"I was never informed," muttered Ares. "I've only borne witness to magick once at a performance, but I scarcely remember it."

"If you can't remember, it wasn't real magick," said Luxea slyly.

Ares tapped his mouth. "It was glittery," he said vaguely.

"Maybe it was real then," laughed Luxea.

"Sorcery is rare. With the right knowledge, you can rearrange the world in your favor. When did you discover it?" asked Ares intensely.

"About a year ago. I blew up a gammer's stash of apples — by accident, of course," started Luxea. Ares looked flummoxed. "On the same day, I won a game of Extreme Dragon Stones by —"

" 'Extreme' Dragon Stones?" asked Ares.

"Yes, where the bloodstones are heated first. It was an unorthodox victory with lots of magick involved," said Luxea kittenishly. "Wagers were so high that Avari said we could buy the castle."

Ares scoffed quietly. "Perhaps a dishrag from the castle," he said into his chalice. "And using your magick in Extreme Dragon Stones wasn't considered cheating?"

"I won't argue with my conquest," purred Luxea. "The day after, Avari brought me to the library to test my magick. Sure enough . . ."

"This was a year ago? You didn't know before then?" asked Ares.

Not wishing to bore him, Luxea hurriedly summarized the river, waking up with starry eyes and no memory of her past, and enrolling in the Tzapodian military. Ares was rather absorbed by her story.

"I'm sure magick came as a surprise," he said, stroking his chin.

"Surely," said Luxea. "Even after all this time, spells can be weak. It's so frustrating, but I'll grasp the practice one day."

"A man who has never walked would find himself struggling to run," said Ares perceptively. He looked her up and down. "If you went through so much trouble to discover that you're a sorceress, do you not have a *Magelas?"*

"A what?"

"A tattoo that reads your name in arcanan."

Luxea cupped the right side of her neck, and the blue ink tingled under her palm. "How do you know about that?"

"You *do* have one," said Ares. A shadow appeared on his face. "I don't condone it, but the Joined Hands requires magick-users to be branded in the color of their arcana when it comes to fruition. It's protocol to prevent sorcerers from hiding that they're sorcerers."

"Hiding it? But magick isn't a bad thing," said Luxea succinctly.

"It's for the comfort of those around you," said Ares sourly. "The wars of spell and blade have ended, but many still fear sorcery."

"Why would anyone fear it?" wondered Luxea.

"You've not been taught the history of magick, have you?" asked Ares. Luxea's head shook at once. He poured himself another glass of wine. "I've nowhere to be at the moment, so I'll brief you. In Era two, the use of arcana was in its prime. But as with all great things, those without power found a reason to hinder it."

"Lor'thanin was once home to one of the world's two magick academies. It's still intact at the foot of the Crystal Spire, called Sirah Academy. At the time, Selnilar was under the rule of the old Light Seeker, a man named Vasna Lorreen. He obsessed over the thought that Selnilar would fall into the hands of sorcerers, so he robbed them of the chance. Vasna Lorreen named the arcana as the ultimate impurity that would steer the Joined Hands' downfall, and all men, women, children, and newborns who had the arcana within them were branded by law . . . and most were caged and slaughtered. Erelong, it was common for sorcerers to face execution."

"As the chaos spread, magick-users from the Greatgrace made a pilgrimage to the sanctuary that Sirah Academy offered, and for a decade, they holed themselves up inside. That was until the *Leitha'maen* marched into Sirah alongside Vasna Lorreen. Nearly half of the academy was eradicated, but just when the assailants raised their blades to the last of the sorcerers, Sirah came to life and trapped the attackers within crystal where they remain to this day."

"Sorcerers are rare because we were wiped out?" asked Luxea.

"Indeed," confirmed Ares. "Presently, the free-killing of sorcerers is banned, and you have the same prerogatives as others, but bias lingers in the *Magelas*. In my opinion, that requirement only fuels the delusion that sorcerers should be abhorred."

Luxea rubbed her tattoo. It felt like an enemy.

"They fear you because they can't understand you," reminded Ares. "You're an anomaly. It's impossible for most to see past what beliefs they've been fed all their lives. Any abnormality in society's design becomes a means for disarray. But that never defines you."

Luxea examined Ares' curled horns and jagged talons. "You're as much of an oddity as I am. We're not so different from each other in that sense, yet people adore you, not fear you," she pointed out.

"You would be amazed by how wrong you are," retorted Ares.

Luxea ran her finger along the lip of the chalice. One last query poked at her. "Pardon my asking if this is insensitive, but did something like this happen to your people too?"

Ares' eyes frosted over. "The dragons?"

"Yes," said Luxea. "I've heard that you're the last of Samsamet's cursed children, so I was wondering —"

"— if the rest of my kind were slain like yours were?"

Luxea knew she was treading on fragile territory. "Yes," she said.

"No one had to kill us. We did so on our own," spat Ares. He drank his wine, collected his papers, and turned without a farewell.

Before he left, Luxea blurted out, "Thank you for teaching me about the *Magelas.* I enjoy speaking with you, Ares."

She'd said his name correctly that time. He glanced over his shoulder. "Feel free to finish the wine," he said tersely.

Ares' heavy footsteps gained distance. There was a creak of a door, a slam, and a click of a latch. Luxea flattened into the cushions. The pique that had shown on Ares' face when the dragons were brought into question nipped at her, and she couldn't stop thinking about it.

What must it be like to watch time burn away before his eyes?

What fear must he feel with a monster lurking in his skull?

What loneliness must beset him to be the last?

WICKED OATH
10.KINGSREIGN.25.OSC.3

ARES HAD hardly rolled out of bed in time for a conference with an emissary from the Isle of Varnn named General Torrin. He supposed it had to be a pressing matter because the aestof people rarely left their island. It had been cursed to eternal night by Varnn the God of Bats, so the residents had an extreme sensitivity to daylight.

Ares spotted the general in the shadows of his bureau. His red eyes and sooty hair gave him the mysterious air that all of his ilk possessed.

"Good afternoon, Torrin," said Ares formally.

The general blew smoke past his fangs. "Yer Highness. Thanks for 'avin' me," he said with an overwhelming Varnnish accent.

"My pleasure," said Ares hospitably. "I hope your trip wasn't too taxing. I apologize that the sunlight can be invasive in Tzapodia. Tea?"

"Yea, thanks," said Torrin, flicking ash onto the floor. Ares scowled at the mess. "Eh, the Tehrastar fucks me no matter where she shines. Trip 'ere wasn't bad. Was already in L'arneth."

"How convenient," said Ares, filling a cup. "Are the Masters Vesas and Levelia prospering? I haven't had the opportunity to speak with them for quite some time."

"The Masters are livin' the dream, Yer Highness," said Torrin pleasantly. "Nice to see Tzapodia thrivin'. Wasn't in the best shape last I came 'round here. 'Twas darker than Varnn."

"Because there was a devil on the throne," said Ares, offering the tea. "I'd hope that these lands have improved now that they're mine."

"Yea, you did good fixin' this place up. But I reckon it ain't much of an achievement to lead betta' than yer ol' dad!" laughed Torrin.

Ares drank with a sour smile. "I won't disagree."

After stirring the tea, General Torrin gulped it. "How you been, Lavrenthea? Growin' out yer hair, besides. I heard the Taress girl's outta the picture. Was a good match, that one. Shame."

Breath was snagged in Ares' throat. "Quite the opposite. I'll sooner marry an honest beggar than a lying empress," he said bitterly. "But my platter is too full for that as it is. Recent events in L'arneth have had my stress levels grasping at the sky."

"Sorry to 'ear," said Torrin. "So I take it you got our warnin'?"

Ares stiffened mid-sip. "What was that . . . ?"

"You 'eard me," said Torrin sweetly. "You ain't no 'alfwit. You get it. I know you dragons've got minds s'quick as yer tempers."

"Is it so obvious?" asked Ares, setting his teacup down. "I haven't been informed of the reason for this summoning. In fact, none of my keepers knew why you were coming. Why is that?"

Torrin plopped his cigarette butt into his cup. "S'because I've been savin' this message for yer ears only."

"I don't fare well with obscurities. Why are you here, Torrin?"

"Take a guess, Lavrenthea."

"The fall of Selnilar," said Ares at once.

"As I says: quick mind," said Torrin amusedly. "S'pose I'll jump right to business. This world's takin' new turns, n' She wants you."

The general pulled a scroll out of his cloak. Ares glanced at it without a thought and held his breath. The black wax seal that fastened the parchment bore a symbol identical to the one that had been carved into Rylin O'sara's flesh.

Ares snatched it. His panic grew as he read the first page.

TO PRINCE ARES LAVRENTHEA:

THE WORLD FEARS THE SPIDER, BUT THE SPIDER IS NECESSARY TO CULL THE INSECTS WHO CONTRIBUTE NAUGHT TO EXISTENCE. THE BROOD FIGHTS FOR A FUTURE OF WHICH ONLY THE MIGHTY ARE DESERVING.

JOIN US, FOR YOU ARE ONE OF THE FEW WHOM I DEEM FIT TO REVEL IN THIS NEW ERA. TOGETHER, WE WILL ABANDON THE ILLUSION OF CONTENTMENT, AND I WILL GUARD YOUR LIFE AMIDST THE WINNOWING. OUR INFLUENCE WILL SHAPE AMNIVEN AS IT WAS MEANT TO BE: FREE OF THE WEAK, LEAVING ONES WHO SEE PROMISE IN WHAT WE COULD BE.

PUT YOUR FAITH IN ME, AND I SHALL BESTOW UPON YOU DIVINE GIFTS. I VOW TO RETURN WHAT HAS BEEN STOLEN AND FREE YOU FROM YOUR CURSE. NEVER SHALL YOU FEAR YOURSELF, SHIELD YOUR HAND FROM WATCHFUL EYES, AND YOUR CHILDREN WILL NOT SUFFER AS YOU HAVE. ALL I ASK IS THAT YOU ACCEPT ME.

FOLLOW ME, AND I WILL DELIVER YOU TO PARADISE. SPURN ME, AND YOUR LIFE IS FORFEIT.

LUCANIN, THE WIDOW.

X. _____

"You came here to entice me into purging my people?" snapped Ares. "Have you lost your mind, how selfish do you think I am?"

"Tch, *'selfish'* ain't the word," clicked Torrin. "With the extras outta the way, Tzapodia'll shine like it ain't never shined before. Val'noren n' the Masters took Widow's offer, but She wants you the most. Yer pure of blood, the last of 'em, n' She'll let you keep livin'. S'what's best, besides."

"Don't tell me what's best for my kingdom! You send me a dying soldier, slaughter his comrades, and yet you urge me to give Widow the lives of the rest of my people?" barked Ares, snapping his jaws like a rabid dog.

"Damn, show the Brood Mother this fire yer showin' me, n' She'll be all over you," hummed Torrin. "Look, you sign yer name, Widow'll get them ugly arse scales off yer arm, n' you'll be sane long 'nough to 'ave a nice family one day. That's a fair trade, aye?"

"Shut your mouth, you lunatic," said Ares, shoving him. "I'll stand behind the Widow only when I have a blade at Her neck."

"The Brood Mother said you'd be 'ardest to convince," laughed Torrin. "We'll give you time to think, but I'll be seein' you anon."

Ares tore the contract down the middle. "Pray that you don't. The next path you take that crosses mine will be your last," he warned.

It was rare for the Speaker to leave the Ruby Wing without prior notice, but what was more surprising to the castle staff was the animosity that he wore.

In the vestibule, Ares watched Torrin as he readied for departure. Then came footsteps. It was Luxea returning from the infirmary.

"Yer that spell-flingin' bitch, aren't you?" laughed Torrin. "Raised yer finger n' blinded one of our titantulas. Good show. Impressive."

"Who are you?" asked Luxea guardedly.

"You don't got to know my name, love. But I know yers," taunted the general. "What was it again? Yer girlfriend was screamin' it when her bones broke. Ah, yea, *Luxea.* S'real nice to see you got home alive, Luxea. Let's see how long you stay that way — !"

Ares collared Torrin with his forearm and sank two talons into his belly. "Speak to her again, and your blood will paint these walls." His irises were violet, and his pupils were vertical slits. Two more black scales surfaced upon his wrist.

"For a holy man, yer gettin' aggressive," jeered Torrin.

"My mercy wanes. Tread light in the land dragons made," said Ares, hurling the general. He raised his voice. "I hereby declare the Isle of Varnn as an enemy of the crown! All ties with the Isle are to be severed, and any unregistered aestof discovered within our borders forthwith are to be detained and brought to me!"

"YES, YOUR HIGHNESS!" shouted every sentinel at once.

Ares arched his lip at the general. *"Get out."*

Torrin dashed to a stallion stabled outside and clambered onto the saddle. The steed reared and vanished down the Steps of Sevinus. All was still until the clopping of hooves faded.

The general was gone, but his words scourged Ares. The bribe that Widow had given him was disconcerting, but what hurt the most was that two of The Six had fallen to the sweet temptation of power.

Luxea rushed to him. "Ares, who was that?"

"General Torrin. He was the War General of the Isle of Varnn, but now he's a servant of the Widow," said Ares broodingly.

"Widow? What was he doing here?" wondered Luxea.

Ares shot a wary look around the vestibule; there were too many ears. "I'll explain everything, but only in solitude. I don't want word of the Brood to spread. That would draw Widow's attention. If you have the time, please join me in the bureau," he said quietly.

"If you trust me."

"I do enough."

She strained to keep up with his long strides as they neared the stairwell. They raced upstairs with devils dancing in their chests.

73

The Ruby Bureau was a masterpiece varnished to satisfy only the paramount of royalty. A mechanical armillary sphere was suspended from the ceiling by silver cords, shimmering heaps of coin slathered the tabletops, sculptures swelled out of the floor, and bookcases dominated the walls. There were beaded cushions around an eight-hosed hookah to the right, and the tiles around it were worn.

"Please, take a seat — or stand. Whichever is comfortable," said Ares, locking the door. "I doubt that I'm warranted to disclose this beyond The Six, but all members of the organization are either too far to address or disloyal, so I'll make an exception just this once. You're the only one in Tzapodia who holds as much knowledge on the Widow as I, so if wish for me to tell you more, I will."

"I'd like to know," said Luxea distantly. "As much as I direct my focus onto better things, there's little hope suppressing the memory of Lor'thanin. The screams, the silence, the Light Seeker . . ."

Ares pulled a roseleaf cigarette out of a silver case. "The eye is stained when it looks upon death," he told her, striking a match. "You don't mind, do you?"

"No, go ahead."

"Thank you," said Ares, lighting the cigarette. He leaned against his desk and exhaled. "Widow is pulling the Light Seeker's strings, and after today's events, I see how. He signed a contract that declared him as a beneficiary to Widow's divine gifts and immunity to death. That's why General Torrin came: to offer me the same. The contract is there, on the floor."

Luxea spied two ripped sheets of paper. Beholding them ran her blood black, but they bewitched her fingers. Like she was picking a poison blossom, she gathered the scraps. Ares' eyes scanned up and down as she read the contents. Her stars burned to crimson when she was at the closing.

She whispered, *"Yeth'lavren."*

Blue flames consumed the contract, and only embers and melted, black wax remained. Luxea rid the pads of her fingers of ash and asked, "What will you do next?"

"Widow will hear about my refusal erelong," said Ares, massaging his temples. "It hardly matters what *I* do. All that remains now that the Light Seeker and the Masters are gone is the Lady, the Sun Chief, the Empress, and myself. Lady Peyamo Nelnah would never give up Tarot for personal gain, and I've preserved Tzapodia's freedom for the time being, but if the Brood seizes The Six, I'll be powerless. So to answer your question: I haven't the faintest clue what comes next. I can't win this alone."

"Alone?" echoed Luxea. "May I be frank?"

"Certainly," puffed Ares.

Luxea counted on her fingers. "Avari, Claymore, Skythoan, Peyamo, Oscerin, *me.* It took three seconds to name six friends that will fight for you, and that's not including your army who have vowed their lives for that purpose. You say you don't want word of the Brood Mother to burn out of control, but containing the name of a virus won't hinder the virus from spreading. If you don't raise awareness about Her, She'll do it Herself. Rally The Six before She can! You don't have to face it without aid."

Through a veil of roseleaf smoke, their eyes linked by an invisible thread that neither could sunder, a synthesis of starlight and jade. Ares' throat rippled as he drank in her declaration, and her integrity wetted his tongue with a taste like nectar. There was an irrefutable truth in the way that she spoke from which even the stubbornest of Ares' doubts couldn't hide.

Ares strode desultorily around the bureau. "Yes, thank you for that reminder. I'll reach out to whomever I can, and if that fails, we'll fight with what we have." He stepped nearer. "But, Luxea, apart from the bigger picture, Torrin knew your face and your name, and it's doubtless that he's not the only one who does. You were in a sanctuary when he recognized you, but if you're ever in a place without the eyes of my men or myself upon you, I don't know what those villains would do. Promise me you won't stray."

Luxea's stars were a rosy shade. "I promise you," she told him.

That night, Ares unearthed a ledger and flipped to an empty page. He saturated the vellum with thick strokes.

AMO,

THE SIX CANNOT BE TRUSTED. ANY COMMUNICATIONS YOU RECEIVE FROM SELNILAR OR THE ISLE OF VARNN ARE FROM ENEMIES. IF TAROT HASN'T CAUGHT WIND OF THE NAME, I MUST WARN YOU OF 'THE WIDOW.'

WE SHOULD MEET IF YOU CAN. IF I'VE EVER KNOWN ANYONE TO UNCOVER ANSWERS WHERE I CAN FIND NONE, IT'S YOU.

ARES LAVRENTHEA

Ares tore the page from the ledger and tied it off with a silver thread. He popped a cigarette into his mouth — the fifteenth or so that evening — and grabbed a stick of blue wax. He lit the cigarette and heated the wax with the flame. It dripped, *tap, tap, tap.* Ares blew smoke from the corner of his mouth and pressed the missive with the Tzapodian seal.

"*Hashis . . . hiahisia. . . .*"

Whispers purled throughout the bureau. A shiver seized Ares' arms. He'd spent much of his life studying tongues, but whoever was there spoke in a language that he couldn't comprehend. He listened, and all that he could hear was the sough of waves through his open window until —

"Shasiasi. . . ."

Ares crept closer to a bookcase that stretched to the ceiling and spilled with outdated registries and artifacts so old that they no longer had names.

"HASHISIASIA . . . !" it whispered louder.

Ares tilted his head like a puppy. The voice was coming from *inside* of the bookshelf. He rolled the ladder toward him. It rumbled as the wheels caught on the track. He pressed his weight onto the bottom peg, and it didn't snap, so he ascended to the second to last level near the top of the bookcase.

"Ashia . . . shasi. . . ."

The whispers were coming from the left. Ares gripped a shelf and slid the ladder closer. Whatever was talking to him was within a cubby jammed with parchments, world maps, and a dish of trinkets. Ares adjusted his cigarette in his mouth and swatted away cobwebs. Dust and lint puffed into the air. Toward the back, an unpleasant sensation tore up his arm.

ZAP!

"Agh!" hissed Ares, yanking out his hand. For a moment, his limb was entirely numb. He saw something silver and tilted his head back in recognition. "Oh, it's you. You've been awfully quiet all these years. Why speak now? Unless . . . she woke you up, didn't she?"

The Architect
11.KINGSREIGN.25.OSC.3

AT HALF-PAST eleven, Luxea stretched in front of the mirror and crinkled her nose. She sank a comb into her hair, starting from the slovenly bottom strands and working her way to the summit.

A loud *thump* came from outside of her door.

Luxea scurried across the bedchamber, crouched, and poked an eye through the crack in the door. There was a rectangular item enclosed by silver silk with a note attached. Whoever had left it had zero talent for gift-wrapping. She turned the note in her hands. Nothing was written on it other than her name in velvety penmanship.

But inside —

MISS LUXEA SIREN,

THIS IS A RELIC OF INVALUABLE KNOWLEDGE. I WOULD RATHER IT BE IN YOUR HANDS THAN LOST ON MY SHELF. IF YOU CAN OPEN IT, YOU MAY CALL IT YOUR OWN. THE ONLY ADVICE I HAVE IS: SPEAK TO 'THE ARCHITECT.' IF YOU FIND THE KEY, I TRUST THAT YOU WILL GIVE IT MEANING.

HILIEN ASHTA,
ARES LAVRENTHEA

Luxea peeled back the shiny fabric and was too stunned to move. It was a spellbook. The cover was scuffed white gold embedded with cyclonic, blue arcanan gems.

At the right edge was a lock with no keyhole. She knew precisely what it was: a name lock. This enchanted seal would open only when the tome heard its name. She didn't know its name and doubted that Ares would tell her. She focused in on the third line of his letter.

"Speak to *'the Architect?'*" she mumbled.

There was one place that always had answers: the library. Luxea eagerly stepped into the hallway but stopped and examined herself. She was still wearing her nightclothes.

Donning appropriate attire, Luxea wound to the library and waved at the librarian at the front desk. "Hello, *hilien dam,*" she whispered.

"Good day, Sugar Puff," said the hoary librarian named Girtha.

Luxea darted to the frontmost right side of the library where the *'A-R'* titles were kept. There were many more books about architecture than she'd anticipated. Hundreds about blueprinting, intersecting lines, and historical monuments lined the shelves in a multicolored jeer of bindings. She had to start somewhere, but that somewhere had a thousand possible routes leading to it.

Hours later, Luxea had gutted the library but uncovered nothing but useless information. There had been accounts of Sirah Academy's construction and how sorcerers had helped build some of Amniven's landmarks, such as the Great Bridge, Tarhelen, but as interested as Luxea was in learning, that didn't solve her predicament.

Luxea lifted her head off of the table and peeled Ares' letter away from her sweaty cheek. She reread it for the one-hundredth time, and after the one-hundred-and-first time, she decided to ask for help.

Her stars settled upon Girtha, who was just as old as ever. Maybe she had secrets hidden up her flappy sleeves — or perhaps she was *the Architect?*

"How are you feeling today, Girtha?" greeted Luxea.

Girtha emerged from her enormous hat like a turtle from its shell, and her lips rumpled like a fleshy zipper. "Hello, Pretty Peach," she whistled. "How can I help you? Come to check out arcana volumes?"

"Er, no. I have an unrelated question," replied Luxea.

"Unrelated? How exciting!" exclaimed Girtha, but in a whisper as not to disturb readers. "What do you need, Sweetest Little Pea?"

"In order to open this book, I need to speak to *the Architect.* Do you know whom that might be?" asked Luxea.

Girtha blinked, and her eyelids squeaked like a thumb on glass. "My great grandson is an architect. Best one in Tel Ashir," she said quietly. "I'll give you the address to his workshop."

Luxea squealed, "That would be — !" She caught herself and lowered her volume. "That would be fantastic. Thank you."

Girtha scribbled the address on the page. It was slapdash, but nothing could've impeded Luxea from finding *the Architect* — not even awful penmanship.

Luxea crashed down the Kingslane and into the streets of Yula Montier. She scanned Girtha's unintelligible note as she cruised through crowds and finally made out: *'Velous Direk.'*

When Luxea reached Velous Direk, she was a huffing and puffing mess. The building at which she stopped had a flat rooftop like a sugar cube and a round double-story window. The bell on the doorframe *jingled.* The interior was blank and geometric with nothing but a white counter and a few empty picture frames on the walls. It was somehow pleasing to look at.

Hovering over the front desk was a seroden man with buzzed, orange hair and a forehead as speckled and oblong as a robin's egg. His overalls accentuated his pudgy belly, but it complemented him.

"Good afternoon. Your home is breathtaking," warbled Luxea.

"Thank you," he chuckled. "Name's Ardin. How may I help you?"

"My name is Luxea," she told him. "Your old granny Girtha sent me. Are you by any chance *the Architect?*"

"My husband's the architect. I'll fetch him for you," offered Ardin.

He departed through a revolving door. After a minute, a second man emerged. He was human, lanky, bald, and had a forward-head posture. His loose neck skin flapped like a little flag.

"Sir, hello," said Luxea, cheeks swelling.

"Hello," said the architect. "I'm Pirtha. Granny Girtha sent you?"

"Yes. I have a question for you." Luxea slid the spellbook across the counter. "Girtha says you're the best at what you do."

Pirtha's brow tipped. "Are your blueprints in there?"

"No. Do I need blueprints?"

"I can sketch them up for you if you'd like. What are you looking to construct?" asked Pirtha, unrolling some paper.

"No, no, I just need to open this spellbook. It's enchanted with a name lock, see?" said Luxea, pointing at the latch.

"I don't dabble in books, miss," said Pirtha frankly.

"But aren't you *the Architect?*"

"I'm *an* architect."

"You're just a regular architect? Are you sure?"

"Very sure."

Luxea's shoulders hung. "I misunderstood," she groaned.

Pirtha scratched his head. "I'd try a locksmith. This is in their area of expertise I reckon," he said, jotting down an address. "My sister runs a shop on the far end of the city. Lass can open anything."

"You think?" gasped Luxea.

"Mhm. Tell her Pirtha sent you," he instructed. "But I'd hurry. The Tehrastar's falling, and she closes her doors at sundown."

Luxea skimmed over the address. His handwriting was just as illegible as Girtha's. She thought that this was a counterproductive characteristic for an architect to have.

"I'll hurry. Thank you!" said Luxea, running outside.

Pirtha hadn't exaggerated when he said that the locksmith's shop was at the far end of the city. It was the farthest building in the farthest district of Tel Ashir, Nu Dalajur.

Luxea almost deflated on the road when she arrived. The locksmith's storefront was just as striking as Pirtha's — strikingly ugly. It was a shanty with a big, wooden key nailed over the entrance.

Unlike Pirtha's shop, there was no bell above the door, there was a bushel of radishes. The room had one window the size of a mail slot, and all of the furniture was hammered together from scraps of recycled timber.

A disturbingly beefy hen was walking around, and a teensy old man was curled like a shrimp under a blanket in the duskiest corner of the room. His pencil spine hardly sustained his onion head.

" 'Ello, wee lass," said a brawny woman. Her neck was the same circumference as her head like a human toe.

"Are you Pirtha's sister?" asked Luxea, evading the giant hen.

"Tha's me. M'name's Mirtha. Lemme show ye my colleagues. This 'ere's Kirtha — most folks call 'im *'Pap,' "* said Mirtha, pointing at the old man. She squatted and broke into a yell, "James! Gitchye crease outtae!"

"Comin', Mum," said a muffled voice.

Out came James, an adolescent boy with scarcely any hair and a face brittled with blemishes. He looked as aged as Kirtha — or Pap. Luxea was put off by his startlingly average name.

"N-nice to meet you all," she stammered, unhooking the spellbook. "I'm here for this. It's sealed with a name lock, and I need to open it."

Mirtha gave it a look-see. "It don' even 'ave a lock," she said.

"Yes, I need its name to break it open. I was told to speak to *the Architect,* so I went to Pirtha, and he sent me here," explained Luxea.

"Oiiiii, a'see. Nae a problem. I don' think ye'll needae name fur this'n. I can pop 'er right open," said Mirtha with a knee slap.

"Really? Thank you so much!" exclaimed Luxea.

Mirtha dipped into the next room. Kirtha's — or Pap's — button eyes barely peeked over the hump on his nose, and James hovered with his arms crooked, breathing out of his O-shaped mouth. Luxea smiled, but neither returned the gesture. She powered through the silence until James groaned, "Birtha likes you."

"Who?" hooted Luxea.

"Birtha," said James nasally.

He pointed at the strapping hen that patrolled Luxea's legs like a fortress. It ogled her with its too-close-together eyes. They were at the front of its head, which wasn't where they were supposed to be.

"She does like me, doesn't she?" asked Luxea, disconcerted.

"Birtha is male," corrected James.

Luxea was reasonably sure that Birtha was a female. "Sorry. He's a lovely rooster," she said incredulously.

"Birtha is a chicken."

Luxea strained not to roll her eyes. "A lovely *chicken.*"

"Let's get 'at bugger unlocked!" said Mirtha, reentering the room.

Thankful not to have to speak with James any longer, Luxea spun around and chirped, "That would be grea —"

Her teeth snapped closed so fast that they almost cracked. Mirtha wielded a chisel in one hand and a sledgehammer in the other.

"What are you going to do to it?" asked Luxea, coddling the book.

"What I do to everythin' 'at don' make sense: smack it," said Mirtha unambiguously.

If Mirtha made one wrong move, a historic heirloom would be deemed useless. However, the book had just as little purpose if Luxea couldn't open it to begin with. Although fearful of the outcome, she handed it over.

"Be careful," she gulped.

Mirtha set the spellbook on a table that looked like it might collapse, rolled back her meaty shoulders, and positioned the chisel over the latch.

"Step back, wee quine. This is how a real locksmith does 'er."

Mirtha struck the chisel with her sledgehammer. *CLACK — !*

Blue light illuminated the shop, and earsplitting arcanan screams broke the mail-slot window. Birtha fled for cover. Luxea smacked her hands over her ears. Mirtha's thumb-like silhouette spiraled backward, obliterating a part of the wall. The energetic discharge abated. After all of that, the name lock was steadfast. Birtha reentered the battlefield.

James wheezed, "Mum . . . Mumma? Mum . . . Mu —"

Mirtha rose from the rubble like a phoenix. She was charred, and her patchy, red hair was fanned out like an electrified broom. Smoking at the nostrils, and everywhere else, she roared, "Git gonnae!"

"I-I'm sorry!" said Luxea, snatching the spellbook off of the table. "I didn't mean to cause troub — !" The table's legs gave out.

Mirtha started to chase Luxea, yelling, "Git out, ye stank!"

Luxea bounded to the exit. Birtha honed in on her feet like a dart. She slammed the door before Mirtha or the chicken could follow.

Several days had gone by, or maybe weeks, but Luxea couldn't tell. She slouched in the Amber Lounge, and her starry eyes were grey from sleep deprivation.

Ares strode down the hallway and bit into an apple as he inspected his agenda. He fell idle at the lounge. One of Luxea's eyes was buggier than the other, and scrolls were all over the place. She was plainly at her wits' end, but unfortunately for her, it was one of those days when Ares felt playful.

"I heard about your mishap at the locksmith's," he hummed.

Luxea gulped. She'd hoped that he wouldn't catch wind of that.

Ares tossed his apple into the air a few times. He went on, "I was surprised when I'd learned about a l'arian woman running rampant around my city. I find myself lying awake at night, wondering who might be next. A grocer? A stonemason?"

"I was thinking a carpenter," said Luxea tartly.

Ares let out a devilish chuckle and covered it up by clearing his throat. "They wanted to press charges. But in all truth, you don't seem like a criminal, so I overruled it. You're welcome. I should go. I wish you the best of luck — but do try not to violate anybody else."

As Ares left, Luxea flicked up one finger. He stopped and cleaned apple bits from his teeth with his tongue.

"Ares, are you *the Architect?*" asked Luxea loonily.

"I'm afraid not," said Ares, taking another bite. "Don't look so far ahead. You have the answer right in front of you."

Luxea's stars snapped to her hoard of scrolls.

Ares smirked. "Have a nice day, *ei'mithanen.*"

His emphatic l'arian elvish farewell went through one of Luxea's ears and out the other. Resolve reinvigorated, she plunged into the jumble of vellums.

For the next few days, Luxea cooped herself up in her bedchamber with a tower of books. After reading through every one front-to-back, she began to think that the solution might lie inside the spellbook itself, and she'd been overlooking it. Maybe its name was *'Please.'*

In the dead of night, Luxea glared at the spellbook as it lounged on her sofa like it owned the place. Out of frustration, she blasted it with arcanan fire. It was untouched, but the cushions were singed. She concealed the damage with a throw blanket.

Downcast, Luxea tossed the spellbook onto her bed and flopped next to it. She should've slept, but ten thousand honeybees were in her skull, and they were all screaming.

In the morning, Luxea's last threads of sanity were snapping one-by-one, and she was so tired that her eyes felt like globs of wet paint. Vanquished, she buried her face in Ares' letter for the last time. When she was about to crumple it up and toss it out, or perhaps light it on fire and laugh, she focused on the closing.

HILIEN ASHTA,
ARES LAVRENTHEA

Luxea had previously assumed that Ares had written it in her native tongue because of her ethnic background, and maybe she'd lost her mind, but she had an idea.

She enunciated *'Architect'* in l'arian elvish.

"Usinnon."

The spellbook quaked and slid onto the floor. A swarm of arcanan whispers buzzed to and fro, the gems exploded with light, and bolts of azure lightning arced across the rug. Then — *click.*

The name lock unlatched. Luxea fell off of the bed.

"You're *'the Architect?!'"* A giggle then squirmed out of Luxea's mouth. She smothered the Usinnon. "You're mine, I get it! Speak to *the Architect* — the *Usinnon* — that's your name!"

"Hasiashasasa. . . ." whispered the Usinnon, congratulating her.

Before opening the spellbook, Luxea bolted to the balcony and cupped her palm in front of her mouth as if to drink from it. Through a smile, she whispered an incantation. An arcanan illusion phased out of her hand. It braved the sunrae winds and flew over the railing.

Too eager to sleep now, Luxea opened the Usinnon. It was flooded with a magister's handwritten notes. This was a *real* spellbook.

The Architect — the foundation of magick itself — the Usinnon.

In the Emerald Wing, the Speaker and the Mooncaller Council were discussing new laws in Tzapodia. However, most submissions were preposterous. The current focus was a city-wide ban on canines.

"I said *'no,'* Your Highness, but he's sent fourteen letters," said Keeper Vessias with a hefty stack of missives in his hand.

Jaded, Ares slumped his head into his palm. "We can't ban dogs. Say it violates Tel Ashir city code. People never check," he suggested.

"But, Your Highness, in the instance that he *does* look into Tel Ashir's coding, what actions should we take . . . to . . ."

Keeper Vessias looked up. The council members all goggled at the open window above the Speaker's chair. Ares tipped his head back.

Fluttering about was a ghostly butterfly that sprinkled white dust. It swooped onto the table and swiveled its wings. Ares outstretched his claw, and the butterfly crawled onto it; its legs were as rimy and light as the brush of a frosty feather.

As suddenly as it had showed, the arcanan butterfly twinkled away. Shallow dimples appeared at the sides of Ares' mouth.

"Your Highness, what the hell was that?" asked General Skythoan.

"What?" asked Ares distractedly. He hemmed and whisked the arcanan ash from his finger. "It's nothing. Forgive me, gentlemen."

SON OF THE MASTERS
10.WORLDBREAK.25.OSC.3

SINCE MANAGING to open the Usinnon, Luxea practiced with it daily in the Flame Gardens of Castle Lavrenthea. One evening, she was learning to channel emotion into magick. Other spellbooks had touched on this, but the Usinnon listed it as a staple. It referred to the arcana as a vital organ of the sorcerer. Without the spirit of the user engaged, the spell could lethally backfire.

Time rushed onward. An orchestra of singing crickets, cooing owls, and rustling leaves chimed out of the groves above the Kingscore. Luxea opened her eyes and gazed at the starless sky; it was late. She edged her toes into her sandals and trudged through the grass to the castle's side entrance.

There was a distant utterance. *"Psst!"*

Luxea swept the area. The voice had come from the Aptuli.

"Hello?" she asked, lurking forth.

"Yes! Lady, you've got to help me!"

Luxea poked her head into the orchard and crossed the outline of a figure. She couldn't make out their face. "Who are you?" she asked.

"Names Oliver. I need help!" he said in an outrageous accent.

"What are you doing in the Aptuli?" asked Luxea dubiously.

"The what? That's not important. I'm hidin'," said Oliver jumpily.

"Hiding from whom?"

"Widow!"

Luxea froze up. "Widow? Is She here? Okay, Oliver. Let's get us some light, and I'll help you."

"Wait, light? No, don't — !"

"Amal luciem."

The Aptuli illuminated. Luxea saw Oliver's face infinitesimally before he started screaming. He tripped on a tree's root, keeled over, and curled into a ball. Soon, Luxea was screaming too. For minutes straight, bright lights flickered, and she and this stranger howled at each other without knowing why.

"Who goes there? What's happening, you two?" shouted a castle sentinel, bursting through the tree line with a lantern.

"I don't know!" cried Luxea.

The sentinel crouched at Oliver's side. "Sir, lower your volume. It's late, and you're causing a disturbance. Sir, I —"

"Piss off, I'm hurtin'!" squalled Oliver.

The sentinel flipped Oliver face-up by the collar. Luxea took a peek. He had a waxen complexion, and four of his teeth tapered into fangs. His clothes were torn and bore a pungency of saltwater so ripe that Luxea got dehydrated.

"You caught a criminal, miss," said the sentinel solemnly.

"What?" asked Luxea.

"Yea, what?" asked Oliver.

The sentinel yanked Oliver to his feet and snapped irons around his skinny wrists. "This man is from the Isle of Varnn. His Highness has a warrant out for any of his ilk spotted within Tzapodia's borders."

"That's a bit racist, innit?" asked Oliver, worming around.

Down the Pearl Alley, up two coiling stairwells, through the Emerald Wing, and all the way to the bedchambers in the Amber Wing, Oliver begged for his freedom. For an adult, he made lots of infantile noises. He was a fussy, loquacious, and vulgar piglet.

The sentinel knocked on Ares' door, and Oliver's lips clamped into a dash when it cracked open. The sentinel huffed, "Your Highness, I apologize for waking you at this unholy hour, but an aestof man was discovered trespassing in the Aptuli. This woman captured him."

Ares glanced at Luxea. She pretended like she wasn't there.

Oliver jiggled his arms free from the sentinel's grip. "Can I plead my case? M'sure His Highness will love to hear it."

"Shush," said the sentinel, nabbing him again.

"You shush! Oi, I'm Oliver Kross! Vesas n' Levelia's son," said Oliver, ducking past the sentinel. All traces of sleep blinked out of Ares' eyes. Oliver peeped, "I knew you'd listen. M'no crook, I — !"

"Quiet! Being a Kross does *not* make this better for you," husked Ares. He beckoned them. "Get inside — you too, Luxea."

In Ares' bedchamber, the sentinel shunted Oliver onto the sofa, and Oliver slouched in the shape of a walking cane. Unsure where to stand, Luxea maneuvered to the edge of Ares' bed and plopped onto a chest.

"How do I know you're really the Kross heir?" grilled Ares.

"Easy-please," Oliver's arm contorted down his waist, and he extracted a trinket from his pocket. "Here. I swear, I ain't lyin'."

It was a brooch that bore the Kross family seal: two white hands with the backlit shadow of a bat behind them. Ares snatched it. He was familiar with the seal and took it as enough evidence to prove this stranger's identity, but his rugged expression only hardened.

Ares flicked the brooch onto Oliver's lap. "Luxea, how did you catch him?"

"I heard him calling from the Aptuli. He said he was hiding from Widow, so I checked on him," testified Luxea.

"That's it?" Ares faced the sentinel. "You said she captured him."

"Assaulted me's more like it," grumbled Oliver.

"I was giving us light. I couldn't see you," snapped Luxea.

"Light's crap, love," said Oliver matter-of-factly.

"I see. The aestof peoples are light-sensitive, Luxea. You burned him like as not," said Ares comprehensively. "So, Kross, you're the son of two war criminals in the Joined Hands. I had a very unpleasant visit from a Varnnish general in Kingsreign, and he told me plenty, so don't think you'll get away with hiding truths from me."

"That Torrin toff? He's the only general the Isle's got left. But I don't imagine Widow'll let him live much longer," said Oliver sourly.

Ares secretly hoped not. "And how did *you* get here?" he asked.

"A dinghy."

"You crossed the Blightwater in a dinghy?"

"I never said it was easy."

"Why were you on my property?"

"It was the first place I found after landfall."

"You scaled the cliffs of Motherpoint?"

"Dunno if you noticed, but I'm lookin' worse for wear. Scraped myself up out there. V'had better nights!" griped Oliver.

"And you're not Widow's informant?" hounded Ares.

"Widow's a nutcase! I'm tryin' to get *away* from Her!" insisted Oliver. "I don't support what the Brood is doin' at all. In fact, it's ruined my life all 'round! The Isle's all up in a toss, mate, I couldn't stay there no more, so I slipped out while I could. Tzapodia's closest to us, so I —"

"— thought you could stay *here?*" said Ares expressively.

Oliver looked sheepish, and then he blurted out, "How 'bout this? You lemme stay, n' I'll tell you whateva' I know 'bout Widow n' what She's been up to."

Ares' guise was flat, but he was considering it. A perspective of the Brood's machinations from the other end of the spectrum could be invaluable. He asked, "You want a safe place to hide in exchange for information?"

"Yea," said Oliver. "If that ain't enough, I'll give you all else I got. Please, man, if I've got to, I'll drop to my knees n' let you tickle my tonsils —"

"Stop! Stop talking!" yelled Ares, choking on his tongue.

" 'Kay," sniffed Oliver. "Well, if you want information, I've got some to give. As I says, s'not much, but I'll tell you what I know."

"Then I want that," said Ares, pinching his nose bridge. "But if I find out that you're lying about anything, I'll tie you to a post and leave you in the sunlight. Is that understood?"

Oliver grinned uncomfortably. "G-got it, mate. You won't hear nothin' wicked from me. I can stay then?"

Ares bound his fingers behind his head and spent another minute mulling over the situation. "My schedule is packed, but I have an hour free in a week. On that day, you'll come to me and tell me whatever you know of Widow's plans."

"It's late, and I don't want to bother anyone with this, so you can take the bedchamber at the end of the hall. Changes of clothing are in the wardrobe, so get rid of those salty rags you're wearing. Throw them out — bury them — I don't care which."

"You've got it. I don't fancy these pants much anyhow," said Oliver, unbuttoning his trousers and slipping them down.

"No, not here!" shouted Ares. He said through his teeth, "There's a woman present. Have some decency, for Eletheon's sake."

"Right," said Oliver, taking in an eye-full of Luxea. "Sorry, doll. You're so quiet. I forgot you were there."

The sentinel freed Oliver. Luxea left as soon as Ares allowed.

Four days went by. Due to the aggressive sunlight in Tzapodia, Oliver only ever came out of his room at dusk, so even though he was her neighbor, Luxea hadn't seen him. Instead, she heard him.

As it turned out, Oliver Kross was quite the libertine, and he was downright proud of it. Multiple times nightly, girls passed Luxea's bedchamber door giggling, and after that, all they could do was scream Oliver's name.

For the first time in weeks, the sky was overcast. Luxea spent the afternoon in the Flame Gardens learning to conjure combat familiars. She unfolded the Usinnon and read the division magick segment:

"Division magick has been practiced since the art of arcana begun. It was formulated by soulpriests in Xeneda who would split their souls to create a second being.

In ANA.2, the Scryer of the Akitaji spirit tribe misspoke a word in a soul-binding ritual, and he, as well as the town of Bulaba, was destroyed. Since then, most users of magick have moved on to other division techniques that do not necessitate such critical drawbacks, but there are some who have prolonged the old ways.

To access this subsidiary, one must be inclined to offer a part
of themselves to a temporal body. Doing so allows for summoning
familiars and mirror images, mimicking appearances, and even
raising the dead.
(That exploit is not recommended. Refer to page 432 section 7
for more on revival.)"

Luxea spotted a tree-stump by the castle corridor that seemed to have been dead for a while. She left a stone's throw between the stump and herself and spoke the incantation. The stump sparked, and the trees swayed like they were rolling over in their beds. The spell failed.

The second time, Luxea rid her head of doubts and envisioned an animal. A lion, she thought. *"I'amal ei mathas!"* she shouted.

A bead of blue light ejected from her chest and zipped to the stump. The wood warped, peeled into pieces, and swooped in circles. The scraps then shaped into what she'd pictured.

The lion sounded like wind chimes when it snarled, and sparkling fog spilled from its eye sockets. It bopped its scratchy muzzle on Luxea's palm. She was ecstatic. A piece of her soul was in that beast.

When Luxea pointed, the lion stalked past her and waited. It twirled and stood up on its hind legs as she instructed. But as it awaited its next command, footsteps clacked from the corridor.

Luxea feared that annihilating nature on castle grounds might get her in trouble. The lion sensed the source of her unease in the corridor. It leaped with its claws outstretched, ready to protect her.

"No, no, no!" screamed Luxea.

She heard screeches and clattering wood chips.

Luxea had harmed yet another innocent bystander — or possibly murdered them. Ares wouldn't be so lenient if that were the case. She saw a man in a cloak sprawled on his side with splinters around him.

"I didn't mean for that to happen!" she wailed, nudging the man. "Say something, don't die! Can you stand? Say something, please!"

Thankfully, the man was not dead. As Luxea helped him up, he groaned, "M'I seein' things, or was that a lion? But, wait — ! Tits n' whiskey, this is just wood!"

"Oh. It's you," drawled Luxea.

Before her stood Oliver Kross with his hood twisted all the way around his head. His maroon eyes glimmered. "Lo'lo. Luxea, right? You love hurtin' me, don't you? I fancy a cruel girl. 'Member me?"

"How could I forget? I've only lost four nights of sleep thanks to you and about a hundred women," said Luxea bitterly.

"Apologies, love," said Oliver with a simper. "If I'm ever keepin' you awake, why not join me n' the girls? Promise I'll treat you right."

"Did you really just ask me that?" spat Luxea.

"O'course. Offer's open. So what was that lion? Came outta no place," blabbed Oliver. Luxea was about to reply, but he sooner pointed at her eyes and gasped, "Aw, lookit those! They're twinklies."

Luxea swatted his hand. "The lion was a familiar. I'm sorry it came after you." She tucked the Usinnon under her arm and left.

Oliver bolted after her. "You're a sorceress? That explains a lot. Never met one o' you." Luxea picked up her pace, but Oliver was a leggy man. "We should get to know each other. What's your favorite color? Mine's red, er, crimson more like, but —"

"Shouldn't you be hibernating? It's daytime," snarked Luxea.

"I love daytime. Day*light's* my problem. S'cloudy today, so I thought I'd get out. This dragon place is so bright, aye? It makes me itchy," said Oliver, scratching his side. "So you live in the castle? Are you the Princess?"

"No, I'm not the Princess."

"You Ares' mum? You're a li'l young to be his mum."

"Of course, not!"

"Yea, you don't look alike at all. Are you the Princess?"

"You already asked that."

"Oops," blipped Oliver. "Ohhh, you must be one o' them upper-class whores. No wonder His Highness keeps you 'round —"

Luxea slapped him on the mouth and shoved him. "Pig."

Oliver's pointy tooth had punctured his lip, and it was bleeding. He rubbed it with his sleeve and ran into the Pearl Alley, but Luxea was already gone.

Three days later, Oliver threw on a black dress shirt, rehearsed etiquette in the mirror, and made his way to the Ruby Bureau. The Tehrastar was tucked behind the clouds again, so he deserted his cloak. He rapped on the burnished doors of the bureau and nibbled his fingernails as he waited.

Oliver heard the percussion of boots, and the door swiveled open. Ares wore a black dress shirt like Oliver's down to the last thread.

"Well, you pull off nice clothes betta' than me," joked Oliver.

Ares was already irked. "I agree. Come in. I only have an hour, so we should get started."

Oliver tiptoed inside and sucked in a gasp. "Blissit, you've got it all," he said, poking a prickly plant on Ares' desk. "If I had a room this big, I'd have the Three Ps. Parties, pets, and p —"

"You haven't been picking fights, have you?" asked Ares, noticing Oliver's swollen lip.

"This?" asked Oliver, pointing at his face. "That bird from the other night did this to me. Luxea. She's got the eyes. Magicky one."

"I'm sure you deserved it," said Ares forthrightly.

"Yea. Told her I thought she was a royal doxy. I was 'bout to ask her to try me for size, but she knocked me sideways," laughed Oliver.

Ares was revolted. "You did *what?* Why would you ever tell a woman — ? Do you even know the meaning of chivalry?"

"Forks n' spoons?" coughed Oliver.

"No, that's —" Ares jabbed Oliver in the chest. "I won't tolerate a lech like you harassing my guests. You'll apologize to Luxea *today.*"

"Fine, fine," groaned Oliver, dodging glares.

"Good. Now that you've wasted five minutes of my life, may we please begin the conference?" asked Ares in a huff.

Oliver became more sedated as he and Ares traveled to the cushions by the balcony. He sat in the shade. Ares sparked the hookah and tossed him a hose.

"Start wherever you want," said Ares gravely. "I need to hear why the Masters did what they did, how it began — just talk."

Oliver opened his mouth about ten times. He said bracingly, "Widow showed up seven months ago I think. Dad got a tip from one of his *'officers'* that the world was 'bout to be remade, or some new-agey trash. He turned out to be Widow's mole, and that's when Widow came along. She offered Mum n' Dad a bribe, and Dad took it right away, but Mum was too scared to until Widow talked to her 'bout it more. Then she took it too."

"She also tried to sway me by inducement. That's why General Torrin came to me, to offer me the contract," said Ares blackly.

"Widow didn't give it to you Herself?" asked Oliver, puzzled. "Anywho, after Mum n' Dad signed the Isle away, the Brood came outta no place n' started . . . riddin' of everybody. Widow's been usin' the Isle as a base of operations since all this happened. But then Mum n' Dad got dark n' twisted like She is. Dad does nothin' but eat the food Widow gives him, Mum spends all her time gettin' pampered, n' they never talk 'bout anythin' but the Brood Mother. It's like She crawled into their heads."

"I see. So after the Isle, Widow took Selnilar?" asked Ares.

"No. She took Drenut first, then Selnilar," clarified Oliver.

Ares swallowed a breath. "Drenut is gone?"

"S'been gone a while. You haven't heard 'bout that?" asked Oliver. He took a drag off of the hookah. "In that case, I should tell you 'bout somethin' else. It *really* affects The Six. That rishja bloke who rules Ank'tatra, Gumbo? Gagaman? Gargantuan?"

"Sun Chief Garamat un Gatra?" asked Ares faintly.

"Yea, Garamat. I heard that he got an offer from Widow n' told Her that he'd serve Her n' whatnot," began Oliver.

Ares had a serpent in his stomach. Not only was the Sun Chief Garamat un Gatra a guardian and personal friend to Ares, but he was also the longest-reigning member of The Six and potentate of Ank'tatra, Anunaru's most prominent nation geographically and economically. Without him, half of the most authoritative figures in the Joined Hands remained.

"It isn't just Drenut, Selnilar, and the Isle of Varnn that Widow has claimed, but also Ank'tatra?" asked Ares, aghast.

"Er, no, I wasn't done," said Oliver briskly. "Widow revoked the Sun Chief's contract. Now the Phoenix Gate is blowin' up in riots. Those people are pissin' silly 'bout him offerin' up their lives."

"Why would the Widow turn away Garamat? He's far more esteemed than the Masters, and Tani Renayo of Drenut isn't even a part of The Six," said Ares, confounded.

"Nothin' Widow does makes sense," quibbled Oliver. He cracked his knobby fingers one-by-one. "Might sound odd, but Ank'tatra's people revoltin' makes me jealous."

"Jealous? Why's that?" wondered Ares.

"They're standin' up for themselves. When Widow came to the Isle of Varnn, no one defied Mum n' dad. Our people laid down n' died without debatin' over a thing. They let Widow take everythin'. I wish Varnn's people had started riots too — that they'd done anythin'."

"You prefer mutiny to submission," said Ares reflectively.

"O'course, I do," said Oliver without delay. "When the Sun Chief vowed to the Brood, his people reminded him that they ain't his property. Not one person on Varnn did that. They fought for nothin' at all, n' now the Isle's history. S'all wrong. But take my word for it, you don't want Widow gettin' Her hands on Tzapodia."

After hearing these accounts, Ares thought Oliver was far less nonsensical than he'd made himself out to be. He'd relived the Brood's horrors with the ambition of benefitting Tzapodia, and this discussion alone had given Ares more insight than anything else had.

"Thank you, Kross. You've fulfilled your half of the bargain, so you may take refuge in Tel Ashir. Mark that you will never face Widow's chaos in my lands. I'll have our boundaries bolstered and men stationed at the ramparts around the clock. Tel Ashir isn't easy to break. It was built with dragons in mind," promised Ares.

Oliver was hardly soothed. "You haven't got a clue what you're up against, do you, Ares?"

After the meeting, Oliver slugged down the Pearl Alley and practiced smiling, but his gleeful semblance just wouldn't stick. Forcing himself to discuss Widow had been no simple task, so he thought to uplift himself, and maybe another, by doing the right thing.

As usual, Luxea was in the Flame Gardens hunched over the Usinnon. She turned a few pages, flipped back one, and then forward again, not noticing Oliver until he cleared his throat.

Luxea slapped the Usinnon shut and spun around. At first, she didn't recognize Oliver. She hadn't noticed how slim, clean, and sharp he looked. He was a different man without a cloak. To her, it was as much a part of him as an arm or a leg.

"Can I help you?" she asked icily.

"M'not here to bother you. I wanted to say sorry," said Oliver, kicking one foot back and forth. "Yunno, for buggin' you, callin' you a workin' girl, comin' to you on the pull." He itched his shin with his heel. "Things've been offbeat for me. I was a bit outta line."

"A bit?" snarled Luxea.

"Okay — a lot outta line," said Oliver. "But you don't got nothin' to worry 'bout, I mean it. I've been a right knoblicker since I got here, but I do respect you. I hope we can be mates. See you."

Oliver walked away. Luxea was astonished that he really was leaving her alone. She watched the grass sway where he'd stood, and then she yelled, "Wait! I have a way you can make it up to me."

"Yea? What's your idea?" asked Oliver.

"You'll help me study," stated Luxea.

"Study-study? Or *'study?'*" purred Oliver.

Luxea thrust out her lip. "What do you think?"

"Just checkin'," said Oliver, ear-to-shoulder.

"You're going to be my training dummy," said Luxea puckishly.

"No! Haven't you magick-ed me enough?" whined Oliver.

"They won't be harmful spells," assured Luxea. "I've wanted to practice on a human subject. I'm not punishing you. We can go out on days when it's cloudy so you won't burn, okay?"

"Sunshine or not, that's a scary idea, sweet," said Oliver.

"It's not dangerous," reminded Luxea. "You wanted to get to know each other, didn't you? Perfect opportunity."

Luxea's cheeks puffed up, and a tingle appeared in Oliver's belly. This was the first positive emotion that she'd shown him. "Awright, I'll be your trainin' dummy. Just don't do anythin' wonky to me."

"I wouldn't," swore Luxea. She presented her spellbook. "Before we start, I want you to meet the Usinnon. It'll be working with us."

Oliver fidgeted. "That's just a book, love."

"It's a *spellbook,* so it's like a pet," said Luxea brightly.

"Really? The Usurper? The Onion? What's its name?"

"Usinnon," laughed Luxea.

"Oh. Lo'lo, Usinnon! I'm Oliver. Nice to meet you."

"Hashiaisia . . . shiashia. . . ." whispered the Usinnon.

Oliver jumped in fright. "Did it talk?"

"Yes, it does that sometimes," said Luxea mildly.

"That's adorable. Can I hold him?" asked Oliver peppily.

"No. *That* will hurt," cautioned Luxea. "Let's begin. Stand over there." Oliver scooted across the grass. "Good. We'll begin with Xenedan methods of castration."

Oliver slapped his hands over his endangered groin. "You sadist! I very much fancy keepin' my baby cradle intact, thanks."

"I'm kidding," cackled Luxea. "We'll start with locus-jumping. It's teleportation. You'll be fine. Come on, Oli."

Pining for his man parts, Oliver moved his hands and crumpled up his face. "If you really mean it . . . do your worst."

Oliver Kross had been a hair in Luxea's eye, but she appreciated his willingness to cooperate in her studies. If he exercised restraint, she foresaw herself getting along with him well.

THE LADY'S MISSIVE
6.REDTAIL.25.OSC.3

AVARI RECOVERED, at last. Luxea put her studies on hold and spent every hour with her. Having been out of commission, she updated Avari on many changes, but only positive ones at first.

When Luxea revealed that she'd been living in Castle Lavrenthea, Avari asked innumerable times, *'You've met the Speaker?'* to which Luxea stated wasn't that exciting.

Eventually, Luxea introduced her to Oliver, and his ribald humor was helpful for once. Avari adored his personality, but when he flirted with her, she pressure pointed him in the neck.

In the Amber Lounge, Avari tossed her travel sack onto the sofa and tugged her purple scarf away from her nose to take a whiff.

"Look at this place," she said, hardly grasping that she, Avari Vishera, was inside Castle Lavrenthea's Amber Wing. "You've been staying here the whole time? How royal. Where's His Highness?"

"I assume he's in the Ruby Bureau. And I would get into the habit of calling him by his first name," advised Luxea.

"Call him *'Ares?'* All the time?" wheezed Avari.

"Just be yourself. It's like living in the barracks if the barracks looked and smelled nicer," compared Luxea.

"Excuse you," said Avari, fluffing a sofa cushion. "It's a little too extraordinary here. This is a castle, and it's Ares' castle no less."

"How's that different from another bloke's castle?" asked Oliver.

"I think Avari secretly looks up to him," hinted Luxea.

"Who doesn't? He's taller than anyone's got to be," joked Oliver.

"So what other news've you got for me?" asked Avari, flopping into a seat. "What about the goings-on in Lor'thanin?"

"There's been a good deal of information. I don't know if you remember, but before you fell asleep, you told me to warn Ares about the Light Seeker, so I slipped past the castle sentinels and ran in," said Luxea, exempting the mention of her violent assault.

Avari blinked. "Okay. Well, I assume it all went well considering you're not in the stocks — or headless. Sorry, go on."

Luxea massaged the knots in her throat. "I found Ares and told him everything. He believed me but sent a troop to Lor'thanin anyway."

Dread hit Avari like a bullet. "You told him not to, right?"

"He still sent them," struggled out Luxea.

"But you warned His Highness — Ares I mean — how bad it was, so the guys were careful, and they're fine, aren't they?" Luxea shook her head. Avari wiped the tip of her button nose and muttered, "Who was it?"

Luxea listed the names. Avari had lived in the barracks for years and been friends with all of the fallen soldiers. There was no forgiving or forgetting, but Avari didn't blame Ares even if his order had delivered them to their demises. If there was anyone to whom this tragedy could be pinned, it was Widow.

Avari wept until her pain glaciated into numbness, and her sorrow calcified into rage. Her yellowy aura washed away and exposed a dull, grey slate.

"I want Widow dead," said Avari, deep and toxic. "I'll kill Her."

Sentinels and serving girls gaped at a messenger who sped through Castle Lavrenthea. His filthy, brown hair poked up like a wheat field from beneath his scuffed goggles, and his scrappy, layered clothes had gone weeks without a rinse.

He neglected to fix himself up before an audience with the Speaker; cleanliness wasn't a requisite. The Ruby Bureau door creaked open. Ares poked his head out, glanced left, right and then down. There stood a much shorter seroden elvish man with puppy eyebrows and catlike eyes.

The messenger gave a Tarotian salute. *"Hithas!* I come bearing word from the Lady Peyamo Nelnah of Tarot, Your Highness. I apologize if it's a bit wrinkled." His stocky arm shot out, presenting a dilapidated envelope.

Ares lit up. "I was wondering when I would hear back from her. Please, come in," he proffered.

The messenger stepped inside, and the two sat at the desk. Ares peeled open the envelope and asked, "What's your name?"

"Nika Lecava, Your Highness. I'm the Lady's helmsman and head engineer — but also her quickest rider. Now I'm here," said the messenger animatedly. "It's an honor to meet you. Lady Peyamo speaks highly of you, and often."

"That's relieving. I thought that she only told embarrassing stories about the messes I've made," grumbled Ares.

"Er, she does tell those. I've heard a few myself. Quite silly, Your Highness, but that's just how our Lady is," chortled Nika.

"Always finding humor where there is none," said Ares, slipping the note from the envelope. "How are things in Tarot and the Shifting City? I suspect Amo has been building and building as usual."

"The city is glowing," said Nika pridefully. "In recent years, Lady Peyamo has focused mostly on filtering exhausts, so I'm thrilled to say that Tarot is well on its way to a healthier future."

"Good. The smog was a problem," said Ares stonily. "And how is Peyamo? Chipper, I hope."

"I've never known her not to be. Crushed me just a week ago in an arm-wrestling match," said Nika admiringly.

"I've never beaten her arm either," admitted Ares.

"Not sure anybody will," laughed Nika. He restlessly straightened his vambraces. "Thank you for your apprise, Your Highness. We harked rumors of the Widow from Ank'tatra, and bands of desert rishja have tried breaching our borders past the Dunes of Duhar to seek safety. But before your message, we didn't know what we faced. *Thali ou Tirima* has been buzzing ever since. We've heightened security settings at all perimeters, yet we worry if that'll be enough."

"I've done the same for Tzapodia. The collapse of Selnilar and the Isle were too close for comfort. I'm certain that Ank'tatra's insurgency against the Sun Chief is also trying on Tarot's resolve," said Ares a bit inattentively.

He started to read the Lady's missive. Her handwriting was almost illegible due to her ailments, but he'd trained his eye to make sense of it over time.

My dearest Ares,

I'm overjoyed to receive a letter from you even if its contents are grave. The Six is crumbling, and it's just you and me against the world, but when hasn't it been?

I insist we meet in person — me, you, and the Empress. I'm aware that you hate the idea of seeing her, but, please, face the past for the future's sake.

Annalais is hosting a gala at Villa de Taress in one moon, and you should attend. Not only do us that remain of The Six need to link, but I've also missed you. I hope to see you in Solissium when sunrae sees its last lights.

Forever your friend,

Amo

P.S. Anunaru is cold in redrift, so bring a coat. A real coat, not that pretty one you call a coat. You know which one I mean.

Silent, Ares tossed Peyamo's letter into a pile of other reports that he couldn't have cared less for. Nika frowned at the crumpled page. "Your Highness, may I ask you a personal question?" he asked.

Ares took a deep breath. "Yes, go ahead."

"You're disinclined to attend the gala because of the Empress' scorning of your trust?" asked Nika with care. Ares nodded once. "So your principal concern is facing Her Splendor after so long of refusing communication, correct?"

"Annalais would try to sweet talk me into reminiscing former pleasures or whatever trickery she could manage," said Ares with a cigarette bouncing out of the corner of his mouth. "Anna hates to be ignored, so she makes herself impossible to forget."

"Yes, the Lady Peyamo has mentioned a nasty thing or two about Her Splendor," said Nika. He sat up a bit. "Your Highness, you say that the Empress doesn't like to be forgotten?"

"She suffocates without attention," spat Ares.

Looking conspiratorial, Nika blabbered, "How should I put this? In computing, a file with a certain title cannot continue to operate if another file of the same name is created, it's overwritten, so . . ." Nika noticed that Ares looked royally confused, so he shooed the idea away. "What I mean is, mayhap Her Splendor's advances will cease to be effectual if someone else occupies her position. So if you attend the gala not alone, but with a partner . . ."

Ares narrowed his eyes. "You're suggesting that I arrive with another woman?"

"I — yes. Yes, that's what I'm suggesting," stuttered Nika. He monitored as Ares' cigarette burned. "Ah, listen to me. It's absurd for me to propose a solution so —"

"Excellent idea," said Ares, feeling lighter.

Nika's mouth twitched. "It is? Of course, it is! I'm sure that any woman in the Joined Hands would jump at the chance."

"And Annalais would lose her mind," said Ares contentedly. He rested his cheek on his knuckles. "I'll arrange for my Wing Regent to supervise Tzapodia in my absence and organize a convoy by the end of the week. Tell Amo she'll see me in Solissium, wearing whichever coat I want."

Nika bounced out of his chair and popped his goggles over his eyes. "Splendid! The Lady will be thrilled to hear this. Shall I request an invitation — ?"

"I won't need one. Just inform the event coordinators that I'll be present," interrupted Ares. "Thank you, Nika. I appreciate your insight and effort to journey so far to speak with me."

"It's no trouble. The lush green of the west is a sight for sore eyes. The red rocks of Tarot tend to grow repetitious," replied Nika. "Then I'll be off. Walk with the Moon, Your Highness."

Ares gave a weak Tarotian salute. "Ride with the Sun."

They exchanged bows, and Nika dashed away. As the engineer's sandy outline shrank down the hall, Ares sifted through options of whom to escort to the gala, but his mind was already set on one.

After four days, Ares summoned a handful of his council members including General Skythoan, Lieutenant Claymore, Keeper Vessias, Spymaster Ruri, Priestess Daiada, and Wing Regent Isaak. Ares announced his leave, and the others were unsettled to hear about it.

"What if Widow brings Her forces to Tzapodia, Your Highness? If she learns that we're without your protection, She may engage," said Spymaster Ruri, pinching her elfin chin.

"We don't have to worry about that," said Ares calmly. "Selnilar and the Isle of Varnn succumbed to the Brood only because Val'noren, Vesas, and Levelia tore down their lands from the inside. That's the least of worries we have here."

"What of you and the Lady attending the gala at Villa de Taress? The Brood might strike where three of The Six are gathered," said General Skythoan brashly. "You're the lifeblood of Tzapodia, but you're just asking to be slain. This is an idiotic strategy!"

Ares smiled. "Then you may leave, General. Widow considers The Six as people of power and would sooner acquire us as underlings than name us as foes." Skythoan bent his lip until his gums showed. Ares resumed his report. "The route I've designed eludes Lor'thanin's boundaries. We will cross Tal Am T'Navin by Mountain's Mirror Bridge. From there, we will cut through Storm Plains and Elder's Expanse. Goldenrise will be a straight-shot over the Great Bridge."

"Isaak, I'll need you to take my place. As you all well know, the Wing Regent has maintained his position under Tzapodia's royals for decades. He's faithful and conscious of everything I know and of what actions to take in my stead."

Wing Regent Isaak, an old man carved from ice and stone, dipped his head. "Your people will thrive under my eyes, Ares. Any who threaten their safety will sing for mercy to the steel of my sword. Go and do what you must," he said, voice grey and ashen.

"Thank you, Isaak," said Ares fondly. He faced the others. "I hope that you recognize the need for my venture. The nexus of leaders in the Joined Hands wears thin, and this is the fork that leads either to victory or annihilation. If The Six are to withstand the Brood, we must do it as one, not as six. We come together or fall apart."

General Skythoan and Keeper Vessias swapped sidelong looks. Spymaster Ruri and Priestess Daiada whispered prayers for Ares.

Lieutenant Claymore stood. "May I speak, Your Highness?"

"Proceed," enabled Ares.

"My wife will give birth in several moons," said Claymore with a hint of sentimentality. "I've pledged my life to guarding Tzapodia and will do so until my end, but soon, my child will take its first breath, and it must be taken in a haven. So I'd like to lead the convoy. I must protect what's mine as well as yours."

The hairs on Ares' arms prickled against his sleeves. "If that's your decision, I have no objections. We'll return before your child's time, and they will be born into a sanctuary."

Ares dismissed the Mooncaller Council, and all but Wing Regent Isaak left the room. His aged eyes were warm like steamed milk as he touched Ares' shoulder. "You made the right decision, boy. I'm proud to serve you."

Ares rested his talons upon the Wing Regent's leathery hand.

There remained one engagement to make, so Ares enjoyed some red wine to prepare. After cleaning out his third glass, he strode to the Amber Lounge. When he rounded the corner, he saw a face that he was vaguely familiar with, a seroden woman's with hair like a crimped feather duster, stuffing her giant mouth with an uncut cheese wheel. Luxea sat beside her taking notes, and Oliver was looking in the mirror and poking his bare belly.

"I don't mean to interrupt your . . . activities," said Ares. Caught in the act, Oliver tucked his shirt into his trousers. "If I could have your attention for a moment, I —"

"Your Highness!" said the seroden woman, flinging her cheese.

Ares flinched. "I assume this is Ranger Avari Vishera?" he asked Luxea. If it was Avari, she looked much different without a bandage strapping down her unruly hair.

"Y-yes, Your Highness!" panted Avari.

Luxea tugged her arm out of a salute. "Remember, call him Ares."

"I'm honored, Your H-Highness!" stuttered Avari. Luxea groaned.

Ares inhaled, and upon the exhale, he donned a gentlemanly expression. "Charmed, Avari," he said, bowing to her. "Please, call me Ares from now on."

Avari saluted again. "Yes, Your — !"

"Ares."

"Ar . . ."

"*Ares.*"

"Ares."

"Perfect. Thank you," said Ares relievedly. "As I was saying, I have an announcement to make. In three days, I'll set off with Lieutenant Claymore's troops to attend an event in Goldenrise and confer with two members of The Six." He threw his sights at Luxea. "This is abrupt, but I must request that you accompany me."

"Hm?" beeped Luxea. "I'd love to go, but why do you need *me?*"

"I have an assignment for you," said Ares vaguely.

Luxea had never received an order directly from her leader, and she was brimming with ideas of what Ares might have planned for her. Then she thought about all of the places she'd seen in books and heard in stories: the Western Woods, the Great Bridge, Tarhelen, and the Golden Spire Hildre. She suddenly felt zealous.

"I'll go with you," said Luxea, concealing her excitement.

Ares' chest deflated with a relieved sigh. "Thank you."

"Me too. I'm Claymore's second-in-command," said Avari.

"But you've only just recovered," pointed out Luxea.

"I'm still mightier than thou," joked Avari, squishing Luxea's arm.

"You do seem spry," said Ares. "Avari, if you feel that you're capable, your prowess would be a great help."

"I'll do better than most folks, thank ya very much," assured Avari.

"Oi, what 'bout me? Can I go?" asked Oliver.

"No," denied Ares. "There's danger outside of Tel Ashir that we might be unlucky enough to cross, and I can't afford you getting us all killed with your nonsense."

"Please, mate!" begged Oliver. "I'd be bored out my skull. Won't you feel betta' knowin' I ain't muckin' up your castle unsupervised?"

Ares shot a hiss past his teeth. Oliver would indeed be footloose inside Castle Lavrenthea, and Ares didn't want to think about what he might do without a leash.

"Fine," nipped Ares. "Are you more afraid of Luxea or Avari?"

"You frighten me the most, Ares," admitted Oliver.

"Good, but that isn't what I asked," said Ares feistily.

Oliver's eyes ticked from the sorceress to the ranger. "Luxie's scary 'cause of her magick." He gulped at the many knives strapped to Avari's thigh. "But Avari's scary in general."

"Watch it," snarled Avari.

"Y-yea, I've got to go with Avari," whimpered Oliver.

"Fantastic. Then she'll be keeping you in check until we've made it to Solissium. Thank you, Avari," directed Ares.

"What?" gasped Avari. Her shoulders hung so low that her fingers brushed the floor. "Might as well ask me to nanny a beehive."

Ares ignored her complaint. "Gather your belongings, but pack only what you need. We disembark in three days."

BLACKJAW HOLLOW
21.REDTAIL.25.OSC.3

ON THE third day, Lieutenant Claymore's troops awaited the Speaker on the Steps of Sevinus. There were shield bearers rigged in chainmail and armed with shamshirs, rangers with their heads wrapped by airy silks and longbows on their backs, and two sages with medicine bags on their hips.

Even though it was early morning, Luxea, Avari, and Oliver were already on Ares' bad side. He'd advised them to pack light, but Luxea brought along an overabundance of novels for leisurely reading, and Avari had enough knives in her satchel to supply an army. Oliver didn't have a bag, so he bundled his belongings in a cloak; three times since stepping out of his bedchamber door had his makeshift valise slipped apart and spilled his clothes and shoes.

At the entrance of Castle Lavrenthea, Lieutenant Claymore and his men saluted the Speaker at once. Luxea and Avari did too out of habit. Oliver tried to replicate the gesture but failed miserably.

Lieutenant Claymore trudged to the infirmary sages at the far end of the Porranim Courtyard and stopped in front of Hanalea. She laid her palms on his breastplate and soaked in the heat of sunlight in the steel. Claymore petted her head and kissed it, lingering to remember her fragrance — cinnamon and sugar.

"Kalo and I will be longing for your return," whispered Hanalea.

Claymore's cold eyes melted as he looked at her round belly. He rested his hand on its curve and envisioned holding his child for the first time. Wordless, he touched Hanalea's face and turned away.

Lali poked up out of nowhere. "Look, Hana, it's that drowned lady," she said, motioning to Luxea.

Hanalea wiped her teary cheeks and fluttered her fingers at the familiar, pale woman who stood beside the Speaker. "Best of luck, Miss Siren!"

"Don't go near no rivers!" cackled Lali. Hanalea scolded her.

Luxea had been told about Hanalea diving into Tal Am T'Navin's rapids to rescue her. She was about to express her gratitude vocally, but a shieldmaiden named Drishti blocked her line of sight with a blue-grey dracas in tow.

"Siren, this one's yours," she said, urging the reins into her hand. "Her name is Velesari. It was requested that she go to you. She's small for her age but'll take you far."

Velesari was the hardworking runt of the most recent litter that Luxea and Avari had trained together. She had the lowest statistics, but her attachment to Luxea had grown wildly in their time spent together.

"Hathas, ei'Velesari!" fluted Luxea. Velesari whistled like a bird.

Across the Porranim Courtyard, Avari hid a grin under her scarf.

Next, Drishti brought a dracas to Oliver. Musha, the moody brother of Velesari, had spines on his brow and mouth, giving him a scowl. The dracas bumped Oliver around with his snout and sneezed directly onto his clean dress shirt.

"Thanks. I love 'im already," said Oliver sarcastically.

Ares met with Pveather, the dracas he'd had since youth. She was white with cranberry eyes and horns spiraled like wentletrap shells.

"Me-thois te comme, lalene, jene vu thois," said Ares in draconic; *You're so big, girl, look at you.*

Avari shuddered. Pveather was nicknamed *'finger-snapper.'*

Once farewells had been given, the Mooncallers descended the Steps of Sevinus and rode onto the Kingslane. In the Court of Light, thousands of citizens flooded the streets to see them off. Flowers and folded notes were cast at the dracas' feet, dressing the cobblestones in white, yellow, red, and green. Each body was clad in bright veils; it was a sea of color. People cried out, and all were heard, but few were understood beside the voice of the next person. Tel Ashir was blazing out of control, and each head was a whistling ember.

A barrier of soldiers from the barracks kept the citizens back, but a girl no older than six peeked both ways and ducked under their arms. Her mother threw herself at the barricade and swiped, but her daughter was gone.

The girl floundered beneath the stares of the dracas. She hustled to the nearest rider, who happened to be Luxea, and screamed, "Miss!"

Luxea tugged Velesari's reins and skidded. The girl waved a note with urgency, and Luxea slid down to pluck it from her hand.

"Thanks! Thank you very much!" cheeped the girl.

She ran back to her mother. Luxea unfolded the note, but it was tricky due to about a hundred folds it had. She flattened it out on the saddle.

I wish our
cat will come home

For some, the girl's jotting might have been rubbish, but to Luxea, it looked like she'd spent hours on it. Avari leaned over on Elthevir and told Luxea, "This is common, kiddo. The people of Tel Ashir give messages to Ares to pass to Oscerin. Touching, huh?"

Luxea glanced at the girl's hopeful eyes and then swept over the other papers that coated the streets. She tried to count them, but there were too many to begin. Words written from the cores of those peoples' spirits danced over the stone like fallen flower petals.

"These are prayers . . ."

Two days swished by. The Mooncallers had hiked into Nav Amani Forest, and the white gates of Lor'thanin could be spotted through the slots in the trees.

On the second afternoon, the Mooncallers stopped in a vale roughly ten reaches south of the city of Erannor. The days were abrupt in redrift, so they pitched camp before it got dark.

Soldiers babbled frustratedly as they struggled to fit together lines and pegs, but Luxea had a far less trying time setting up her tent. She loafed on a fallen log eating grapes and reading a romance novel all while tying eaves in place with magick. Her fellow soldiers approached her one-by-one and bathed her in pleas to fix their sites for them. Close by, Oliver balanced his ridgepoles in the dirt with his feet, and then his tent collapsed.

Once Oliver had gotten his tent set up, Avari dragged him off to teach him how to use knives. A few times, she almost decapitated him, and a few more times, she called him pathetic. After half an hour, Oliver finally figured out how to grip the haft.

"Wimp. What are you gonna do when someone's ready to stick you in the dome with a pike, huh?" asked Avari candidly.

"Die," sniffed Oliver.

Feeling sorry for him, Avari gifted him the tiniest of her knives. "This one's easy to learn with. Take it, so you've got somethin' pointy on you other than those buckteeth."

Oliver grinned at her. "I feel dangerous."

"Yea? Learn to use it. Giving a mouse a sword doesn't make it a fighter," said Avari as she tossed a knife without looking; it cleaved the offshoot of a tree right down the middle.

In the interim, Ares wove through the camp with a ledger, ducking under Tzapodian banners and tallying heads; there were fifteen men not including himself. He spied three rangers loitering.

"You three," called out Ares. He gestured to a downhill path. "I'd like you to scout along the main road. It passes close to Lor'thanin, and we can't have encounters with the Brood during our journey."

The rangers gathered their weapons, swathed their heads, and hopped onto the saddles. The dracas sped down the trail.

Hours later, the sky was black, and Nav Amani Forest chattered with nature. Luxea stripped in her tent. As she pulled her tunic over her head, the girl's note slid out of her breast pocket. That child probably thought that Oscerin had heard her wish, but She hadn't. Luxea untucked her hair from her collar and looked past the tent flap.

It was challenging through the smoke from the campfire and the frosty breaths from the mouths of her comrades, but Luxea saw a tent across the way with Tzapodian banners on it. She whispered a spell, and the girl's note quivered and fluttered away. She hoped that it wouldn't fly into the fire pit.

Ares sat on his cot with a lumpy pillow supporting his back; it smelled like a bag of peanuts and felt like one too. He skimmed two books of financial accounts and copied the numbers from one to the other, but he was so tired that he accidentally wrote *'eleven'* instead of *'seven.'* He scratched it out. Just then, he heard something outside like the buzz of insect wings. He set his paperwork aside and peeked through the flap.

A singed note was stuck to the line of his tent. Ares brushed off bits of ash and unfolded it. His leafy green eyes darted back and forth as he read it once, twice, thrice. This was only one of the countless prayers that he'd received in his lifetime. After a while, the heartfelt wishes of his people had started to affect him less and less, but there was something about this one that kicked his emotions awake.

Ares' hand slithered into his collar and touched his pendant, and when it did, the Irestar came out from behind a cloud. This was the first time that he'd asked Oscerin about a cat, of all things, but it made him smile.

"Your Highness! I come bearing your patrol report," yelled one of the three rangers.

Ares swiftly hid the note in his talons. "Yes, what of it? Was there any sign of the Brood?"

"Nay, the road is clear of enemy numbers, Your Highness, but Mountain's Mirror Bridge has been washed out, surely due to traveling storms from the Iris," said the ranger uneasily.

Cursing his bad luck, Ares stalked back into his tent and unrolled a map. "Is there no other way across Tal Am T'Navin?" he asked.

"Not a way across, but there is a way around," suggested the ranger. He tapped a convergence point on the map. "If we reroute west, Tal Am T'Navin drops into underground caverns roughly here. This region of the Western Woods is unmapped, yes, but if we keep our eyes on the Tehrastar, we would add little over ten hours to our schedule at most."

There were multiple routes to take that either brought them too close to the Brood's territory or strayed too far from their initial course. If they were to cut up the center of the Western Woods as the ranger had suggested, they wouldn't alert Widow or risk elemental peril.

"I'm relieved that you caught this. We'll take leave at the break of dawn and move west. Relay the word at once," declared Ares.

The ranger vacated the tent. Ares inked the new course on the map.

The next morning, the Mooncallers collapsed their tents and equipped their armors through the dimness of dawn and the crust of sleep in their eyes. Not an hour after waking up, they mounted and rode into the Western Woods.

These paths were uncharted; seldom did they see men, and seldom did men see them. The forest was thin and peaceful. Tiny birds hopped from twig to twig, willow trees older than time dangled their branches, and a vivid, white and blue mural stained the sky.

An archer sat backward and swung her legs on either side of her garnet dracas' saddle. A melody thrummed from her throat to the rhythm of footsteps, and she crooned an old bard's tale.

"O, Lemuria, Thou fare alone,
wont to no stars or place to call home.
Little Thou speak and much dost Thou wish,
till Thy lost heart grants Thee a gift.
Giveth Thy hand and taketh Thy quill,
the ink of Thy world shalt breathe at Thy will.
Thou art creator to the lady of Sun,
the first voice therewith darkness hath sung.
Her light is Thy child, and Thou art Her mother,
but She is a daughter who yearns for another.

Giveth Thy hand and taketh Thy quill,
the ink of Thy world shalt breathe at Thy will.
Now there is Moon, but tears dost She cry,
absent of fire to brighten Her eyes.
'Fear Thee not,' dost the Sun's lady incite,
'a sister is meant to share Her own light.'
Giveth Thy hand and taketh Thy quill,
the ink of Thy world shalt breathe at Thy will.
'Shine,' quoth the day to Her kin of the eve,
'mirror my light, and hence Thou shalt see.'
White glows the Moon under Sun's golden blaze,
and smile dost She, know She the way.
Giveth thy hand and taketh thy quill,
the ink of thy world shalt breathe at thy will.
At peace is Lemuria as Her children doth grow,
spreading Their warmth ere creating Their own.
Reign high for all time doth Sisters Sun and Moon,
blessed by Their mother's first greatest boon.
Giveth Thy hand and taketh Thy quill,
the ink of Thy world shalt breathe at Thy will."

The sunshine on the archer's face felt sacred to her when she finished. Little was she aware that the Speaker had been listening. The tale of Lemuria and the Sisters of Sun and Moon had been one of his favorites when he was a child. His mother had once sung it to him before he slept.

Morning phased into afternoon, and the atmosphere became wilder. The trunks of trees were entrapped by rocks that had twisted into the bark. Fissures lined the ground leading to caverns or vertical drops. Dense canopies swallowed the Tehrastar and left but a shred of brightness, but the midday heat lived on through the humidity.

The convoy descended a steep hummock where Tal Am T'Navin River torrented into a rift. They proceeded over the chasm, and then Ares halted the dracas. Lieutenant Claymore cantered to him, and the two surveyed the roads ahead — all five of them.

Claymore looked up. "The leaves are too thick, and we cannot follow the day star. Which way do we go, Your Highness?"

Stumped, Ares whispered, "The roads in these woods are unmapped. I don't know what lies ahead."

"*Your greater concern is what is behind you,*" squawked a voice.

The stretch of a bowstring groaned from the trees.

The Mooncallers searched, but there wasn't a soul to be regarded. Avari grasped leerily for a weapon, but then an arrow flew through the undergrowth and pierced the dirt at Elthevir's feet.

"*Keep still, lest you find an arrow in your skull!*" barked another.

"*Their ssscent is dirty. It ssstings the throat!*" hissed a third.

Luxea heard a *crunch* in the soil to her right, and her mouth fell open. Snarling at her from far above was a blood red wolf twice the size of a horse. Its shoulder was painted white with the rune of the Wolf God Fenne.

Seated on its back with a cedar wood longbow was a woman with waist-length locks the same red hue spilling over her swarthy shoulders where was also the mark of Fenne. The woman and the wolf shared amber irises, haunting like sunlight through wildfire smoke.

A serpent of the same unbelievable size wound out of the bushes on the left with scales of emerald green and eyes identical to those of the rider in a basket on its neck. On the reptile's forehead was a berry red symbol of the Serpent God Sithess; the mark was also on the throat of the rider.

Lastly, clawed feet scratched to the front. A sallow, middle-aged woman with black hair down to her rawboned knees rode the most gigantic creature of the three, a raven. The two possessed the same lavender eyes, and the mark of the Raven God Raveth claimed the faces of them both.

The raven stopped at the head of the convoy and snapped its beak. The rider nodded to Ares' shamshir, and he dropped it on the ground. She detached a chained sickle from her belt and ran the arch under Ares' neck. Claymore gripped the hilt of his broadsword, but Ares ordered him to stand down.

The raven rider said haggardly, "I take it you are their leader."

Ares examined their captors. Their eyes matched, the beasts were much too big to be born of natural conditions, and all three bore the symbols of the bestial gods with which their mounts corresponded.

"I am, and you are Riders of the West."

"If you've heard of our tribe, you should have known better than to tread on sacred territory," rasped the raven rider. "What is your name, and from where to do you hail? Speak quickly, or Skye will rob you of a head."

Skye squawked and ruffled her feathers.

"We ride from the city of Tel Ashir in Tzapodia, at the sea's edge," said Ares without delay. "My name is Ares Lavrenthea, and these men fight under my name and that of the Goddess of the Moon Oscerin."

"Lavrenthea? That name is blighted, *Dragon!*" wailed the serpent rider. His beast uncoiled and hissed with the volume of a lion's roar.

"Calm that accursed snake, Syervis," ordered the raven rider.

Syervis stroked the serpent's spine. "Hush, Cheyale."

The raven rider cawed, "I know of you, Dragon. You're the only son of the Heavens Devil. For what purpose have you come?"

"There was no path for my men and me to take across the river to the east. Our destination is Solissium where we will attend an event. That is all our journey entails, I swear on my life," said Ares, glancing at the sickle. "Forgive us, raven rider. The location of your hollow has been unspoken for decades; we didn't know that these trails were forbidden. Please, I beg that you let us take our leave. There's no reason for —"

An earsplitting screech sounded from above the trees; something was patrolling the sky. The raven and the wolf riders passed each other distressed glances.

"Hehehe! Too late does the fire-breather's sssly tongue plead. Gajneva caught your ssscent," said Syervis, eating the Mooncallers' fear. "I cannot wait to tell her the newsss!"

Cheyale slithered into the brush.

"Syervis!" shouted the raven rider. The serpent and the rider were gone. She jabbed Ares with the sickle. "Horned-one, you and your people will come to our hollow, but not as guests. Leave your lizards, blades, and arrows."

Luxea pulled her skirt over the Usinnon; it was only a book, right?

The red wolf bounded forth, and the wolf rider barked, "Omnia, wait! Ruka and I taste no lie in Dragon's words. Look at these men. They tremble in fear for living, not with lust for blood. If they vow to keep our secrets, we can allow them to —"

"No, Briell. We cannot hide it now," denied Omnia. She lowered her voice. "You know what Gajneva would do if we let them go."

Skye tucked her choppy wings.

Briell petted Ruka, and his ears flattened. But Omnia was right; there was little that they could do now that their chieftain knew of the Mooncallers' intrusion. Her fingers angrily curled into Ruka's fur.

"You heard her, Dragon. We ride for Blackjaw," throated Briell.

The Mooncallers' wrists were bound by scratchy ropes, and they were led to the riders' hovel, Blackjaw Hollow. Ares told his men to go quietly. He believed that resistance was a natural reaction to danger, but when danger had a mouth as big as Ruka's, it was best to abide.

Past the thicket, the air was soddened like breathing through a hot, wet rag, and it was so quiet that one could almost hear the heartbeat of the person next to them. Warriors ducked to avoid giant bugs and spiderwebs that tied branches together like twine.

Luxea hastened to the front of the group. "Ares, what are the Riders of the West?" she murmured, glimpsing at Briell.

"Tribesmen of the greenwood," began Ares, eyes ahead. "These beasts that they ride, Ruka, Skye, and Cheyale, were once humankind. They were someone that the rider held attachment to — a parent, sibling, or a spouse. When a loved one dies, the rider sacrifices half of their soul to bring life to a second vessel. The spirit of the lost is bound to the celestial body of the beast that coincides with their star sign in life."

"The Riders' practices reverse the permanence of death, but the rider and their beast are linked in all ways from that day on. If the rider dies, the beast dies with them; if the beast dies, the rider dies with it. They're two sides of the same coin."

"Division magick," gulped Luxea. "So these beasts —"

"— are human in every way but the body," finished Ares.

Luxea cautiously faced Ruka, and he detected her. The wolf's eyes were bestial, but as he blinked, Luxea noticed something childlike about them.

Syervis and Cheyale slid through Blackjaw Hollow and into a hut. Syervis swung out of his basket and slunk to Chieftain Gajneva.

"Hm? Syervis," croaked Gajneva in words crisp like old paper. "Unwelcome feet tread on our lands; I smell them still. Is that why you have come, Serpent's Lover? *Taga osu.*"

"Yesss. Omnia bringsss them now," confirmed Syervis. "But there is sssomething you should know. Fate hasss brought you a gift."

"Ah? *Cagh!*" coughed Gajneva. She spat. "A gift? What gift?"

"One of them isss . . . the Lavrenthea child."

Gajneva bared her greying gums. She couldn't shake a smile.

Omnia slowed in a grassy meadow where an immense boulder stood with the Tehrastar shining upon it through a break in the leaves. Skye hopped closer, and it seemed like she would run into the rock, but then she disappeared past a slight left turn. Ares advanced, and the boulder revealed a hidden pathway carved only to show when standing in the right position.

Ares trudged down the walkway with the Mooncallers behind him. The tunnel steepened and spiraled, and windows in the walls showed glimpses of Blackjaw Hollow past the overgrown sheets of moss that hung over them.

The way flattened out and expanded into a cavern with an opening at the pinnacle. Lichens and fungi carpeted the ground, and lustrous minerals glittered under the roots of trees that had cracked through the ceiling. One tree reached all the way down to the floor where its gnarled branches spread like fingers over a glowing, green pond; it was the arcanan reservoir.

Rider children splashed nude in a natural spring with their young animal companions, and grottos were formed in rocks where riders slumbered as one. However, the majority of the tribesmen had congregated in the middle of the hollow to await their captives. They trotted alongside them on the backs of beasts the sizes of Ruka and Skye; a stag, a bear, a rabbit, a fox, and some others.

A lopsided hut sat on a stump up ahead, pasted to the wall by thorny ivies. Stone had encrusted the roofline, and yellow fungi reflected on the wicker.

The flap of leathery wings flew past, and a screech identical to the one that the Mooncallers had heard above the trees scored their ears. Suspended upside down over the hut was a bat; it was without a doubt the most sizable beast in the hollow. Its eyes enlarged as it scanned the faces below, and then it dipped into the shadow behind the hut.

Omnia slid from Skye's back and fitted her large nose into Ares' neck to whisper, "The chieftain will have you, Dragon, but I must warn you . . . she is rishja of the mountain kind. Gajneva and her sister suffered in Naraniv ere her sister became that winged rat. Grudges pass by blood. Be wise in your supplications."

"Thank you for the warning," said Ares, gnashing his teeth.

The hut was unlit except for the center where a twiggy throne stood, and atop it rested Chieftain Gajneva of the Riders of the West. As Omnia had said, she was an elderly rishja woman from the mountain ranges of L'arneth. She was gigantic, leonine, and had skin like gravel. She smoked a fat cigar, and her grey hair clung to the bone bangles on her wrists like cobwebs.

Gajneva leaned in like she was inspecting the Mooncallers, but she wasn't — she couldn't. Under a scalp scarred by burns, the front of her skull was exposed, and her bare sockets were empty. Gajneva was blind, but the Mooncallers sensed that she was watching them.

"The interlopers, *ilcniak thavesh,*" groaned the chieftain, weaving tongues of common and rishjaan. "Come, Veshra. Let me have a look."

A screen of dust engulfed the throne from behind as the bat limped around the side of the hut. Veshra acted as the chieftain's eyes, and when she latched her sights onto Ares, she lumbered closer until she was hovering over him. Ares held his breath to avoid the stench of mildew in her fur.

Cigar smoke surged through Gajneva's misshapen nostrils. "So it is true. Never did I foresee the crownless king of the dragonlands in my hollow — and as a prisoner!" Gajneva motioned to her riders. "Briell, Reychar, bring them to their knees."

Briell and a bear rider named Reychar pushed down the Mooncallers. Reychar trapped Ares and Claymore under his hands and huffed like a bear.

Ares looked into the bat's eyes, and in the politest tone that he could muster, he said, "Chieftain Gajneva, our intrusion wasn't intended. You permit me to plead our purpose, but I must ask you a question first. If you have eyes on your territory, then surely you've caught a trace of the one called '*Widow,*' am I wrong?"

Gajneva's forehead wrinkled above her bone. "Yes, *aku,* but why speak of that she-demon here?" she asked, sucking the damp tip of her cigar.

"If you strived for your tribe's safety, you would free us," said Ares unwaveringly. "I kneel at your throne by reason of a quest to oppose the Widow. We hunt to reclaim Amniven from Her before it's stolen."

"You cannot stand against the spider. She would have you in Her web before you knew it, *bas belak dracona*," said Gajneva, calling him a stupid dragon.

Ares ignored her insult like a fly buzzing by his ear. "Not if She is drawn out. When a spider is unsheltered, She can be crushed," he stated boldly.

"And when the spider has an army?" grunted Gajneva.

"We take the army from Her," answered Ares. "The secret of your location will be withheld, and my Mooncallers and I will fight for your kind like our own. We are equals, and if one day you wish to battle alongside us, we would welcome the Riders of the West."

Briell and Ruka exchanged glances.

The chieftain tapped her inches-long fingernails on her throne as Veshra scanned the Mooncallers' faces. With each wavering eye and bead of nervous sweat that she saw, Gajneva's mouth distorted. Finally, she guffawed.

"Aha! *Cagh-caghcagh!* The Riders fight alone, here at Blackjaw, not for you! The Widow will fall as all villains do, and we shall thrive as we have for centuries — without your help."

"Until She finds you! A spider's favorite place to capture Her prey is in the dark," snapped Ares.

"You dare strike me with such threats?" asked Gajneva hostilely.

"Perhaps Dragon speaks the truth," blurted out Briell. "Ruka and I have tracked the spider's underlings from the brush. They only grow nearer as the Irestar turns, and their numbers scatter in all directions. If Dragon guards us, could we not also guard — ?"

"Stamji'dal! Lock your jaw, Wolf! The dragon lies to spare himself. Only we will protect us!" screamed Gajneva; phlegm spattered on her rotten teeth.

Briell shrank back, and Ruka's tail tucked between his legs. Smoke from Gajneva's cigar twisted around her skeletal hand as the last traces of manipulative spirit dwindled from her face. Now there was vengeance.

"Lavrenthea, you try to sway my hand with fear, but there is no chance for you now that you are bound before me, *drajn'lach o dracona'ji,* dirty child of dragons. We are not in your kingdom, *Basu Hajanazj,* we are in mine. Tell me, what will you do if I refuse your liberty? Would you show your true face, would you raze us without mercy and leave nothing but ash? To save yourself, is that what you would do?"

"If you wish for me to kiss the ground and weep for our bonds to be cut, then I'll do that. Taunt me if you crave it, but you'll see no fire unless you force it out of me," said Ares, tolerance waning.

"It's lucid that you hold us here as a means of self-satisfaction, not out of concern for your tribe. The evils outside of Blackjaw Hollow are ones that transcend importance to your enmities, Gajneva. There has been bad blood betwixt our peoples, but —"

"Bad blood?!" roared Gajneva.

In a rage, she pitched her cigar and launched from her throne; her misaligned legs shook, and her bones rattled like she was made of sticks. Veshra and Gajneva loomed over Ares, and Gajneva's flesh-bare ocular cavities bored into him like a child to an insect, ready to squash him just because she could. She scratched her fingernails into his hair and yanked his head back.

"That silver tongue of yours was well trained to beseech your innocence, but there has never been a shred within you," said Gajneva loathsomely. She pointed to her empty sockets. "Do you know what the last thing my eyes saw was before they were stolen from me?"

Ares clenched his teeth as she wrenched his hair. "No," he said.

Gajneva inclined until her breath soaked his nostrils; it stank of ash and sour meat. "The last thing they saw was my sister burning alive at our home in Quaritan, laid to waste by the flames your father blew upon Naraniv. Now my sister, *mak rakgun,* is a beast!" she cried, cracking her hand toward Veshra. "The blaze ate my eyes when I tried to save her, and we are broken! We are broken because of your family — no — because of *you!* Oh, what I would not have forfeited to butcher the last of you devils from this realm, but now . . . here . . . you . . . *are.* You will never leave this place."

Gajneva tore her fingers from Ares' hair. "Cage them! Watch this monster and rip the flesh from their bones if he so much as breathes a spark."

Reychar hoisted Ares and Claymore off of the ground while Briell and Omnia gathered the other Mooncallers. As he was dragged off, Ares glared into Veshra's eyes.

"Bas vanje tilnulac kitia'ji!" he spat; *'you make selfish mistakes!'*

"Luz ra'na tua dracona'ji," said Gajneva; *'so did the dragons.'*

Rakgun

Tl)e Mooncallers were crammed into two wooden cages, and their arms were tied to bolts above their heads. Ares damned himself for having let this happen. Out of all of the enemies they could've stumbled into, the Riders were the last he'd predicted.

Syervis and Reychar guarded the tunnel, and Briell had volunteered to watch over the prisoners. She leaned on Ruka's flank and carved new arrowheads with her eyes fixed on the cages.

At nightfall, the riders retired to their dens. Blackjaw Hollow was quiet save for the sough of the arcanan reservoir beneath the root cover. With the coast clear, Ruka nudged his nose into Briell's arm.

"Stop it," she snarled. Ruka grumbled and poked her two more times. "Yes, I heard you. Fine, but don't let your eyes stray."

Ruka wagged his tail. Briell crawled to the cages on her hands and feet. The Mooncallers squirreled away from her, and Avari's eyes narrowed into a glare that could slit throats. Briell crouched like a canine outside of the bars where Ares was napping. She hissed sharply, but he didn't wake up. Briell looked over her shoulder, and her locks swayed, and then she hissed again.

Ares' eyes blinked open; violet first, and then green. "What?"

"If we speak, will you spit fire, Dragon?" asked Briell.

"No, and I'm not *'Dragon,'* I'm *'Ares,'*" he said irritatedly.

"You made a remark about the Widow earlier, *Dragon,*" said Briell emphatically. "Is what you say true? Do you mean to engage Her?"

"I'm planning to eventually destroy Her, but I now feel that chance might elude me," said Ares, rattling his bound wrists on the cage.

"I sense frustration in you," mentioned Briell.

"Do you really?" asked Ares sardonically.

"Yes," said Briell surely. "I share your yearning to protect this world, but Gajneva views only what her barren eyes wish to."

"You could have joined us had we not been dragged here," nipped Ares. "But in the woods, you wanted to let us go, didn't you? Your superior wouldn't sanction it."

"That's not it," said Briell. She looked at Omnia and Skye as they slept under a fallen log. "Omnia once crossed a peddler in the woods and released him. Gajneva took a blade to Skye's wings for it. The fat bird can never fly again. If we had let *you* go, Dragon, she would have roasted Skye for a meal or skinned Ruka for fells on her bed. I'll not let that fate meet my brother. You must understand that freeing you was no option."

"It sounds like Gajneva wants your people as pets, not kinsmen. Could you not run away to live on your own?" wondered Ares.

"Running equates to death. Legs are no match for wings. The bat rules these skies, and if we left with the secrets of Blackjaw in our heads, Gajneva would take them from us," whimpered Briell. She fixed on Ruka. "Wolves are not born to be trapped in a hole; holes are for worms and rats. We're born to run in fields with sunlight on our backs, to look upon the moon, and to warm our loved ones when the snow falls. Most of all, we're born to fight for a pack."

"This isn't a place for a free spirit," said Ares mutedly. "I won't let my men die here, but I fear that there will be no escape without bloodshed. That is unless you help us. If you sever our bonds and —"

"No fleeing," spat Briell. "If I assisted you, Ruka and I would suffer the consequences in your stead. You are Gajneva's prize. If I cost her that, it will cost us greater. I cannot help you for my own sake and my brother's. If that's selfish of me, I'm sorry."

Dead ends were at both Ares and Briell's predicaments. He had less sentiment for Briell than his men but was reluctant to imperil her and Ruka. The scales on his wrist prickled; fire was the only way out.

Meanwhile, Gajneva relaxed in her bed, and Veshra dangled from the rafters with her wings folded like a chrysalis. Her sloughy eyes were guilty.

"*I mean not to offend, Sister, but the outsiders may be right about the Widow. I've seen Her armies from above and listened in the night. They're demons, these things, and I'm frightened of them!*" wailed Veshra; her voice sounded only inside Gajneva's head.

"Do not flood our thoughts with angsts, *Rakgun,*" said Gajneva, puckering sourly. "That filthy dragon is getting to your head just as he meant to. Never have you feared what lurks in the wood, and you shouldn't now."

"*But if the dragon will lay down his life to resist Her, do you not think it wise to permit it?*" asked Veshra timorously. "*Dragons are the most terrible creatures. He could be our ally in the world above.*"

"You think we should let them go? That it would be to our benefit joining that pitiless fire-breather, *nil ignija-bahjnazil?* He is the offspring of your killer! Have you forgotten that?" seethed Gajneva.

"That boy is not responsible for what I am!"

"The dragons have stolen everything! *Tatamat int funtilaj azun uba!"* said Gajneva, cupping Veshra's thatched face. "It was not his flame that doomed us, but his veins house corruption. For that, he is guilty!"

Veshra's wings flew open. *"The Lavrenthea child could not have been a day older than three when Naraniv fell! What guilt is there in that?"* she contended. Gajneva staggered, and Veshra calmed down. *"I don't want to quarrel. The choice is yours . . . but you must hear my concerns."*

"I have heard them, but no more will I listen," said Gajneva, swatting Veshra like a housefly. "Your devotion is weak. You would let this horned villain tear us asunder with decorated words. Whisper no more of dragons and spiders, *mak rakgun.* The fire child will pay the debt he owes, and we will go unseen by the many eyes of the Widow."

Veshra tucked her mashed snout into her wings and blinked at the ceiling. *"I only care for your life, Gajneva. So long as you're safe, I'll not question your verdict. Forgive me."*

That night, Briell slept curled under Ruka's paws, and the Mooncallers struggled to untie themselves. They kicked, tugged, and scratched but were only given rope-burns. Hopes plummeted, and most ceased their attempts — except for Luxea.

"Oi, will you do me after?" peeped Oliver.

"Stop asking. Give me a minute, won't you?" grouched Luxea.

"We could've done this a bit earlier," asked Oliver.

"No. Any sooner, I'd have put us in a worse situation," grunted Luxea. She whispered the unbinding incantation, *"Lu'vasa in."*

Her arms came loose. She waved at Oliver. His ties came undone.

"Divines' tits. Finally. Thought I'd never have feelin' in my fingers again. Poor li'l lads," he moaned.

"We don't have time for comfort. Start freeing the others. I'll share our plan with Ares," whispered Luxea.

"Got it, love," said Oliver, scooting away.

Luxea crawled across the cage floor and scanned past the bars to refresh her scheme in her head. It wouldn't be simple, but she had just the right amount of tricks up her sleeve.

The ties above Ares' head disintegrated when Luxea touched them. His hands fell from the bars, and the motion shook him awake. Ares looked both ways and whispered, "Luxea, what are you doing?"

"I can get us out," said Luxea abruptly.

Ares glanced at the tunnel. "Their eyes are closed, but it's too much of a distance to cover without exposure. If it were one or two of us, maybe, but there are sixteen."

"I've counted. I need your help, Ares. The others have to know exactly what I require of them," insisted Luxea.

She nestled at his side, unhooked the Usinnon from her hip, and said its name. She flipped through it and tapped on a paragraph.

"This is how we'll do it," said Luxea. "A concealment shroud will make us undetectable to the naked eye. I can keep the arcanan link fastened, but . . . I'm not familiar with this spell on a mass scale."

"It says: *'if the essence of the arcana lacks in the user, subjects beneath the shroud must remain in close contact for the incantation to hold effect.'* This isn't something I can cast on my own; it involves everyone. If one finger breaks the line, they, and every person behind them, will be out in the open. At that point, I can't help them."

Ares surveyed Blackjaw Hollow through the bars and found a clear shot across the cavern. "Tell me what to do," he said.

Restraints were severed, and Ares relayed their method of escape to the soldiers. The design consisted of cooperation, silence, and caution; without any one of those, they could find themselves face-to-face with a beast.

Luxea unlocked the cages, but the clink of the locks woke up Ruka. He caught the Mooncallers in the act but didn't howl. Instead, he prodded Briell's head.

"Ruka, please," she groaned.

"Brie, the dragon and his men broke out," whimpered Ruka.

"What?" gasped Briell. The blood left her cheeks at the sight of broken binds and open gates. She bounded to the Mooncallers and spat, "Dragon, what are you doing? I don't understand —"

Ares pressed a finger to his lips. "Our sorceress freed us. We'll get out if we're careful. I hope you can honor our actions."

Briell shook her head madly. "It's impossible. Eyes in this place are too sharp for sneaking. Dragon, there's much to be lost for you and for me if you fail!"

"Then we won't fail," said Ares with sureness.

He stepped past Briell, but she nabbed his arm. "What of Ruka and me? If you run, we will suffer," she reminded.

"You said yourself that protecting those important to you is selfish at times. This is one of those times," said Ares, wrenching his silken sleeve from her hand. "I'll offer this once. Run with us. If you long to fight for a pack, fight for ours."

Briell was speechless. The possibility of breaking out played an alluring tune on her heartstrings, but those strings broke fast. Ruka nuzzled his snout to the back of her head, but she disregarded it. His ears drooped; he knew her answer.

"I can't. Gajneva will find us," said Briell, eyes quivering.

Ares walked away. "I pray that your freedom comes swiftly. Briell and Ruka, if your feet ever cross the forest's edge, know that you have friends there."

He set his hand on Luxea's shoulder, and a single-file link was created by the soldiers. Luxea whispered, *"Tashetha'hil."*

A bubble of indigo light swelled around the Mooncallers, and all of them vanished. Briell and Ruka watched their footprints fade out of the moss where they'd stood. Their only chance had evanesced before their eyes, and they realized that staying behind was a mistake.

Ruka passed amber thoughts to his sister. The wolf, a creature bred of strength and ferocity, wallowed in the shadow cast by a bat's wings. This wasn't what Briell wanted for Ruka. Instinct drew her forward.

"Wait! Please, wait!" said Briell as tears wetted her cheeks. "Take us with you! No, please, don't go. Wait . . . wait. . . ."

Their hearts galloped while they waited for a response. Briell's muscly legs weakened as dread crept up their length, but just when they were about to give out, a small, dirty hand phased through the concealment shroud. Briell's limbs regained feeling. She tugged Ruka's scruff, and they disappeared from sight the second that her fingers closed around the disembodied wrist.

Avari squeezed her hand. "Don't let go of your dog or me."

Briell nodded feverishly. "Thank you, Small One."

The Mooncallers, Briell, and Ruka prowled with Ares behind Luxea, Oliver behind Ares, and the rest trailing after. Luxea was unsure which direction to take, so Ares whispered to her where to step. They sneaked over mounds and through bracken, avoiding rocks lest their feet spoke loudly.

They outflanked a cluster of sleeping riders. All that was left was a hillock, Syervis, and Reychar. At the tunnel, Luxea stopped. The path was narrower than she'd predicted. With a serpent to her left and a bear to her right, there remained space for three persons abreast. Ares signaled his men to compress into file formation.

Luxea tensely moved past the slumbering beasts and into the tunnel. Half of the Mooncallers stepped into the entryway, and the probability of rising to the surface unscathed looked promising.

Briell scratched Ruka's fur. When they passed that corridor, the face of freedom from which they'd been chained would smile upon them on the other side.

The way was almost clear, but Drishti wasn't paying attention and caught the toe cap of her sabaton on a root. She crashed into the wall, and her armor echoed down the tunnel like pots and pans. The link was broken, and all at once, Drishti and the four behind her popped into the open — including Briell and Ruka.

Ares spun around and slapped Oliver's hand into Luxea's. Oliver squeaked in opposition, but Ares had already burst out of the shroud to meet Drishti's aid.

Syervis and Reychar snapped awake, and the bear named Kodan laid his bright, blue eyes upon Drishti. His fat, black lips flapped. He sank his incisors deep past her steel grieves. Her bones snapped.

As Kodan shredded Drishti's legs, Ares hooked his fingers onto his shieldmaiden's breastplate and swung his left hand. His razored talons left four, bone-scraping slashes across Kodan's snout. Ares dragged her away as Kodan and Reychar roared in shared agony.

Gajneva flew up in her bed, and Veshra's eyes opened to give her sight. The chieftain's flesh-bare brow twisted into a raging mess as she limped to the hut's door. The bat shared the image of the tunnels. Reychar was on the ground, Syervis was climbing into Cheyale's basket, Briell and Ruka were cowering on the path, and Gajneva's prized captives were free.

"*Ganac naaj!* Get them!" she screamed, lashing her frail hand. Veshra crawled through a hole in the ceiling. Gajneva frothed at the mouth. "*Ganac naaj, Rakgun!*"

"Luck is no longer with us. Veshra is coming!" howled Briell.

The bat's glass-breaking screech woke up all of the riders. A stag, a fox, and a rabbit bounded out of their dens. The white fox yipped. The rabbit thumped its feet. The stag was ready for a fight.

Beneath the fallen log, Omnia vaulted onto Skye's back, and the two dashed along the shadowed cavern wall.

Cheyale's tail wound around Avari's legs and tugged. Avari tried to roll away, but in seconds, she was dangling upside down. Luxea bolted out of the concealment shroud, and every soldier was exposed, but she couldn't stand idly by while Avari faced danger.

Luxea yelled, "*Amal luciem!*"

A flash crashed into Cheyale's face and threw her back. Syervis shrieked and held onto the serpent. Luxea knelt to assist Avari but was distracted by Veshra's towering silhouette as she clawed out of the hut, casting a shadow where there had already been so little light.

Kodan suddenly bowled Luxea over into the dirt. The impact unhooked the Usinnon from her hip, and the spellbook wailed as it slid across the stubbly grass and fell into a rocky niche.

The eyes of Syervis and Cheyale were irritated as they rose again. Cheyale constricted Avari's legs and cracked her against the ground, reviving the pain of her fractured bones. Obligation struck Oliver like a glass bottle on the head. He patted the lining of his cloak and ducked under bestial arms and legs, straight into the chaos.

Kodan's footsteps rumbled. Luxea shrank into a corner, petrified by the bear's curled lip and loose skin as it jiggled with each slogging movement.

"Amal luciem!" she cried out.

Light flashed, but Kodan and Reychar had closed their eyes. Luxea wriggled like a worm from a bird. Kodan slammed a gigantic paw onto her belly and felt her organs squish. As he drooled on her neck, she gasped for air and reached for the Usinnon.

Luxea smacked Kodan with the spellbook. Bolts of arcana ejected from the Usinnon and permitted the slightest yelp to slip from the bear's throat before he and Reychar flopped over paralyzed. Luxea held her aching middle and kissed the Usinnon's cover.

Veshra swooped down and picked off soldiers like mice. She flew to the ceiling to tear them apart, and blood rained. Gajneva tottered down the steps of her hut.

Meanwhile, the stag, Tyfus, galloped at a pair of unsuspecting warriors. He impaled one on his antlers, and innards dribbled down his tines like sap down branches. As the stag was about to strike again, Lieutenant Claymore knocked the other warrior down and rolled. Tyfus faced them and shot like an arrow. The lieutenant ducked, and the warrior sidestepped, but Tyfus had been expecting it. He bashed the warrior onto the ground, and his hooves crashed like boulders onto the bend of his neck. The warrior's spine shattered, and his eyes bulged from his skull.

Claymore was brimming with the vigor to avenge. He pulled the stag rider, Dolses, down by the leg and smashed his gauntleted fists into his face. The beasts were fierce, but alone, their riders were just as vulnerable as anyone else.

He beat Dolses until Tyfus came to his rescue. The stag smacked his hooves into Claymore's side and paddled over his head, ready to trample him. Foreseeing his own death, Claymore envisioned Hanalea's rosy cheeks — and then he saw black hair.

Ares latched onto Tyfus' antlers. The stag swung its head, and Dolses yanked Ares down and threw him. In a moment's fragment, Ares was straddled by Dolses and pummeled. As blood leaked from his nose and lip, he thrust his talons into his assailant's throat. In sync, the rider went still, and the stag smashed down to the dirt. Ares winced when Dolses coughed hot red onto his face. Tyfus' body disintegrated into ash.

"Ssstrike her, Cheyale!" spat Syervis.

The serpent flicked Avari back and forth like a toy. She'd planted several punches but was struggling with her knives amiss. Cheyale raised her up high, and her massive jaws unhinged. Avari's scarf bunched up as she stared into the serpent's quivering throat.

Then she heard a scream — Oliver's scream.

Oliver was crouched, jamming the tiny knife that Avari had given him into Cheyale's middle. The serpent dropped Avari as her body went into shock. Oliver toted Avari away by the collar of her vest.

"Kross? You had a weapon all this time?" she gasped.

"Small 'nough to hide in my cloak," said Oliver nervously.

"Go, my sssweet!" groaned Syervis.

Cheyale slithered after them, refusing to lose no matter if death came for her. Oliver somewhat regretted his involvement until red fur dashed past him. Ruka clamped his jaws around Cheyale's head and snapped the ropes that secured the basket. Syervis tumbled out.

"Cheyale! My beloved Cheyale," he said, giving all of the strength that he had to reach his serpent before they both died.

Syervis' fingers grazed Cheyale's scales, and then an arrow pierced him between the eyes. His head rocketed back, and the tip that Briell had carved that evening ruptured from his nape. Life languished in his eyes. Cheyale dissolved into embers in a coil shape.

Briell's mind swarmed with images of what Syervis' last thoughts might have been. She fell onto her behind. "Forgive me, Syervis."

Omnia had been watching Briell and Ruka. She slid from Skye's back and said to Avari and Oliver, "Leave us now!" When they were far enough, Omnia snatched Briell's longbow and shoved her. "What do you think you're doing?"

Briell's lip trembled at Syervis. He'd died reaching for the wife he'd lost a decade before, Cheyale. Syervis had been one of Briell's tribesmen but also Gajneva's servant. As Briell recalled all of the trouble that he and Cheyale had begotten, her brow leveled out.

"I'm fighting," she said, stealing her longbow back.

"For the prisoners?" squawked Omnia.

Briell climbed onto Ruka's back. "Yes. There's no difference between them and us. I'm finished being a pet to Gajneva!"

"Girls?" said Oliver from close by.

"The wolf in you cannot be tamed, Briell, but you must bethink what consequences you'll face. Gajneva will have Ruka slaughtered for this betrayal!" exclaimed Omnia.

"Ladies," said Oliver again.

"I'm sick of belonging to her!" said Briell, drawing an arrow.

"We all are!" said Omnia, grabbing Briell's legs. "I've suffered her wrath, I know. But if you expect to run off without her —"

"Oi! You broads!" belted out Oliver.

Briell and Omnia showed him their teeth. Oliver pointed behind them. "Th-the b-bat — it's the bat, get out of the way! Move — !"

Veshra slammed down in the middle of the fray. The floor of Blackjaw Hollow quaked, and winds were cast from her wings. The riders scampered away, and the Mooncallers who'd endured the battle braced themselves to face the most menacing beast yet.

The bat's swampy eyes met with Ares' as she discarded the mutilated corpse of one of his soldiers from her jaws; the warrior's ribs poked from his torso like pins in a cushion. Veshra prowled nigh, but Ares didn't back away from her. Gajneva doubled over laughing.

"Look what you've done, Dragon," she said. "You think yourself a redeemer to the lives of men, yet all you raise is devastation. *Drajn dracona'lach,* now you pay the price for the pain you've caused us!"

Veshra lunged, and Ares pulled back his sleeve. Scales stretched up over the ball of his wrist. "Unless you wish for me to refresh your memory of what calamity a dragon can bring, concede now, Gajneva!"

"Blighted maggot. If you drive your savagery upon me, you will face atrophy. Killing me is killing yourself. You won't do it," said Gajneva.

"Will I not?" asked Ares, scales climbing. Veshra whimpered.

"We shall see," chuckled Gajneva. *"Fatna naaj!* Kill them!"

Ares' skin crackled with cinders as Veshra charged, but then she wobbled in place and stopped. The smokes of draconic transformation abated from Ares' arm as Veshra tripped on her wings, unable to hold herself up.

Gajneva clapped her hands to her bony sockets and collapsed, swiping for Veshra and screaming, "I cannot see! *Rakgun, os nagi'je mastak! Rakgun? Moku na fajanidaj?* I cannot see!"

"She severed their vision. Never has Veshra done this," said Omnia tensely. "Look at her eyes. They're at their whites."

The bat's eyes were blank like an empty shell. Incredulous, Ares rolled down his sleeve and circled Veshra, but she was as ignorant of him as the screams of her sightless rider.

"Something's wrong with Veshra," yipped the fox rider.

"Is she ailing?" squeaked the rabbit rider.

Veshra screeched and wheeled toward Gajneva. Feeling her sister near, Gajneva waved her sagging arms and sniveled, "Where are you, Veshra? It's all right. Come to me now . . . *mak rakgun?"*

Silent, Veshra stretched out her wings and locked her needle-like teeth onto Gajneva. The Mooncallers recoiled in shock, and Briell and Ruka were stone stiff.

"What is she doing?" yowled the fox rider.

"Gajneva!" roared Reychar after he recovered.

"Veshra, stop! You'll die too!" shrieked the rabbit rider.

Deaf to admonishment, Veshra chomped Gajneva and punctured every inch of her ancient body. The chieftain's delayed screams were released amidst the sound of her bones cracking.

"Veshra, why do you do this?" she asked, head dangling like a pendant. *"Os notu bas . . .* I love you still . . . *Rakgun."*

Gajneva's fingers slipped out of Veshra's scruff, and the bat flung her. Blackjaw Hollow plunged into total silence, but even that was loud when Veshra's eyes flickered back to muddy green.

The bat sniffed and gurgled at the sight of Gajneva's corpse. Death had taken her second half, and it would take her too. She dragged herself to her sister as her body disintegrated from the feet up.

Veshra died. Her ashes crumbled upon Gajneva's chest.

THE FREE WILDS
25.REDTAIL.25.OSC.3

OMNIA WAS the first to move. Hanging off of Skye's back, she and the raven slowed at Gajneva's remains. She crouched, and her sheet of hair picked up some of Veshra's faint, green embers. She dipped her hand in the bloody ash, and it streaked her palm.

"If you want to run, run!" shouted Omnia.

The rabbit wriggled its nose, and its rider stroked its narrow head. The beast *thumped* its feet and shook its cottony tail, and its bent legs sprang off of the walls. The rabbit rider had watery eyes and kissed one of the rabbit's long ears as they bounced into the tunnel.

Next, two orange foxes sprinted from their dens, and a second stag trailed after them to embrace liberty without punishment.

Briell meant to desert Blackjaw as well, but her curiosity for Gajneva's death was more immediate. Ruka circled the chieftain's body, and Briell jumped off of him.

"Veshra killed her. Why?" she questioned.

Omnia knelt to consider. "That look in her eyes, she was no longer herself," she said, turning the chieftain's head with her sickle. "Veshra loved Gajneva. I don't know why she did it."

"Was she rabid?" suggested Briell.

"Possibly," said Omnia. She glinted sidelong at the Mooncallers. "But it seems odd to me that Veshra fell to madness the same day these strangers arrived."

"I saw nothing out of the ordinary except for the spell-flinger and the dragon," remarked Briell. "But I had my eyes on them, so did you, and Dragon didn't wish for Gajneva to die."

"I don't feel that this was their intention, but these outsiders brought something with them. Whether it's blessing or curse," Omnia looked at the sky through the pinnacle, "it has rescued us."

The Mooncallers gathered their dead and wounded. Four had fallen from conflict, and three were injured too critically to endure the journey to Solissium. They were prisoners no longer, but the fight with the riders had cost them half of their numbers.

After assisting Claymore with steadying a ranger, Oliver jogged to Luxea and Avari outside on the path. "You awright, loves?" he asked.

"Peachy," said Avari, rubbing her thighs.

Luxea hung her shoulders. "This shouldn't have happened. I thought I had the spell secured, and now . . ."

"Stop that crap," said Avari, jostling Luxea. "It isn't your fault that Drishti tripped out of the barrier. You did great, kiddo. We owe you."

"Yea. You saved all our arses in the end," added Oliver. "I knew magick could do all sorts o' damage, but blissits."

"What are you talking about?" asked Luxea.

Oliver laughed gawkily. "What else would I mean? Big, ugly bat eatin' that ol' crone alive? M'glad you never tried that one on me."

"Of all ways to win a fight, that's one for the books," said Avari. "Didn't know you could do things like that, Luxie. Guess you really did learn a lot while I was caught under Mollah's itchy blankets."

"That's kind of you to say, but I didn't do anything to the chieftain or her bat," confessed Luxea.

Oliver squeaked, "What? But — ?"

"You didn't? Then what happened to them?" cut in Avari.

"You know as well as I do," said Luxea uncomfortably.

"Dragon!" said Briell, riding to the tunnels. Ares withdrew from his men and approached her. "I'm glad to speak with you without bars between us, but I pity the loss of your men. Omnia will take up the mantle as the Chieftain of Blackjaw. The others agreed."

"Your tribe has a worthy leader now," said Ares, but his tone wasn't the least bit positive. "What of Gajneva? Has a beast turned on its rider before?"

"Not that I've heard. A rider eliminated by their counterpart makes little sense," said Briell, answerless. "We think Veshra was ill, or that she and Gajneva had an altercation in secret. No one understood them in any case. Some suspect that you and your spell-flinger did it, but Gajneva's death is too new to tell. We may never uncover more than this."

"It wasn't Luxie," said Avari, trotting closer. "Kross and I thought it was her too, but she swears it wasn't, and I believe her. No matter who did what, your chieftain got what she had coming."

"You speak facts, Small One," remarked Briell. Avari scowled, hating her new nickname. "But now those who are left fear that an incident like Veshra's will happen to our own. I cannot put my Ruka in the path of risk. I disdain lingering in this place."

Ares inspected Briell, Ruka, and the last men who vacated the hollow. "If you'd like, my offer still stands. Our ranks could use passion like yours and Ruka's. I would be honored to name you as Mooncallers."

Ruka's tail wagged, and he nestled his muzzle into the side of Ares' head. Ares' cheeks dimpled a bit, and he ran his thumb along the wolf's ear.

"Your path couldn't be worse than the one we've been walking, Dragon. If my brother yearns for your pack, we will follow," said Briell fondly.

Ares bowed his head charmingly. "Then I welcome you, Briell and Ruka. May we walk with the Moon — together."

Briell and Ruka tailed the Mooncallers to the surface where Lieutenant Claymore and his injured men waited. He sent one of the two sages to accompany the wounded back to Tel Ashir and offer medicinal aid until they could be committed to the infirmary.

The dead, however, required a dracas of their own, which robbed another soldier of a mount. This was predicamental at the start, but Oliver volunteered Musha for the position and said that he could share a saddle with Luxea or Avari. Elthevir and Avari forced the short end of the stick onto Luxea. From Blackjaw Hollow to Solissium, Oliver would ride a pillion on Velesari's back.

Briell steered them out of the Western Woods along the somber trails. Hours later, she called, "Dragon!"

Ares snapped Pveather's reins and met Ruka. "What is it? And my name is Ares, so if you could please —"

"The trailhead is just beyond that hill, Dragon," said Briell. "You go on. Ruka and I must say goodbye to the trees."

"Take your time," said Ares, motioning for the lieutenant to pass.

Ruka trotted aside. As the Mooncallers scaled a knoll, Briell flopped onto his haunches and soaked in the scent of dewy moss and dusty tree bark. While the forest had been a cage, it had also been their home.

"Will you miss Blackjaw, Brother?" whispered Briell.

"A little. Our den was warm. Plenty of bugs to look at," said Ruka.

"Yes, it was. But we will find new dens. Lots of them with soft cushions and blankets, or big ones with a fire inside and more bugs than you could ever imagine," said Briell, stroking his pelt.

"I want to see cushions and blankets," panted Ruka. He sniffed. *"Brie, do you think we'll be happy with these strangers?"*

Briell watched the last dracas as it scampered down the road. "Dragon says they will guard us as their own, so I'm going to believe we will," she said hopefully. "If we don't find joy with them, we will find our own. But do you know what else we will find?"

"What? Chickens? Or fenlaig?" asked Ruka, licking his lips.

"We will find those too," chuckled Briell. "But sooner, we will find the world — just past that hill."

Ruka bounced around. *"Can we go? I want to run!"*

"Run far and without fear; there's none to be had now."

The wolf bounded to the trailhead and slid to a stop where inches ahead, the dirt was warmed by the Tehrastar. The expanse of the Storm Plains swelled as the wind pushed the tides of gold and white barley. This was the realm yonder the trees that had stood like bars. Ruka took his first steps as a beast into the wild. His paws *crunched* on pebbles, and his muscles tensed.

"Can I?" he asked, ears flying up.

"Yes, Brother." Briell gripped his pelt. "Run."

Ruka leaped into the meadow and ran fast, feeling the sunlight on his back and his sister clinging to his fur. His legs delivered him at speeds that he'd never thought he could reach, no longer constrained by tight-knitted woodlands. As his heart drummed, Briell's played to the same rhythm. This was the life that she'd always dreamed of for Ruka — for them both — and now they had it.

Briell's eyes sparkled as tears kissed her umber cheeks. She threw her arms into the air and howled. Ruka howled too, and they did so until they ran so far that they couldn't be seen from the trail.

The Mooncallers stopped at twilight at the north border of Dundis Angle. A few soldiers rested their heads the moment that cots were made available, and others prepared a fire for cooking.

Oliver and Avari scavenged for hares or foxes, but wildlife was scarce in the Storm Plains. They managed to uncover a bushel of dustapples, but Avari told Oliver to move on as the taste of dustapples was as the name suggested: like dust. They headed back to the camp with their satchels empty.

An eery howl blew on the wind. Poking up from the pasture to the west were red ears and two pairs of eyes glowing like lightning bugs. Ruka huffed and slowed by the fire pit.

Oliver waved at them. "Welcome ba — !"

Briell pushed a horselike carcass off of Ruka's back, and it walloped the dirt. The animal had a slender snout and a lion-like mane.

"The 'ells is that thing?" asked Oliver, hiding behind Avari.

"It's a yulacai. Hard to track, harder to kill, but their meats are worth the challenge," said Briell, ripping two arrows from the creature's throat.

Ares moved a wet rag from his black eye and was visibly impressed by the kill. On the other hand, Avari and Oliver were ashamed. It hadn't been a day, and Briell had outshone them.

"Dragon, take this," said Briell, tossing a leather sack. Ares nearly dropped his daybook but was able to hook the bag with his talon. "Sweet plainsberries for the yulacai. Sugar and smoke make friends on the tongue."

"Thank you," said Ares, pleased with the Mooncallers' new member — aside from her perpetual denial of his proper name.

As preparations for supper were made, Briell and Ruka relaxed. The wolf twirled three times and plopped down, and she laid on his flank. A scrawny archer glowered at her through the fire smoke.

"You stare too much, Rabbit," Briell told him.

The archer sat up. "What did you call me? *'Rabbit?'*"

"You're jug-eared, and your eyes are too far apart," said Briell bluntly. "You were born under the sign of Mamaku, the Rabbit. You're a rabbit."

A swordsman at the archer's side elbowed him. "You're a rabbit? That's cute. No wonder you're always runnin' scared."

"You're little fiercer, Fish Boy," said Briell to the swordsman.

"He's born under the stars of Ocaranth, the Winged Koi," said Avari, munching on a barley stem. "How'd you know their signs?"

"It's like telling colors apart. A soul is born with two or more traits exact to the god of their sign," said Briell as she slid two wolf fangs into her sagging earlobes. "Like you, Small One, you're resilient and have wide feet. That makes you a child of Nall, the Mammoth."

Growing used to being called *'Small One,'* Avari nodded. "That's right. I'm Nall." An idea boinked into her brain, and she mashed the unsuspecting face of Luxea into her shoulder. "What about Luxie? Can you tell what her sign is?"

"She's curious, quick-witted, and has narrow wrists. She was born under Wynd, the Stag," said Briell at once.

Luxea's stars turned pale yellow. Due to her warmth, her lifeday had always been celebrated in sunrae, assuming she'd been born under a Sun sign. However, she'd never known her real sign.

"You're certain?" asked Luxea excitedly.

"It's doubtless," said Briell.

Avari patted Luxea's hair. "Damn, finally. I guess you're not a sunrae baby after all."

Briell found that statement hilarious. "Her, *a sunrae child?* Never! Children of sunrae are ill-humored dandies — like Dragon for example. He's Theryn, the Lion."

Ares lowered the rag from his eye. "Excuse me?" he growled.

"Well, is she right? Were you born under Theryn?" asked Luxea.

"I — yes. I'm Theryn," admitted Ares.

Briell pattered her feet, proud of her excellent intuition.

"If you're Theryn, wasn't your lifeday not long ago?" asked Avari.

"Yes. 28.Kingsreign. I also turned twenty-eight," informed Ares.

"Your golden lifeday," beeped Avari. "When you turn the same age as the day you were born, it's special. This'll be a spectacular year for ya!"

"So far, it hasn't been very spectacular," said Ares sourly.

"Why didn't you say anything? I would've given you a gift," said Luxea, guilty that she'd missed such an important day.

"You did," said Ares. Luxea almost asked, but he drove the conversation elsewhere. "What about you, Briell? Under what stars were you born?"

"I'm Fenne like Ruka," said Briell. Ruka wagged. "My brother and I were made under the same sun before his human body was surrendered to Fenne. We looked quite alike."

"You're twins?" asked Avari.

Joining the group at the campfire, Oliver purred, "Twins? Nice."

Ares asked Briell, "You've lived your whole lives in Blackjaw?"

"No, but close," replied Briell. "When Ruka and I were pups, we had a cottage in Avi Yeromin. Our father cared for us for a few years, sewed our clothes, and tracked creatures of the wood for us to eat, but we cannot recall his face now. He left one day and never came back. After that, Ruka and I hunted on our own — rats mostly. From time to time, a caravan of merchants passed through with food and supplies aplenty to take. We were careful all but once, and once was enough."

"What went wrong that once?" asked Avari, accidentally ingesting her chewing straw.

Briell nestled into Ruka's shoulder. "A band of traders from Northreach was importing harvests to Nan Jaami, and Ruka and I had been planning for days to snatch all we could from their cargo. By Landheart, we frisked the carts in the night and filled our sacks, but a patrol officer caught us and mistook us for armed and dangerous. He shot without eyes."

18. SNOWHOWL.3.OSC.3

Smoke rose from the pistol's barrel, and his fingers trembled on the trigger. He'd only loaded one bullet, and now that bullet was lodged in a skull. The gun tumbled from his hand. He kicked sand onto his victim to hide what he'd done, and then he ran.

Briell peeked her head through the sprigs of the bush in which she hid. The world darkened. All she saw was the still face of Ruka with his tight, red curls and swarthy cheeks coated in white grains.

"Ruka? Come here," called out Briell, stepping through a clump of beachgrass. "Brother?"

The sack of thieved goods slid from Briell's fingers. Apples and salted meats spilled, and her hempen sandals flew off as she dashed to her brother. She turned him, and his brown eyes stared up at the night sky. Blood twirled down his ringlets and wetted the sand.

"Ruka . . . Ruka!" screamed Briell, shaking him. "Brother, answer me! Please, say something! Ruka! Say something!"

Briell's lips stretched out as a muted sob strained to breach her throat. She pressed her ear to Ruka's chest, and his heart said nothing.

In the morning, Briell swatted at carrion birds with beaks hungry for a pick at Ruka. She flew through the sand with her missing baby teeth bared.

"Get away! Go!" she said, kicking and falling on her back.

A shadow blotted out the Tehrastar. The vultures' tongues clicked, and they vacated the dunes. Briell threw a handful of sand after them.

"Pissers! Don't come back!" she screamed.

A huge raven with a black-haired woman on its back landed behind Ruka's body. The raven flared its wings, and the woman jumped off. Briell was scared, but she wouldn't let them touch Ruka. She uncovered a chunk of driftwood from the sand, snapped it, and pointed the jagged end at the raven.

"Leave, or I'll kill you!" yelled Briell, swinging the wood.

The raven screeched, but the woman hushed her. She knelt to Briell's level and examined her. Briell's curly hair was so red that it looked like she was wearing a hat made out of currants. That made the raven woman smile.

"You have a wolf in you, girl," she said. She pointed to Ruka's lifeless face. "You two look so similar. Was he your brother?"

"He still is," hiccuped Briell. She swung again. "Now get away! I won't let you take him!"

"I'm not here to take your brother from you. My name is Omnia, and this is Skye. Young wolf, do your parents know what happened?"

Briell shook her head. "They're gone."

Omnia looked at the far-off Western Woods. "Will you believe me if I say I can bring your brother back? He wouldn't look like he does now, but beyond that, he'll be the same in every way."

"That's impossible," cried Briell.

"Nothing is impossible," said Omnia, touching her raven's feathers. "I've lost someone dear to me as well. My daughter was born with an illness that she couldn't fight, so she died. But now she's right here and just as much my baby as she was then."

"That's a bird," said Briell sharply.

"She looks like a bird," said Omnia, trailing her hand down Skye's chest. "But in her heart — right here — she's my daughter still. You're a fighter, child, and my people need fighters. If you come with me, I promise you'll get your brother back."

Briell propped up Ruka's head with her free hand. He'd never been so quiet. He'd once had a loud mouth, but now he was motionless, and it made Briell not want to exist. But Omnia and her bird daughter swore they could reverse what had happened. Briell dropped the driftwood and picked up Ruka.

"I want my brother back."

Skye carried Briell and Ruka to Omnia's home, Blackjaw Hollow. The raven drifted into a chasm at the cavern's vertex and landed in front of a shimmering, green pond. Omnia set Briell and Ruka on the mossy floor and said, "I must speak with the chieftain; he will help us bring Ruka back. Skye will care for you while I'm away."

Skye ruffled her feathers and nested. Briell crawled under her wing with Ruka. Omnia strode to a crooked hut across the cavern. Once she'd discussed her discovery with the chieftain, a burly man named Yaemin and his giant, white lion returned with her.

Chieftain Yaemin peeked past Skye's glossy feathers. Briell glared at him. In a voice as hot as freshly baked bread, he said, "Get on your feet, girl. A wolf doesn't hide. If you do this, you will forever be bound. You will not be individual, you will be child and beast. Are you willing to give half of yourself for his sake?"

"I want him back. Bring him back right now!" snarled Briell.

"Enter the water. Don't let go of him and don't lose breath," said Yaemin. "When you breach, you and your brother will be reborn as one. Now go, young wolf!"

The moment that Briell's toes dipped past the viridescent surface of the arcanan reservoir, the back of her scalp tingled like her ringlets were being played with.

She submerged and waited for something to happen, but then Ruka's body started to evaporate. Briell screamed his name as her fingers slipped through his fading body. She savored the memory of his face, and then he disappeared. A fiery, orange orb floated where he'd been. Somehow, it looked just like him.

Weeping into the water, Briell cupped Ruka's light. Yellow smoke escaped her lips and melted into his. The two shades blended into hot amber. Briell's eyes burned; it was a scraping pain like claws. When it subsided, her brown irises were stained that same amber.

She looked up, and floating before her was a blood red wolf pup with a pelt fuzzy and premature. His big paws twitched, and he blinked sleepily. He stared at his sister with eyes the same shade as hers.

"Brie? I had a dream and couldn't wake up," he whimpered.

Ruka sounded the same way that he had since they'd learned to speak. Briell threw her arms around him as the pond drained.

Then and always, they were child and beast.

Briell finished telling her story. Ruka lapped his tongue up her cheek.

Oliver rested his elbows on his knees and goggled at Ruka. He asked, "So there's really a li'l lad in there under all that fluff?"

"Yes. He's the brother I always had," answered Briell. "That's why we could stay no longer in the hollow. When Yaemin was Chieftain of Blackjaw, he let us roam and treated us with respect. But after he vanished, Gajneva took the throne, and we riders were caged."

"And where'd that Yaemin fellow run off to?" asked Avari.

"Some think that he and his lion were unlucky during a hunt, but others think that Gajneva was responsible," said Briell grimly.

By then, the yulacai was cooked, so Briell tore a piece from it and tossed it into Ruka's maw. She said warmly, "Your pack is built on trust, not fear. That's why Ruka and I will protect you as we protect each other. As long as my brother is with me."

Two days dragged by. The Mooncallers trailed into the Elders' Expanse by early afternoon, but then storms from the Cove of Tar cracked over their heads. They took cover in a cave amidst the Screech Rakes at the bend of Gut Leak River until it passed.

Briell and Ruka had been consistent in hunting along their journey, so the Mooncallers started a fire to cook a meal. There were two hawks and a falscreamer, and there had been a wild fenlaig, but Ruka devoured it.

Luxea loafed at the river's edge with a book she'd brought. She dug her toes into the cold, hard sand as she flipped the pages. A way down the stream, Briell squatted next to Ruka in search of fish. Just then, she noticed a strange object sitting on Luxea's lap.

"Don't give up, Ruka. I'll return," said Briell, stare unmoving from Luxea's lap-friend. The wolf took a seat to carry on fish-stalking.

The rider advanced as if she was closing in on a foe. Luxea saw her instantly. "Hi, Brie. Any luck with fishing?"

Briell shook her head. "That there. It looks like an insect with too many wings. What is it?" she asked.

Luxea raised the book up and down to flutter the pages. "You're right. It does look like that. But it isn't an insect, it's a book. It has stories inside of it."

With her wits about her, Briell crouched and gazed at the book. Tiny, black figures marched over the pages like a colony of ants in single-file lines. Briell rubbed her eyes. Luxea humphed and set the book down.

"Brie, do you not know how to read?" she asked bluntly.

"I've never seen this . . . book," growled Briell. "You say there are stories inside, but what do they say?"

"Books say infinite things," said Luxea enthusiastically. "Do you want me to read something for you? This is a love story, so all of it is exciting."

Wheels spun in Briell's head as she turned the papers. Thinking hard, she picked out a line and poked the page to squeeze sound from it. "I want this one. What does it say to you, Starlight?"

Luxea's face suddenly had color. "Ah-ha, that part? You're certain you don't want me to read something else?" she coughed.

"Yes. I want this one," said Briell, tapping the line again.

"O-okay. It says, *'She bared her flesh. As he cornered his prey, her hands sneaked down and traced h-his . . .'* That's it. It doesn't say anything else," fibbed Luxea.

After articulating something so lewd, Luxea's cheeks were numb, and she was questioning her morals. For a member of the Speaker's convoy, she was godless. Briell, however, had a tickle in the pit of her belly that she craved.

"Tell me what she does next. I must know," said Briell adamantly.

"How about I just teach you how to read? That way, you can read as much as you want," said Luxea, fanning herself.

"Teach me. Teach me as fast as you can," said Briell crossly.

Luxea wiped her sweaty forehead and set her filthy book aside. "How about we start with your name? Do you know how to spell your name?" she asked as she picked up a twig. Briell's head shook. Luxea etched a capital *'B'* in the sand. "Your name is *'Briell,'* so it begins with *'B.'"*

"Buh?" asked Briell.

Letter by letter, Luxea taught Briell how to spell her name and how each vowel and consonant was pronounced. When *'BRIE'* was drawn out, Briell was mystified that the *'E'* made no sound. Luxea explained that when that letter was at the end of the word, it became silent. Briell declared *'E'* as her favorite letter.

Luxea spelled *'BRIELL,'* and Briell was flabbergasted.

"Br . . . ie . . . ll," she said, touching the sand. "If I put the *'E'* after these lines, will it be a quiet one?"

"That's right! So if you want to spell your name like this, it'll be spoken the same way, but it looks different. Do you like it better like that?" asked Luxea, spelling out *'BRIELLE.'*

"Yes, I do. *'E'*'s are sneaky," said Brielle happily.

Luxea underlined Brielle's name. "Then you'll spell your name as *'B-R-I-E-L-L-E.'* How about we spell *'RUKA'* next?"

"Show me Ruka," said Brielle, enthralled.

Luxea taught Brielle the common alphabet, simple words, and how to read and write them until the storm let up. When the Mooncallers departed, Brielle told Ruka all about how she knew how to spell his name. Luxea lent her one of her easier books for practice, and Brielle had her eyes stuck to it until it was too dark outside to read.

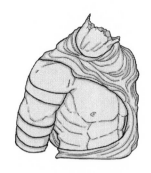

Lust for Gold
3.Nightspeak.25.Osc.3

After passing through the city of Tarhelen, the Mooncallers trekked over the Great Bridge. It shot across Eternity's Ocean, connecting L'arneth and Anunaru as the link of the Joined Hands.

It stretched for three hundred reaches, and fog as thick and dark as black sheep's wool concealed whatever end there was. Rain and hail raged, and heaven-scoring waves from the sea far below sprayed over the parapet. Many stones on the road were crumbling from the harsh elements, but men and women in overcoats worked around the clock to replace them. Canvas tents crowded the roadside belonging to travelers who couldn't wait for Eternity's Refuge, the city built from stone in the center of the Great Bridge.

Luxea saw a monstrous hurricane not too far off from the Great Bridge. It was an aerial nightmare of lightning, cyclones, and rain that twisted inside of a reaches-wide funnel of slate-colored clouds.

"Avari!" shouted Luxea over the storm's roar.

"Enjoying the rain, kiddo?" called back Avari.

"Not really," said Luxea a bit sourly. "Should we be worried about that hurricane? It could wipe out the whole bridge."

Avari faced the hurricane, and her hood flew off. "We're already inside the storm. What did you think all this rain was? It won't be coming any closer. It's been there for a thousand years. Doesn't ever move. It's Sh'tarr's Iris, you dope! Haven't you ever looked at a map?"

Sh'tarr's Iris could be spotted on every map, but Luxea had been under the impression that it was an archipelago, not a storm. Horrified, she said, *"That's* Sh'tarr's Iris? It's huge!"

"Most folks think it's where Sh'tarr Herself lives. Wouldn't be surprising. Where else besides the ocean would you go if you were the Goddess of Storms? Probably nowhere," said Avari with a shimmy.

"Has anyone seen Her in there?" wondered Luxea.

Avari snorted loud enough to overpower the rain. "No, and I don't think anyone will. No one alive's been close to Sh'tarr's Iris. Sailing within even a hundred reaches would destroy any ship in a heartbeat. From the Great Bridge down to Harpy Pass, people curse taking to Eternity's Ocean because of the pissin' Iris. So I don't think anyone's seen Her, but I'd wager She's a spooky one!"

It was astounding to Luxea that something so untamed had been thriving in Eternity's Ocean all of this time. As she squinted, she thought that she saw a face laughing inside of the Iris. She blinked, and it was gone.

Solissium possessed natural and materialistic beauty beyond any that most of the Mooncallers had seen.

Rolling hummocks and green pastures swirled over the land, and dispersed along the skyline were towns and villages big and small. The

Golden Spire Hildre, like the Crystal Spire, was so tall that only the base could be seen over the Timeless Mountains.

The buildings were made from ivory plaster, and their entablatures were trimmed with gold. Luxuriously dressed city-folk stirred in the streets. Clothing, food, and jewelry shops had their windows open, and customers buzzed like bees in a crate.

Solissium was built around a plateau, and atop it was incomparably the most gorgeous piece in the region. It was Villa de Taress, the home of Empress Annalais Taress and the Mooncallers' final destination.

The dracas carried the Mooncallers along, and every pair of eyes gravitated to them — especially Brielle and Ruka. They gawked at her and the wolf as they trotted, but the peoples' focus was diverted when they realized that they were accompanying the Speaker's convoy.

Ares didn't give them much to be excited about. He waved and gave quick smiles every few minutes. Lieutenant Claymore cruised beside him, and a tidbit of fascination showed in his dull eyes.

"Solissium is breathtaking, Your Highness," he complimented.

"That opinion is likely to change momentarily," said Ares.

Deeper into Solissium, Ares' negative remark made sense. Minds did change, some for the worse, others for the better.

The marble streets deteriorated into alleyways of grimy flagstone, and the arcades of the rich were overtaken by the shanties of the poor. Doors swung open and closed with the endless stream of clientele, and the upper stories of each building had topless women draped in cheap metals, blowing farewell kisses to their patrons.

Whorehouses weren't a rare sight in the Joined Hands, but there was a disturbing quantity in Solissium. Every other establishment overflowed with bare skin, packed to capacity with men and women who either lusted for more or begged for less.

Oliver — as everybody had assumed — harnessed the nature of the slums to his advantage. "M'sure glad I came along," he said, whistling to two women who passed by.

Pleased to have drawn attention from a man in the Speaker's convoy, the working girls scurried alongside Velesari and parted their silken dresses to show their bulging breasts. Soldiers howled in approval and commended Oliver. As women crowded Velesari, she stumbled. Luxea cracked her elbow into Oliver's ribs, and he shrieked in the least masculine way.

"Do it again, Luxie," piped up Avari. "Men spring like rabbits. Do so much as open your mouth, and they try to stick something in it."

The working girls began calling to Ares from their balconies. They waved scarlet silks and offered complimentary dances, dreaming about how much money would come from a royal patron. Their determination to bed the Speaker was inspiring.

Perhaps if Ares had been in a better mood, he would have visited the girls. That wasn't the case today. He aggressively puffed his cigarette and retrieved a single gold piece from his pocket. He flicked the coin into the street. It *clinked,* and the road ahead was suddenly empty. He spat and tossed his cigarette into a puddle.

"Kas nenoix," he ordered in draconic.

Pveather bolted. The Mooncallers yelled *'An talah!'* to their dracas. Brielle patted Ruka, and the wolf sped past the others. The Solissium slums were deserted, but they were one gold piece richer.

The convoy ascended the plateau to Villa de Taress. Their guest wing was located at the southwestern edge overlooking the city, and the Empress' wing was on the northwestern sea cliffs.

The guest wing was spun from solid gold. Sculptures of Asrodisia the Goddess of Fertility sprang out from between columns, and palms brushed the lintels and shaded the thirty-stepped front staircase.

The Mooncallers dismounted and shook out the stiffness from their arms and legs. Brielle frowned. "Exorbitant. Are the divines within?"

"Don't think even the divines are this excessive," snorted Avari.

Oliver peeked out. "Ares, this makes your castle look like sh —"

"Does it? You can stay here then," snapped Ares.

A woman in scintillating, golden raiments traipsed down the stairs. Her braided hair was streaked with grey, and her expression reminded Luxea of an itchy sweater. She curtsied to Ares.

"Your Highness, welcome to our guest wing, Haven de Asrodisia. My name is Madam Lilivae Alanis," she enunciated her name like she loved hearing it from her own paper-thin lips. "Us at Villa de Taress were over the Irestar to learn that you would grace our lands again!"

Ares flashed her a well-mannered smile. "Madam Alanis, charmed. It's a delight to be back," he lied.

Madam Alanis extended her hand. Ares looked tart as he struggled to make a pecking motion past the excess of colorful rings on her fingers. Madam Alanis said, "A refined prince, as you're reputed. If you would please allow me to escort you and your associates inside, Your Highness."

Brielle clicked her tongue to call Ruka. Madam Alanis spun around. "Forgive me, miss, but we have a no-dog policy here at Haven de Asrodisia, I'm afraid," she said, shooing Ruka.

If Ruka had to sleep outdoors, Brielle would too. "Go on, Dragon. We will find a den where uppity cats cannot govern us," she barked.

Madam Alanis pouted to say *I hope you understand.* Brielle spat, and Ruka showed his yellow teeth before racing to the sea cliffs.

The Mooncallers entered a colonnade. The friezes were carved with men and women being fanned by giant feathers, fountains spilling teal water lined the walls, and flecks of gold in the floors dotted sparkles on the underside of palm fronds.

Up ahead was a maiden in a harness and a gold choker. She poured wine of maroon into the mouth of a loutish Goldenhand and kissed him when the bottle was empty. She spotted Ares and the Mooncallers and hastily asked for her lover to retire to a room with her. As they departed, she refused to meet eyes with the Speaker.

Madam Alanis leered at the woman. "We've reached the atrium of Haven de Asrodisia. At our left are the gardens where you will find pleasure in the botanicals and lounging quarters."

Down a short flight of steps was a garden with flowers of exotic sorts twisting up from the gravel. Gold effigies of Asrodisia germinated like poppies amidst the grounds. The Fertility Goddess was depicted in the pistil of a blooming firelily with a lover's nautilus shell in Her right hand, and Her left hand resting upon Her pregnant belly. The look etched into Her metallic guise was one of vanity.

After a brief overview of the atrium, Madam Alanis proceeded to a strand of semicircular alcoves. "These are your chambers. I suppose you're weary, so I'll leave the rest of Haven de Asrodisia for you to explore. We have kitchens plentiful with delicacies, and the hot springs are at the northern sect of the villa. Lastly, Heart of Haven awaits you with a prime selection of courtesans to bestow upon you whatever it is you desire."

The bedchambers of Haven de Asrodisia were spacious and overdecorated. Luxea couldn't even see the mattress because it was buried in embroidered cushions. But over the terrace's quartzite balustrade was a stunning view of the Golden Spire surrounded by snow-capped mountains; wind swept the cold white from their peaks.

Luxea lallygagged face-up on the heap of pillows as twilight took rest over the eastern world. She was stuffed full of boredom. The headmistress had said that guests were permitted to amble, so Luxea thought, what better to do?

She plucked one of the complimentary chiton robes from the armoire and slipped it on over her head. It was a marvelous raiment, airy and comfortable, but the sides were slitted from her chest to her hips. Luxea unbuckled the cape from one of her shoulders, wrapped it around her middle, and refastened it. Pleased with her impromptu tailoring, she skipped through the door.

Luxea inhaled through her nose at the tropical gardens. The air in Goldenrise felt like sucking on an ice cube, which woke her up, but the whirring of insects made her sleepy again, so she moved on.

She almost stepped inside of the commissary, but her feet adhered to the threshold before she did. Some men's laps were being ridden by courtesans despite others who were enjoying a meal. Luxea walked away. She would come back later but hoped there wouldn't be legs unfolded in front of her dinner plate by then.

Beside the commissary was a hall packed with sculptures of men and women, not of Asrodisia like everywhere else. They were carved of white marble, not gold. Luxea admired the sculptor's attention to detail and read the plaques at their feet.

Isabelia Taress. Genntric Taress. ————. *Annalais Taress.*

Luxea stopped at the last platform, the only one that portrayed two figures and two names. She recognized the second name as belonging to the current Empress of Goldenrise, but the first had been violently scratched out.

Luxea rubbed away dust and made out the name: *Rowan Taress.*

The sculpture on the left was a half-naked man without a head. It was broken after its creation but had once been complete.

That had to be Rowan.

She stared at the empty space between his shoulders and wondered why no one had repaired it. She reread the plaque. Below his name, it said that he'd died in 18.OSC.3.

Leaving alone the mystery of Rowan, Luxea carried on.

UNBLOSSOMED

AT THE northern end of Haven de Asrodisia was an entryway with flashy, scarlet curtains. Luxea peered inside, and her stomach dropped so fast that she thought she'd heard it hit the floor.

It was Heart of Haven, the den that Madam Alanis had mentioned. Courtesans writhed on top of their suitors, and their jewelry clinked, but what they wore weren't necklaces or bracelets — they were manacles. Stakes and rings poked out of the walls, and attached to them were chains, tethering men and women. A stocky headmaster unhooked several workers in stringy underthings, jerked their leashes, and prodded them toward their clients.

Just when Luxea thought that the scene couldn't get any more despicable, it did. A crying girl with peachy-blonde hair was shunted out of a side room. Her frail body crashed into a table, and the contents of a wine decanter splashed on the tile. A tall headmaster battered her, and her beaded chemise slipped; she hadn't even grown in her breasts. This girl was too young to be in a place like Heart of Haven, but her occupation was apparent despite that.

Luxea resisted the temptation to barge in and scoop the child up off the floor. Never had she seen this occur in Tel Ashir, and it made her wonder what sort of person Madam Alanis was to condone such abuse.

The curtains opened, and the tall headmaster stepped out. A dimple was drilled into his chin, and his brown curls bounced without him even moving.

"Evening. Forgive me, but observing the works of Heart of Haven is prohibited unless you're a customer," said the headmaster crossly.

Luxea glanced at the weeping child as she slid her silks up over her bruised torso. She blurted out, "I am a customer! I want that one — the small one with hardly any meat on her."

The headmaster knew of whom she spoke. "That's Unblossomed, my lady. I'm uncertain if she has learned her way around a woman yet," he laughed. "But while I would normally oblige, Unblossomed is reserved for handling by our most honored guests. *You* can't have her."

"How about money? I'll give you all that I have."

"No. Unblossomed is for celebrated names — *not you.*"

"Magick? I'll do magick for you!"

"I don't want your tricks. You can't have her."

Luxea uttered an imprecation. There wasn't much that she could do without getting herself into trouble. If the headmaster would deny her *'business,'* she would have to get more creative.

"Would you be willing to make another sort of negotiation with me, master?" asked Luxea, unfastening her waist sash and baring her pale flesh.

Interested, the headmaster peeked past the curtains to be sure that none of his colleagues were watching. "Such a covetous woman. What's your name, flower?" he asked, closing in on his prey.

Luxea's eyes darted left and right. "Velesari," she lied.

"Ah, it suits your fairness. My name is Pertia. If you pay *my* price for Unblossomed, I think I can be flexible," said the headmaster. "You will come inside and ride me until your legs give out. Understood?"

Luxea pictured Unblossomed weeping. "I can't meet every desire at once, master. Where's the excitement in that?" she asked slyly.

"Hm, you're right. You seem innocent. I wouldn't want to spoil the pleasure too quickly. What a smart girl," he moaned. Luxea looked away as his hand glided to her chest. "I get a taste now, and if you sate me, I'll give you Unblossomed. But after that, I get the rest of you."

He was wrapped around her finger. For now, Luxea would give Pertia what he asked of her. After sparing Unblossomed from an evening inside Heart of Haven, she would worm her way out.

"I get Unblossomed *tonight,*" said Luxea quiveringly.

"You must earn it, Lady Velesari," reminded Pertia.

The headmaster combed his rough fingers through her hair and tugged. Their lips fought like enemies. With her head snared to the wall, Luxea's eyes flitted to Unblossomed sitting on the floor of Heart of Haven.

Pertia withdrew. Luxea asked, "Have I earned her?"

"I suppose you have," said Pertia, running his thumb down Luxea's cheek. "You've left me wanting more, and that's not easy to do. Fair is fair, my lady. I shall deliver Unblossomed to you this evening, but when the morning comes, you know what you owe me."

"No, I've already forgotten," said Luxea testily.

Once she was out of Pertia's line of sight, she spat in the garden and wiped her mouth on her skirt.

It was almost midnight. The sky was black, and the lamplight from Solissium's streets emanated a hazy glow onto Eternity's Ocean.

Luxea studied with the Usinnon to take her mind off of Pertia. Ingredients were scrawled on the top of the left page for a potion that could make the imbiber sing better, and on the right were notes describing a term that Luxea had never heard before.

Spell-eater: Users of the arcana who cannot be harmed by another's magick. Instead of coming in direct contact with the spell, they absorb it, or eat it. Their opponent's energy is transferred unto them where it remains theirs and adds potency to the spell-eater's incantations.

"Spell-eater? That sounds terrifying," murmured Luxea.

A loud knock made her jump. She tucked the Usinnon under a cushion on the bed. At the door, Pertia stood with Unblossomed beside him and her chain in his palm. Unblossomed stared at the ground and clasped her small hands in front of her. Since Luxea had seen her, her hair had been neatly braided, and her youthful face had been washed.

Pertia smiled desirously. "It's delightful to see you again, Lady Velesari. As promised, here is Unblossomed." He shook the chain, and the child flinched. "Greet the client. You're hers for tonight."

Unblossomed looked at Luxea with her low-set hazelnut eyes and was entranced by the starlight. She bowed her head, and her manacles clinked. "Lady Velesari, I hope I please you," she said robotically.

"Get inside," said Pertia, kicking Unblossomed's ankles. He came closer and twirled Luxea's hair around his forefinger. "I had to pull many strings to allow someone like you to claim one of our more revered girls, so you will pay whatever dues I ask of you." He brought his lips to her ear. "Tomorrow."

Luxea retracted. "Tomorrow," she said tartly.

She dove into her bedchamber and fell against the wall. Her cherry red stars rose up and transitioned to pale blue. Unblossomed was alarmingly calm for having had been handed over like a product. The chain was suddenly heavier. Luxea couldn't stand holding it.

"Is there any way to take this off?" she asked.

"No," said Unblossomed.

"Oh. Let's sit by the window. Here, hold this," said Luxea, presenting the chain. Unblossomed obediently took it and became her own prisoner. Luxea asked, "Do you want water? Snacks were brought earlier, some fruits and steamed veggies, but I'm not hungry. You can eat them if you want."

"Lady Velesari, you're offering me things. Why?" whispered Unblossomed, staring at the chain lying over her fingers.

Luxea crouched to eye-level. "Want to know a secret? My name isn't Velesari, it's Luxea Siren. Will you call me that?"

"Lady Luxea?" gulped Unblossomed.

"Not 'Lady' anything. Luxea Siren," said Luxea kindly.

Unblossomed inspected the starlight. "Luxea Siren."

Luxea softened. "Thank you. Will you tell me your name?"

"I'm called Unblossomed," she answered.

"But is that your real name?"

"No."

"Can I know your real name?"

Unblossomed looked grim. "I'm not allowed to say."

"What? You can't say your own name?" asked Luxea sullenly.

"Names give too much power," said Unblossomed.

Luxea was tongue-tied. "How old are you?" she managed to ask.

"Ten," said Unblossomed plainly.

A sigh trickled from Luxea's lips like she was blowing into a flute. She thought she might be sick. "Have you always lived here?" she asked next.

"I was born here, and Mama also lives in Heart of Haven. She's called *'Slumber.'* Mama was once called *'Chariot'* because she has hair like gold, but she got sick and sleeps too much. Now she's called *'Slumber,'*" said Unblossomed monotonously.

"I'm sorry your mother isn't well," said Luxea dolefully.

"She's still pretty," said Unblossomed admiringly.

"Can you and your mother go anywhere else? Do you have family who can take care of you both?" asked Luxea thoughtfully.

"Mama has nobody," said Unblossomed, hanging her head. "It doesn't matter. We have to stay in Haven until our work is done."

"When will that be?"

"When Madam says we're finished, or death comes."

Luxea couldn't remember what she'd been like at age ten, but even if she could, she would have trouble imagining a life with a chain around her neck. Not once since Unblossomed had arrived had she smiled, and the manner in which she spoke was like she'd accepted that this was all that she would ever have.

As Luxea sulked at Unblossomed, she recalled the happy face of the boy in the Sapphire Bazaar who'd spectated the illusionist. She thought that she might be able to raise this child's spirits in the same way — but better.

"Have you seen magick before?" asked Luxea keenly.

Unblossomed tilted her head. "Magick isn't real," she stated.

"Yes it is," said Luxea excitedly. "What's your favorite animal?"

"A bird," answered Unblossomed.

"What sort of bird?"

"They're small and fly fast. The ones that sing."

Luxea envisioned a small, fast-flying bird. She then requested Unblossomed's hand. The girl trapped her chain between her knobby knees, and Luxea's palm hovered over hers.

Luxea whispered, *"Nav'in ei th'luneth."*

Blue light emitted through the weaves of their fingers. The second that Luxea withdrew, the chain fell from between Unblossomed's legs and coiled on the floor. Hopping on the child's hand was a translucent songbird with white mist trailing its every movement.

The songbird cheeped sweetly and flew in circles above their heads. It fluttered onto Unblossomed's bare shoulder, and bumps poked up on her arms and legs. She tucked her chin to look at the bird's face. It fluffed its tiny feathers and sang a song for her.

Tweet-eet! Tweetle! Tweet-twee! Tweet! Tweee!

Unblossomed's impenetrable frown shattered into a smile.

Over the next few hours, Unblossomed told Luxea all about her mother, growing up in Haven de Asrodisia, and how she'd begun working as a courtesan. However, she didn't reveal her real name.

Luxea also shared what she could remember about her life, and Unblossomed laughed for a long time about the exploding apples. Luxea concluded with the mention of the gala, and the Speaker being the reason she ended up in Solissium.

Unblossomed looked contemplative, blinking over the balustrade. She asked, "Can His Highness really hear Oscerin's voice?"

"If he says he can, he can," said Luxea, swelling her fingers at the Irestar. "I have trouble believing in Her, but maybe someday I will."

Unblossomed swept for the Irestar too. "Oscerin is my favorite divine. She smiles like Mama does." Her expression fell. "You're lucky to know His Highness like you do. You stay in his castle, wander the world, and Oscerin is so close to you. All of the girls in

Haven want him in their bed. He hasn't come to us yet, but it would make no difference if he did. We in Haven de Asrodisia are forbidden from touching Ares Lavrenthea."

"Why is that forbidden?" asked Luxea briskly.

"He belongs to the Empress," said Unblossomed right away.

"Belongs to her?" asked Luxea, volume low without intent.

"Yes. Her Splendor says not to go near him even if he begs for it. Looking at him makes him think we'll please him, so we can't do that either. If we do, we'll never see the light again," said Unblossomed.

Suddenly, Luxea hated the Empress.

In the wee hours of the morning, Luxea shoved the mountain of cushions off the bed and tucked Unblossomed under the covers. She fell asleep not a minute after laying her head.

At dawn, the fast-flying songbirds that Unblossomed adored whistled and flitted to and fro above the terrace. Luxea slumped on the chaise after a sleepless night. Her head was swarmed with misgivings about Haven de Asrodisia, Empress Annalais, and Ares too.

She peered across the bedchamber where Unblossomed lay peacefully with a sham covering her mouth. Luxea was glad that she could offer her a night of repose. However, that relief was abruptly stolen by a knock at the door. Unblossomed's eyes opened like she hadn't been resting at all.

"Lady Velesari, I'm here for Unblossomed," called out Pertia.

Luxea scampered across the room. "Just a moment!"

Unblossomed was already prepared for departure. She stared at the ground and clasped her hands in front of her like she'd done when she came. She slugged to Luxea and presented the chain. Luxea loathed the very sight of it, but the headmasters could never find out that a courtesan had been roaming boundlessly.

When Unblossomed bowed to Luxea, tears bubbled up on her waterline and spilled over her flushed cheeks. Luxea hugged Unblossomed; her hair smelled like tobacco and potpourri.

"Lady Velesari, my patience isn't great," pressed the headmaster.

Luxea smacked the door. "Shut up and give me a minute!"

"I don't want to leave — !" hiccuped Unblossomed. She clung to Luxea's clothes until her knuckles were drained. "Thank you for everything — thank you so much — Luxea Siren."

With her sleeved bunched up, Luxea wiped Unblossomed's tears from her blotchy face. She then stopped and whispered, "If I get you and your mother out of here, will you tell me your real name?"

Unblossomed sucked in her breath, let go of Luxea, and stopped crying; even the tears that had already stained her skin vanished. Luxea's stars were inky blue, and the hue looked like a promise.

"Okay," said Unblossomed meekly.

Luxea held the chain in her hand like she'd had it all along and unlatched the door. Pertia's arms were tangled impatiently, but he half-smiled at the appearance of his promised bedmate.

"Good morning, Lady Velesari," he said, ignoring Unblossomed and snatching the chain. "If you could join me at Heart of Haven, flower, I do believe that you have something for me."

He captured Luxea's wrist. She wrenched herself out of his grip. "I don't want to do it in Heart of Haven. You'll get distracted from me. I want you to have me in my bedchamber."

Concern appeared in Unblossomed's eyes as she fitted the pieces together. Luxea twinkled her stars at her for subtle reassurance.

"Hm. I could have more fun with you here. So be it, Lady Velesari. I must turn in Unblossomed, but I'll come back for you. Tidy up and undress. I want to see every inch of you," said Pertia, sliding the strap of Luxea's robe off of her shoulder.

"There won't be a silk containing me, master. Go quickly. Don't make me wait," said Luxea, fixing the strap again.

"Five minutes," said Pertia, jabbing Unblossomed forward.

The second that they turned the corner, Luxea slammed the bedchamber door and sprinted. Notwithstanding her new suspicions about him, if anybody could help, it was Ares. There was no sign of him at the far end of the atrium, so Luxea doubled back. Out of an alcove came Oliver, and she barreled right into him.

"G'mornin', Luxie. Lookin' lovely," he said, chipper.

"Thank you, but I don't have the time for compliments, Oli. Have you seen Ares?" asked Luxea, glancing behind him.

Oliver bent his thumb over his shoulder. "Yea. He's got the spot by mine. Why you need him? You doin' awright?"

"No, and I —" Fast footsteps were nearing. Pertia was striding in their direction. Luxea yanked Oliver into a niche. "He's coming!"

"Who's comin'?" asked Oliver, peeking around the corner.

Luxea tugged him back. "Just help me!"

Right when Pertia passed by, Oliver pushed Luxea's head down and threw his cloak over her. The headmaster stopped walking and made a twisted face at Oliver. His legs were svelte, but his torso was robust. Detecting nothing fishy about Oliver apart from his top-heavy frame, Pertia stormed away.

Oliver ripped his cloak away from Luxea and asked, "Who's that bloke? Why's he lookin' for you?"

"I'll explain, but take me to Ares first," begged Luxea.

Oliver bolted with Luxea behind him. They hightailed past three alcoves and zigzagged by a column into a group of bedchambers. They were headed to the door on the far right when they heard footsteps approaching again. Frenzied, Luxea pounded on the door with both fists, and then it opened. Ares was a mess. He'd clearly been napping.

Luxea ducked underneath his arm and dragged Oliver inside. Ares was driven awake by her atypical behavior. He opened his mouth to ask, but then Pertia hurried by. The headmaster was averse to crossing the Speaker, so he kicked on to the next alcove with all speed.

Fixing her robe straps again, Luxea stumbled out onto Ares' terrace without an explanation. Her cape twirled in the wind, as white as milk, but that grace was annulled by the storm cloud that brewed over her head.

Muddled, Ares and Oliver joined her. Ares gave a roseleaf cigarette to Oliver, and he smelled tobacco on Luxea already, so he held out a second one for her. She didn't react. Taking that as a 'no,' Ares set it on his lips and frisked his pocket for a match. Luxea snapped her fingers, and the cigarettes ignited in arcanan fire.

Ares blew smoke out of his nose; it was tinted blue. "Would you care to enlighten me as to why you two were running from that man? Don't tell me you damaged property."

"I don't even know the gent," said Oliver innocently.

Luxea didn't look sheepish like the past few times she'd made a mistake. Instead, an air of fury rose from her like steam. This worried Ares. He connected to her stare, and the nebulas that were usually shades of pink, yellow, and blue churned with red and black.

"What happened to you, Luxea?" breathed Ares.

"Last evening, I shared my bedchamber with one of Heart of Haven's most popular courtesans," said Luxea tonelessly.

Oliver choked on smoke. "Did you just — *cagh, cagh!* Biscuits. I didn't expect that. The tables've buddin' turned. Who was it?"

"A girl," said Luxea. Oliver gagged harder. "A ten-year-old girl."

Ares was a statue. Oliver held in his hacking.

"Kids are workin' here? A li'l girl?" asked Oliver, ill in the belly.

"She's called Unblossomed. That man outside was a headmaster. I happened across Heart of Haven last evening and saw him striking her," said Luxea darkly. Ares almost snapped his cigarette in half. "I pretended to be a customer, but he refused to give me Unblossomed, so I had to . . . negotiate with him."

"He was tryin' to find you 'cause you owe him," said Oliver.

"Tragically. But I had to do it. She's forced to do the same every day, and I couldn't leave her there," said Luxea. "That hardly matters. These people aren't permitted to leave until death or warranted release, and it's unlikely that they'll ever see that. It's illicit to say their own names, they wear manacles, and they are slaves. We have to help them."

"M'not goin' nowhere till that girl's outta here," declared Oliver.

Ares' cigarette burned his fingertips. "Have any of them agreed to this?" he asked unfeelingly.

"Unblossomed is ten, Ares," said Luxea darkly.

Ares flicked his cigarette butt over the balustrade. Numb in his mouth, he said, "I'll address this with Annalais at the gala. I'm sure she's unaware of what has befallen her guest wing."

"Is that so?" asked Luxea foully. "Because Unblossomed also mentioned that the Empress has enforced a rule for the courtesans to stay away from *you* specifically."

"*Me?*" asked Ares, floored.

"You heard me," said Luxea frigidly. "They're not to go near you even if you beg to be pleasured. The Empress claims that you belong to her, and anyone who disobeys that rule will never see the light again. Don't believe me? Try approaching them. They'll run from you like cats from a dog."

Oliver sized up Ares. "What's all that, Ares? Have you known 'bout all this too?"

"Of course, I didn't," said Ares, backing up.

"Then why's they bein' threatened with your name?"

"I don't — !"

Ares cut himself short and slid out a second cigarette. His fingers trembled on the roll as he lit it, and he inhaled so deeply that it dizzied him. A beat of his heart died with every crestfallen memory that darted through his brain. After the tobacco mollified his pulse, he explained.

"Annalais and I were engaged to be married a long time ago, but she forbade me to get near — no — to even look at other women. I dealt with her restrictions until I discovered her with another man in *my* home. Two years she'd been seeing him. That wasn't the only man she'd visited, might I add. She's a heartbreaking whore with a black soul and a gold crown. Every time I pick up the pieces, she slaps them out of my hands again. That's why I was wary of coming here, and also why . . ."

Ares swallowed his words. "It's why I brought you here, Luxea. I thought Anna would refrain from exhuming dead intimacies if she saw me with someone else," he admitted.

Luxea was unsure what to think. She was confused, hurt, or maybe relieved, but she struggled to tell which. She'd believed that she had more to offer than being a replacement, but now she wondered if she'd been wrong. She watched the sky, and her eyes shaped the clouds into Tel Ashir's horizon. A part of her wished she'd never left.

Oliver broke the silence. "M'sorry, mate. You don't need Annalais, that sloppy drab. Also, sorry for bollockin' you."

"Your motive was sensible, but I promise you both that I had no knowledge of Heart of Haven," said Ares hoarsely. The resurfaced anguish left his system. "Kross, switch rooms with Luxea forthwith. I don't want the headmaster stalking her again."

"O'course. The rat won't find her," said Oliver readily.

"Thank you," said Ares. He looked at Luxea with guilty eyes. "Luxea, thank you for putting yourself after Unblossomed to get her out of that hell. One night spent with you will change her life forever. This isn't my kingdom, but I'll cross whatever roads I have to. Whether or not the Empress approves, we won't leave Solissium while those slaves are still slaves."

Whispering Birds
8.Nightspeak.25.Osc.3

The sunset carried the gala on its back. Coaches jammed the road in front of Villa de Taress and oozed lavish peoples onto the staircase. Aristocrats, war veterans, theater stars, philosophers, three of The Six, and countless others were expected to make appearances.

Empress Annalais loitered on the second floor with a glass of red wine as guests flocked into the atrium on wings of silk and fur. Her dazzling, blue eyes were vindictive of every made-up face and custom gown. None saw her, but she saw all.

A party of pale-skinned lords and ladies from the cabinet of the Wraiths strutted about like peacocks of black and scarlet. The men sported capes and looked debonaire, and the women's bellies were laced by steel-boned corsets into a number eight shape.

Two rishjaan nobles from the Phoenix Gate of Ank'tatra sauntered in, and their elitism shone as brilliantly as the sands from which they hailed. Their red-brown skins juxtaposed to the teals and yellows that were draped over their muscular bodies and painted their faces.

The desert rishja were like oil and water to the other guests. The Ank'tatra Dominion was governed by the Sun Chief Garamat un Gatra, who hadn't seven months earlier offered his people to the Widow and birthed hideous riots. In spite of being scarred by diabolical politics, the desert rishja walked with their heads held high.

Annalais was about to return to her sanctum when she heard the hollow thunk of metal. Entering was the Lady of Bronze Peyamo Nelnah. Tarot, the nation over which she reigned, wasn't as visually striking as Goldenrise, but the Lady was reputed to be the most revered leader in Amniven's history.

Peyamo Nelnah's flaws were like the scuffs on an antique. Her skin was sun-stained, and her greasy, blonde hair was all over the place. Her right eye, arm, and leg had been replaced with mechanical prostheses after she lost her limbs. To her, they weren't ailments, they were trophies.

The Empress' eyes were rich with antipathy for the universally loved mother of sunlight and machines. She strode off with her lacy, white dress swishing across the floor.

Luxea left her bedchamber in a blue gown that collared her neck. Long gloves constricted her arms from the wrist up over her elbows, and a chiffon drape hung down her back that reminded her of wings.

Nerves scored her belly like she'd swallowed thorns. She couldn't put a finger on what wound her so tightly, but it was one of five or six hundred factors. She was most bothered that Ares wanted her to ward off his lover of yore, but he was her leader, and she was obligated to heed to his decree. Because of that, she would give her best effort to meet his expectations.

"I thought you'd never show," said Ares, resting against a column.

If it could be believed, his mien was more princely than usual; he really was the son of a king. Luxea thought he must've spent all day in front of a mirror — and he probably did. He wore black Tel Ashian regalia with tiny silver plates sewn into it, and the pendant he ordinarily kept secret now dangled as a statement over his chest.

Ares came closer. The clicking of his heels amplified the emptiness of Haven de Asrodisia. Luxea caught the scent of his clothing. His suit had been packed in a bag since leaving Tel Ashir, and it smelled like jasmine and sandalwood. It made her homesick.

His eyebrows slowly raised as he evaluated her vibrant, blue gown. "Well done," he said, requesting her hand.

"Color makes the picture perfect," said Luxea a bit quietly.

Ares looked down, and her fingers made him think of snow. He gently kissed her knuckles and told her, "I prefer black and white."

Avari and Brielle had already ridden Ruka to the gala, but Oliver waited at the front staircase of the guest wing. "Lookin' shaggable, mates. Those legs, Ares. Kick me," he said.

Luxea's eyes ticked like a metronome, examining Oliver. He wore a jacket with a ruff. A red handkerchief with white embroidery hung from his trousers. Varnnish formalwear suited him, but his hyperactive conduct clashed with the sophistication of the attire.

"So dapper, *Lord Kross,*" purred Luxea.

"Oho! How formal, *Lady Siren,*" chuckled Oliver.

"I'll admit, I expected less," said Ares.

"What's that mean?" asked Oliver. "Eh, I can't be bothered. Let's be off, yea? Don't want to miss the whole do."

The three passengers bobbed up and down as the carriage bumped up the road. Once the wheels stopped turning, Ares stepped out and scowled at Villa de Taress, pushing back memories as they crashed into him.

"I'll escort you," he said, reaching for Luxea's hand.

Ares' palm was hot like touching somebody with a dangerously high fever. When Luxea took his hand, she felt breakable. Four of her fingers fit into the web from his thumb and knuckle.

"Wellp, I'm headin' in. Be good, you two. Cheeries!" said Oliver with a cottony grin. He bowed inelegantly and bolted into the villa.

"I pray he keeps in mind that he's *my* responsibility," said Ares.

"Watch him get kicked out before we reach the door," said Luxea.

At the top step, Luxea's gut plummeted. Pillars coated in pure gold lined the villa like the smiling teeth of a divine mouth, and just beyond that was an atrium filled corner-to-corner with guests from all walks of life — if their path was a wealthy one.

Dancing girls and fire-eaters entertained onlookers, and acrobats swung from aerial silks of yellow, red, and orange that burst around them like solar flares. Extended down the middle of the atrium was an impluvium with effigies of naked women pouring water from ewers, and at the far end was a three-story-high, gold statue of the Empress.

The instant the Speaker entered, a ripple effect began. Whispers came from all mouths, and many eyes focused on the woman at his arm. It drove Luxea into a box. Ares let go of her hand.

"You must trick yourself into confidence," said Ares, lifting Luxea's chin and tapping her shoulders to fix her posture. "Events like this are staggering, but no matter what presentation we give, the wheels will spin. I do nothing but feed you affirmations, yet all they see is a reason to wag their tongues. Remember, the secrets of whispering birds hold meaning only to those who thirst for the nectar of a lie — not us."

For over an hour, Ares and Luxea mingled with aristocrats and smiled to those who were too afraid to talk to them. There were more reproachful faces than welcoming ones, but after several flutes of champagne and lessons on decorum, Luxea faced the glare of the public eye excellently.

The two wandered to the back of the atrium by the ballroom stairwell. Both were in good moods, and Ares abandoned his taciturn disposition and was quite talkative. Maybe it was the atmosphere, or perhaps it was the multiple bumpers of bubbly, but they found pleasure in what they'd feared would be a means for stress, until —

"The son of Mountain's Fall. How frightening!" announced a man.

Ares pulled Luxea to a halt, and his joyous expression sank into a glower black enough to douse the Tehrastar like a candle. Luxea looked past him.

Two rishja of desert ilk, a man and a woman, stood taller than all those around them; Luxea wondered if they could even fit through normal-sized doorways. Both had leonine facial features and hot orange eyes; the whites were amiss, a distinctive rishja characteristic.

Ares' lips upturned, and he faced the nobles with a courtly mask adorned. *"Desal pajacitua.* I don't think we've met," he said.

"Hupado, Your Highness. Nay, we have not," said the nobleman. "I am Tahnos Litaan, son of Yurok, and this is my sister, Rhiari Litaan, daughter of Minrala."

"It's an honor, Your Highness," said Rhiari with a curtsey. She held out her hand, and Ares made a kissing motion above her knuckles.

"Charmed, Tahnos and Rhiari Litaan. I imagine I needn't introduce myself. I gather that you already know who I am," said Ares tartly.

"Ares Lavrenthea. The name of the last dragon is not easily forgotten," said Tahnos spitefully. His enlarged irises flitted down to Luxea. "And who is this snowy maid?"

Tahnos asked for Luxea's hand. She politely rested hers upon his. She'd thought that Ares' hands were large, but Tahnos' could've pulverize hers.

"My name is Luxea Siren," she told him.

Tahnos laid a rather wet kiss on the back of her hand, and Luxea almost whisked it away. According to Ares, a man is not to make oral contact with the woman's skin at their first meeting out of respect for her. Ares noticed his social faux pas as well and wasn't pleased.

"The l'arian elves are rarely seen in these days of trial, especially not ones with stars for eyes," said Tahnos flirtatiously.

Rhiari beheld the night sky. "Goddesses, take me, they're stunning!" she said, showing her humungous teeth; it was a marvel that she'd been hiding them behind her little lips.

"Thank you. That's so kind," said Luxea politely.

"I didn't foresee denizens from the Phoenix Gate gracing this event," said Ares next. "I've caught word of the chicanery that has burdened your kind. Your Sun Chief made a blunder that he didn't think through."

Tahnos and Rhiari's visages iced over. "He is not *our* Sun Chief. He is a coward with a crown," rectified Rhiari. "We came to remind the Joined Hands that this is Garamat's downfall, not Ank'tatra's."

It was no secret that the Phoenix Gate had been hurt by its leader's exploits. Had there been any misstep, they could've ended up in the same predicament as Selnilar, Drenut, and the Isle of Varnn. It was a miracle that Widow had censured the Sun Chief's devotion, but the desert rishja were thusly robbed of a leader and left with diminishing faith.

"My mistake," said Ares judiciously. "Silence me if I pry, but what possessed Garamat to give up his lands?"

"Fear," said Rhiari. "When the spider requested his allegiance, he panicked. Mayhap he dreaded a war with the Brood, rightfully so, but that put him under the illusion that his only option was extermination. The Sun Chief held a public address at the Phoenix Gate and defined himself as a servant of the spider, but the spider did not answer. She deserted Garamat while Garamat deserted us, and that was his final error. Perhaps She came to see him as the dastard he is, but whatever reason She has for casting out the Sun Chief remains Her own."

"What happened to him since then?" asked Luxea.

"That is no answer I have for you," said Rhiari darkly. "When the revolts in the Phoenix Gate worsened, Garamat disappeared — fled for his life I envisage. We are not anarchic per se, but we might as well be. Since the Sun Chief's desertion, the announcement has been made that Ralvesh un Gatra is to become the new *Yaz Magia.* Ralvesh is no longer a boy, but he is scarcely a man. It troubles me. If the Brood Mother can tantalize men like Garamat, Vesas, Tani, and Val'noren, what could She do to a child? I pray that Ralvesh suffers not from his father's volatile heart."

Rhiari's orange eyes struck Ares. "Withal, the blazes of mutiny recede, but there is a new crux for the Phoenix Gate. Some think that the Brood Mother pities our injustice, but such theories have resulted in dire circumstances. There are coteries of worshipers unseen, Your Highness, chanting Her name in deification."

"They exalt Her?" asked Ares breathily.

"Yes," validated Rhiari. "They think Her a savior who holds more mercy for our souls than Garamat. Our fates are unforeseen, but the adoration these infidels give to the spider runs thin the sands of time for us all."

"The Widow will surely come for us eventually," sighed Tahnos.

Some bystanders' heads turned to listen in on them. The entirety of the Joined Hands was aware of Widow by now, fearing in silence the evils that stirred behind the name of a faceless divine.

"Do not repeat it, Tahnos. The air turns foul," pleaded Rhiari.

"Widow," said Tahnos balefully. He inspected Ares' horns and claw next, and he looked wicked. "This is only the start. She will come for you too. But apart from that, I am thankful that Ank'tatra is not faced with worse problems . . . such as the savagery of you dragons."

Ares never wanted to hear the word *'dragon'* again. Tahnos' vindictive quips about his kind had turned from stale to rotten. Luxea's mouth acted faster than she could think.

"Yet Tzapodia has had better luck with dragons than Ank'tatra has with Sun Chiefs, hasn't it?" she said, sinking a barb into Tahnos' side.

"Never should a woman speak to a man with venom!" bit Tahnos.

"Respectable men — if they're lucky," said Luxea.

Tahnos spat on Luxea's feet. Ares tugged her behind him and gave Tahnos a warning glare. Just as Tahnos stepped closer, a raspy voice said, "A woman is a weapon, and it'd do ya well to remember that."

Ares smiled and shooed Tahnos. "Impeccable timing, Amo."

Tahnos tugged his sister's arm without farewell. Rhiari gave Luxea an apologetic pout, and the two blended into the crowds.

Approaching was the Lady Peyamo Nelnah. The bronze half of her husky body swayed with a limp, but she made it look like a sashay.

She sneered at Ares, and the pipes stretching down her neck spit steam. They clapped their hands together.

"Ares," said Peyamo through her teeth; one of them was gold.

"Amo," said Ares, eyelids crinkled.

Peyamo strapped his limbs down at his sides and lifted him up off of the ground like he was a feather. The points of Ares' boots brushed the tiles as he squirmed. He grunted, "Put me down."

"I'm already on your nerves? Beat my record," laughed Peyamo.

She planted Ares like a war flag. He brushed the dust off of his suit that had been transferred from her unwashed vest.

"You gorgeous bastard, I've missed you. Look at that hair, you stallion." Peyamo pinched his shoulder. "You've gotten bigger. Think you can beat my arm yet?"

"No," said Ares truthfully.

"That's what I wanted to hear," said Peyamo competitively. She faced Luxea. "Who's this li'l spitfire, eh? Tall, for a girl. Pale too."

"Forgive me for not introducing you," said Ares abruptly. "Her name is Luxea Siren. She's a Mooncaller and a friend."

"You've got a clever mouth on you, Luxea," chortled Peyamo.

"You should see what else she can do," said Ares. Peyamo's mechanical eye zoomed in and analyzed his trousers. He went rigid. "That's not —" He turned away.

Peyamo roughly patted Luxea. "Sorry, girl, I like to play with his head. It truly is a pleasure, Luxea. My friends call me 'Amo,' and any friend of Ares' is a friend of mine."

"I can do that. I've had plenty of formalities," said Luxea tiredly.

"M'with you there. These gents n' dames have got enough sticks up their arses to start a vineyard. I'm only here for the ale and the hearsay," said Peyamo. She grimaced at the Annalais statue. "How's about we migrate? I don't want that thing peepin' at me no more."

The crowds in the golden belly divided for the two of The Six until they arrived at an empty terrace outside of the villa. With privacy aplenty, Ares and Peyamo shed their respectability. She soaked him with questions, wrung out answers, and cracked jokes whether it was a serious matter or not.

After Peyamo guzzled down several ales, she started to tell Luxea her favorite embarrassing stories about Ares, and he hated it. Luxea, however, couldn't get enough. The Lady began with how he'd failed to hold his alcohol the first time she'd given him wine.

Ares groaned, "May we stop?"

"Naina," said Peyamo; *'no'* in seroden elvish. "This lass ain't stupid enough to think you're tellin' the truth, Ares. Just admit it. You heaved your guts after ten minutes at most."

Ares took a generous gulp of champagne, proving himself. "I was only thirteen, and you gave me oilshine black for my first drink. It's a wonder I didn't die."

"My first drink was bourbon straight on my eighth lifeday. Go on, pretty boy, tell me again it's my fault you purged," snarked Peyamo.

"It's your fault I purged," said Ares puckishly.

Peyamo obliterated her seventh ale. "Bah, I've had enough of fresh air. Let's make for the ballroom!"

"You're going to dance? That's new," remarked Ares.

"Hells no," said Peyamo. She thrust Luxea to Ares, and Luxea almost flew over the balustrade. "You two can dance. I'll sit back n' watch."

En route to the ballroom, the Lady wolfed down a few sippets and cleansed her palate with a pint. At the curve of a wall, a couple gave up their seats, mindful that her prostheses must've tired her.

Peyamo flopped down, and an attendant refilled her flagon. "Get on with it, you two. Fire up the mayhem."

Dancers dispersed like ants around a leaf as Ares guided Luxea to the dance floor. They stood in front of each other, and Ares hemmed. "You've been doing it all night, but I should point out that you're slouching." Luxea hastily fixed her posture. "Better. Are you familiar with the Wraithian Wisp?"

"Whom?" asked Luxea, slouching.

Ares straightened her. "Not 'whom.' It's a dance practiced in the Wraiths. It's one of the more simplistic," he informed.

"Do the dragons have a dance?" wondered Luxea.

"Yes, and it's dangerous," said Ares casually. "Well, let us try the Wisp. Your left hand will be in my right, and my left will be at your hip like so."

As he instructed, he moved her arms around, but Luxea dithered.

"Every other woman has the man's left hand," she pointed out.

"Traditionally, it is that way, but . . ." Ares trailed off and curled his scaly talons. "I would never make you touch my left."

Luxea reached out. "I want your left," she said candidly.

For half a second, Ares looked impossibly afraid. Gulping a few times first, he forced his talons into her right hand. "The steps consist of pivots and travels, both of which you'll perform on the balls of your feet. I travel, you pivot. Follow when I pull you like this." Ares pulled her back, but Luxea instantly tripped over his boot. "This might be harder than I anticipated."

Ares steered Luxea backward, and she shadowed him crookedly with her eyes on his feet. Ares dimpled at her and said, "Had I not known that you've never danced, I might've called you an expert."

"Yes, I excel in the art of wobbly legs," said Luxea with a smile.

Ares looked roguish. "Smile at me again, and so will I."

At the sidelines, Peyamo clapped and drank, but far above her was someone who enjoyed Ares and Luxea's performance much less.

On the second floor, Empress Annalais watched Ares as he took genuine pleasure in a dance with a nameless commoner. Her blood scalded. She caught a glimpse of the white-haired woman's face; she looked happy. Annalais bit her bee-stung lips until they leaked red.

The music slowed, and the dance was finished. Peyamo trudged to Ares and Luxea, reeking of stale alcohol. "Less chaotic than I'd imagined, but enjoyable nevertheless."

Luxea focused on Peyamo's metal leg, and a memory nipped at her. She said, "Amo, in the Tel Ashir barracks, there's a dance that requires one foot."

"How does anyone dance on one foot?" mused Ares.

"Most are either getting drunk or too drunk to use both."

"I s'pose I could give that a shot," burped Peyamo.

"Bring your ale, because it's also a drinking game," said Luxea. She snatched a champagne flute from a passing server and skipped onto the dance floor with Peyamo. Ares sat down to spectate.

"There are very few rules. First, we stand on whichever leg is most comfortable," said Luxea. The Lady chose her metal leg, so Luxea balanced on her right. "Now, hopping on our toes, we swing our left leg forward and back, and with our free hand upturned, we drift left, dive down, rise up, and jig twice."

Peyamo's eye scanned Luxea's movements, and she mimicked them. Nobles on the dance floor scowled and scampered away from their barracks horseplay, but Ares couldn't have enjoyed it more.

"Outstanding," said Luxea. "We then spin on our foot and take a drink — but if you spill, you have to finish the rest. Got it?"

Together, Luxea and Peyamo moved through the steps and twirled in sync. As Luxea swilled her drink, Peyamo shunted her, and the champagne sloshed into her face. Ares laughed out loud.

"Drink up, Starlight!" bellowed Peyamo.

"Sabotage," said Luxea playfully. She polished off the flute.

Empress Annalais derailed in her sanctum. She smacked the door until her anger had been expelled into the wood, but it pulsed right back into her. She broke into a cold sweat and dashed to her vanity to dab her face, but she delayed in front of the mirror. She brushed her hands over her bejeweled waist wrap and hated it all.

Raging, she wrenched the gown off of her chest and rived the gold chain from around her neck. She slipped off her undergarments. Her eyes sparkled with tears at the sight of at her naked reflection.

"No one can replace you . . . can they?" she cried.

Her fingertips traced the grooves of her delicate collarbones, under the crescent of her pert breasts, and down her lissome waist. She lifted her left hand to her face, and a ring on her finger told her that she had nothing to fear. The longer she gazed, the steelier her eyes became.

The Empress sped to her armoire and rifled through her hoard of apparel. Long dresses and glittering shawls were cast away. She unearthed a racy gown with skirts slitted to the fold of her thighs. She worked it up over her body and let a twirling lock of her strawberry-blonde hair bounce free. She extracted a jar of viscous reagents and ruby dust from her vanity drawer and spread two thick coats onto her puffy lips.

She stepped back and loved it all.

"A treasure. You can never be replaced," she told herself.

When she turned to leave, a gust of wind swung inward the double doors of her balcony. The glass panes shattered against the wall, and the white curtains *cracked* as they were strewn about.

Annalais spun around, and every one of her hopes died.

Error Code: 70600

Ruka lay on a haystack. The Goldenhands had prohibited a wolf of his stature, or any wolf at all, to enter the villa, so he'd gone to the stables instead.

The wolf tore a branch from a tree and munched on it to pass the time. The wood *snapped* as he broke it into pieces with one of his massive paws. He established a goal to obliterate it by dawn.

As his teeth sank into the core, a scent passed by on the breeze. It was thick with a warmth like rotting flesh and a sourness like stomach acid. Ruka lurked out of the lamplit stall, and the fur on his haunches bristled. This was no miasma of a carcass or a stomach-ill guest.

Not feeling safe in the open, Ruka slunk into the thicket by the cliff. He harked for danger as he relayed his qualms to his sister.

Avari, Brielle, and Oliver had met with each other earlier in the night. The first hours of morning approached, and two of the three were assaulting wines. They migrated to the ballroom where there was much to occupy their intoxicated minds. However, Oliver's groin was suffering.

"I've got to find the loo. 'Bout to break the dam," he whined.

"Ew. Go on then," said Avari, picking at a cheese plate.

"Hurry. Pissing yourself is an irredeemable defeat," said Brielle.

Oliver pouted. "I'll be back. Don't go leavin' me."

He teetered into the crowds of decorated heads. Avari and Brielle spectated the dancers that whirled past. The flashing of jewelry and sailing of gowns was hypnotizing.

"Sister, come to me," said Ruka's little voice in Brielle's head. *"There's something here. The scent hurts. I'm scared!"*

Brielle launched out of her chair and nearly spilled her drink. "Come. Ruka is asking for me," she said, tugging on Avari's scarf.

"What about Kross? We can't leave him," said Avari resistantly.

"Yes, we can," said Brielle, pulling again. "I must go. I don't know what's wrong, but something is. You won't come with me? Fine. But I can't leave Ruka in harm's way. No."

Avari stared in the direction Oliver had gone. "Okay, but let's be quick about it," she sighed.

"Run with me," said Brielle.

They laced their fingers together and bounded out of the villa. Both were glad that they'd opted for pantsuits instead of gowns.

On the landing above the sea, sky-sailors loitered and drank sooty ales aboard the Lady's airship *Matha ou Machina:* Daughter of the Machine.

Nika Lecava kept score as his crew members battled their brawn in a game of arms. A man named Scotsmel let slip a vicious roar as he slammed down his opponent's hand.

"That's another for Scotsmel," said Nika, kicking out his legs.

"Your arm never fails to impress," commended his rival, Jiala.

"Thank ye," said Scotsmel, shaking her hand. "If I keep this'n up, I'll be able to compete with the Lady hersel —"

An alarm blared from abaft, and a red light flashed. Nika scampered to the command center but had trouble interpreting the complication. A warning on the screen blinked: **ERROR:#70600**.

Cursing, Nika typed in the command to override the alarms and entered it with a flick. The ringing stopped, but the screen yet flashed. Fixing it the old-fashioned way, he cracked his fist against the glass. It warped, but the warning popped up again.

With one finger on the intercom button, Nika said, "Command to generator, do you copy? Over."

"Generator to command. We hear you. Is everything all right up there, Lecava? Over," said a voice through the speaker.

"We have an energetic field error, the code number is 70600. Reset the detection cache and reboot the CPU for the anti-gravity chamber. Thank you. Over," said Nika, watching as the hands of the energy meters trembled.

Two minutes later, the operator said, *"Cache is clear, but the CPU for chamber AG is already offline. All systems are inactive, hydraulics are sealed, engines and anti-gravity chamber are dormant. Whatever's going on up there isn't coming from down here. Over."*

"Then where's it coming from? Over."

"Sorry, sir. I don't know what else to tell you — !"

Suddenly, the airship heeled at starboard side and crashed noisily into the docking area. Nika clung to the control panel and planted his feet on the scrappy floorboards until the vessel balanced out.

"Lecava, what the hells just happened?"

"I don't know. I'll find the Lady," said Nika worriedly.

Nika glanced at ERROR:#70600. If there was a malfunction with *Matha ou Machina* that he couldn't fix, the Lady could. He hopped onto the docking area and peeked over his shoulder. The hull was abraded from the accident. The Lady wouldn't be pleased.

All was merry inside the villa, but Ares and Peyamo were perturbed that there had been no sign of the Empress all evening. They claimed that Annalais craved idolization from her guests, and it was remarkably out of character for her to hide away. Apart from their questions, neither Ares nor Peyamo wished to search for her.

The Lady shared information about her current inventions, but Ares and Luxea had no idea what she was talking about. She told them about her new thermal cameras, bio-dome experiments, and single passenger copters. Ares inquired as to what a *'copter'* was, and she said it was a tiny airship. All that Ares and Luxea could envision was a sailboat with one seat.

After that, Peyamo expressed her anger about the postponed construction of her locomotive, *Desha Dunali*: The Iron Dart. The project had been put off due to the pyroclastic clouds in Tarot, but she thought that volcanic gas was an absurd excuse.

"Alls I'm sayin' is, if and when we've got to hop 'round the Joined Hands, the steam engines I'm buildin'll deem coaches and those lizards you've got as a part of a bygone society," said the Lady, finger wiggling. "It's all in the design. If I don't do it, who else — ?"

"Lady Peyamo!" interrupted Nika. With his hands on his knees, he huffed, "It's *Matha ou Machina.* She's having a bit of a major malfunction."

"Did you try turnin' her off and on again?" suggested Peyamo.

"That's just it, My Lady, she wasn't running in the first place. All of our meters are going haywire. It's an energetic field error, code number 70600," said Nika cluelessly. "Additionally, the ship nearly tipped from the loading dock. She's a bit . . . scratched."

"Blasted — !" Peyamo thumped Ares' shoulder. "I'll be back. I ain't losin' my babe to the sea tonight."

Peyamo limped off with Nika. Luxea and Ares were alone together for the first time in hours. "I enjoy Peyamo," she remarked.

"She's quite the nonconformist," said Ares, swirling his drink. "She's my best friend, like a sister, or I suppose *'brother'* is fitting. I'm more of the sister."

"Just a little," teased Luxea. "How did you two meet?"

"I've known her well-nigh all my life," said Ares reminiscently. "My parents took me to Tarot when I was seven, and my maolam insisted I meet Peyamo even though she was seventeen. Peyamo was in an office mapping blueprints for an airship — the airship that's now broken. All of her limbs were in place back then, but she looked the same otherwise. She had an infectious energy, like sunlight. The first thing she said was, *'ever head-butted anyone? Want to try me?'*"

Luxea giggled at a mental image. "So did you head-butt her or not? You can't leave that part out," she said kittenishly.

"Yes, and she flattened me," chortled Ares. "She helped me up, but I got into a world of trouble for it when my —"

Ares' voice was stolen, and his eyes rolled back to their whites. He staggered, and his talons scored the marble wall. Luxea's heart ripped into a sprint. She inched toward him and shook his arm. His wineglass fell and broke.

Come to me, child! RUN!

Ares' eyes flared open. He gasped like he'd been asphyxiated. He tried to look at Luxea, but there were four of her. The amount of champagne he'd consumed didn't help the dizziness. He pressed on his eyelids and recited the Moon Goddess' words in his head, but the phrasing She'd used was riddling. Oscerin dwelled far away, in the realm of spirits, and there was no way for Ares to go to Her. He'd never even seen Her except for in a —

"Of course. Follow me," said Ares, clasping Luxea's wrist.

"What's going on?" asked Luxea, struggling to keep up.

Ares didn't answer. Chasing time, they carved through the crowds and stopped at a roped-off doorway behind a pillar. He tore down the barrier and shouldered the door three times, forcing it open.

"Go," he said, nudging Luxea.

"Ares, just tell me what —"

"Go!"

Luxea went. Ares sidled in after her without looking back at the amassing throng of gossipers. The colonnade was vacant, and not one brazier flickered within. The only visibility came from the moonlit fog that floated in from the courtyard.

In the dark, Ares and Luxea loped around many corners. Soon, they met an impasse with a standalone entrance. Dust coated Ares' palms when he pushed open the door; no one had been there in a long time.

It was a house of worship.

They entered an eery basilica strung with inches-thick cobwebs. An ambulatory led past ten stone apses, each of which had lancet arches with stained glass windows depicting female figures. Through her awe, Luxea studied them.

A glowing woman beneath a white orb clutching a gold guisarme: *Tirih, the Sun.* A smiling woman with dusky skin and a downturned, silver crescent at Her back: *Oscerin, the Moon.* A female child with red hair and a flaming globe in Her hands: *Ka'ahn, Fire.* A faceless woman coated in liquid gold, strumming a harp in Her lap: *Anatatri, Time.* A sneering woman with kelpy hair stalking a ship from the ocean's depths: *Alatos, the Sea.* A floating woman formed of clouds with bolts spraying from Her palms: *Sh'tarr, Storms.* A dancing woman with green skin and flowers blooming from Her hair: *N'ra, Nature.* A naked woman flaunting Her swollen belly beneath Her hand: *Asrodisia, Fertility.* A winged woman with Her hands overflowing with riches: *Himhre, Wealth.* A muscular woman with a long braid and a downturned battle axe: *Daetri, War.*

They were the ten goddesses, the essences of Amniven personified.

Situated in the divisions amid the panes were stone effigies in the shapes of animals. Their sacred names were carved into Their plaques.

A stag with crystal antlers, as curious as He was gentle: *Wynd.* A bear with His black lips parted, a protector of what was His: *Ganra.* A serpent with His neck fanned out, the sly trickster: *Sithess.* A mammoth with corkscrewed tusks, a stubborn warrior: *Nall.* An owl with a heart-shaped head, the master of self-reflection: *Ostriseon.* A raven with His wings open to take flight, the father of secrets: *Raveth.* A lion with a long, braided mane, the most prideful of beasts: *Theryn.* A rabbit ready to leap, quick on His feet: *Mamaku.* A koi with gossamer wings, a being of persistence: *Ocaranth.* A fox with pointed ears leveled to His head, a maven of fleeing, not fighting: *Rin.* A bat with broken wings, the unseen predator of the night: *Varnn.* A wolf with six bushy tails, the warrior of unbending love for His kin: *Fenne.*

They were the twelve gods, the rulers of the stars.

Ares advanced. Luxea pursued him. The divine guardians watched them with eyes of glass and stone. He stopped in front of the Moon

Goddess' image and pressed his palm to the glass. His viridescent irises that were so often spiritless now bled faith.

He said Her name like it was breakable. "Oscerin?"

🦋

Brielle and Avari vaulted across a rolling meadow and skidded down a hill behind the stables. Avari caught a pebble in her shoe but ignored it for time's sake. Brielle rounded the stalls to a sparse grove, and in the thicket, she saw two lights like candles.

"Brother!" she exclaimed.

Ruka emerged. Brielle grabbed onto his neck. His pupils then expanded, and he backed up to take in the air. Her head snapped left, but she wasn't looking at anything in particular.

"This scent is evil," said Brielle. "Have you seen anything?"

"I saw an owl," answered Ruka.

"That's exciting, but owls don't carry death in their feathers," said Brielle portentously. She asked Avari, "Can you smell that too?"

Avari sniffed twice, but the zest of the beach trees and the bite of the sea air was overpowering to her senses. But just then, a fetor like raw meat and bile hit her. She flinched and nodded. Something so faint couldn't have been detected inside of the villa where it smelled like wine and perfume, but out here, it stank of hate.

🦋

Even the Lady Peyamo was unable to find the reason behind *Matha ou Machina's* malfunction. She'd reprogrammed the antigravity chamber CPU and was able to counter the energetic field error for about two seconds, but the notification reappeared: `ERROR:#70600`.

Theorizing that it was an irregularity in the hardwiring, she popped open a hatch in the floor. Her head bobbed in and out of the works as she fondled wires and cursed.

"Bitch of a ship," said Peyamo, wiping her face. A pasty smear was left on her cheek. "I can't figure this out. She don't want to cooperate!" She slugged a pipe, and it whistled.

"It began so suddenly, My Lady. Do you think the salt in the air could be affecting her performance?" wondered Nika.

"I've sealed her in n' out for salt erosion. I can't think of nothin' that'd send her this out of whack. See these gauges? They're goin' batty." Peyamo tapped a glass meter below deck.

Nika knelt and looked over the instruments, but then his eyes caught onto something odd. He murmured, "My Lady, your arm."

Peyamo did a double-take. The power gauges implemented into her prosthesis were oscillating out of control. She pivoted to another angle, but the meters refused to point anywhere but Villa de Taress. It was evident that there had never been anything wrong with *Matha ou Machina.*

"My arm's done this before, but I spent years buildin' up *Matha's* environmental resistance," said Peyamo. "To affect the antigravity chamber to this extent, you'd need one *hells* of a —"

"— magnet," finished Nika.

Luxea gazed at Oscerin's portrait and wished She would speak, but She didn't lend them a word. Ares looked like an abandoned child who could hear his mother's voice but not find her face.

"I must have misunderstood. I thought She wanted me to come here, but . . ."

Ares retracted his hand. The mist from his body heat was absorbed into the rippling glass. Luxea looked up, and although she thought that her efforts would be for naught, she touched the window.

"I'm sure You know this, but my name is Luxea," she said, pale stars swaying. "If there's something You need from Ares, please say so. We heard You, Oscerin, so hear us."

A minute went by without a change in sight or sound inside of the house of worship. Ares' eyes trailed up to Luxea's face. The indigo glass radiated onto her white hair and skin, painting her like a canvas.

"Thank you," said Ares, smiling weakly. "Oscerin gives us nothing more, but know that She heard you. She'll always hear you."

Luxea admired Ares' faith in Oscerin even when She refused to answer. She lowered her hand to her side, but before her misty fingerprints had the time to dissolve, the ground quaked.

There was a muffled *crack*. The frame of the house of worship shifted, and some of the decaying interior along the domed ceiling toppled and broke into pieces with impact to the floor.

Tens of subsequent tremors came as rapidly as a heart's beat after running. Through Oscerin's translucent smile, orange and yellow lights flashed onto Ares and Luxea's faces. She grabbed onto his shoulder as a spray of pebbles cracked the windows.

"Havan'ha neila — !"

An explosion in the courtyard muted Luxea's shouting. Every stained glass shattered at once. The splinters of sacred faces pierced the air. A firestorm blazed in through the empty windowpanes, bullets of rubble hurled, and a wave of smoke saturated the house of worship.

Villa de Taress was annihilated.

Flames stained the starless sky. The grove where Avari, Brielle, and Ruka were hidden lit up. Avari dashed toward the hill, but the ground was tar. Even if she could've gotten there fast enough, she feared that all of her friends were already lost. Ruka ran past Avari, and Brielle hoisted her up onto his back by the arm.

Matha ou Machina's sky-sailors shielded their eyes as the scalding heat blasted their faces; it felt like kissing the Sun.

The energetic field error flickered out. The meters flatlined. Whatever force that had tempted their iron fingers was gone.

Peyamo's machine was functioning, but that was the last thing on her mind. She'd watched Ares grow from a boy into a man, taught him all that he knew, and wanted to share many more years doing so.

The blood abandoned her remaining limbs and rushed to her heart to heal it. Nobody could've survived a blast like that — not even a child of fire.

ONE CROWN LESS

LUXEA CLEARED her lungs of embers.

During the last explosions, she'd chanted the heaviness incantation, *'havan'ha neila,'* to pull Ares down. The ash had flown over their heads, and the debris had collided with them minimally.

Ares clutched her head beside his, and she could feel his hot breath on her neck. Her fingers scratched the stitches on his suit. She thanked fate for survival that had been a blink away from demise.

She rose up, and her hair dangled around their faces. They were both charred, but he'd hardly been injured. A single shard of glass from Oscerin's portrait was embedded into the recess of his clavicle.

The weight of life in Ares' chest crushed him. Luxea had looked so chagrined when he admitted that she was present only to ward off the Empress, but now she was the reason he drew breath. His lips pressed into a line, laced with guilt.

"Thank you. I owe you my life, Luxea."

"Your life isn't a debt. It's a life," remarked Luxea.

She touched him and dispelled the heaviness enchantment. Ares stood and pulled her up with his good arm. They stared through the melting framework of the window and saw that the sanctum and the ballroom were partially intact, but the atrium where they'd been not ten minutes before was in ruin.

Oscerin had known they would be safer inside of the house of worship, and they only had so much time to run. Had She spoken out any later, they surely would have perished.

As Ares and Luxea ran, silence roared from the atrium's skeleton. Even the waves over the cliffs made no sound; nature was speechless. The colonnades were obstructed by collapsed pillars, so they scaled the debris into the courtyard. They slowed outside of the atrium. Pebbles crunched beneath their feet as they ascended the wrecked staircase.

At the top step, Luxea's gut turned. Broken pillars coated in pitch black lined the villa like the teeth of a devil's mouth, and just beyond was a necropolis. Dancing girls and fire-eaters were husks of ash anchored by bones, and arms and legs poked out like weeds from underneath the rubble. The gold statue of Annalais had melted into a haunting shape, and the water filling the impluvium was red.

Luxea doubled over, unable to stomach the image.

As Ares waited for her to recover, he saw the vestiges of couples dancing and heard the whistling echoes of flutes. The dragon blood in his veins was meant to burn, but it was frozen with terror.

The floor was a messy painting, and it was a challenge to keep their shoe soles from stepping upon the dead. All was quiet, but that didn't negate the possibility of evil eyes watching.

There was a distant *clank,* and Ares and Luxea jerked in a start. He spun around and expelled a sigh like a shot. It was only Peyamo. The

Lady slid down a slab of marble and landed with a crash like a drum cymbal.

"You ploughin' bastard!" she said, swinging her arms around Ares' waist. "Don't know how you did it, don't care how you did it, but you're one lucky bastard. I'm so glad."

"Oscerin told us to run, and Luxea covered me," said Ares, darting a beholden glance toward Luxea.

Peyamo embraced Luxea. Wiping her tears away, she said, "I'm sorry for dumpin' this on you so soon, but where's Anna been? I hate to point fingers, but somethin' ain't right about her not showin'. You know her best, Ares. Do you think she was involved?"

Ares didn't want to presume treachery regardless of the deep-seated antipathy he held for the Empress, but given the facts, he had a similar outlook.

"Do not give the Empress my credit, Lady," thundered a fourth voice; his accent was as torrid as the desert sands.

The three spun back-to-back. *Ticks* and *whirrs* spouted from Peyamo's prosthesis as it converted into a barrel. She picked bullets from her belt like cherries and popped them into the chamber.

"Show yourself!" said the Lady, aiming to open fire.

"Your eye needs repairs, Lady. I am right here," said the voice.

Peyamo's heat-seeking lens pinpointed a giant figure on the second floor. Ares and Luxea rotated, and he looked heartbroken.

They saw a desert rishja with skin like red clay and exaggerated features like the drawings in children's books. His golden braid swept the floor as he neared the balustrade with a loaded crossbow.

"Garamat? You're responsible for this?" asked Ares lividly.

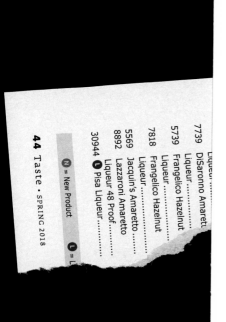

The Sun Chief's laughter was surprisingly paternal. "No, I was not responsible, my boy. Their deaths are Her music. I played the notes, but She wrote the symphony."

"I thought Widow turned you away," pointed out Peyamo.

"Yes, but She came back!" said Garamat boldly. "It is the second birth, and this was the trial of my proving. The Widow sought me out for this accomplishment, and I am Her paragon. Goldenrise was never meant to fall, but it had to. It is as She commanded!"

As an altercation amongst the three leaders grew heated, Luxea's ears twitched to a shift within the rubble at their backs. She saw movement in her peripherals. Her legs started to tremble.

"Never meant to fall? What does that mean?" needled Peyamo.

"The Widow is merciful. She would not bring harm without purpose, no. However, the Brood Mother was at a stalemate. She had no choice but to take action! But I . . ." Garamat lifted his weapon and fused his pained, blue eyes with Ares'. "I am afraid that you have seen too much."

"You must face the consequences of your actions. Stand down, and I'll spare your life, but don't you fight us!" wailed Peyamo.

"Ares," said Luxea, tapping his back. He swatted her hand.

"I am sorry, Lady, but I am sworn to Her," said Garamat. "I must fulfill my role at all costs, and if you get in my way, I will not let your lives be prolonged!"

"You don't mean it!" said Ares, out of his mind. "You're afraid, Garamat, but you aren't a faithless man. Some part of you must sense that you worship a false divine — !"

The Sun Chief launched a bolt at Ares' feet. "I must do this! How dare you give guidance when you know so little? If I do not act, I — !"

Peyamo shot two bullets and skewed her aim on purpose. The wall behind Garamat was demolished. "Don't you make a move!" she shouted. "I'll be damned if I've got to take your life, but I

"You think me a soldier who battles alone?" ask loading another bolt. "You will be very disappointed then,

"Ares!" exclaimed Luxea.

"What?" snarled Ares. He turned around and tensed up in frigh

An army of hellish creatures arrived to aid the Sun Chief. The were as black as obsidian with four pairs of white eyes running vertically down their tapered heads. A steaming trail was left as they crawled up the walls at horrifying speeds.

A second, formidable abomination plowed over the wreckage and crushed marble beneath its elephantine feet. It was a titantula like the one Luxea and Avari had encountered in Lor'thanin. Its craggy paunch festered with goiters, and its lumpish head slacked upon a bludgeon atop its shoulder.

Garamat leaped, and Ares dodged his bolt just in time. "Amo, take that one down. Luxea, you get the rest. Go!" he instructed.

Peyamo nudged Luxea aside. "Don't be afraid. I'll cover you!"

She fired two hollow-point bullets. The titantula staggered but proceeded with its sluggish advance. The crawlers flanked them, and Peyamo vacillated over which to target.

"Yeth'lavren!" blurted out Luxea.

Ribbons of blue arcana slithered forth and engulfed the crawlers. Their tarry flesh liquefied, and then they were puddles.

Peyamo shaved eyebrow twitched. "So *that's* what you can do."

Ares heaved his claw, and the Sun Chief upthrusted his crossbow. The two *clashed.* "This is wrong! What about everything that you taught me? The Garamat I once looked up to would have never succumbed to this madness," said Ares.

"I taught you all that I did because *my* son would not listen. You are right. Never would I serve a mother of hatred without reason, but there is plenty to justify my choices that you cannot understand," said Garamat secretively. He glanced past Ares. "If you and the Lady run now, I will let you go. But the starry-eyed woman stays with me."

The statement caused Ares' arms to weaken. He readjusted himself quickly. "Why do you want Luxea?" he rasped.

"No questions. Do you want to live, or die?" asked Garamat sadly.

"Die. I won't let you have her," said Ares loathsomely.

Garamat's eyes lost their vibrancy. "Then you will die. But before we go on, allow me to give you my final counsel. You are a good man, Ares, but duty is not everything. Know when to deviate. When your only path leads you to doom, walk it proudly."

Ares' talons *scraped* down the side of the crossbow, and he lurched. Garamat nimbly eluded and slid twin scimitars from the scabbards on his back. "Blade and claw. You fight just like Heavens Devil. You are more like him than I thought."

"Provoking me is not in your favor," said Ares warningly.

"No? After Mountain's Fall, the desert rishja adopted a saying. *'Tua desana agaz'tad fatna dracona na'tad mandu int'magmak: the best way to kill a dragon is to make it angry,'*" recited Garamat.

The crawlers leaped at Luxea. She yelled, *"Sheishan'in!"*

A shield surrounded her, and the crawlers smacked against it. The veil would diminish soon, and Luxea would be vulnerable. She thought back to the Usinnon. The solution hit her — division magick.

Taking two breaths first, she dropped the barrier. The crawlers jumped for her. She gasped, *"Eluva eshas;"* *"mirror the face."*

In an instant, she looked exactly like the crawlers. They turned to her, and she peered around as if she was searching too. Knowing that one of them had to have been an imposter, the spindly crawlers sprung upon each other. Luxea ducked out of the way and hid as they tore themselves to shreds.

"Dammit!" said Peyamo, losing the fight.

She had to change her tactics. Her arm altered into a barrel with a greater circumference. She tugged a missile from her belt. It was a prototype, but there couldn't have been a better time for a stress test.

The titantula elevated its club, and the Lady unleashed devastation. As her arm cooled, she could see her opponent's outline through the smoke. A portion of its torso was missing, but it yet lived.

Luxea noticed that Peyamo's battle was proving difficult to win. She sprinted around the impluvium, and her stars darted up to the Annalais statue. She inspected the arcana sparking from her hands and rerouted toward the Empress.

As the Sun Chief charged, Ares swiped up a snapped banner pole and hindered the scimitar. Garamat gripped the rod and slammed him into a column, snaring his throat with preposterous strength. Ares' feet dangled above the ground, and his eyes spoke fear.

"Come, this cannot be all you have to show me. Your father did it right. He won every battle because he was not afraid to!" roared Garamat. "Here I am, Ares. Show me the flames that my brothers and sisters of the mountains faced. Do you not lust for it?"

"You're not worth a dragon's fire," husked Ares.

"I should be! Do not make me beg!" shouted Garamat.

"You would be begging for death."

Giving Garamat what he wanted, Ares spat a tiny orb of dragon fire — which Garamat hadn't known was adherent. He dropped the banner pole. The purple flames stuck to him and spread as he screamed and covered his eyes. Ares ripped his claws across his face and sliced his hands. Blood squirted from Garamat's fingers. Their tips dangled from ligaments like ornaments from red ribbons.

Ares knelt and gripped the Sun Chief's vest. "Tell me now, why have you chosen to serve Widow?" he asked.

The Sun Chief was struggling to speak through the dragon-fire that dripped down his face. For the sake of receiving answers, Ares wiped away the flames and flung them onto the floor.

"You will not understand, Ares, for you are not a father," wept Garamat. "I could not deny Widow — I cannot, for his sake!"

Luxea maneuvered to Annalais's statue and crouched. She placed her hands on the chain that fastened the figure to the wall. Her fingers burned as the metal heated up and began to soften. She counted down in her head, and then the chain *snapped.* The statue swayed. In seconds, it would fall.

"Ares, Amo — MOVE!" screamed Luxea, turning tail to run.

Peyamo looked up as the statue teetered. "GET DOWN!"

Ares threw his arms over his head and bolted for cover.

The statue cracked away from its marble plinth and descended as slowly as time seemed to be moving. The distorted, gold face of Annalais was all the titantula saw before it was squashed. The ground cracked under the statue's unthinkable weight, and the bloodied water inside of the impluvium sprayed across the atrium.

When the dust and mist settled, Luxea peeked. Beneath Annalais's breast was the lifeless body of the titantula. All it had taken was a barrage of bullets, a missile, and one egocentric decoration.

Ares raced to Luxea. "That was symbolic," he panted.

"Thank you," said Luxea tiredly. She scanned the area, and the sweetness of victory turned sour. "Where is Peyamo?"

"You almost had me," said Garamat weakly.

The Sun Chief had one clunky foot stomped onto the barrel of Peyamo's arm, and his mangled hand was in her hair. Blood from his missing fingers trickled down her forehead. With his free arm, he teased her throat with a scimitar.

Luxea lifted her hands to cast a spell. Garamat spat, "No. No more incantations, little spell-flinger. A single word leaves your mouth, and I'll take her head."

Ares batted down Luxea's hand, refusing to gamble with Peyamo's life. The Sun Chief nodded to the upper level, and more enemies approached. They were more human than the others but just as deadly. Bows and arrows targeted Ares and Luxea, and knives were poked into their necks.

Peyamo clutched the scimitar. "Ares, kill him."

"No," said Ares without delay.

"Kill him," restated Peyamo.

"If I move, he'll kill you first," said Ares grievingly.

"I know, but if you don't do somethin', we're all goin' down. It's me or all of us, and I ain't lettin' you die. Do it."

"You can't ask this of me!" shouted Ares.

"Dammit, Ares! Just kill him!" wept Peyamo.

"A dragon too soft to take a life?" laughed Garamat. "The Lady is right, Ares. You could have a chance. Otherwise, you are all going to the same place."

Two enemies fell from the second floor, but only Luxea noticed.

Garamat whispered, "How touching. But I do not have all evening. You fought well, but in the end, Widow will reign — !"

A red blur flashed out of the shadows. The Sun Chief was consumed by frothing jaws. The assassins tore their blades away from Ares and Luxea's necks. He grabbed her, and they inspected the fallen. Hand-carved arrows were in their skulls.

Brielle was slinging projectiles from above. Each shot was precise. One in the neck, one in the heart, one in the mouth. At her side, Avari tackled an assailant, slammed daggers into his eyes, and rode him onto the ground. She knocked another onto his back with a swing of her leg and slit his throat.

Ruka flung Garamat. A skid mark of red was made as he slid across the tile. His spine broke against a wall. His arms and legs were bent like an insect's that had been stood upon.

After Brielle sniped the last enemy, she jumped from the second floor. "No more, Brother," she said.

The wolf licked his teeth and receded. Brielle plucked an arrow from her quiver and stretched it on the bowstring. "Speak the words you hide in your foul mouth, Sun Chief. You have ten seconds."

"Yes, yes," gurgled Garamat. His filmy, blue eyes shifted to Ares and Peyamo. His shredded fingers twitched, and the signet on his finger glinted. "Forgive me, friends. . . . Please . . . tell Ralvesh that it was all for him. . . . I die a man of faith."

Brielle aimed beneath his mandible.

"No. You die a fool."

ROSENBLOOM RED
9.NIGHTSPEAK.25.OSC.3

EVERYONE BUT Luxea and Peyamo brushed themselves off and recounted their means of survival. Luxea drank in the faces of her fellowship. Ares, Avari, Brielle, Ruka, Peyamo — but not Oliver.

"Where is Oli?" she asked.

Avari and Brielle frowned. "Last we saw him, he was pissing himself. He ran to find relief, and that's when Ruka called us. This was in the ballroom," said Brielle.

"I'm going there. I have to find him," said Luxea as she left.

"Us too. The Empress' Goldenhands have set up cots for survivors. It's the best place to start," said Avari, hopping onto Ruka's back with Brielle.

"If we search together, we can cover more ground," added Ares.

"I'm stayin'," said Peyamo, taking a knee at the Sun Chief's side. "I'll fly Garamat's body to Ank'tatra. His people might not want him, but Ralvesh will. Go on. I'll find you soon."

Ares patted Peyamo's back. He spent a moment reading the history written in Garamat's creased flesh, but his book of life had been closed. He rested his fingertips on the Sun Chief's forehead.

"Nisele vene, dalnemes," he said in draconic; *sleep well, brother.*

The ballroom was packed with victims wounded, weeping, and lifeless. Luxea found this area worse than the atrium. Her colorless stars traveled to the healers who mixed serums and threaded surgical needles, but most injuries were irreparable.

A maiden in a sequined gown rested on a cot. With all the make-up she wore, she looked like a bluebird, but the left side of her head had been scalded from the blasts. She screamed to the healers that her husband would never love her again. '*I'm a monster!*' she would say. Luxea wished she could tell her how pretty she really was.

Nearby was a man with healers circling his bed like vultures. His eyes were unfocused, and his arms were curled against his chest. Although he would survive, his consciousness wouldn't return. He was a living shell with a dead mind.

Luxea glanced at Ares, hating what all of those people had been forced through. He started to console her, but a vaguely familiar scream cut him short.

"*Nashta! Mak rakgun. Nashta gi'je tatam'naani!*"

Tahnos Litaan of Ank'tatra had one arm outstretched, but everything past his elbow had been amputated. With vestigial fingers, he swiped at the nearest cot where his sister, Rhiari, lay in halves.

A mender pulled a sheet over Rhiari's remains. The light left Tahnos' eyes. Blood splattered on the floor as his incomplete limb flopped onto the cot's edge.

"Death only gets crueler the longer you look," breathed Ares.

Luxea hid her starry eyes behind her lids. Their feet slowly drove them onward, but it was difficult to remember where they had and hadn't been. By the minute, more beds were placed with more bodies upon them, and their course became an ever-shifting labyrinth.

Peyamo Nelnah had delivered the Sun Chief's remains to *Matha ou Machina*. She hobbled toward Ares, but a Goldenhand seized her ear before she could make it to him. Her mouth gradually opened, and then she saluted the Goldenhand and moved on. Her neck burned with angst from what she'd been told, but also with the dread of relaying it to Ares.

"Sorry for interruptin', but Annalais was found unscathed," said Peyamo darkly. "She's in her sanctum. If we're goin' to uncover what she knows about all this or forge any union, we've got to do it now."

Ares was queasy, but he couldn't tell if the feeling was in his throat, his stomach, or his heart. Luxea was suspicious. The sanctum was the only region that had been entirely avoided by blasts.

"Go. I'll keep looking for Oli," said Luxea, nudging Ares along.

"You're sure?" asked Ares.

"Yes, but don't forget Unblossomed," reminded Luxea.

Ares nodded once. "I haven't."

The Speaker and the Lady advanced to the back end of the ballroom. Wood chips flittered down as Ares tore the door away from the damaged frame. The first staircase was battered in some places, but the third floor looked as if no calamity had ever taken place. Doors were on their hinges, and lamps shone brightly. However, all of the tables that had once been arranged with porcelain and finery were now bare and tipped askew.

At the sanctum, puzzles appeared in Ares and Peyamo's eyes. Tens of utensils, candelabras, and platters were heaped around the door.

The Lady turned the handle, and the tableware on the ground sent *clatters* down the hallway. Peyamo entered with ease, but Ares felt like he was stepping into an iron maiden.

The Empress' sanctum was in splendid disorder. A fountain sloshed with roses on the water, but beside it was a splay of broken glass from the balcony door. To the right was the bedchamber, and the mattress was bigger than some peasants' homes. But in the center of the room was a chaise set before a crackling fireplace with a woman lounging upon it, and that woman bore a beauty so unrivaled that it could've swelled the hardest of men's hearts to burst.

"What a surprise. It's the world's favorite bucket of rust," said Annalais to Peyamo; her words were curled like her tongue was a pretty bow. She approached Ares, and he could see how fast her heart was beating within her breast. She trailed her eyes from his feet to his head. "I missed you, Ares. It has been too long."

"Not long enough," said Ares blackly.

"Always the quickest to decline kindness," said Annalais wantonly.

The Empress strode to her vanity and poured three glasses of wine into a set of lover's nautilus shells. She casually handed the first to Peyamo, who took it at once, and stepped like a swan back to Ares.

Swirling the lover's nautilus beneath his chin, Annalais purred, "Rosenbloom red with the essence of blackthorn. As harsh on the tongue as it is sweet. Your favorite."

Ares glared downward, and a nail was driven into his heart. Annalais's left hand was graced with the ruby engagement ring that he'd gifted to her nine years prior.

Back then, he'd called her 'my treasure.' He'd chosen a day and had it engraved under the ring's jewel. When he'd given it to her, he'd asked her to marry him on that date and to remember that she was his treasure each time she read the message: 11.LM.17.

Now all Ares saw in Annalais was a devil dangling a lure.

"Enough with pleasantries," said Ares gruffly. "Peyamo and I came here for a coalition, but after tonight, our purpose has changed."

The Empress sat. She took a delicate sip and crossed her legs, baring her thigh through the slit in her gown. Repulsed by her ignorance, Ares ripped the lover's nautilus away from her lips. "How are you so mellow after so much blood has spilled? Are you aware of anything that has happened, or were you too busy pampering yourself to notice?"

"Ares!" yelled Peyamo. She pushed him aside. "Annalais, you were nowhere to be found all night. It'd be in everyone's best interest to hear the truth. This is no accusation, but where were you?"

"I was here. Where else would I have been?" asked Annalais. She reclaimed her wine from Ares and drank. "You don't think that I have something to do with this, do you? That this was a plan to jeopardize my own empire and bring eyes back to Goldenrise? What a dull way of thinking, Lady. You wish to learn the cause of my absence? My reason is simple. Widow."

Ares motioned to himself. "You think we aren't aware that the Brood Mother is accountable? Speak plainly, Anna."

"Fine," spat Annalais. "Widow was here — in this room."

A chill settled upon the sanctum. Even the flames inside of the hearth weakened. Ares exhaled sharply like his breath had bitten his tongue. Peyamo watched the white curtains buffeting as her heart relearned to thump.

"You're certain it was Her?" asked the Lady distantly.

"Clearly you've never seen Her yourself. The Widow isn't one who can be mistaken for another," said Annalais standoffishly. "Midway through the evening, I was leaving to start my presentation when She invited Herself in. The room was rumbling like She was pulling the world toward Her."

An image of *Matha ou Machina* aslant against the loading dock blasted off in Peyamo's head. She glanced at the platters and utensils that cluttered the floor; all of them were metal.

"Like a magnet?" she asked quietly.

"Exactly like that," said Annalais indisputably.

"But how? It's impossible. A human body couldn't even come close to handlin' that level of —"

"Widow is *not* human," said Annalais with a whimper. "The air around Her twisted, and She smelled of black death. Whatever doubts Amniven may cling to of Her claims to be divine are void. She is divine. Of that I have no doubt — and you shouldn't either."

Needing it, Ares scooped up his neglected shell of rosenbloom red and gulped it without savoring the taste. More pacified, he inquired, "Why assault the gala? What purpose did it serve?"

"I don't know," said Annalais with a swill. "No matter what I could have said to Widow, we would have suffered the same outcome. When She came, the first thing She told me was that She planned to raid the event. Shortly before She departed, the fires ignited. The road to sanctuary was impassable all along. I pray you understand that She is smarter than all of us, and She is resourceful. She knows my weaknesses, both of yours, and She knew the Sun Chief's."

"Knew?" repeated Ares. "We never mentioned Garamat's death."

"Widow did," stated Annalais.

"You claimed that Widow came before the assault," said Ares.

The Empress' eyes dropped into her wine. "She said you two were meant to survive the initial attack, so I take it you were the driving force behind Garamat un Gatra's death?"

"That's right," said Peyamo warily.

"Then the Sun Chief perished the way he was intended to," said Annalais sharply. "Ravaging Solissium was not Garamat's true function. He was not led into this game to prevail, but to be erased."

"How do you know this?" asked Peyamo.

"The Brood Mother told me," said Annalais straightforwardly. "She'd surmised that you would live, and that the Sun Chief wouldn't reign victorious against big guns and bigger dragons. Widow has wanted Garamat out of Her way from the beginning. He was an obstruction. But the Sun Chief's undoing was not the core of Widow's purpose. She yearned for something, although I don't know what. But since She has ended Her onslaught, I assume She has attained it."

Ares recalled Garamat's request to surrender Luxea to him. He hated the idea that she could've had anything to do with this, so he ignored it. "What did Widow want from you?" he pried.

"What She wants from us all — loyalty," said Annalais.

"And did you give it to Her?" badgered Peyamo.

The Empress' fingers tightened around the shell. She was anxious, reluctant to speak. The warmth left Ares' hands. He crouched to survey her. If anyone could pull the truth out of her, it was him.

"Anna, say you didn't give your oath to Her," he pleaded.

The Empress tried to cover her mouth with her lover's nautilus. Ares lowered it. She snapped her head away. He turned it back. She started to cry. The sight of her tears hurt him in the same addictive way it had so long ago.

"Anna, please. Did you sign your name?" whispered Ares.

Annalais kicked Ares and pitched her lover's nautilus at him. "Yes! Yes, I signed! She had me in Her web, Ares. *'No'* was not an answer I dared to give Her! I couldn't turn Her down!"

Ares watched as rosenbloom red filled the cracks in the tile and saturated the white tail of Annalais' gown. Unless they could earn Ralvesh un Gatra's loyalty, only two of The Six were left. Widow had stolen the third right from under their noses. Since the fires began, Ares and Peyamo had unknowingly been inside of enemy territory.

In a monsoon of tears, the Empress rushed to a desk with a scroll sitting upon it. She gave it to Ares. The black wax seal was broken. Imprinted upon it was the same symbol that Ares had seen in Rylin O'sara's skin. He read the contents. Every word was exact to the contract that he'd been offered months before, except this one only had one page, and the bottom half had been burned.

"What happened to it?" asked Ares, touching the singed edges.

"I threw it into the fire. She took it out," said Annalais. She cried and laid her head against Ares' chest. "I failed myself, failed you, and failed my empire. I don't know what to do."

Out of an undead habit, he set his claw upon her head. She swatted it and reached for his right hand.

"Have you told anyone about this?" inquired Peyamo.

"No," hiccuped Annalais.

"Tell no one. Say nothin' of Widow's presence here or of your oath to the Brood," said the Lady. Ares flashed her a disagreeing look. She disregarded it. "You vowed loyalty to Widow, but so long as you don't adhere to Her, we're still your allies."

"I cannot defy Her! She will have my head and damn my soul if I don't give Her what She asks of me!" said Annalais, releasing Ares.

"You'll choose Her or us," said Peyamo unequivocally. "If you assent to persist cooperation with The Six, you'll have our aid and our secrecy. If you decline, don't expect us to keep your meetin' with the

Brood Mother hidden or treat you any differently than we treated Garamat."

"But — !"

"Protestin' will only cost you more," said Peyamo severely. "It's up to you, Annalais. We'll part ways as allies or enemies."

The Empress gazed up at Ares. His expression was no more pardoning than Peyamo's. She squeezed tears between the gaps of her eyelashes. "I don't want you as my enemies. My empire hangs in the balance no matter which turn I take, so please help me. Speak of this to no one, and I will do whatever you say. I swear to you."

"Then the Empire of Goldenrise will have the protection of Tarot and Tzapodia as well as the discretion of The Six," said Peyamo, slackening her shoulders. "This can't be disclosed to anyone — and I say that to both of you. Tonight's been a shit-show, I think we can all agree on that, but we'll deny Widow of further chances to strike. If we're on the same page, let's —"

"There's one other condition," said Ares. "Before we depart, you will sign warrants of arrest for the hired hands in Heart of Haven and authorize the release of the courtesans who reside there."

"What? I've lost my villa and my prestige, and you wish to rob me of Haven de Asrodisia moreover?" shrilled Annalais.

"If you won't uphold, an alliance with Tzapodia is nonnegotiable. I refuse to provide my guardianship if you continue to endorse inhumanity," said Ares reproachfully. He bit his lip. "And don't you *ever* again speak my name as if I belong to you."

The Empress was blinded by anger. "Let me guess. That white slut you were dancing with is one of them, and now you want to take her home with you. Is that right? If so, no!"

Ares was so dumbstruck by her asinine guess that he laughed. "That's not at all the case. I say this from a moral standpoint, not for my own benefit. I'll provide the courtesans with legal backing until they can carry their own weight. Say *'yes'* or be named an adversary of the Kingdom of Tzapodia and *me* forthwith."

The investments that Annalais had poured into Heart of Haven were substantial, but Ares and Peyamo calling her their foe was a more damaging penalty. She stared into Ares' eyes and knew that if she refused, she would never do so again.

"If letting those cocksuckers roam the streets helps you sleep at night, take them," she barbed.

As the Empress tore through her shelves, documents drifted to the floor and soaked up rosenbloom red. She scribbled names and her signature onto each page and slapped the stack against Ares' chest.

"I do this for you, not them," she grated.

"As long as you're doing it, I don't care," said Ares. "I'll deliver these and discharge the courtesans from duty. From here on, I vow to offer my aid and secrecy by the bond of The Six."

Peyamo blew air out of her cheeks. "Right. Since that's all out of the way, let it be pledged," she said, picking up Annalais's quill to ratify the agreement. "We fight the Brood as one and impart nothin' that'd harm Annalais's standing as a member of The Six. All in favor, jot down that pretty name here."

ḪAVEN ÐE AṢROÐIṢIA

ARES AND Peyamo egressed with the arrest warrants. She would depart for Ank'tatra apace, so she said farewell before parting ways.

"Ares, if returnin' to Tel Ashir ain't imperative, I insist you come to Tarot for a few days," she said with a hug.

"It's necessary, Amo, we have much to negotiate, but it would take me weeks to get back to Tzapodia from Tarot. Isaak didn't agree to fill my role for that long. I can't put that on him," said Ares glumly.

"You know who you're talkin' to, Ares?" laughed Peyamo. "When we've concluded our business, I'll fly you to Tzapodia; *Matha* needs her exercise. Please. Close to nothin' was achieved here."

Ares patted Peyamo on the head. "All right, all right. It can't be for long, but I'll hire transport through the Wraiths and have a select few Mooncallers accompany me. If all goes smoothly, you can expect me in Tarot in little under a sennight."

"Thank you, Ares," said Peyamo. She started to trudge to the airship landing but stopped after a few steps. "I know meetin' with

Anna was rough on you, but that aside, keep what we discussed tonight between us. Not even your Mooncaller buds can hear about it."

Ares hesitated but slowly nodded.

Peyamo winked. "I've got to get goin'. I'll brief you on Ank'tatra when we meet anon. Be safe."

Dawn was blooming when Ares reentered the ballroom. White rays of sunlight spilled through the gaps in the ceiling and made the pools of blood glitter. What a harrowing clash of ruin and beauty, he thought.

Brielle was sprawled across Ruka's back, and Avari was curled into Luxea's chest. Ares neared sluggishly and knelt.

"Luxea," he whispered her name. She looked up, and the stars were grey and motionless. Ares presented the documents. "These are warrants of arrest for the headmasters in Haven de Asrodisia, authorized by the Empress. You discovered those people and took the right measures to help Unblossomed. I don't deserve to be the one to free them — you do."

Luxea's stars regained light for a split second before fading again. She sifted through the warrants and saw Unblossomed's face in the ink. Knowing that the slaves would be released brought her peace, but all other happiness had been irreparably ground to smithereens.

"Thank you," she said.

She set down the warrants and shuffled around behind her back. Refusing to behold it, she exhibited a burnt scrap of red cloth with white embroidery. The elation of freeing the courtesans slipped through the cracks in Ares' heart.

It was Oliver's handkerchief.

Ares buried his face in his hand and regretted every time that he'd treated Oliver like a nuisance. He wished he'd laughed at his jokes and found joy in his foolhardiness, but it was too late for that.

Avari sobbed, "Ares — I was s'posed to protect him — like you told me to. I'm sorry — I'm sorry — !"

"It was in a pile of . . . others. Any one could've been him," said Luxea. She blinked mournfully at the handkerchief. "Ares, may I ask something of you?"

Ares peeked at her over his forearm. "Anything."

"Tell Oscerin to take Oli to the brightest place She can find. I want him to know what the light is like," sniffled Luxea.

"I will," said Ares grievingly.

Brielle upraised Avari onto Ruka. Luxea walked alone to any exit she could find amidst the crumbled walls. Ares watched as they left and made out Oliver's vestige bouncing by their sides. He squeezed his pendant and whispered, "Carry him."

No carriages waited for them at the front steps of Villa de Taress, but after the loss they'd suffered, walking distances was the least of their troubles. Ruka kept his pace slow to let Ares and Luxea limp beside him. Luxea hugged the warrants to find relief in the pages. Ares mindlessly cradled her upper back every few minutes.

Despite the catastrophe that had occurred so close by, not a sound came from within Haven de Asrodisia. The Mooncallers trudged around the thirty-stepped staircase.

Something beckoned Luxea's stars upward.

A person in a black cloak was hunched over on the steps. Luxea's feet locked, and then her legs broke into a run without her permission. If this was a mirage, she wanted to catch it before it rippled away.

The figure looked at her. There and then, tears came gushing out of Luxea's eyes. It wasn't a mirage — it was Oliver Kross.

The instant her first sob sneaked out, he hugged her. The impact yanked his hood down, but he bore through the sunlight. Without the

Mooncallers' awareness, he'd been pining for their lives as much as they had for his.

"I thought we'd lost you, Oli," said Luxea, clinging to him.

Oliver frowned but tried to smile. Next Brielle crashed into them with a bear hug, and Ruka licked Oliver's face lovingly. Avari tucked herself into the gap between Luxea and Brielle.

Ares stepped up last. He gazed at Oliver like he was a miracle and pulled his scrawny figure toward his own. Oliver was stunned. Ares shook him, welcoming him back from the death that never took him.

"Dunno 'bout you, but m'spent with parties," said Oliver gawkily.

"What happened? We searched all night and only found this. We were sure it was yours," said Luxea, revealing the handkerchief.

A blush took over Oliver's cheeks. He swiped the handkerchief. "It *is* mine. Bit of a long story," he said, rubbing his neck. "See, I went off to look for the loo but couldn't find it quick 'nough — n' it was an emergency, I swear! So I took a leak in a plant . . ."

"And?" sniffed Avari.

"*And* it was the Empress' prized rosebush," said Oliver bashfully. "One o' them hoplings saw me n' took a grab. Fellow swiped my hankie. I ran but got tackled anyhow. They kicked me out n' told me never to come back. I wandered here, and then the place went up in flames."

"You lived because you pissed in Annalais's roses?" asked Ares.

"Guess you could put it that way," coughed Oliver.

Ares' eyes narrowed, and his dimples plunged into his cheeks. He folded over and laughed so hard that no sound came out. When he gathered himself, he was still giggling boyishly inside of his mouth.

"Her bushes deserve it," said Ares cheerfully.

Claymore and his soldiers loitered beside the garden. They'd kept vigil throughout the night in wait for the Speaker to return, but they feared the worst. The lieutenant had prayed whenever he heard footsteps in the hall, but each time, he'd been let down. Another set clacked along, and he almost thought not to turn.

Ares and the others rounded the corner. Claymore sprinted to him as fast as his cuirass would allow. The lieutenant clasped hands with Ares, and then he, and every soldier, saluted.

"Thank Oscerin for sparing you — all of you," said Claymore pensively. "Forgive me. I told our men not to decamp. I thought you would have elected safety over risk."

"It was the right choice. That place is a graveyard, and I wouldn't have liked to find any of you among the dead," said Ares grimly.

Claymore glanced past Ares. "Pardon my questions if the wounds are too fresh, but what was the meaning of this terrorism? Who is responsible, what do the Empress and the Lady think, and are we safe here?"

Ares almost leaked the truth, but the dotted line on the indenture he'd signed forced him to stonewall the lieutenant. "Garamat un gatra acted as a pawn to Widow for reasons unknown, but he's been eliminated. The Lady and I convened with the Empress, but Her Splendor is just as nescient. Presently, there's no danger for the Empire of Goldenrise, but that doesn't negate the possibility," he lied.

"I understand, Your Highness. It's a pity that there was no fallback to ending the Sun Chief's life. I hear that he was a figure of import to you," said Claymore consolingly.

"Nothing good lives forever," said Ares, but he was more apprehensive than grief-stricken. His guise hardened. "Aside from the Sun Chief's besiege, there's a more immediate affair that requires our focus. First and foremost, our plans for the homebound journey have been altered."

"What changes, what can I do, Your Highness?" asked Claymore.

"There's an excess of fifty slaves inside Heart of Haven, and some of them are children," said Ares. Claymore's hands scalded as he recalled the warmth of Hanalea's belly.

Ares pointed at Luxea. "Miss Siren has warrants of arrest certified by the Empress for every headmaster employed. Tidy yourselves with haste and ready the dracas with carts and rations. From there, you will join me for the liberation of Heart of Haven. Then you and your men will depart for Tzapodia with anyone who asks for a new life in my kingdom. Upon your arrival, you will arrange for them work, homes, and anything else they need. Is that clear?"

A shieldmaiden blurted out, "What about you, Your Highness?"

"I still have work to do in Anunaru. The Lady Peyamo will transport us to L'arneth via airship as soon as fortifications for Tzapodia and Tarot are finalized. Worry not about our safety. *Thali ou Tirima* is unbreakable. Pray tell Wing Regent Isaak to proceed in his duties, and that I will retake my position within a moon."

Avari's little eyebrows almost flew right off of her face. She scooted in front of Ares. "We're goin' to Tarot? Really?"

"Verily. We will make for the Shifting City posthaste," said Ares. Avari hadn't visited her homeland for thirteen years, and the thought sent her mood sky-high. Ares went on, "If all is in order, let us move. Go quickly, gather what you came with. We will reconvene when you're ready, and then we march for Heart of Haven."

Disinclined to join his men in the hot springs, Ares retreated to the bath in his bedchamber. Ash was caked into his hair, and his suit was bonded to the minor lacerations Garamat had given him. As the steaming saltwater soothed his muscles, he viewed his claw through the fogginess. Traces of Garamat's blood twisted away from his talons like smoke.

Ares had only been a member of The Six for a decade, but he'd come to know the Sun Chief well in that time. He'd once thought it a bother how patronizing Garamat was, but he'd grown to admire that part of him. It had been in his nature as a parent.

When they'd first met, Garamat had only ever had wrinkles when he smiled, but that had been often. Ares had thought that his voice was like warm milk when the Sun Chief had told him, *"My boy, when a father's hatred burdens the land, the son must lift it."*

Garamat had sounded just as warm when he'd told Ares to die.

Soaking strands of black hair snaked around Ares' eyes, nose, and lips. He languidly peeled them from his face and sloshed to the side of the tub that overlooked the northern districts of Solissium. Those lands belonged to Widow, and not a single person apart from three of The Six had a clue.

He bathed in enemy water, breathed enemy air, and swept his eyes across enemy terrain. The uptown brothels ate enemy coin, and lovers pranced down enemy promenades.

Ares began counting the homes, temples, and theaters below. Mollah had once told him to focus on numbers to bring stasis to rumination. Twenty-seven, twenty-eight, twenty-nine — suddenly, the city was in flames. The plateau was scorched, and orange and red branched down every street all the way to the sea. It was as if the world had never known anything but fire.

He harshly rubbed his eyes. When he opened them again, the fire was gone. He held his breath and submerged to forget.

Later, the Mooncallers traveled to Heart of Haven. Along the way, Luxea saw a pack of Goldenhands skulking in a circle. She hurried to them and asked, "May I have your assistance?"

A hoplite slumped into his cushion and yawned, "We're resting. Tragedy has befallen our empire, miss. Give us time to mourn."

Luxea made a sour face. "I don't recall seeing you at the villa where your comrades spent all evening recovering the dead. Did you fight by their side, or mine?" She showed the warrants. "I have official orders from the Empress. You serve her, right? Then get up."

The Goldenhands were shaken by Annalais's signature. Chewed fruits were kept inside of their mouths and smoke in their lungs. With one accord, they dropped everything and rose for duty.

More hoplites were recruited as the Mooncallers went, for there were too many slaves and headmasters to handle without them.

Madam Alanis spotted them as they passed by the commissary.

"Goddesses, be good, I'd feared you perished," she said, catching Ares' arm. She surveyed the Mooncallers and Goldenhands, and her nose crinkled. "What is this? Is there something the matter, or anything with which I can assist?"

Ares smacked her hand. "If you'd be so kind as to join us at Heart of Haven, we have news you should hear," he said as he left.

Madam Alanis was confounded. "Heart of Haven? But, Your Highness, I don't — !"

Ruka bared his bloodstained teeth, and Brielle strummed the string of her longbow. The headmistress babbled, "Who let the dog inside?"

"I did!" said Ares from far down the colonnade.

The Mooncallers blasted through the scarlet curtains of Heart of Haven without herald. As was the norm, men and women were chained to the walls, and patrons were taking their fills of intimacy.

When the Speaker and his soldiers entered with a wolf and Goldenhands in tow, they withdrew, and the headmasters went rigid.

"All clientele, you've had enough!" shouted Ares at the top of his lungs. Shaken men deserted their escorts, buckling their trousers and pulling down their tunics as they flew for the exit.

Madam Alanis zoomed to Ares with a florid face. "What do you think you're doing? This is a private establishment. You have no right to tell our customers what to do!"

Ares didn't respect Madam Alanis enough to spell it out for her. He motioned to Luxea. She meandered to the middle of the den where Pertia, the headmaster, coincidentally stood.

"By order of the Empress of Goldenrise, every headmistress and headmaster employed by Heart of Haven is to be ironed and imprisoned," said Luxea with the warrants raised.

Madam Alanis grabbed Luxea's hair. "Get out! Get out, you l'arian pig! I forbid this!"

Luxea shoved her. "Shut up," she growled.

Before Madam Alanis could attack again, Luxea sifted through the warrants and forced the one that said 'Lilivae Alanis' into the headmistress' hands. Madam Alanis went still. A hoplite clamped shackles around her bejeweled wrists, a new ornament to add to her collection. The warrant slipped onto the ground.

"No . . . NO! Stop! I don't understand!" wailed Madam Alanis as she was yanked to the door.

"Come off it, ol' bawd. You know what you did wrong," said Oliver. The headmistress kicked him but missed. "Don't worry, Madam, there's a throne fitted for your dusty moal in Sithe. Rot, you daft twat."

Pertia goggled at Luxea as she slid his warrant from the stack and read his full name out loud. "Pertia Voulet!"

As he was cuffed, Pertia's temper snapped at all seams. "You double-dealing witch! How dare you use me?"

"I hope your years inside a cell have mercy on you. One day, may you understand why I did what I did, master," seethed Luxea. She tossed the warrants up into the air as Pertia was manhandled through the door.

Ruka blinked at Brielle. *"Sister, can I help too?"*

Brielle patted his behind. "Yes, Brother. Go on."

Enthralled to contribute, the wolf bounded with his tail wagging to a group of slaves hooked to the wall. He bit down on the chains, and the stake ripped out, taking a part of the wall with it. He panted happily at the slaves, but they cowered in fear of him. He backed away with his ears flattened.

"Brie, these people are scared of me. Am I scary?"

Brielle jogged to Ruka, who had his tail tucked between his legs. She kissed his snout and laughed, "You can be scary sometimes."

The slaves shied away from Brielle when she knelt beside them. She recalled when the Mooncallers had come to Blackjaw Hollow. Although the Riders of the West had been able to protect themselves, they'd also been afraid. She now empathized with how Ares must've felt when he'd offered her freedom.

"My brother and I were trapped too. Our lives were spent inside a cage where we could never look upon the day," said Brielle somberly. "I've not yet been to Tzapodia, but I've been told it has lots of sunlight and places to run. You should go. We mean not to scare you — especially not Ruka. He has a big head and bad breath, but inside, he's a little boy who knows fear. He'll never hurt you."

A very skinny woman with curled, black hair shifted closer. She laid her quaking fingers on Ruka's snout, and he stayed stock-still. An invincible joy uplifted the corners of the woman's lips. She exposed her smile to the others.

"He is soft like cotton!" she said fondly.

Her fellow slaves approached, and Ruka was drowned in affection. He rolled onto his side to ask for belly scratches. Brielle rested her elbows on her knees and thought that Ruka had never looked so blissful. Under a fortnight ago, they'd been trapped inside of the Western Woods, and now they were freeing ones who'd had just as little liberty. Brielle was sure then that the Mooncallers was the right pack to follow.

Three curtained nooks were at the back of Heart of Haven. Luxea poked her head into the first two and found nothing, but in the third, Unblossomed was huddled into a corner with a boy and a girl her age.

She blinked at Luxea. "Luxea Siren?"

"Yes, it's me. Don't be afraid," said Luxea calmly.

She waved two fingers, and the collars and shackles came unlatched. The children's throats were irritated in a strip. They brushed their fingers down their naked necks, the first time they'd felt relief from restraint.

Unblossomed crashed into Luxea. "What — *hic* — is this? What's happening?"

"I said I would get you out of here, didn't I?" asked Luxea softly.

Unblossomed had never known that she could cry and feel joy at the same time. "I don't know what to say. Can Mama come?"

"Everyone can. Go to your mother and take these two with you. I'll find you again, okay?" directed Luxea.

"I will," said Unblossomed, head bobbing like a spring. She tugged the little boy's arm. "Come. We can trust Luxea Siren!"

The children took her hands and vacated in a rush.

Haven de Asrodisia was pandemonium. Employees scattered like bugs in a rainstorm, and the freed peoples of Heart of Haven cheered their thanks to the divines. Over half of them elected to travel to Tzapodia, and the rest arranged to return to their families.

The dracas pulled three carts loaded with supplies, blankets, and rations aplenty for the soldiers and those who were immigrating. The Mooncallers gathered there. Ares, Luxea, and Avari extended their farewells to their dracas. Luxea sneaked Velesari a strawberry, and Ares promised Pveather he would take her riding when he got home, but Avari struggled to leave Elthevir.

"I'll miss you, you stupid lizard," she said quietly. "Remember to stay away from dairy — you know where that goes — and don't let no one else ride you. Got it?" Elthevir licked her cheek. She cringed and rubbed it with her scarf.

Ares and Luxea ascended the staircase. They'd made it halfway up when a high-pitched voice yelled, "Luxea Siren!"

Luxea was almost bowled over by a tiny, peachy-haired child with a violent hug to give. Ares was able to guess who she was without an introduction.

"I want you to meet Mama!" beeped Unblossomed.

She almost tripped on her way to a frail woman with golden hair. Slumber gaped at Ares as she approached, and then her gaunt face dampened with tears at the sight of Luxea.

"You're the one who saved my little girl," she whispered.

"She's Luxea Siren, Mama, like I told you. She's so smart and can do magick too. It's real — she showed me!" squealed Unblossomed.

Slumber stood crookedly. Her quivering lips struggled to open. She clasped Luxea's hands and fell to her knees. "Bless you! I don't know what I've done to deserve this, I don't know what divine has heard our voices, but you've given my baby a life I could not. Bless you, Luxea Siren, and you, Your Highness!"

She pressed a kiss to Luxea's palms. Unblossomed helped her to stand up. She took Ares' hands next. She searched his face with eyes of ochre. "Perhaps it was Oscerin then. She was listening all along."

"All prepared for departure! Any who desire transport to Tzapodia, speak now!" said Claymore, breaking up the moment.

"That's us, Baby," said Slumber, touching Unblossomed's blueberry-sized nose.

They started down the staircase. Unblossomed let go of her hand and said, "Wait, Mama."

She waved for Luxea to bend lower and cupped her pointed ear. Ares observed as Luxea's starry eyes ignited into bright pinks and yellows. There was a cosmos within her.

"It's beautiful," whispered Luxea.

Unblossomed faced Ares. They blinked at each other, and then she jumped to hug his waist. She was incapable of reaching her arms all the way around him. Ares staggered and looked down, startled.

"Thank you, Your Highness! Take care of Luxea Siren!" shouted Unblossomed, although muffled by Ares' stomach. He chuckled once, and she bounded away. She turned at the bottom step and yelled, "Will I see you again in Tel Ashir?"

"Yes!" called back Luxea.

"Promise?"

"I promise!"

Unblossomed and Slumber moved onto the dirt road. Oliver and Brielle hoisted them onto the carts. Ares and Luxea stared at the freed children of Haven de Asrodisia as the mild afternoon wind blew their black and white hairs toward Eternity's Ocean.

Ares' eyes drifted to Luxea. "What did she tell you?"

"Their real names."

"What are they?"

"Slumber's name is Estalyn. Unblossomed's is . . . Runa Faust."

Ares felt firecrackers under his skin.

"Runa," he said dotingly.

THE RIDDLING ROADS
13.NIGHTSPEAK.25.OSC.3

FOUR DAYS had come and gone since Ares had departed from Goldenrise with Luxea, Avari, Oliver, Brielle, and Ruka. Their carriage rumbled through Solissium, swerved through the endless moors, and breached the northern border of the Wraiths. It was estimated to take five days to wind through the boglands and reach Tarot on the other side.

Spirits were higher since the liberation of Heart of Haven, but only to the extent their hearts allowed. One good thing didn't neutralize the shadow that had been cast. Goldenrise did a balancing act over grounds of grave and sanctuary, the Sun Chief had faced his demise, and Ares was overstuffed with secrets about Widow's hidden purpose and the Empress' unstable loyalty to The Six.

This day was just as rainy as the last. Oliver relished the overcast skies, but his companions hated it. Luxea and Avari tugged him away from the carriage window and slammed it shut every other minute to cut off the flow of the scent of muck.

Oliver unlatched the window once more, and Avari moved as far into the corner as humanly possible. Oliver soaked in the muted colors of the scenery, but then he jumped in surprise.

A copse of four trees popped up through the swamp with eery designs grown into their bark — human faces. Some were screaming, others had their timber lips sealed, and a few had squinty, hollow eyes.

"Oi, those trees've got faces," said Oliver, shuddering.

"They're Wraith Houses," said Ares, his first words all day. He pulled the curtain aside. "They're a vital part of the initiation to the army of the Wraiths. As the entirety of the Ghostwives are female, whether by genetics or otherwise, it's a tradition for their husbands to be buried alive in the mud beneath a tree. If his face appears in the trunk or branches, the wood has accepted his soul and will then bestow upon her periodic immortality. If not, she isn't worthy of becoming a Ghostwife."

Oliver was even more disturbed by the trees than before. "That's just creepy. Crazy broads," he said.

"Most Wraithian men consider it a great honor to partake in the Ghostwives' traditions. Dying for their spouse's extended life is seen as the sincerest form of respect," informed Ares.

Shivering, Oliver looked out the window, but then his expression screwed up. Sailing by was a copse of four trees with eery designs grown into their bark — human faces, and all of them were the same as the ones they'd already passed.

"Did we turn 'round?" he wondered.

"No. We're riding straight south," said Ares confidently.

"Either you're wrong, or I'm seein' things, 'cause we're passin' those same wraithies right now."

"Many trees in the Wraiths share similarities."

"No, no, they're definitely the same ones."

"No, they're *not.*"

"Mate, I ain't kiddin' you!"

Brielle knocked on the window. "Dragon, Kross is right. Ruka says he's seen those faces three times, and we've made no turns. These trails are tangled."

Ares yanked the curtain aside, and his sleepless eyes became alert. All four trees were identical to the other ones. Just then, the crackly voice of the horse master, Alucard, sounded from ahead.

The horses dug their hooves into the mud, and the carriage braked. Ares jumped out, and his feet slid. He stared down the road and thought his eyes were tricking him. Ahead of the horses were hoof trails, unbroken wheel tracks, and Ruka's paw prints.

Pitying his leather boots, Ares slopped to the front of the carriage and pulled himself into the driver's seat. Alucard peeked up from a flimsy map. "Forgive me, Yer Highness. I ain't meanin' to throw us off schedule, but I've got to review the maps. Might've taken a wrong turn."

Alucard scratched under his cap and messed up his two or three scraggly hairs. He tapped on the map and said, "We came in through 'ere and should've reached Apparition by now. There's no trails nowhere that go in circles. See, we're on the Riddling Roads 'round 'ere, and —"

"The Riddling Roads?" asked Ares worriedly. "Tell me there isn't some reason of significance behind that name."

"Eh, well, they may 'ave a reputation for gettin' folks lost," said Alucard sheepishly. Ares covered his eyes.

Alucard went on, "These swamps rise in the evenin', y'see. Some paths sink, the rest resurface. Oft travelers who pitch camp 'round these parts wake up to find one route gone and another in its place. If all'd gone right, the Riddling Roads would've gotten us to Apparition fastest, but . . ."

Ares took the map and listed four settlements that were sprinkled down the Riddling Roads: Palvitae, Snake's Head, Witchsleep, and Apparition. If Alucard was correct, they'd gone by the first three and were somewhere in the middle of Witchsleep and Apparition.

"Brielle! Ruka!" said Ares, quieted by the air's density.

The wolf trod forth, and his dinner-plate paws made new prints over old. Ruka wiggled his nose. Brielle asked, "What is it?"

Ares pointed down the Riddling Roads. "I want you two to scout ahead and report back to me what you find. Right now, all that should wait for us is Apparition. If you discover anything odd, I must hear about it."

"Consider it done, Dragon," said Brielle resolutely.

Ruka kicked sludge against the carriage. Brielle flattened her body to his as he trampled down the Riddling Roads. In moments, the wolf's massive silhouette dissolved into a wall of fog.

For half an hour, the two roved about with their wits high, but this area wasn't unfamiliar. They were following their own tracks, after all.

"Brother, stop," said Brielle out of the blue.

"What is it, Brie?" asked Ruka.

"I see a sign."

Ahead was a wooden road sign swinging from one hook; the other had been snapped off the post. Brielle tried to read the words engraved on it, but it was especially difficult for her due to the weathered paint.

"It says Wi . . . t. Wit . . . ch. Witchsl . . . ee. . . . Witchslee?" she whistled up a tempo. "P — ah, I see. It says *'Witchsleep.'"*

There was much smaller text beneath the giant *'WITCHSLEEP'* that Brielle strained to read. After a few minutes of exercising her brain, she, at last, made out *'The best lodging in the Wraiths!'*

"Is it a town?" panted Ruka.

"Yes, but unless my memory betrays me, I swear Dragon said there was one town ahead — Apparition, not Witchsleep," said Brielle suspiciously.

As they waited, Luxea and Oliver started feeling adventurous. They climbed onto the carriage's hood and dangled their legs, breaking twigs off of low-hanging branches and throwing them into the mire.

A hair-raising howl then vibrated the air. Luxea and Oliver craned their necks to look down the Riddling Roads behind them. They were sure that Brielle and Ruka had been scouting *ahead.*

Bewildered, Ares asked, "You came from behind?"

"These roads are a loop, Dragon. Their limit doesn't exist," said Brielle distrustfully. "I cannot tell you the way out of this cycle, but the town of Witchsleep lies ahead."

"Witchsleep is behind us," said Ares, getting a headache.

"What's forward is backward," asserted Brielle. "The day burns dim. We should enter Witchsleep and rest our heads for the eve. They have the best lodging in the Wraiths. I know that because a sign said so. I read it."

"Great job, Brie!" said Luxea, plopping onto the muddy path. "Em, might I also mention that the bog is rising? The water was at the roots one hour ago, and now it's lapping at the trunk."

Ares inspected the swamp. After what Alucard had said about the muck swallowing the paths, he didn't encourage taking any risks.

"We'll stay in Witchsleep for tonight," he agreed.

Alucard claimed that he'd also seen that sign for Witchsleep reaches back, but he complied with Ares' demand to proceed up the Riddling Roads.

The clopping of hooves upon the herringbone street petered out. Avari prated on about how opposed she was to spending the evening in a bog-town, but when she wormed her scarfed head out of the window, she gasped, "Wow, this town is adorable."

Witchsleep was composed of draping trees, smoke-stained gaslights, and lopsided buildings. A park was in the middle of the town with a bright red gazebo in it, presumably for live performances.

This place was too small to be called a city, but it was congested despite the size. It was abuzz with merchants and couples dressed in dark attire. The Wraiths had been colonized centuries ago by immigrants from the Isle of Varnn. Those who ambled in Witchsleep were pale of skin and smoky of hair, similarly to Oliver, but it was transparent that he bore purer aestofian blood.

The Mooncallers nearly launched themselves out onto the street when the carriage drew up. Ares stepped out last. Although he was dressed a bit less flamboyantly than usual, his curled horns and general regality robbed all of the attention.

"How twee is this place?" gasped Oliver.

"Huh. I wasn't expecting something so quaint," said Ares as a woman in a corseted dress tried to touch him. He took one step away from her.

Brielle and Ruka retreated to a hunched over tree that stood in a meadow nearby. The others carted their belongings and followed signs to what was the supposed *'best lodging in the Wraiths.'* As they scooted along, Luxea noticed a marketplace on the edge of a canal.

Pointed marquees sprouted over the hedges that reminded her of the Sapphire Bazaar in Tel Ashir.

They reached a building that looked like it was about to slide off of the foundation. A crooked sign above the door read *'WOODGATE INN.'* Most structures in Witchsleep were charming, but this one was very, very unattractive.

"If this is the best lodging the Wraiths have to offer, I don't want to find out what other inns are like," said Ares, dead inside.

"Seems hospitable if you tip your head to the right," said Avari.

A dented summoning bell sat atop the front counter. Ares bopped it with a talon, and it made a lamentable *gak* sound. An innkeeper with a dusty beard, a white toupee, and a bear-claw nose zoomed to them.

"Hello, my name is Bizzner. It's been a while since we've had company here at Woodgate. What a delight!" he bellowed.

Ares grimaced. "A pleasure. My name is Ares Lavrenthea, and these are my associates. We fare from Solissium and require rooms."

The innkeeper Bizzner blinked at the speed of a hummingbird's wings. "Lavrenthea? Surely you wouldn't mean — ?"

"Yes," said Ares curtly.

"Oh, Your Highness!" wheezed Bizzner. When he bowed, his toupee flipped up at the back. Luxea and Avari snickered. Ares mouthed *'shh'* to them.

The innkeeper jotted down notes in his ledger and munched on his quill every few letters; the feather was nearly barb-bare. How disgusting, thought Ares. A question then popped into his head.

"About the Riddling Roads to the southwest," he began. Bizzner ogled him with his tiny, shark-like eyes. "Is it common for them to send travelers riding in circles?"

"It's very common, Your Highness. In fact, the Woodgate Inn owes most of its customers to those roads. They sink into the mire at night which makes it difficult to track where you're headed. That's why we have the Day Trail and the Night Trail in Witchsleep. Only use the one that matches the time."

"And what about going in *circles?*" emphasized Ares.

"Oh, sure. The Riddling Roads can make you think you're going 'round in circles, indeed," said Bizzner with a piece of feather stuck in his teeth.

The innkeeper was overlooking the literal sense of the question. Once Bizzner, at last, completed their check-in, Ares slipped out of Woodgate Inn to seek Alucard. The Mooncallers had lodging for the evening, but that was of little meaning if they were unable to circumvent the Riddling Roads' orbit.

Ares knocked on the carriage door. Alucard reacted promptly. "Yer Highness. Is aught amiss? Need transport?" he asked.

"Thank you, but no," said Ares as he sat down. "I wondered if you'd uncovered any solutions regarding the Riddling Roads. I don't want to be caught in that loop a second time."

"Nor do I," said Alucard. He produced a heap of vellums and unrolled them. "I swiped a few maps from 'round town n' gave 'em a once-over, but they ain't much different from my own. Some folks said we might've taken the wrong trail, but that don't help much I reckon."

"You speak of the Day Trail and the Night Trail?" clarified Ares.

"I see you heard 'bout 'em too. S'pose it's possible. 'Twas rather late when we rode in," said Alucard, scratching his chin.

"Paths don't go in circles, so I fail to see another explanation."

"I agree, Yer Highness." Alucard squinted at the twilight sky. "The eve'll erelong thrive. I'll take a look-see down the Night Trail to get a lay of the land afore mornin' comes."

"I'll go with you," said Ares at once. "My curiosity is an itch on my back. Bring a lantern. I imagine we'll need it."

Inside of her inn room, Luxea stripped, rinsed in the baths, and wound her damp hair into a bun. She was keen to stop by the marketplace before the Tehrastar fell too low, so she left in a hurry.

Avari didn't want her to go alone. She gave her an excuse that she wanted to buy something for Elthevir to chew on, but Luxea knew that she was coming along to sate her overprotective tendencies.

They went headlong into the swarm of Witchsleep's townspeople. They hopped over bushes and nearly cleared a bridge, but Luxea tarried at the keystone, affixed onto something familiar. Lune lilies were pirouetting along the surface to the river's current. She hadn't seen her favorite flower since leaving Tzapodia, and being so close to them while so far away from home was bittersweet.

"Hurry up, beanbag," said Avari, tugging Luxea's arm.

In the marketplace, Avari ravaged three plates of sample cheeses that a seller had laid out, and Luxea browsed the knickknacks and raiments for sale. The apparel in Tzapodia was garish, crowded by detailing, and purfled with nonessential bells and charms, but the items for sale in the Wraiths were reserved. Everything was grey and had little variation in design. There were petticoats, shoulder capes, laced underthings, and medallions with a single jewel.

After a while, the peddlers began to store their wares and draw their drapes. Luxea and Avari had been miserly, so they stuffed their pockets with the few purchases they'd made and set off for the bridge.

At the roadway, Luxea spotted a tent beneath a tree that she didn't recall seeing earlier. Completing a transaction was a merchant in a threadbare suit, maybe the only one he'd ever owned, with colorless skin. He looked like cold weather — something Luxea had only ever seen in herself.

"Is that a l'arian elf?" she asked, tapping Avari blindly.

Avari snorted. "No, especially not out in the Wrai — but that *is* a l'arian elf. Let's talk to him!"

"I wouldn't mind saying hello," said Luxea timidly.

Avari dragged her by the wrist to the tent. The l'arian merchant's light pink eyes enlarged, and he fretfully organized his wares for presentation.

"Hilien leloh, ei'mithanen," he said in a windy voice.

"Au un, ei'masthanen," said Luxea as Avari casually strolled off.

The merchant removed his newsboy cap, and soft, white curls sprang out from beneath it. "My name is Cherish. What's yours?" he asked politely.

"My name is Luxea," she said kindly.

"I'm Avari," added Avari.

"Luxea and Avari. How lovely. It's wonderful to meet you," said Cherish. "Well, are you looking for something specific, *Luxea'mithan au Avari'alu?"*

Avari was enthralled that he'd addressed her in seroden elvish.

"Not entirely. Do you mind if we browse?" asked Luxea.

"Peruse to your heart's content. I intended to close shop, but the arrival of such lovely flowers has changed my mind," said Cherish with a wink. "Fetch me if you're burdened. I'll be glad to assist."

He withdrew to the trunk of the willow and lit up a thin cigarette. He frequently passed rosy eyes to Luxea, and she passed them back. It was the first time she'd crossed another l'arian elf apart from the devastation in Lor'thanin, so it was challenging to turn her sights away from him.

The options Cherish's booth had were more various than those at the others they'd seen. There were charms of Selnilarian, Tarotian, and even Tzapodian make, all of which were winsome, but a tray of unusual rings reeled in Luxea like a fish on a line.

The circular heads had tiny clocks upon them like a timekeeper for a finger. Luxea selected a blue ring with white accents and slipped it onto her right forefinger; it was conveniently in her size. However, the hand was ticking counterclockwise.

"Luxie, I'm getting this for Elthevir," said Avari with a raggedy mouse plushie in her hand. "But my belly's growling, and we should head back."

Cherish crushed his cigarette with a wiggle of his foot. "Have you found anything you fancy?" he asked charmingly.

"We have," said Luxea, swiping the mouse toy. "How much will it be for this and the ring?"

"Oh, that timekeeper is unlucky," said Cherish bashfully. "I hadn't realized that the hands move backward until I'd packed for sale."

"I like it because it's backward," said Luxea buoyantly.

"I'll not stop you then," said Cherish brightly. He tallied the prices off-hand. "Typically, this would be forty-four sterling, but meeting one of my ilk has made my evening. So, for you, twenty sterling."

"That's thoughtful, Cherish, but I couldn't," said Luxea guiltily.

"You'd best pay me before I charge you double," purred Cherish.

"Fine. Thank you," said Luxea with a tingling in her cheeks.

She reached for her coin purse. Turning her head exposed her *Magelas.* Cherish's eyes tacked to the blue ink in an instant. "You're a sorceress? I knew there was something off about you!"

Luxea recalled when Ares had said that some people were opposed to magick-users. She worried that Cherish might be one of them. Sharing a like mind, Avari spat, "Yea, and she's a ploughin' good one. Taught herself from the bottom up. If you don't like it, we'll take our business elsewhere."

"I meant no disrespect, it merely shocked me," said Cherish. He peeled back the collar of his shirt where inked upon his chest was a grey *Magelas.* "I can also access the arcana."

"Can you really?" exhaled Luxea.

"That's just nutty," said Avari, rattling Luxea dangerously hard. "You've got to do tricks together, Luxie. I have to see it!"

"I thought you were hungry?" reminded Luxea.

"I'll eat twice. Do something!" insisted Avari.

Entertained, Cherish waved his slender fingers over the tabletop. A lily of white arcana materialized beneath his palm. Luxea spoke an incantation, and a blue lily appeared beside his. The flowers bent toward each other.

Cherish tenderly brushed the petals of her illusion. "Do you see how they look at each other? If there are no akin essences with which to resonate, the arcana becomes lonely. But when faced with another's, their energies gravitate like erstwhile friends."

After a while, Cherish decided to give them their items free of charge. The cloudy sky was black when Luxea and Avari scaled the bridge back to Woodgate Inn.

Cherish removed his cap, sparked a cigarette, and massaged his neat goatee. He laughed at a thought, and with a swish of his hand, the tent, table, and his products magickally shrank into one briefcase.

🦋

Ares and Alucard trudged with a lantern, but it hardly let them see past their noses. Half an hour brought them to a fork with two signs pointed inversely. The left road they'd traveled down that afternoon said '*DAY TRAIL.*' The right read '*NIGHT TRAIL.*'

Ares veered right, and Alucard went after. In five minutes, they could barely make out a barrier of fog as solid as the rampart of a city.

"That's the Riddling Roads. If we're facin' west, Apparition is a straight shot southeast," said Alucard, squinting at the map.

"I don't mean to find Apparition, I mean to find what's steering us in circles," said Ares, scoping out the area. "Let us go left as you said, but if in an hour we end up back here . . ."

They moved jointly to the wall of fog and couldn't so much as hear their footfalls through its density. Ares took the first step, and all of a sudden, nothing was underfoot. His leg plunged into the swampy water up to the middle of his thigh; to most people, this was hip-level.

"I thought this was the Night Trail!" yelled Ares.

Alucard's wiry mustache twitched. "It is, Yer Highness," he said, tugging Ares out of the mud. "This is the way folks take durin' the evenin', but it's a tad deep for carriages. The horses would sink."

"No, would they?" snapped Ares. He batted his trousers, but the mud was in his boot and fused to his leg hair. "There's nothing here, but there has to be. Are you sure we turned right?"

"Aye. I remember it 'cause '*right*' rhymes with '*night,*'" said Alucard indisputably. "Mayhap we should give the Day Trail a chance? The signs could've been swapped, or —"

"Fine. We'll attempt the Day Trail," said Ares testily.

With one slimy boot, Ares and Alucard backtracked down the Night Trail and stalled at the crossroad sign. As the horse master had claimed, *'right'* was for *'night.'* Nettled, Ares kicked the post and stormed left.

The Day Trail was lengthier than the Night Trail. After ten minutes, they spotted the same boundary of fog. Ares reviewed the map under the lamplight. The Day Trail wasn't oriented west like the Night Trail, it was south, yet the haze bent around them both as if Witchsleep was inside of a dome.

Alucard tried to advance, but Ares held him back. "A moment. I don't entertain the possibility of ruining my other boot."

Sweeping the trees above, he picked out a branch and jumped to grab it. His weight snapped it from the trunk.

By the fog, Ares poked the offshoot into the mist and planted it upright. As he'd dreaded, it dunked low into the mud. He extracted it and extended his muddied leg beside it. The water level on the branch was up to his belly, indicating that the end of the Day Trail was deeper than the Night Trail.

Ares dropped the stick. There was no way out of Witchsleep.

CRUELTY AND LOVE

IT WAS late, but Luxea didn't feel drowsy. As she ambled around the Woodgate Inn, she spotted a glimmer of light at the end of the hall. She found Ares lounging with a journal on his lap and one leg hanging over a sill with no railing; it was too narrow to be a balcony. A candle and a bottle of wine sat beside him.

"Evening," he said insouciantly.

"Good evening. How are you doing?" asked Luxea.

"Well, I never want to touch mud again," groaned Ares.

It was better not to ask about it. "Er . . . may I sit?"

"If you'd like," said Ares without looking at her.

Luxea hung her leg over the sill too and set the Usinnon next to her. Ares sluggishly rolled up his sleeves and kept working. She peeked over and noticed that the veins in his forearms were quite prominent. She secretly wanted to poke them.

Luxea eyed his journal. "You're mapping the stars?"

"I am. They look different in this part of the world," replied Ares.

She leaned in. He rotated the journal to show her. The map of Amniven depicted the other planets around it and the three stars, Tehra, Ire, and the dwarf, Ka'ahn's Fire. Amidst them were hundreds of dots connected by thin lines, the constellations.

"This one looks like a fish. Is it Ocaranth?" asked Luxea.

"That's correct," said Ares. He motioned to a cluster of stars to the northwest. "He's right there. Those three stars are His tail, and the biggest star is the top of His head."

"I see. He's flying to the right."

Ares started to feel better. He glanced at his journal and directed Luxea to the northeast. "This one is Ostriseon: the Mind-Father. The two largest are His eyes, and the others make up His wings." Luxea followed his point to the next. "Here's Ymarana: the Smiling Blackwood. It's the only constellation with parallel lines." He gestured directly above them. "That smaller one is Novis: the One-Eyed Cat."

"What about those orange ones? What are they called?" asked Luxea, squinting to a congregation of lights just above the tree line.

"Those are called street lamps," said Ares, grinning.

Luxea looked at the Irestar next. Ares faced it too. As they drank in the silver light, their eyes became talkative. She then chose to ask a question that had been digging a hole in her head.

"What does Oscerin sound like?"

Ares had been nagged about that topic all of his life, but there had never been an explicit answer. Sometimes, Oscerin's voice was a lullaby, and others, it was thunder. He gave Luxea the closest comparison that he could manage.

"Hearing Her voice is like feeling my own heartbeat."

Luxea pressed her middle and index fingers to her wrist; her pulse was quicker than usual. She wondered next how Ares had reacted when Oscerin had initially communicated with him. He acted sedated usually, but that must've given him a scare.

"How did it feel when you first heard Her?" she inquired.

"I've never smiled more," said Ares, fiddling with his sleeves.

Luxea relished the smallest details of her companions' pasts. Without a history of her own to explore, it made her feel included. She was fully conscious that her curiosity could be bombarding, but that didn't stop her from asking her next question. "Will you tell me about hearing Her in the beginning, what She said to you, and how it all happened?"

The instance flashed through Ares' head in reverse. Many years had passed since he'd been vocal about the start of his tie with Oscerin or his childhood. Something inside of him screamed to swallow it and say nothing, but Luxea's starry eyes screamed the loudest. Although he felt cornered, his guard dropped.

Preparing himself, Ares gulped his wine and lit a cigarette.

"It was a year after the war with Naraniv had ended. My father won it unfairly — no — inhumanely. He leveled three of Naraniv's most populated settlements to the ground, and to this day, his fire burns in the ruins. The bulk of rishjaan territories were then esteemed parts of Tzapodia. As you've gathered empirically, the rishja haven't forgiven my family even if I've tried time and time again to return their lands."

"I digress. The people of Tzapodia hated the King for his actions even if Naraniv had been our foe. Our kingdom was crumbling from the inside out, and that only made conditions worse for those of us within the castle. That's when Oscerin came to me, when I needed Her the most."

✹

11.LIGHTSMEET.1.OSCERIN.3

King Naiv Lavrenthea hauled his son down a corridor with light dotting the floor through the barred gaps in the wall. He thrust open an oaken door and suspended the Prince by one of his small horns.

"When you've recompensed me, I'll have you released. If you fail to, don't expect me to stop you from dying here."

The Prince kept his teary eyes low. Naiv trapped Ares' head against the door with his crimson talons, and the chipped wood drew blood from his skin. "Look at your king!" screamed Naiv. Ares fixed upon him. Naiv shook his head. "You make me do this, my son. One day, may you honor me enough to understand that."

The king latched the door. Ares swabbed his eyes and winced, disturbing the splinters in his eyebrow. He pulled his hair over the wound and lay on the sopping ground.

To the tempo of dripping water, he sank into a paralyzing slumber. The nothingness was comforting. Time passed. He gasped in surprise when a warmth curled up beside him. He believed that he'd woken up, but he was still sleeping.

"My parallel," whispered a woman's voice.

"Who's talking?" asked Ares, searching the blackness.

"My light graces your world with each night that comes to pass. I am Oscerin," said the voice, volume pulsing with every word.

"Oscerin?" echoed Ares. "I know you from the books Mea reads. You're a divine — one of the greater."

"You are very bright," said Oscerin proudly. "Prince Ares, tell me, what future do you desire?"

Ares had never considered. For a moment, he imagined going outside to play on a sunny day, but his mind was made red. Instead, he was blinded by dragon-fire, ashy skies, and crimson scales.

"You have not seen what I have seen. Tell me," urged Oscerin.

"I want a world where no one cries," said Ares quietly. He pushed past his doubt and yelled, "I want no one else to burn! I don't want Mea to be scared anymore!"

"I was right to choose you," said Oscerin. Her timbre changed. "I sense that one day my children will suffer, and I will weep for their enfeebled faith. When that time comes, you will not prevail without me. But I cannot help you if we do not share a vision."

"You will grow into a guardian of the land, but a true king is a man who hearkens the cries of those who need it, not of the rapacious. Never let go of charity, compassion, and selflessness, Ares. Sustain this, and I shall forever protect you as you protect those around you."

Ares scarcely understood any of the big words Oscerin used with him, but by some means, he knew what She was telling him. "You want me to care about people?" he asked.

Oscerin chortled. "Yes. That is all I want."

"That's easy. I'll do it if I get to be with You!"

An image of the Irestar glowed white before him. Oscerin thundered, "Then I shall make it so. Amniven must heed that you are the one I have chosen. They will shun such claims from a child, but you will prove to them their wildest imaginings."

"Gather your people and bid them to turn their eyes to the sky at moonrise on the third night, and I will make the Irestar disappear. Together, we will observe as our promise becomes doctrine."

The moonlight flickered to black and reappeared upon Ares' chest. "This is my gift to you. It is your Felastil — your key to the Irestar. While you have this, you will always be heard. Three nights . . ."

Ares was chilled awake. In his little hand lay a pendant, a relic forged in the Irestar's fire, inlaid with a gem that glistened like the stars. He started to laugh, and he couldn't stop. He stretched the chain around his neck, and it swung over his tummy. He would grow into it.

It wasn't the turnkey who rescued the Prince from the dungeons; it was Isaak. The Wing Regent was usually tolerant of King Naiv's decree by onus of his role, but there were instances where he broke the rules for Ares and his mother's sake.

Isaak rapped on the farthest northern door of the Amber Wing. The Queen of Tzapodia, Manalaei Lorcé-Lavrenthea, stepped out. Her leafy green eyes were magnetic to her child.

"Nach lathene! There you are, my son!" she wailed.

Manalaei cupped Ares' plump cheeks and brushed his hair out of his face, exposing his scrapes. Her freckly skin burned red, too familiar with who drew the blood. She hoisted him onto her hip and smooched his nose.

"Stay with me. You're all right now. What do we say to Isaak?"

Ares twinkled at Isaak. "Thank you very much."

Isaak rustled Ares' hair. "You're welcome, Ares."

The Queen turned shoulder-to-shoulder with Isaak. "The next time he lays his hands on my son, I'll kill him," she said in a whisper.

Manalaei knelt at the bedside and dabbed Ares' forehead with a wet rag. She was surprised when he began to giggle uncontrollably.

"I do love that smile. Why so joyous, Ares?" she asked.

"Mea, something impossible happened to me!"

"Tell me about it, Baby."

Ares brought his mouth to her decorated ear. "Oscerin came to me. I heard Her speak. She told me She'd protect me so I can protect everyone else — even you! But I need your help."

"Anything. What is it?" asked Manalaei, although irresolute.

"In three nights, I need to go outside," said Ares. The Queen frowned. "Oscerin wants it. She's going to make the Irestar disappear to show people that She chose me."

Manalaei set the rag aside and tucked Ares' hair behind his ear. "Nach lathene, faith is sweet, I know. Oscerin watches over you, as She does all of Her children, but I cannot do that."

"But I can't say 'no.' It'll hurt Oscerin's feelings, and I won't get to talk to Her anymore! I made Her a promise!" cried Ares.

As he sniffled, he unveiled a mysterious pendant. The starry gemstone mirrored in the Queen's eyes, and bumps whisked up her arms. It bore an aura pure enough to verge her to tears.

"Where did you get this, Ares?" she breathed.

"Oscerin said its name is 'Felastil, the key to the Irestar.' She said no one would believe me. That's why you have to help," Ares told her.

Manalaei's sinuses twinged. Only one assessment penetrated the knot of questions within her skull: never had she seen Ares smile like this. That couldn't have been from a dream or a scratch on the head.

That night, Queen Manalaei sidled through Castle Lavrenthea to consult with Mollah in the infirmary. She surreptitiously told the sage everything from the beginning. Mollah was skeptical, at first, but the truth in Manalaei's beseeching stare was impossible to refuse.

After some thought, Mollah avowed that she and her husband Willem would spread the word of Oscerin's oath to the Prince.

The third night closed in. Queen Manalaei wrapped Ares' head in a veil to allow for an unnoticed getaway. They scurried through the *castle and avoided the eyes of King Naiv and his sentinels. A few were stationed at their posts, but Manalaei had memorized where they would be and when.*

The Queen and the Prince entered the infirmary. Mollah signaled to the other sages to clear the wing and keep lookout perchance the royals had been tailed.

The shadows upon Manalaei's brown skin vanished when she unraveled her veil. She gingerly passed Ares over to Mollah and rested her jewel-coated hand over her child's heart.

"Go, my son. Show them."

"Will you watch too, Mea?" asked Ares hopefully.

"It's a promise. Iu lemi thois," said Manalaei, softly kissing Ares' forehead. She told Mollah, "Take care of him."

"Always, Your Mercy," said Mollah.

Ares, Mollah, and Willem scaled the rampart and cleared the Porranim Courtyard to the Steps of Sevinus. They darted past two sentinels on guard as the Irestar reached its high. Willem scooped Ares into his arms and sprinted to get him to the Court of Light in time.

There were fascinated coos upon their arrival. Willem hefted Ares up onto his shoulders. Mollah revealed his face from beneath his indigo veil.

The public had never been permitted to see Ares Lavrenthea before. Now many failed to give credence to his claims about Oscerin. All they could deduce was that a child's imagination had gone rampant, that they'd left their beds over a faith that was simply make-believe.

A sea sloshed inside of Ares' stomach under so many pairs of eyes. He questioned himself. Regret was a hand held over his mouth, and he could no longer breathe.

Suddenly, his limbs went numb, and his eyes reeled back. Mollah saw his head tipping to the side. She rushed behind Willem to catch him.

I am here, Ares. Do not be afeared. Look up.

Ares grabbed onto Willem's hat. He was hyperventilating, and his vision was doubled, but he was sure of himself after hearing the voice of the Moon Mother once again.

"Look up! She said to look up!" exclaimed Ares.

Whispers rippled as rain on a pond, some cynical, and others believing. Ares' wide eyes gleamed as he stared skyward.

The Irestar flickered out, and the world was black.

On her balcony in Castle Lavrenthea, Queen Manalaei's legs gave out. She raised her hands and cried, "Thank You, Oscerin, thank You! Don't ever leave him, I beg — !"

The King barged into her bedchamber, irises violet, pupils in slits.

Tel Ashians fell to their knees before the Prince. Men, women, elders, and children alike bombarded him with prayers that had gone unsaid for their whole lives. Windows lit up, and doors opened around the city. Soon nobody else could fit inside of the Court of Light.

Faith had a face, and that face belonged to a sickly little boy. Talk of the child Speaker was a wildfire, one that burned to every corner of Amniven.

❀

Ares drew the Felastil from his collar. "It's because of cruelty that Oscerin willed me to become who I am," he said redolently.

The jewel that shimmered between the cracks in his fingers was similar to Luxea's eyes. She'd never known that he'd walked such an abysmal road. Now she admired him more than she ever had.

"I'm sorry," she said quietly. "I can't believe your father did —"

265

"I shouldn't be pitied," said Ares, but no edge was in his tone.

Luxea gazed at the Felastil. She envisioned Manalaei Lorcé-Lavrenthea staring at it too. In her head, the Queen looked just like Ares.

"Your mother sounds like a lovely woman. You're lucky to have such fond memories of her," said Luxea breathily.

Ares looked like he'd been pricked by a pin. "She deserved the best but was given the worst. I yearn for her to see all that I've done to repair what he destroyed — but I also want *him* to see. It would kill him. His people follow me just like Oscerin augured, and he failed to believe."

Luxea pointed at the Irestar. "And the Moon still watches over you. It's no wonder that you worship Her."

"I owe all things beautiful in my life to Oscerin. I've never worshiped Her, only loved Her," said Ares earnestly.

"Love is worth more than worship," remarked Luxea.

Ares glanced at her. "Love is worth more than anything."

Ocaranth's Tears
15.Nightspeak.25.Osc.3

The Mooncallers had stayed in Witchsleep for two nights. It was morning. They conversed around a table in the lobby of the Woodgate Inn. Ares briefed the others about his experience with the the Day Trail and the Night Trail.

Luxea, Avari, and Oliver munched on breakfasts from two plates; one was a cheesy biscuit, the other was a mushroom and potato medley. Luxea snatched a potato chunk and crammed it into her mouth. Oliver tried to swipe a slice, but Avari made him forfeit it.

"That one's mine," she said, devouring it.

"Meh meh meeeh," mocked Oliver.

"For Eletheon's sake — may I have your attention?" asked Ares, tapping on the map. "We must find our way out of Witchsleep if we want to proceed to Tarot."

"Let's go back to Tel Ashir. S'nice place. I miss it," yawned Oliver.

"It's wonderful that you think so, but can we focus?" begged Ares.

As they planned out their route, lightsome footsteps creaked down the staircase at their backs. The feet belonged to a lean man in a threadbare suit with stark white hair.

"Luxea'mithan! Hathas mahnan, hello again!" sang Cherish. He waved at Avari next. *"Avari'alu ta, an's delenen.* It's a pleasure."

Luxea and Avari turned in their chairs. Oliver snatched a potato unnoticed. Avari yipped, *"Ein ta!* You're at Woodgate too?"

"Just down the hall. But I'm leaving Witchsleep today. I'm happy to have found you before then," said Cherish, striding to the table.

Ares snapped their map closed. "Who is this?" he asked.

"This is Cherish. He's a traveling merchant." Avari inclined over the table. "And a sorcerer! Can you believe it?"

"A sorcerer?" echoed Ares.

"Indeed," said Cherish with a spellbinding smile.

Proving himself, he summoned a glittering image of the Tehrastar over the tabletop. Oliver fanned it away and continued eating.

Cherish gasped, "How rude of me. These must be your friends."

"They are. This is Ares Lavrenthea, and that's Oliver Kross. We have two outside as well, Brielle and Ruka, once tribesmen of the Riders of the West," said Luxea pleasantly.

"You're the one Bizzner has been maundering about," said Cherish, beguiled by Ares. He took off his hat. "Your Highness, it's an honor to meet your acquaintance."

"That's very kind," said Ares standoffishly. "You're a merchant, you said? A sorcerer selling novelties in the quagmire. Eccentric."

"I realize that my status is idiosyncratic," said Cherish agreeably. "It can be a challenge for those of mine and Luxea's disposition to acquire respectable occupations. Employers don't delight in the risk of unstable arcana in their workspaces, so selling wares of my own accord is currently my last resort. But I'm blessed to say that I love what I do."

"Lucky you," said Ares snidely. "It was a charm meeting you, Cherish, but I'm afraid we have many troubles to overcome."

"What kind of troubles? Perhaps I can help," suggested Cherish.

"We're trying to get to Tarot but can't determine how to get out of Witchsleep. Ares says the roads are missing," said Luxea worriedly.

"Missing?" asked Cherish. "Have you traveled the two trails —"

"Yes," said Ares irksomely.

Cherish stroked his goatee. "If you're voyaging to Tarot, I'd be thrilled to escort you through the Wraiths. Coincidentally, I'm fixing to depart for Halfbend, a day's ride past the Shifting City. If the Riddling Roads are amiss, I'll need to uncover them too."

"I don't think that's a good idea," said Ares guardedly.

"It isn't — it's a *great* idea," said Avari avidly. "The Riddling Roads were winding us in circles for hours. I'm not about going through that again. Do you know the Wraiths well?"

"I've explored them many times. The roads are familiar to me — even the riddling ones," said Cherish with a wink at Luxea.

"Come with us! I don't want to die in mud, thank ya. And you and Luxie can share magick tricks," said Avari rapturously.

Ares looked alarmed. "Avari, we don't know anything about —"

"I would love to join you," interrupted Cherish.

Ares garnered what he could about Cherish. Friendly, cultured, dashing smile, courtly temperament, rare talent. He looked at Luxea next. Her stars were rosy with a sense of belonging that they didn't usually have. Ares' stomach twisted a bit. He wanted to deny the company out of ill will, but Cherish's guidance would be beneficial.

"Fine. Get us out," he said laconically.

The Mooncallers and Cherish egressed Woodgate Inn. Brielle and Ruka were introduced to their new companion in the town square. She informed him that he smelled like maple.

Cherish sat in the driver's seat until they reached the end of the Day Trail. Ares and Alucard were bewildered to find that the Riddling Roads were right in front of them. Apparently they'd overlooked the capstan at the roadside. Cherish claimed that someone must've forgotten to draw the bridge over the moat.

The Riddling Roads were being incredibly cooperative. Within an hour, Cherish sent them rolling into Apparition. He explained that it was all about riding on the correct side of the road. If one stuck to the right, there were less unexpected occurrences.

According to the maps, their last stop before Tarot would be the capital of the Wraiths, Anathema, but it would take several days to reach it. Cherish insisted that Anathema was an urban gem with many delectable food choices — which Avari was ecstatic to hear.

Three days in, the carriage pulled into a place called Ocaranth's Tears. The area looked more like a fairytale kingdom than a swamp. Willows grew like weeds, and the lavender sky filtered through the branches. Starlites whizzed about and blinked shades of pink and yellow. The water in the marsh was crystalline blue and clear to the bottom of the biggest pond. Swishing in the depths was a school of koi fish nearly as lengthy as Ruka. Their ribbony whiskers undulated behind them, and their glassy skins exposed their bones and organs.

The Mooncallers found a dell with plenty of room to pitch tents. The two sorcerers combined their efforts, and the camp was laid out within a minute; it often took an hour manually.

Ruka dove into the tall grass and dug in the dirt. Alucard lounged in the driver's seat and nibbled on stale bread as he spectated the wolf doing whatever it was that he was doing.

The trees in the area were nothing but targets to Avari. All that could be heard from her direction was *thunk* and *shick* as she struck the wood and removed the knife for another pitch.

Having some much-needed privacy, Ares relaxed at the water's edge and lit a cigarette; he hated how much he'd been relying on them.

Luxea, Brielle, and Cherish chatted on the opposite bank. Cherish beckoned the two to the shore.

"Do you know the story of this marsh?" he asked.

"I don't," said Luxea.

"*I* do," said Brielle cockily.

"Should I interpret it, or would you like to, Brielle? I imagine that the Riders are unsurpassable storytellers," said Cherish flatteringly.

"I wish to hear you speak it — but yes, we are," swaggered Brielle.

"Okay. Luxea, do you know about Ocaranth?" asked Cherish.

"Father of the Flying Koi — the god of the first redrift sign," said Brielle quickly. She poked Cherish's chest. "You remind me of the Koi, but you're under the sign of Varnn. It's odd to me. Bat Children are mavens of affliction and recklessness, but you're gentle and intuitive like Ocaranth. I suspect you were born in a year when the stars were misaligned. Offhand, I might guess 87.TIR."

Cherish's eyes bugged. "Goodness, that's impressive. I am, and I was. My lifeday was a sennight ago," he said, bewitched by her reading. "But, yes, it's fabled that Ocaranth was born in this marsh."

"Were the gods born like mortals?" wondered Luxea.

"I believe so. I've heard tales that the gods roam Amniven as men of the wilds. They say that the gods look just as human as any one of us," said Cherish.

"And They die the same," said Brielle intellectually. "The divines aren't immortal; They only have more lives to spare. Like a cat. Cats have eleven."

"Do they?" asked Luxea. She thought of the little girl who'd lost her cat and hoped it was true. "So if the gods look like us, how do you know if you've seen one?"

"That's a good question," muttered Brielle.

Cherish went on with the myth. "Well, Ocaranth was born here long ago. Over time, He grew too big to fit. He longed for the ocean but feared that He couldn't breathe without this pond. He wept for a thousand years, and His tears flooded the land."

"But one day, Ocaranth faced His forebodings and swam to shore. It took all of His courage, but when He breached, wings of silver sprung from His back. Ocaranth had dreaded the air, but His yearning for freedom was so great that the Lemuria blessed Him with flight. He fell in love with the sky and never returned."

"But there's more. The most magical aspect of Ocaranth's Tears is the evidence of His presence. These koi are His children. When the water is disturbed, they light up to celebrate the chance of Him, at last, coming home."

Cherish grazed the water's surface, and the koi flashed. Every stone, root, and cavern in the abyss illuminated. Vibrations rippled from the mouths of the koi like whales singing.

On the opposite bank, Oliver popped out of the thicket. The starlites on the branches scattered. He swatted them with both hands.

"Mate!" he called out.

"Where have you been?" asked Ares with a passing glance.

"Wanderin'. Wicked lookin' tree stump over there. Saw a squirrel diggin' up a nut too," said Oliver joyously.

"How exciting," drawled Ares.

Oliver stared across the marsh where Cherish was busy enchanting their friends with pretty words and pretty magick. He cringed. "Watch him sell 'em faerie dust n' unicorn eggs next. We're loads o' fun. The lasses like us more than Cherish, right? Right, Ares?"

"Mm," grunted Ares.

Pouting, Oliver turned away. He parted his legs and unbuckled his trousers. "Blissits, I've had to piss for hours."

The koi flashed. Luxea, Brielle, and Cherish scowled at what was alerting the fish. Ares, however, couldn't contain his laughter.

"Sacrilege," said Ares with a puff of smoke.

After desecrating the marsh, Oliver played fetch with Ruka using oversized mushroom caps. Alucard retired early, and Ares gave him his tent for the night. The Speaker secluded himself inside of the passenger car with a candle and a forsaken stack of paperwork.

Luxea, Avari, and Brielle lounged around the fire pit with Cherish and swilled rum from the bottle. Avari sat on a stump and tied Brielle's locks into a bun — which was the size of a melon in the end. Cherish and Luxea rationed space on a log. The girls had been listening to his bottomless tales for hours. This one in particular was about the time he'd commandeered a donkey.

"The damned things all look the same. I hadn't a clue that it wasn't mine until I was three reaches from town!" laughed Cherish.

"The supreme ass-burglar," said Brielle, a pundit of animal humor.

The black sky wept. The campfire sizzled as water splashed upon the coals. Avari opened her mouth for the rain to land on her tongue, but Brielle pouted as it splatted upon her bare arms.

"I hate it. We're going in," she said, lifting up Avari.

"You really gotta carry me?" sighed Avari.

Luxea ran after them. Cherish doused the campfire with a magickal swish of his hand and chased them. Brielle bowled Avari into their tent like a ball, and Luxea passed into her own.

Cherish looked adoring as he waited for her to go to sleep, but when the light of her lamp went black, so did he. He glowered at the bolts of rain that pierced down from the sky and jogged to the carriage.

Ares, who was smoking outside, passive-aggressively simpered. Cherish crept a cigarette of his own into his mouth and snapped his fingers. Silver sparks ignited the tip and slowly waned.

"Evening, Your Highness," he said pleasantly.

"Evening," said Ares minimally.

"I've not had many turns to speak with you. You're a thought-provoking individual. I'd like to get to know you better," said Cherish smokily. "I hope it isn't in bad taste to ask, but I'm dying to learn about your condition."

Ares revealed his talons, asking if that was the 'condition' to which he'd referred. Cherish nodded once. Ares tucked it back under his arm and asked, "What about it?"

"What's it like?" asked Cherish, eyes gleaming. "Dragons are the most deadly creatures in existence. You must feel such enormous power from —"

"Try fear," said Ares dourly.

"What do you have to be afraid of?" asked Cherish insensitively. "You're an authoritarian male with a priceless name and world-breaking flames. You could harness it for your behoof. You strive for the reality that you want, don't you? Then take it. Your ancestors did likewise."

"Abusing either of those properties would deem me a knave," said Ares. His freckled nose glowed orange as he inhaled. "I could lay waste to all things if I wanted to, but I don't lust for exploiting my capability. That's what sets us apart, Cherish. You were blessed with a gift, and I was damned with a curse. Practicing your abilities might advance you, but doing the same would kill me — and truly? I'm not fanatical of that probability."

"Kill you? Draconism doesn't kill. Will it drive you to insanity? Yes. But kill you? By all means, no. In my eyes, missing a few pieces of your mind is worth the rush," said Cherish presumptuously.

"Is there a difference in losing my mind and losing my life?"

"You make a just point. If you face such fear, then why don't you take action to stop the affliction?"

"Even if there were any dragons left to utilize for that benefit, I yet wouldn't go to that extent," said Ares acerbically.

"The selfless man. So commendable," taunted Cherish. "Ah, but there's *one* dragon left. How upsetting that after all these years, he is still the King of Tzapodia."

Ares' muscles knotted up. "How do you — ?" He crumbled his cigarette between his knuckles. "If you're so enamored by exchanging theories about dragons and the Lavrenthea dynasty, pester someone who cares to lend their time to you."

"Oops, I struck a nerve," tittered Cherish.

He stepped out into the rain and shattered into water droplets, becoming a part of the storm. Ares searched, but couldn't find him.

Like every day, Cherish taught Luxea new components of the arcana in the carriage. After a few hours of lessons, he retrieved his spellbook. Metal accents decorated the black leather cover, shifting from violet to green. It made Luxea think of a beetle's shell.

Cherish's spellbook had a name lock that came unlatched to the name *'Nightingale.'* The Nightingale and the Usinnon edified in vastly different ways. The Nightingale told of chaotic magick that ignored energetic balance and focused on gamble and risk. Cherish said that this approach was dangerous but granted more power. He compared it to air and fire. Both were effective, but wind flourished flame when faced with the other.

"You have a spellbook too, correct? May I see it?" asked Cherish.

Excited to show him, Luxea rummaged beneath the carriage seat. The Usinnon whispered sleepily when she picked it up.

"This is the Usinnon," she said proudly.

"Hashiasiahia. . . ."

"It's chatty," laughed Cherish. "This is valuable. The architect of magic, as its name suggests. From whence did you obtain such an artifact?"

"Ares gave it to me — but made me work for it."

Her statement instantly grabbed the Speaker's attention.

"What a gift," said Cherish, locking eyes with Ares. "This must be Era Two, perhaps? And it survived the book burnings of old. Your Highness, you were right to provide it to such an adroit sorceress."

"Would you like to see it?" asked Luxea, presenting the Usinnon.

"Absolutely!" said Cherish animatedly.

Luxea held out the spellbook. Cherish grasped it without hesitation. The carriage illuminated in blue light, and arcanan screams cracked every window.

"HASHIASHIAISHIAISA!" warned the Usinnon.

Luxea dropped the spellbook. Avari and Oliver woke up from their naps at once. Ares' instinct burned a hole in his censorship.

"Spellbooks bite those who can't use magick, but you show off yours each time you open your mouth. Why can't you touch the Usinnon?" he asked suspiciously.

In a snit, the Usinnon whispered, *"Hasishiaisi — !"*

"It's because the Usinnon adores Luxea!" interrupted Cherish. "It's uncommon, but sometimes spellbooks grow too attached to a single subject. See, the Usinnon only wishes to be touched by its master."

"Pity that you're not as popular with spellbooks as you are with women," laughed Ares.

"Ares!" yelped Luxea.

Oliver snickered. Ares sank into his seat.

No one talked for a long time.

THE PHOENIX GATE

19.NIGHTSPEAK.25.OSC.3

NIKA SUBMITTED a command into the *Matha ou Machina* database. The airship descended under a billowy cloud, and an alarm trumpeted from the speakers on the hull.

Peyamo Nelnah limped to the handrail and soaked in the view. Ank'tatra was an arid nation where towns were few and far between, but the Phoenix Gate was a gem amongst coals. It rested in the shadow of the Sandstone Spire Ilsemet whose essence bled into the dazzling, teal rivers that entwined around the city. Fifty reaches north, the deltas let out into Sandblood, an estuary leading into Eternity's Ocean.

Crowning the Phoenix Gate was the Phoenix Palace, a landmark fashioned from tiger's eye. Sky-high effigies of the female titans of Anunaru guarded the rampart.

The Goddess of War Daetri reminded Her onlookers that while war was a concept brought about impetuously, it was also inevitable. The second was the Goddess of Wealth Himhre who endowed Her prosperity onto those that dwelled within the Phoenix Gate.

Peyamo's eye flickered to the sheeted body of Garamat un Gatra. She called to mind the time he'd invited her to the Phoenix Palace to discuss the black market smuggling that had been occurring betwixt their nations. He'd devised a scheme to cease iniquity for the victims of the trades. He'd fought by Peyamo's side to undermine the operations. He'd been there when her arm was sundered in battle. He'd cupped his hand to her shoulder and toted her to the front lines.

Never had Peyamo surmised that, one day, she would aim the arm she'd lost at Garamat un Gatra as her rival.

Far below *Matha ou Machina,* a cloaked rishja touched their torch to a pyre. The flames devoured the wood and sent up a smoke signal for the sky-sailors to see.

"We're cleared for landing. Keep your sky-legs, My Lady," said Nika, lowering his goggles over his eyes.

Matha ou Machina surged vapor as it settled into the dock at the Phoenix Palace. The shell of the ship altered into a rested state. The sky-sailors turned a capstan, and a metal ramp extended from the hull. They collected iron killicks from cubbies and anchored the airship.

As Peyamo and Nika trudged down the stairs, they heard the pattering of feet from within the Phoenix Palace. The outline of a middle-aged rishjaan man came into view. His shaven hair and expansive irises were the color of a crow's feathers.

"Peyamo, the Lady of Bronze!" bellowed the manservant. He bowed in a scatter. "My name is Martnir. If I am to your liking, I will be representing you."

"Thank you, Martnir, but I'll not be visitin' long. We ain't here for pleasure, I'm afraid," said Peyamo breathily.

Six men positioned themselves around Garamat's stretcher and strained to lift his weight. Gooseflesh rose up on Martnir's arms.

"He gave us no choice," said Peyamo regretfully.

Martnir was stiff with shock. *"Rakma'ji,"* he said, beckoning two Phoenix Sons. *"Lampa vadu ma tad Yaz Magia Ralvesh. Gavo, gavo!"*

Peyamo recognized the phrase *'Yaz Magia'* as *'Sun Chief,'* but also Ralvesh, the name of Garamat's only son. She had many queries, but if Ank'tatra had adjudged it necessary to crown Ralvesh as the new Sun Chief so presently, that was their verdict.

The hypostyle hall beyond the landing had walls lined with murals depicting Ank'tatra's history. The Lady had been to the Phoenix Palace many times and remembered it as a joyous locale with energy coursing through every papyrus plant that grew along the aqueducts. Now there were frowning servants, sneering members of the Phoenix Sons fanned by said servants, and the essence had left the vegetation.

Martnir toured Peyamo and Nika by grand terraces and catacombs of Sun Chiefs past with Garamat's body carried alongside them. They descended a helical ramp into a courtyard.

The courtyard declined into a quadrilateral ditch where sand spread over the floor. In the middle was a barbed obelisk with a chain fastened to it. This was called a *'deathbed.'* A prisoner would be locked in the center and made to combat the opponent of the arbiter's picking. In the instance of their survival, the walls would part and unleash sand, burying the victor prematurely.

The three neared the throne room referred to as the *'Khabeptah.'* The stone door scraped open with a sound like chewing on sand. Peyamo's eye buzzed to the *khabe* at the opposing edge of the room.

Ralvesh looked nothing like his father. His skin was sienna brown, his braided hair was canary yellow, and his blue eyes were effervescent. But he was cold in all of the places that Garamat had been warm.

Sun Chief Ralvesh patted the orange and white striped tiger beside his *khabe* and, in a voice like a god, said, "The Lady Peyamo Nelnah! When was the last time I saw you? I must have been, what, seven?"

"Aye. Congratulations on your coronation," said Peyamo. The Phoenix Sons carried Garamat's body into the room. "I'm sorry, Sun Chief, but your father —"

Ralvesh laughed, "Don't look so mousey. He is dead, I know."

The Sun Chief ripped the pus-stained sheet away from his father's corpse and inspected the deep, crusted lesions. Around Garamat's nearly-detached middle finger was the Sun Chief's signet, a ring handed down through the generations of Ank'tatra's royals. Ralvesh slipped the band from his father's dead finger and admired it.

"Sayshi, *lampa,*" he ordered. His tiger, Sayshi, prowled nigh and nuzzled her head into his thigh. He said, *"Tagida ib naano."*

Feast on him.

The tiger clamped her teeth into Garamat's flesh and lapped up the last of his blood from his fibrous veins. Peyamo and Nika were daunted. They'd made such an effort to keep his remains intact only to meet this fate.

"Father always hated Sayshi. Silly," said Ralvesh, swiveling the Sun Chief's signet onto his own finger.

"Will there be no Rite of Fire for him?" asked Peyamo, aghast.

"A Rite of Fire? Of course, not," said Ralvesh frivolously. "A traitor like him doesn't deserve it. A Rite of Fire is a ceremony to carry the dead into Eletheon, but Eletheon is a realm for virgins and heroes. My father was neither of those. I honor him not with a Rite of Fire because there is naught to honor."

"I . . . I understand," gulped Peyamo. "But, Sun Chief, what'll you do now? Ank'tatra's sufferin'. From the sky, I could see the smoke from the riots. I fear for your safety and theirs."

"I will train them who is in control," said Ralvesh. He raised his enormous hands and watched as Sayshi devoured his father. "Hearken! I will make the Ank'tatra Dominion greater than it has ever been. The Lemuria will envy the world we have created, the divines will adore the paradise in which we bask, and never shall any man dare oppose us. Where once my ancestors stood feeble — Tajukhet, Tatamen, Athavos, Nastet, Hamsesh, Damkhet, and *Garamat* — *I* will embody the might that Ank'tatra should have always had. I will be the champion who carries the world on his shoulders. Around us will be walls grand enough to keep the unworthy from polluting us!"

"Walls mean little when the rot is from within," hissed Nika.

"There is no rot here. My people will love me," stated Ralvesh.

The Sun Chief escorted Peyamo and Nika back to *Matha ou Machina.* He babbled about structural developments, renewing ancient rishjaan traditions, and repealing the laws that had done nothing for Ank'tatra's prosperity. Peyamo was hardly listening. At the dock, she sent Nika onboard and saluted Ralvesh.

The Sun Chief beamed and said, "I thank you from the bottom of my heart for returning my father to me, Lady."

"You're welcome, Sun Chief," said Peyamo vacantly. "I apologize for not stayin' longer. The Speaker is makin' a journey to Tarot, and I've got to get back to *Thali ou Tirima* afore he arrives."

"We rishja scum say *'zasteau,'*" spat Ralvesh; *'hello'* in draconic.

The Lady turned away. Without facing Ralvesh, she said, "Your father told me he did it all for you."

Ralvesh didn't even blink. "How sad," he whispered.

Robbed of hope, Peyamo trudged onto *Matha ou Machina's* ramp. She then halted, stricken by a realization. "Ralvesh, how'd you know Garamat was dead 'fore I got here?"

She heard Ralvesh let out an exasperated sigh. His footsteps came closer until he towered behind her, nearly twice her height. She kept her arm ready, but the Sun Chief didn't appear aggressive.

As if he were addressing a child, Ralvesh squatted to her level. "Do you know what bargain Widow gave to my father?" he asked.

"No," said Peyamo defensively.

"She told him that if he refused to serve the Brood, She would kill me — his only son. My father took the bribe out of desperation and publicly announced his allegiance to Widow. But Widow betrayed him, no? Why do you think that is, Lady?"

"I don't know."

Ralvesh grinned. "Because She had already made a deal with *me*, long before She approached my father. All we needed to do was push him off the throne. He committed political suicide for my sake, but that was only the start. We assaulted the Empress' gala and sent my father to his death, guaranteeing my place at Widow's side. So, Lady, I thank you and that mangy wolf rider for destroying my final obstacle."

Garamat, Peyamo's lifelong friend, had been tricked into serving Widow. He'd done it for his son — but his son had been behind it all along. Her arm couldn't have altered any faster. With the barrel of her gun pointed between Ralvesh's eyes, she tipped her head toward her airship.

"By the power of The Six, I declare you an enemy of the people of the Joined Hands. You're comin' with me, Sun Chief. Get movin'."

Ralvesh didn't react. Peyamo cocked her arm to fire but noticed that her meters were swiveling. The alarms at *Matha ou Machina's* command center went off, and metal scraped against stone. The airship was dragged toward the Phoenix Palace at an alarming speed, and the crewmen could do nothing to stop it.

"If you value your life, you should leave," said Ralvesh blackly.

Suddenly, a spider's leg the same length and circumference as the airship's masts pierced through the Phoenix Palace's archway. It scored the polished ground, and then seven more appeared.

Panicking, Peyamo stumbled backward. She knew to whom those legs belonged, and she dared not fight Her alone.

"Begin ascent!" she screamed at her sky-sailors.

With Nika at the helm, the airship rose from the dock. Peyamo's arm shifted into a hook. She clung to the hull and pulled herself onboard. As *Matha ou Machina* flew away, she saw a grey-skinned woman with a long, bald head and four black eyes in the shadows of the Phoenix Palace.

It was Her.

DEATH KNELL
20.NIGHTSPEAK.25.OSC.3

HACKNEY COACHES strung down the streets of Anathema. The row-houses were so squashed together that it looked as if each block had been built under a single blueprint. The rooftops were lofty wherever the eye went, but a clocktower with a rusty bell and a ticking face on all four sides stood the highest.

The Mooncallers vacated the carriage. Excitement blossomed upon Luxea's face as they entered the Famous Tamistier Lodge. Cherish had told her that there was a library inside, and she was keen to rummage through it. At the front counter, she dashed away to search for the kingdom of books.

Cherish tipped his hat to the innkeeper, a bow-legged man with one eye, who greeted him likewise. "We require six rooms," he said.

The innkeeper flipped the pages of his check-in ledger. "My apologies, but we're three rooms short. Storms are rollin' in, n' folks everywhere are lookin' for a place to keep from the cold."

Cherish tapped his finger on his lip twice and brightened up again. "It's no matter. We'll take the three vacancies you have."

"Three isn't enough. We'll find another inn," said Ares at once.

"Don't think you'll have luck there. Bookin's filled most places. S'always the case durin' Nightspeak," pointed out the innkeeper.

"It's all right. We can share chambers," said Cherish, patting Ares. The Speaker rolled his shoulder away from him.

"I'll den with Avari," said Brielle. "Ruka enjoys the outdoors. He says there are rats. He loves rats and wants them all to himself. He's feeling greedy today."

"Perfect," said Cherish. "Your Highness, if you'd like to divide space with Lord Kross, I'll extend a bed in my room to Luxea —"

"No," snapped Ares. He gestured to Oliver. "I would rather you take a room with Luxea this evening."

Oliver's eyes flitted back and forth. "Me? Sorry, mate, you're askin' *me* to share a room with Luxie?" He fidgeted. "Well, awright. I promise I won't do nothin'. She'd kill me anyhow."

"Damned right, she would," warned Avari.

Ares spat eye-fire at Cherish. "Excellent. Then Cherish and I will take the last room. That would be so much fun, wouldn't it?"

"I'd love to. Mayhap we can better acquaint," said Cherish bitterly.

Affixed on Ares, Cherish shuffled through his pocket and slung five gold pieces onto the counter.

Luxea followed the signs to the library. Doors on either side of the hall led to unknown places, but the last had a stack of books shoring it open. The library was smaller than Castle Lavrenthea's, but there were just as many books.

Four musty walls were packed with a thousand volumes and a thousand more clocks, most of which were cluttering the floors and tables. Luxea glanced at the timekeeper on her finger. The time was still wrong, and the hands still ticked backward, but none of the clocks in the library were set correctly either.

The books in every aisle were disorganized, mistreated, and coated in dust. Luxea had wanted to explore whatever sections this library had to offer, but there was no structure for her to follow.

She unhooked the Usinnon and placed it on the floor. As she reached for a book, the Usinnon sparkled at her. Luxea tickled its face and said, "Don't worry. You're still my favorite."

With the Usinnon sated, she flipped open a random book. The pages assaulted her nostrils with the scent of pine. There were no pine trees in the Wraiths that she'd noticed, so she wondered from whence the book had originated. Her feet shuffled as she flipped through the sections and read down each, and then she stopped at the last page.

There was a single-line poem.

"Leaves may grow and fall away,
but roots forever will remain."
- Anonymous

It made Luxea feel peaceful but also sad. She had new leaves, but not roots. She'd learned Avari's roots, Brielle and Ruka's, and even Ares', but she hadn't unearthed her own. Her feet stopped moving. She hadn't thought about it in a long time, but she wondered if she would one day find out more about herself.

Her stars flitted to a gap in the bookshelf where she saw a wizened librarian scanning a catalog. She quietly tore the poem out of the piney book, folded it in half, and tucked it into the Usinnon's cover.

Shortly after settling in, Cherish took to the baths. Ares started filling out paperwork on the windowsill. He tapped the quill against his chin and glanced outside.

Silver light painted the mire. The bent shadows of the trees stretched over the mud, grasping at Ares. As the darkness crept up the outer walls of the lodge, his talons clicked against the window, grasping back.

The bath door swung open. Ares' fingers closed into his palm. He could feel Cherish's pale pink eyes upon him, teasing him from across the room. He fought shy of a conversation, but his wish was abruptly denied.

"Ah, the Irestar," said Cherish, pulling on a pair of worn-out trousers. "Oscerin's voice must be so soothing to you, Your Highness. How unfortunate that you can't look upon Her face."

"The greater divines dwell in the realm of spirits. If seeing Oscerin requires my death, hearing Her is plenty for me," droned Ares.

"You'll behold Her one day then," said Cherish with a forked tongue. He came closer to the window and admired the spray of stars in the sky. "Luxea is a jewel, isn't she? As charming as she is gifted." Ares said nothing. "You don't agree? I thought you surely would. See, it startled me when you'd shot down my generous offer to give up my bed for her. I'd only wondered if you felt —"

"I don't trust you, Cherish. Like the hells I was going to let you spend a night with her," said Ares like a spike.

Cherish snickered. "I'm curious. Luxea has relayed to me the stories about her awakening in Tel Ashir. Bizarre, no? How did you meet her? A cadet, and the Speaker himself? Quite divergent."

In retrospect, Ares experienced meeting Luxea. He'd just concluded a conference and hadn't slept the night before. He'd been feeling weary, so he'd fetched himself a hot drink. He'd taken one sip before Luxea had ripped around the corner and spilled his tea.

Ares almost smiled. "We happened to cross each other."

"At last, a real answer to one of my questions," said Cherish snidely. "I see. Chance meetings are the best sort."

"Or the worst," added Ares.

"Verily. Fate's path is a labyrinth," laughed Cherish.

A flame sparked between Ares' eyes. His brows creased to extinguish it, but it branched too rapidly to contain. He replayed the week from the start. Goldenrise, carriage, Wraiths, circles, circles, circles, Witchsleep, Cherish.

"I could even call it a *'Riddling Road,'*" suggested Ares.

"That wasn't fate's course, it was mine," said Cherish proudly.

The sorcerer had deliberately jumped right into the trap Ares had set for him. Ares stood and shot a transient stare at the shamshir that leaned against the wall. "Who are you, Cherish?"

"Just your everyday traveling merchant," taunted Cherish.

Ares snatched up his shamshir and swished it toward Cherish's throat. "Liar! You led us to Witchsleep. You knew we could be coming from the start," he accused.

"Don't fret, Your Highness. I'll not be an impediment to you for much longer. Let's make peace for tonight," said Cherish benevolently.

"There will be no peace. Tell me the truth!" barked Ares.

Cherish became the shadow of a man. "So be it. I'm here to finish what Garamat started — what Widow started," he confessed.

"What are you going to finish?" asked Ares, jerking the blade.

"You haven't figured it out? It's your fault that Goldenrise fell," said Cherish blackly. "Had you not taken advantage of Luxea's loyalty and roped her in as your safeguard, the empire might still belong to the

Empress. You have yet to be honest about what really occurred that night, even to yourself, and you call *me* a liar? See, Luxea has long been destined to be culled from the Brood Mother's design, for she is the reason behind doom in totality. So, in light of Garamat's miscarry, I will eliminate her."

"Why Luxea? She's less of a hazard to Widow than —"

"— than what? Than *you?*" cut in Cherish. "I wish for you to understand, but I doubt you could. Even if I shared with you all of the knowledge I have on Luxea Siren, your mind's eye is too blinded by her witchery to make any sense of it. Now, I enjoy our talks, but there's work to be done."

Cherish strained to free himself, but Ares was steadfast. "The last thing I'll do is let you out of my sight," he seethed.

"Perhaps it will be the last. Time is ticking, and Luxea will suffer whether or not you kill me. You know, your ignorance is laughable, but your *fire* would compliment the Brood superbly," purred Cherish.

Ares gave a lethal swing of his shamshir. The blade sliced through the wall, but Cherish was gone. There was a tap upon Ares' shoulder.

Cherish grinned. "You shouldn't play with magick."

White light flashed. Ares was blasted through the upper-story window, but he didn't hear glass shattering or feel himself falling. In a blink, he landed in water, and his skull cracked against stone.

"This li'l pigs covered himself in feathers like a chicken," said Oliver, showing Luxea a picture book he'd found in a trunk.

Luxea took a peek at the drawing of a pink piglet slathered in feathers. "I wonder why a pig would do that?" she humored.

"The lad just wants to fit in. Maybe he wants to fly 'round n' sit in the trees like the chickens do," said Oliver sentimentally.

Luxea wondered if she was the only person on Amniven who possessed valid information about chickens. She was close to debating over nearly-flightless birds and even more flightless pigs, but she resolved to let Oliver have this one.

There was a knock at the door. Luxea scuttled to the entryway.

"Good evening, Luxea — and Oliver," said Cherish jovially. "I came to ask if you'd like to join me at the clocktower ere the storm arrives. There's a stunning view from the observatory."

Luxea glanced out the window. The sky was clouding over, but it hadn't started raining yet. "I'd like to see it, yes," she said, but then she looked distressed. "How's Ares? I haven't seen him all afternoon."

"His Highness has gone to bed. He didn't sleep a wink last night. We should allow him to rest," said Cherish with a pout.

Luxea said farewell to Oliver and departed with Cherish.

After a while, Oliver got bored with his pig book and left to seek out a brothel. He whistled as he strode through the Famous Tamistier Lodge, but then he saw a slightly open door toward the end of the hallway. It was Ares and Cherish's room.

Oliver knew that Ares would breathe fire if he were walked in on, but he snooped anyway. He poked his head inside, and the room was lightless. He dared to twist on a lamp. Neither of the beds had been touched, and Ares' shamshir was embedded in the wall.

"Shit." Oliver hopped backward and bolted down the hall.

When Ares woke up, he groaned and clutched the back of his throbbing skull. The sloshing of water startled him. He rubbed his eyes. Wherever he was didn't appear to be anywhere close to the Famous Tamistier Lodge.

He trudged through knee-deep water and stared through a metal grate overhead. He was in a storm drain. He tore to one side of the cell and patted the slimy stone. He spun the other way and felt the opposite wall. Water trickled through drains at his feet, but there was no likelihood of him fitting even a hand through them.

Cherish had sent him to a place where he could no longer interfere.

An hour had passed. Oliver had checked everywhere inside of the lodge for Ares. He'd asked the innkeeper if he'd seen a *'tall, dashing bloke,'* but the innkeeper said he hadn't. Since then, he'd traced every alleyway and was now in the ghettos of Anathema.

Meanwhile, rain blasted through the grate above Ares' head. His hair bled down his face and left streaks of silt on his cheeks, and water rose up his legs and chilled him to his core.

He suddenly heard, *"Ares! Where are you, mate?"*

"Kross?" Ares boomed as loudly as he could, "Oliver! Come to me, follow my voice!"

Oliver spied a circular vent in the ground with runoff torrenting into it. He peeked inside. Ares tilted his head back in relief.

"I've been lookin' all over for you! D'you got any idea how much I hate runnin'?" screeched Oliver. He cringed. "Ain't that poo?"

"What — no!" said Ares, not so relieved anymore. "It's a storm drain, and even if it was — ! Kross, where is Luxea?"

"Went with Cherish to the clocktower," said Oliver worriedly.

Ares' skin blanched. "Get me out! There isn't time to explain, we have to get to the clocktower!"

Oliver's gangling arms trembled as he lifted the grate from the setting. He reached out, and he and Ares brushed fingers. Eventually, Ares jumped, and his weight nearly yanked Oliver down with him.

"Blissits, you're heavy!" wailed Oliver.

"I'm aware, and I'm sorry — now lift me!" shouted Ares.

Oliver pulled Ares out of the drain. By the time he'd captured two breaths, Ares was already halfway down the street.

At the top of Anathema clocktower, Luxea and Cherish had been admiring the view of the city together in silence. For a time, he'd looked as soft as he always had, but then he grew sharper, jagged.

Now wind raged, and rain splashed Luxea's ankles. But the cold was of no comparison to the swollen, exhausting heat in her gut. She felt unsettled by the way Cherish was looking at her. There was something off about his smile, something crooked. His laughing eyes made a joke out of her.

Luxea's stars turned violet, and the hairs on the back of her neck became needles. "You aren't a merchant, are you?" she asked almost inaudibly.

Cherish plucked off his hat and fluffed his hair. "No. I'm shocked it took you so long to notice," he said, tossing his cap over the ledge.

"Then who are you?" whispered Luxea.

"Who are *you?*" asked Cherish harshly.

The chain attached to the bell *jangled* as the tower-keeper a few floors down readied to sound the hour. Cherish appeared complacent.

"Your death knell tolls."

The bell rang, and the air buzzed. The timekeeper ring around Luxea's right forefinger altered. She was pricked by something sharp within the band. An excruciating pain slashed up from the ball of her wrist to the crook of her neck. Black veins branched onto her cheeks.

The timekeeper ring wasn't broken — it had been counting down.

"What did you do to me? What is this?" coughed Luxea.

" *'The Nightmare Venom.'* You'll have to shred yourself to pieces to reverse it, so I wouldn't waste my time if I were you," said Cherish.

"Why pretend to be so kind if this was your intent all along?"

"If you think kindness equates to honesty, you have much yet to learn. But my job is done, and after all of this, you still don't recall a thing. You don't remember me, Luxea? Not in the slightest?"

Luxea couldn't speak. Cherish looked anguished, and then, as if he were lecturing her, he rasped, "No point in hiding it now. Do you know how irritating it's been to tolerate all of your boasting about educating yourself in the art of the arcana? No sorceress could possess the abilities you do without guidance. You've excelled as an artist of your caliber, but give credit where credit is due. *I* was your teacher!"

24.Riverspell.19.Oscerin.3

By the curve of bookshelves stood a slender man with frigid, pink eyes.

A faceless figure said, "This is Magister Cherish Ven'lethe. He'll be your instructor from now on. Go."

Cherish circled Luxea with a rimy expression. "Strike me."

"Magister?" gulped Luxea.

"I said strike me."

Luxea unsurely lifted her hands and whispered, "Yeth'lavren."

A wispy, blue flame slithered to Cherish. He locked his stare onto it, and it dropped like a stone. It hit the ground and engulfed the room in a ring of white fire.

"Mediocre. She'll do," sighed Cherish.

4.Snowhowl.20.Oscerin.3

Luxea and Magister Cherish stood upon a cliff above a roaring river.

Cherish asked tonelessly, "What is deflection?"

"Hitting spells away, Magister," answered Luxea.

Cherish cracked open the Nightingale and strode away. "That's right. Turn your back to the cliff. You're going to deflect my spells when I attack. Otherwise, I'll knock you off, and I promise the drop will kill you."

Luxea was afraid to do so much as breathe. "Yes, Magister."

Noiseless, white bolts sprang out from Cherish's hands. She threw her arms up and gasped, "Sheishan'in!"

Her heels dug into the dirt. She listened as several pebbles clacked down into the ravine far below. She opened her eyes. His spells had deflected off of her shield.

Cherish smiled a little bit. "Very good, Luxea. Again!"

17.Softstep.21.Oscerin.3

Magister Cherish's guise was adoring. "You've done so well, Luxea. I can hardly believe you're the same girl."

"Thank you, Magister. Will I see you soon?" asked Luxea brightly.

"It's doubtless. You're my most excellent student. So, if you agree, I'd like to make you my disciple," said Cherish thoughtfully.

Luxea almost popped. "Of course! Yes!" she exclaimed.

Cherish was proud. "Then I'll teach you all I know."

31.Nightspeak.23.Oscerin.3

"Good morning, Magister," greeted Luxea. "I finished the homework you gave me. I think I'm finally grasping the concept of —"

"Keep it," said Cherish, refusing to look at her.

Luxea clutched the worksheets. "Is everything all right?"

"I can't teach you anymore," said Cherish emptily.

Luxea's heart snapped in two. "Why not? Have I done something wrong? I'll try harder, this is so important to me, and — !"

"Nothing you say will change my mind. Now go!" spat Cherish. He looked at her only for a second. "You were a wonderful student." He deserted her. Luxea dropped her workbook.

12. CLAWSGUARD. 24. OSCERIN. 3

The shatter of glass from the next room sent Luxea's heart running. She shot up, and her quill bled all over her magick notes.

Footsteps, the stride of a perfectionist. The door opened.

"Magister Cherish? What are you doing here? And . . . how did you find me?" questioned Luxea.

Cherish admired her studying space, knowing he'd taught her well. He braced himself and, in a soft voice, said, "The butterfly mustn't meet the spider's eyes. Forgive me."

He clapped his hand over her mouth and locus-jumped them away.

Luxea's heart was a stone, and it was scratchy. "You're Magister Cherish Ven'lethe. I was your disciple," she said emotionlessly.

"So you do remember. Delightful," said Cherish bittersweetly.

"If I was your student, why hurt me?" asked Luxea woefully.

"Why not ask Ares?" said Cherish. He grimaced. "That is if you survive long enough to find him."

"Find him? What did you do to him?" husked Luxea.

"Something," laughed Cherish.

Fury blasted into Luxea. She lashed out with the most potent incendiary spell that she could conjure. The flames devoured every inch of Cherish's stature — but he was unscathed. Her magick had no effect on him whatsoever. She tried over and over again. Then she experienced the greatest fear that she had all evening.

"Spell-eater," she whispered.

Cherish's eyebrows flew up. *"That* you learned on your own." He held his arm out, and his magick blew Luxea backward.

In the interim, Ares and Oliver ran down the flooded streets. Through the blur of rain, wind, and orange leaves were crackles of arcanan static in the observatory. Ares broke in the clocktower door and bounded upstairs with Oliver practically stepping on his coattail.

Cherish struck Luxea again. She was in too much shock to heed how close she was getting to the ledge of the clocktower. Her heel slipped, but she rolled forward. In Cherish's next assault, she shielded herself. His magick thrashed the barrier, ricocheted, and hit the clocktower bell.

The ringing was dizzying. The sound blew Luxea's mind into the past. Deflection. She revisited the Usinnon's notes about spell-eaters.

"Cannot be harmed by . . ."

Cherish's fire rushed forth. Luxea erected a smaller shield at an angle. His magick was deflected right back at him. His white arcana grazed his middle, and he was painfully scorched.

"That's it. A spell-eater can only be harmed by their own spells."

Cherish was in pain but looked impressed. "Very, very good! You were always so perceptive, Luxea," he said, glory bruised.

"I learned from the best," she quipped.

"Indeed, you did," said Cherish amusedly.

"What's going on?" shouted the tower-keeper, ascending the staircase with a lantern. "This isn't a place for foolin' around — !"

With a flit of his eyes, Cherish turned the tower-keeper to ash. The man's hat *piffed* into his ashes, and the lantern shattered on the stairs. Oil dribbled down the steps, and a trail of fire snaked after it.

Cherish splenetically kicked the tower-keeper's remains and thrust Luxea against the wall. The force of his magick only increased with his anger. It deflated all of her breath and felt like her bones were about to snap.

Just then, two figures prowled up the staircase beyond the flames. Ares wiped up the oil with his bare hand, and a gap in the wall of fire was created. The second it was clear, Oliver ran.

Surprising everyone in the clocktower, especially himself, he leaped onto Cherish's back and gouged his fangs into his throat. Cherish gripped his wet hair and heaved him off. He smeared blood from his lips, and his murderous eyes were the same shade of red.

Cherish cupped his wound in disbelief, but when he saw who had been the one to defeat him, he started to laugh. "Oh, that is *funny!*"

He watched as his blood saturated his shirt. "That was memorable. I thank you for the exhilaration, but I've had my fill. I wasn't trying to kill you in any case, Luxea; the venom will do that for me. Farewell, and use the time you have left wisely. It isn't much."

White flames licked Cherish's boots. His blood sprayed the ground as he vanished in a flash.

FALSE GUARDIANS

ARES INSPECTED Luxea. "Are you all right?" he asked.

Luxea secreted her hands. "I'm fine," she said curtly.

"Well, I neva' want to do that again," huffed Oliver.

"I didn't think you had that in you, Oli," said Luxea feebly.

"Neither did I," said Oliver, spitting traces of Cherish's blood.

He tucked Luxea into a hug. When she wrapped her arms around his waist, Ares caught a glimpse of her right hand. He snatched her wrist and examined it. Veins writhed under her skin, and the stretch from her fingertips to her forearm was pure black.

"What happened?" asked Ares, eyes melancholy.

Oliver's expression mimicked Ares'. "Did your hand always look like that, Luxie?" he squeaked.

"Of course, it didn't," snarled Ares. "Luxea, what is this?"

Luxea stole back her hand. "Cherish said it's poison. He also said there's no way to reverse it."

"There has to be a cure," said Ares adamantly. "I'm not familiar with poisons, but if anyone is, it's Avari."

"She excels in poisons," said Luxea, looking away. "General Skythoan would scold her whenever she made her own in the barracks washroom. She isn't any good at concocting them, but she knows how they work."

"That's better than nothing," said Ares under his breath.

The three returned to the Famous Tamistier Lodge where Ruka rested outside. The wolf sniffed the air and happily trotted to them. Luxea tried to pet his head, but he scampered away at once. His amber eyes were hooked on her palm as if it were an enemy.

Right when they stepped through the front door, Brielle ran to them with her face glistening with sweat. "Is Ruka all right? He was afraid so suddenly. He wouldn't tell me why," she panted.

"He's safe," said Ares concisely.

Brielle took in their straggly appearances and peeked out the door past them. "The sorcerer isn't with you?" she asked.

"Cherish is a traitor. Sent Ares off someplace, n' I had to track him down. In the meantime, he stuck Luxie with poison," explained Oliver.

Brielle then noticed Luxea's hand. She took a step back, fearing it like an animal to a wildfire. Luxea hid it in her sleeve.

"Where's Avari? We need her help," she asked.

"She's in the den playing with knives. I'll take you to her, but you go first. Three levels up and that way," said Brielle, pointing right.

Ares started to follow Luxea and Oliver, but Brielle wrested his sleeve. "Dragon, the shadow in her fingers bears the scent that Ruka and I caught in Goldenrise. It's like death. What is it?" she asked.

"I don't know, but I hope it isn't that," whispered Ares.

Brielle let them into her room where Avari sat at a table with blades laid out on a sheet of cloth. When her companions entered, she said, "Hi, you! How's — wait. What's happened? You're a mess, and you smell."

Luxea plopped onto the bed across from her. "Firstly, Cherish tricked us. Secondly, I remembered something," she said in a daze.

"All right. Well, I want you to tell me all about Cherish. But that's great that you found somethin' about yourself! Do you know how many moons we spent looking for you in L'arneth's registries? Much longer than I'd have liked to keep my nose in a book. What'd you remember?" asked Avari timorously.

"I remembered Cherish," muttered Luxea.

"You knew him?" blurted out Ares.

Luxea explained. The news was startling to all, but mostly Ares.

Now mindful that Luxea had once been involved with one of Widow's underlings, Ares' questions concerning the evils within the Joined Hands harrowed him. He backtracked to Oscerin. She'd struck him so confrontationally with demands to guard the stars back then. She must've been cognizant from the start that Luxea would be perilous to the Brood Mother — maybe before Ares had even met her.

Avari furiously babbled, "If Cherish was your instructor, what the hells was he doing following us around all creepy-like? I can't imagine you were that bad of a student, Luxie."

Luxea shook her head. "He didn't tell me why —"

"He's Widow's servant," said Ares, not wanting to be heard.

"What? How do you . . . ?"

Dubious, Luxea's stars darted around Ares. He lowered his eyes to his muddy boots. She didn't want to ask him then, but she would later.

Avari yowled, "I'm glad Cherish is gone then — damn! I would've kicked his scrawny arse straight into the spirit realm if I knew. No. I won't let Cherish touch you, and not Widow. Never you!"

Luxea presented her blackened hand. "They already have. Cherish called it the *'nightmare venom.'* He said there's no way to nullify it. It's poison, so I thought you'd have some insight."

Avari sought answers in Luxea's fingers. After a while, she pinpointed a microscopic speck on the back of her index finger. "He stuck you right here. How did that happen?" she inquired.

Luxea unearthed the timekeeper ring from her pocket. Avari flipped it upside-down and saw a cylinder the circumference of a human hair within it. Timed pressure, that's how Cherish managed it.

"All right," said Avari, running her finger along Luxea's hand. "A part of this formula was deployed instantaneously, but I don't know *what.* Up here, at your elbow and shoulder, I see veins just as dark as the ones in your hand. That would suggest that it's spreading — but it shouldn't be. The injection point isn't located over any veins, it wasn't administered into your bloodstream . . . but they're black too."

Oliver laughed, "Did the dickhead miss?"

"I think he missed on purpose," said Avari gravely. "Luxie, can I try something? It'll only hurt a bit. I promise."

Luxea let her. Avari picked out her slimmest blade and positioned the tip over a black vein in Luxea's arm. Luxea distracted herself with the rain on the window as Avari nicked her skin. The swelling bead of blood was black like Avari had expected it to be.

"I have to make one more. Don't move."

Avari targeted one the bluish veins in the crook of Luxea's arm and pricked it. The blood was as red as it should've been. Avari's eyes turned to glass. She tossed her knife onto the table. A bolt came loose from the haft and rolled off the edge. She slumped into her chair, washed out.

"Cherish was right. It can't be removed from your bloodstream because it hasn't touched it. That isn't a bad thing, but it's not a good thing," she said, clearing her throat often. "I think it's almost like a parasite. It isn't affecting you yet 'cause it isn't finished growing."

"The thing is —" Avari hemmed and crossed her arms, "— it created a second circulatory system right next to your original one. Cherish didn't worry about hitting your veins 'cause that's not how the compound was structured to perform. This was made to give you new blood. Introducing it into your bloodstream might've killed you instantly. It wasn't, so it'll hit you slower . . . but it'll still hit you."

Avari bent over into her knees and cried, "I don't think I how to fix this one, Luxie."

The discussion about poisons ended in tears. After that, Ares, Luxea, and Oliver dragged themselves to their rooms. Oliver tried to make them laugh along the way, but even he was having trouble finding humor at a time like this. Ares suggested that he and Luxea switch rooms, allowing her to have her own.

At the door, Ares stalled. "Luxea, may we speak in private?"

"I think that's a great idea," she said suspiciously.

At the end of the hallway was a balcony with an awning. Ares lit the only one of his cigarettes that hadn't been soaked down to the last shaving. That moment was peaceful, a moment of rain without words.

"You know something that I don't," said Luxea, breaking the quiet.

"Yes. That's why I asked you here," said Ares bracingly. He fumbled with the rings on his fingers. "I shouldn't reveal this, but for what happened tonight to make sense, I have to. At Villa de Taress, Amo and I were informed that Widow was there with us."

"What? At the gala? But what do you — ?"

"Please, wait to ask me questions," implored Ares. "Widow came to proffer a contract to the Empress. I regret to say that Goldenrise has been signed away, but now that I've spoken with Cherish, that's the least of —"

"So when we freed Runa from Haven, we were stumbling around in enemy territory? And now that we've left Goldenrise vulnerable, it *still* belongs to Widow?" asked Luxea heatedly.

Ares burned most of his cigarette in one tense inhale. "That isn't the point. I assume you recall what the Sun Chief told us? Goldenrise was never meant to fall. Something forced Widow to act, a threat. Cherish said the same to me tonight. He rearranged the Riddling Roads, led us to Witchsleep, and revealed to me that the threat was . . . you."

Luxea's stars blew out to black. "Me? But that can't be true. The reason all of those people died was so that Widow could kill *me?* And now everyone in Goldenrise will . . ."

The physical pain that Luxea had felt transformed into guilt. She hid her face in her blackened hand and started to cry. Ares touched her head and said, "Luxea, I tried to stop Cherish, I swear —"

She pushed him. "This isn't about me, it's about Goldenrise! You didn't see Lor'thanin, but *I* did. Now we've left Solissium to meet the same fate because you told us the empire would be safe. We shouldn't be going to Tarot, we should be getting those people out! I thought the Mooncallers stood for offering help to others. Was that a lie too?"

Ares flicked his cigarette into the rain. "Peyamo and I vowed secrecy for Annalais's sake. If her people learned of her oath to the Brood, they would overthrow her. That would only make it easier for Widow to take what She wants! Hells, Luxea. I shouldn't have shared any of this if all you're going to do is —"

"— if all I'll do is be honest?" asked Luxea belligerently. "You lied to all of us, Ares. I can't wait for Goldenrise to burn. Maybe then you'll realize that your silence is what started the fire!"

Ares knew Luxea was right, but the despair in her eyes stole his voice and hurt him in ways that cuts and poisons couldn't contest. She creaked open the door and gave him one last show of her smoky cherry blossom stars.

In hardly more than a whisper, Luxea said, "Oscerin once told a sad little boy that a true king is a man who acts in the best interest of the needy, not of the rapacious. No wonder you aren't a king."

✺

Two days passed. The angst in the carriage was dense enough to touch. Ares and Luxea weren't necessarily angry, but it ached to be near each other. Her words had left him with a darkening bruise. He'd tried to remember that The Six must take actions of which others have no understanding, but he started to slip away from that belief the more that he pushed it upon himself. He really was a liar. He'd known it from the start but thought that he was the only one who could see it.

It had been raining nonstop in Tarot, but somehow, the terrain was bone dry. The region consisted of jagged, red rocks and rifts in the ground that showed rippling, petrified lava.

In the Shifting City, the carriage tilted back on an incline and slowed beneath the Lady Peyamo's fortress, *Thali ou Tirima* — the Throne of the Sun.

The size and mechanics of the structure hardly made sense. It hovered, and all that was keeping it afloat were gilded wings and springy posts around the bottom radius. The midsection lit up the city beneath it in a rose-golden glow, and the crown was made of glass paneling.

Peyamo Nelnah waved her mechanical arm as the Mooncallers vacated the carriage. She approached Ares with the intent of giving him one of her breathtaking hugs, but she backed down when she noticed the darkness under his eyes and the lifelessness in his face. She patted his back instead.

Luxea approached. Ares left to unload the carriage. Peyamo told her, "S'a pleasure to see you, Starlight. How're you farin'?"

"I'm fine," said Luxea, obscuring her hand.

"Let's get you all inside, hm? I'm sure you're tired. I'll show you 'round and grab you ales if you'd like," offered Peyamo.

The Mooncallers dragged their bags to *Thali ou Tirima*'s platform where above were accordion posts. Peyamo yanked on a lever that was hooked to a copper box with blinking red, green, and yellow lights. The platform lurched as it ascended vertically.

They were let out into a boiler room where all things turned like clockwork. The grinding of cogs and sprockets was startlingly loud. Soot-coated workers scurried up rickety scaffoldings and commuted along platforms to and from their stations.

The rest of *Thali ou Tirima* was just as lackluster visually but more extraordinary in every other respect. Spare weapons, ammunition, escape pods, first aid kits, rations, and survival necessities were packed into glass lockers along the walls.

After touring the army and mender wings, they were led to a parlor that was more of a cozy storeroom. It had velveteen couches with mismatched pillows, ale kegs and wine casks stacked askew, and a stage with a metal pole in the center. The Lady's explanation for this addition was *'sometimes my men get drunk and start to sing.'*

The commissary could be reached through a giant tube. Peyamo introduced her head chefs, a pair of rotund twins with glistening, bald heads and curlicue facial hairs named Kurloy and Bavani. Neither of them could get the name of the Lady's visitors right.

Kurloy called them *'Mooncrawlers.'* Bavani corrected him by saying that they were called *'Moonscholars.'* After a few minutes of bickering, the twins agreed that the word was *'Mooncobblers.'*

Peyamo reminded the Mooncallers that she'd employed Kurloy and Bavani to work in the kitchens for a reason. Their culinary skills were sound, but they had shortcomings with just about everything else.

They crisscrossed bridges into the core of *Thali ou Tirima.* Such heights allowed them to see every curvature of the interior. The fortress was divided into vertical segments like the slices of a tangerine. The most eye-catching sector was the botanical unit. Mist poured over the railings, and dewy petrichor floated on the air.

Lastly, Peyamo showed them where they would rest their heads. The sleeping enclave was puzzling. Rather than separate chambers, the quarters were made up of scaffolds that stretched up to the roofline. Luxea counted eighteen stories.

Some without a word, the Mooncallers retired to their lofts. Avari took the second level, Oliver the third, Luxea the fourth, and Brielle and Ruka were given a space on the bottom floor that was usually a public lounge.

As Ares was about to claim his own area, Peyamo asked, "May we speak? I have a thing or two to tell you, and I'd like to know what's on your mind. It's as plain as a slice o' bread that you're upset."

The Lady's eye buzzed as the lenses switched. Ares spat a *'tshh'* through his lips. He hated it when Peyamo scanned his vital signs.

"My infrared sensors say your body temperature is high. It usually is for you, but this is up there — one-eleven point three. Not good.

Your heart rate is restin' 'round one-forty too. Either you're feverin', chuffin' too many darts, or somethin's buggin' you," listed Peyamo.

Ares booted his bag to the loft ladder. "Fine, but let it be quick. I pray whatever you have to share is something good," he growled.

The Lady Peyamo's office was more of a vault. A hatch to the right led to nowhere but a 200-foot drop, a smoky, clunking furnace was on the left, and a bronze armillary sphere hung from the ceiling. It made Ares homesick. Peyamo had built the silver armillary sphere in his Ruby Bureau years ago.

Peyamo batted the coals inside of the furnace and sat in a patchy armchair across from Ares. She poured them each a bumper of oilshine black, a seroden elvish wine considered a delicacy. Ares despised the stuff, but it packed a punch, and that was all he cared about. He gulped the whole thing.

Now Peyamo was positive that there was something very nasty on his mind. Never would he drink oilshine so greedily in any other case. She filled a second glass, but he took his time with this one.

"I'll give you a minute. Let me have introductions," said Peyamo, binding her charred fingers over her stomach. "I transported Garamat to the Phoenix Palace, and there's somethin' wrong there."

"What of Ralvesh? Assuming you met him, were you given the opportunity to pass on your worries?" asked Ares with a swig.

"He's the problem. The boy's demented," said Peyamo grimly.

"Ralvesh and I conversed four years ago during a memorial service. He's strong-willed, sophisticated, well-rounded," listed Ares.

"Yea? Well, somethin's changed. You think a 'well-rounded' man would choose Widow over The Six?" growled Peyamo.

Ares froze with a draft of oilshine in his mouth. "He's considering siding with the Brood? Then . . . we can't call him our ally. Ank'tatra's affiliation is vital to The Six, but giving a madman the key to constitutional power would lay another brick on the road to catastrophe. We're well supplied with that as it is."

Peyamo huffed, "You ain't hearin' me. Ralvesh has already got the key, he's already Widow's servant. I *saw* Her, Ares. She's human and spider — She's stunning, but in a way that terrifies me."

"Look, Ralvesh conspired with Widow to set up Garamat. They used Ralvesh's life as an incentive, but Ralvesh made a deal with Her before then. They turned Ank'tatra against Garamat and sent him to Solissium with the intent of us killin' him so that Ralvesh could snake 'imself into the throne."

"When I got to the Phoenix Palace, Ralvesh took the Sun Chief's signet off Garamat's finger and tittered n' cooed like a love-tickled maiden while his blasted tiger ate whatever was left. That ain't nothin' you do to your own blood. Ralvesh has got a screw loose — or ten. The Six ain't got a relationship with Ank'tatra no more."

Ares now understood why Garamat had done what he did. He'd only feared for his son, but Ralvesh had been playing bait. Garamat had died for villainy when he'd thought he was dying for love.

Furthermore, The Six now had such scarce leverage that it could no longer be a federation. Goldenrise and Ank'tatra were Widow's property, and Tzapodia and Tarot were the last two leading societies free of Her influence. Ares' perspicacity whispered to him portents of a highly flammable scenario.

"I take from your lack o' words that you get it," said Peyamo after a spell of silence. She nervously loosened a bolt in her forearm and tightened it again. "Listen. Tzapodia's in more of a shit sandwich than we are, so I think it's best if I stay in L'arneth when I take you n' your friends home. I'll extend technology to you that'll make or break your chances — and I've got to get that locomotive done."

"It'll be necessary," said Ares, kneading his head. "Any support is welcome. I doubt Tzapodia has much to offer you, but if the Brood closes in on Tarot, *Thali ou Tirima* has a home in my country."

"Ha. Thank you, Ares, but if I don't got to move *Thali,* I won't. Takes a lot of energy to lift this babe," chuckled Peyamo. "I'm done botherin' you with all that. I want to hear what's eatin' at you."

In one swill, Ares finished his oilshine and helped himself to the decanter. Discussing Ralvesh's treachery and emergency measures had somehow calmed him. He affixed to the flames inside of the furnace. A log shifted, and a swarm of embers sailed out of the air vent. He pretended they were stars.

"The threat," he said desolately.

"The what?" asked Peyamo.

"The reason Goldenrise suffered when it wasn't meant to, the one that Widow fears. I know who it was," said Ares, resting his mouth on his hand. "Is it me, you, or Anna? No. The one She fears is Luxea."

"Starlight? How's Widow know about her?" gasped Peyamo.

"I don't know. When She failed to eliminate her at Villa de Taress, She sent a servant after us," briefed Ares. "Luxea was inflicted with a poison called *'nightmare venom.'* It's very likely that she'll die."

Peyamo frowned. "But she seemed well n' good earlier. Didn't she? I looked her right in the eye, and she told me —"

"If you were at death's door and asked *'how are you doing?'* would you answer truthfully?" snarled Ares. "She scarcely talks, her legs shake, she was once the light of the stars, but now she's the emptiness in-between."

"Amo, the one thing I —" Ares shut his eyes, a sting, "— the one thing Oscerin demanded I keep safe will be gone. Every turn we've taken has buried us deeper in this mess. We should've known that night at the gala that it would only get worse — hells, I *did* know! And still, we left the empire vulnerable, and I lied to all of them for The Six's sake. Now The Six is broken. It wasn't worth the untruth. I don't want to do it anymore."

"Where's all this comin' from? You're never this dithery. I hear you, Ares, but the decisions we made in Goldenrise were for the welfare of the empire. Don't you lose hope even if we lose Luxea. You've lost before, you can do it again," encouraged Peyamo.

She touched Ares' hand; it felt like a burn. Ares ran his thumb over the Felastil and searched for warmth within the jewel, but there was none.

Of What is Real
23.Nightspeak.25.Osc.3

Avari and Luxea made an outing. Since the day they met, Avari had envisioned roving through the Shifting City with Luxea. They might have gone sandling fishing, roof-jumping, or Luxea could've put on a magick show in the exchange. But she could barely walk.

Luxea had never seen a place like the Shifting City. It clashed with the world that she was used to like orange and blue. The concrete was slippery with grime and oil slicks, the buildings were trussed by wooden planks, and the dips of the corrugated metal roofs were crusted with verdigris.

The first place they went was the Cookery District. Luxea wasn't surprised. Avari's palate outshone everyone else's. Mobs of residents and tourists commingled at the roadside. Luxea was baffled by how many seroden elves looked just like Avari. The bulk wore odd contraptions on their heads alike to the mechanized eye that Peyamo had implemented into her skull, but these had round, colorful lenses.

Avari stopped in front of a tiny bakeshop that was far over the maximum capacity. The wooden sign over the door had the seroden name written in peeling, green paint. *'Tafida Dekda,'* or *'Welcome Bakery.'* Inside, Luxea stood awkwardly taller than everybody else. She started to wonder if this was how Ares felt, but she extracted the thought of him from her ear.

There were two-person tables with crocheted mats draped upon them, and desert air-plants swinging in front of the circular windows. Beyond the line of hankering customers were plump bakers dressed in red garments with matching hats.

The display cases were packed with muffins, buns, puddings, cakes, pies, and also some sweets that Luxea couldn't have possibly cared less for. She cringed at the *'decadent sandworm éclairs.'* The sandworms were ribbed, coated in roasted, beady eyes, and Luxea wanted them far away from her.

"This was my favorite shop when I was small," said Avari, feasting her honey-brown eyes upon the bleached-out wall hangings. "My cousin Vina and I would skip our lessons and end up here. The head baker gave us free pastries before sending us off again."

Somehow, Luxea's vision of a young Avari still had a scarf wrapped around her head. Her stars explored the cramped spaces between the tables, and she could almost see two girls scampering beneath them.

"Does that baker still work here?" asked Luxea.

Avari stood up on her tiptoes and gasped, "Yes! There he is! The one on the left with no hair 'cept for in his ears. See him?"

Luxea did see him, but she was more interested in the first bit of joy that Avari had conveyed in days.

If she could smile now, she would be able to even after Luxea's time had ended. As Avari shuffled excitedly, Luxea wondered if this would be their last adventure together.

Avari waved at the baker, and it took him one catch of her rodent teeth to remember her. "Is that *Avari'alu?*" he asked with floury lungs.

"Vatha. Hithas, Terin'amu!" greeted Avari.

Terin embraced Avari. His girthed arms made her look even smaller than she usually did. "You've gotten so big!" he chuckled.

Avari drummed upon his tomato belly and joked, "So have you!"

The two began catching up. Luxea dawdled. As she surveyed the shop, her head throbbed, the walls melted, and the voices of the customers muffled. She applied pressure to her eye sockets, and the pounding gradually let up.

Luxea opened her eyes, and a little girl was standing in front of her. She was l'arian elvish and looked like Luxea in all ways. White hair, pointed ears, round cheeks, bowed lips, but her irises were pink.

The child beckoned Luxea to the front door. Luxea eyeballed Avari; she hadn't even noticed the girl. Too curious for her own good, Luxea followed her into the hectic street.

The little girl walked like a marionette, twitching and jointed in too many places. She took a turn into a dead-ended alleyway packed with empty boxes, trash, and steam vents. At the farthest wall, the little girl hung her arms at her sides and tipped her head back. Her eyes were unhighlighted like an old doll's.

"The butterfly mustn't meet the spider's eyes," she whispered.

Luxea's teeth chattered. Cherish had said the same thing to her so long ago, in a memory. "What does that mean?" she asked.

Without an answer, the little girl pointed toward a crack in a pile of wood. In the crevice, Luxea saw a blue butterfly in a seamless web. A shiny, black spider skittered over the blanket of gossamer. It trapped the butterfly with its spindly legs and needled it with its venom. The butterfly's erratic movements subsided in paralysis.

"Hehehe!" the little girl giggled and bolted out of the alley.

Luxea yelled at her, "Come back! Why did you show me — ?"

Something tickled Luxea's hair. She brushed the back of her head, and it crunched. She went grey in the face. Tiny cotton balls were matted into the strands. She removed her hand. Thousands of spiders filled the spaces between her fingers. She batted herself. The spiders drifted to the ground and skittered up her legs again. The more she swatted away, the more appeared.

The egg sacs in Luxea's hair burst and let loose a legion of bulblike abdomens and angular legs. The spiders hooked onto her mouth and trickled down from her hairline like droplets of water. Innumerable legs closed in around the corners of her colorless eyes.

Luxea covered her face and waited for it to end.

"Hey! Wake up!" shouted Avari.

Luxea's eyes broke wide open. She inspected her hands. Not a single spider remained. She looked up and saw that it was dusk. She swore that she'd only been gone for a few minutes.

"Who was that?" asked Luxea, wiping black blood from her nose.

"Who was *who?*"

"The little girl who came to the bakery. She was here a second ago, Avari, she looked exactly like me. Who was she?"

Avari wanted to say that there was no little girl, but she didn't want to scare Luxea. She helped her to stand. "I'm not sure, kiddo. Don't worry about it, okay? Let's get back to *Thali ou Tirima.* You've got blood on you, and it's gross," she laughed.

It was nighttime when they got back to *Thali ou Tirima.* Luxea didn't interact with Avari and went straight to bed, but Avari went straight to Ares.

She located him with Brielle and Ruka inside of the commissary. Brielle was feeding Ruka fenlaig pies, and Ares was enjoying a fruit bowl. When Avari stepped over the threshold, her eyes slopped over with tears.

"I need — to talk to you — Ares," she choked out.

"What's the matter? Sit. Ruka will warm you," said Brielle.

Avari flopped onto the wolf's flank and sobbed. "Luxie isn't doing good. I took her into the city this afternoon — I've wanted to for so long. We went to a bakery, and she just vanished! She never runs out on me! Never! I looked around for her for hours, and no one had seen her. S'not like it's hard to find her in Tarot, her head sticks out like a bare arse, but she was gone!"

"I climbed onto the rooftops, and thank the gods I did. I found her curled up on the ground in a blind alley. I asked her what she was doing there, and I don't think she knew why. All she asked me was *'who was that little girl?'* But there was no little girl! She swore someone'd led her there, a girl that looks just like her. But there was nobody! It wasn't real!"

"She's having hallucinations?" asked Ares.

"No. She's having nightmares," said Brielle, tapping her palm.

"I don't care what she's having! Now she won't talk to me! She's pushing the world further and further away," cried Avari, scratching her knees through her leggings.

Brielle and Ruka swapped glances. They'd witnessed Luxea's behavior in nature many times. Brielle whispered, "When an animal accepts that it's dying, it finds relief in isolation. It fears that it will be a burden to their pack, or it might starve for the peace of wasting away alone. But at times, it simply cannot bear to say goodbye."

Two days later, Ares draped over the edge of his loft. He heard the scrape of curtain hooks, and Luxea surfaced beneath him. His slender legs dangled over her head, but she didn't notice them as she left the enclave. Ares thought that she was going to the botanical unit; he knew that she favored being in nature.

He slid down the ladder to the fourth level. It was daytime, and call girls were in short supply in *Thali ou Tirima,* so Oliver was like enough not anywhere but his loft.

Oliver answered, but his eyes were so inflated with sleep that he could barely see. "Need somethin'?" he moaned.

"Yes . . . for Luxea," said Ares a bit shyly. "Go to the botanical unit and talk to her. She's partial to being alone, but it's killing me to see. Check on her and do whatever will make her happy."

"Anything for Luxie. Makin' her laugh's my favorite thing to do." Oliver went bitter. "But why don't you do it, mate?"

"I'd bring her more misery. Don't ask me why," said Ares guiltily. "You know how to make her smile; I've never seen you fail. Please."

"No worries. She'll have the cheesiest o' cheesin' grins when I'm finished with her. I promise," said Oliver, collecting his cloak.

"Thank you, but keep your hands to yourself," said Ares gallantly.

The artificial world inside of *Thali ou Tirima*'s botanical unit was remarkable, but Luxea pined for tall trees, blooming flowers, and babbling rivers. This was the closest she could get.

Her gloomy stars trailed around the synthetic foliage. The spectrum of green, rose-gold, and aqua was made all the more vibrant by the afternoon sunlight that melted in through the windows.

Layers of water-dwelling plants swayed beneath the surface of the water reservoir. Luxea spied a tuft of riverroot in the shadows by her feet. Mollah had always had riverroot laying around the infirmary.

"There's the starry princess. Blissit, s'real pretty in here," said Oliver cheerily. He settled down at Luxea's side. His legs were slightly longer, so he shimmied back to keep his toes from grazing the water. "Sorry if I'm buggin' you. I just miss you."

"I've missed you too," drawled Luxea.

"Don't sound too serious. Try again, love."

Luxea smiled a little. "Sorry. I missed you too, Oli."

"There we go," giggled Oliver. "Yunno, m'always here if you need me, Luxie. Always. We don't got to talk 'bout bad things. How 'bout I give you a piggyback ride? It'll be fun, I promise —"

"It's all right," said Luxea disconsolately. "I'm sorry I'm so quiet. I've just been straining to make sense of everything. Anything. I can't determine what's real and what isn't."

Luxea wasn't referring to the nightmare venom. Death was closing in, but she had a harder time stomaching her involvement with the Widow, Goldenrise's fall, and Ares' retainment of information than how thin time ran. Luxea wondered if she was still the only one who knew the truth about that night at the gala.

"Did Ares tell you?" she wondered.

Oliver scratched his head and sighed, "Fine . . . I came here 'cause Ares asked me to check on you. He's just worried. But I have missed you, Luxie, I swear!"

"That's not —" Luxea swallowed. "He asked you to come here?"

Oliver bashfully swung his legs. "Yea. He wanted me to make you smile. He thinks if he gets near you, it'll make you sad, so he sent me." He twitched his brow. "Wait, if that's not what you meant, what'd you think Ares told me?"

The answer was knocking at the back of Luxea's teeth, but indecision sucked it back into her throat. Her stars lowered to the water. "It's nothing. Sorry. I was just confused . . ." She trailed off. Where her reflection should've been rippled the little girl. "Oli, do you see her? The little girl."

All that Oliver saw was Luxea's mirror image. Spineless, he retracted his legs and squeaked, "Don't joke 'round like that."

"I'm not joking," said Luxea vacantly.

The little girl pressed her palm to the underside of the water, and her fingers blew wavelets across the surface. Luxea extended her blackened hand, meeting with the reflection's. When her skin kissed the shallows, the little girl ruptured out of the reservoir and yanked Luxea into the realm beneath.

Oliver saw Luxea tip into the water. She floated for a moment, and then she splashed feverishly. He ripped off his cloak and jumped in after her.

The little girl drove Luxea's head to the bottom. Luxea scratched her hands to pry them off. The little girl's eyes spiraled madly. In a voice that could've cut metal, she shrieked, "STOP SCARING HER! STOP SCARING HER! STOP SCARING HER!"

Lanky arms folded around Luxea's stomach. In moments, she was back in the botanical unit. Oliver fell backward and shook out his hair. He looked into Luxea's face and saw black veins forked through the skin beneath her eyes. Only a few stars were left within her irises.

Oliver inhaled and exhaled slowly, saying, "Breathe with me, aye? Don't got to hurry, love. Just breathe slow."

Shivering, Luxea took in a gulp of air and let it out in a stream. She swept the water and found merely her own soaking reflection staring back. The little girl was gone.

Once Oliver had helped Luxea back into her loft, he climbed up the ladder to the fifth level and knuckled the wall. Ares' face appeared in the gap between the curtains moments later.

"Can I come in?" asked Oliver at once.

Ares inspected Oliver's drenched hair and clothing before sliding open the curtain. Oliver crawled into his loft and noticed that there were tens of textbooks about poisons strewn across Ares' bedroll.

Oliver sat crosslegged, and Ares tossed him a rag. Oliver began to dry himself off and shaking droplets out of his ear. "I talked to her. Didn't go too good. She was all jumpy, confused, n' went n' tipped right into a pond. Thought she saw a little girl in the water."

Ares shut his eyes, looking distraught. Oliver stopped swabbing himself and asked, "But are you doin' awright?"

"I'm . . . no," said Ares under his breath. "If I could change anything, it would be everything."

"Well, if you really want to change somethin', why don't you go n' talk to Luxie?" questioned Oliver. "I hate to admit, but you might not get anotha' chance."

"It's better for her if I say nothing," said Ares grievingly.

Oliver's expression darkened. He flung the rag back toward Ares and asked, "That day in your bureau, I told you everythin' I thought'd help you out — 'cept for the most painful part. Wanna hear it?"

"Yes," said Ares quietly.

Oliver blinked at the floor. "While ago, I used to see this girl. Her name was Tell. I ended up givin' her a kid, but back then, I was too scared of that commitment shite — hells, I never won't be — so I left her. Nine months later, she had a daughter. Named her Rosamie."

"On Rosamie's fourth lifeday, I brought her a present. Wasn't nothin' good, I don't know what kids fancy. When I held her for the first time, she poked me in the eye. But I didn't care. I still loved her. Then Tell kicked me out n' told me to stay away from them, so I did. I thought it was best."

"When Widow came, I knew those two weren't safe. Didn't care much for Tell, still don't, but Rosamie . . . I wanted to go to 'em, but I thought Tell wouldn't want me there."

"Couple weeks later, I gave in n' ran to their flat. When I got there, all that was left was ash. I spent hours tryin' to figure out which bones were theirs. I'd stayed away from Rosamie all those years 'cause I thought it'd make her life betta', n' look where she's at now. All 'cause I didn't get to her fast enough."

Oliver's glare cut through Ares. "You know what I wouldn't give to have the chance to say goodbye to my daughter? To look at her face one more time? And you're scared of talkin' to Luxie when she's sleepin' ten feet under us — still breathin'? Come off it, Ares."

CRYSTAL STRANGERS
26.NIGHTSPEAK.25.OSC.3

ARES HAD a dream. There was an ocean. White sparked, and thunder quaked. He was suspended inside of a killer storm. A low, buttery voice seeped into his ears. It was Oscerin's.

"The stars have little time left. Death hungers for her, and you have failed to prevent it. Your truth wanes, and duty blinds you to what is right. I cannot help you while that is amiss."

Ares shut his eyes tight. "You're going to leave me, aren't You?"

"I am not abandoning you, Ares," said Oscerin mercifully. *"I've come to grant you one chance to reverse a stroke that has befallen my grace. I reveal this to you so that you might stop the shadow ere it consumes her. There is a reason that evil cowers in her light. If she dies, your world dies with her."*

"But how am I to stop it? Tell me what Widow wants with Luxea, why her survival is so critical. There's so much I don't understand, and You keep Your silence! I deserve to know why this — !"

Ares was stricken still by the echoes of Luxea declaring the same.

"You grasp her anger with you. Good," said Oscerin contentedly. *"There is much that you cannot see, but I will bestow upon you a glimpse. You are white, the Widow is black, and the starlight is my sacred divide. If you strive for Amniven's fortitude . . . take her to Sh'tarr's Iris."*

Trembling, Ares looked into the funnel of clouds above. "What hope is there for her inside of a storm?"

"The Iris is not a storm, it is a mask," said Oscerin.

The cyclones surrounding Ares unlaced. Beyond their crashing and thrashing was an island. The terrain was carpeted with colorful vegetation, and white crystals spiraled upward from the crust.

"What is this?" mouthed Ares.

"The forgotten strand of Mythos," informed Oscerin. Beyond the mantle of storms loomed the Crystal Spire, attached to the island at the base. *"In ancient days, Sirah gave birth. They were named 'Sil'simani,' Sacred children, but have also been called 'Mythics.'"*

At the foot of the Crystal Spire, Ares shaped out the silhouettes of tall, crystalline beings, but he couldn't see their faces. Dubious, he asked, "Mythics? But I've never heard of anything like this."

"The divines intended for them to be lost. Man craved their flesh, and when the pollution of greed impended the Mythics' doom, Alatos pulled Mythos into the sea."

Eternity's Ocean expanded, and the Crystal Spire gained distance from Mythos until it was enveloped by storms.

"To preserve their innocence, Sh'tarr conjured a storm around Mythos. For millennia, Sh'tarr and Alatos have remained the sworn protectors, and the Mythics have been impervious to modern influence. Never has a mortal soul beheld them, but that cycle must be broken."

"The Mythics read energy like you read books. They will know you are coming long before you arrive. Think of a tree. Every leaf is a separate entity, but the roots make them one."

A tree materialized in the clouds, transparent to expose the shimmering veins that pulsed through the branches.

"These creatures are a single soul divided into a nexus of minds. Their purity makes them capable of performing miracles. The growth of nature, temporal manipulation, inter-locus travel, and healing. That is why you must go, or watch all life burn away."

"It's impossible to make it through that storm alive, Oscerin. It would kill us all!" wailed Ares. "Even if I tried to convince Peyamo to do this for me, she would never oblige. She thinks our survival is critical to repairing The Six, and no ship could withstand the — !"

"Silence! I did not choose The Six to serve at my behest, I chose Ares! No ship, no aid! The irons bodies of man's make are weak, but you are not!" screamed Oscerin louder than thunder.

Ares was inside of the eye. Far away, the Irestar sailed above him.

"In three days, my Irestar will course over Sh'tarr's Iris. You must reach the storm at that moment, no earlier, no later, and I will thereby grant you passage to Mythos."

The Irestar halted over Sh'tarr's Iris, and the storms died instantly.

"The tides of sea and air are the Moon's to control when I stand over them. Sh'tarr and Alatos will be deemed powerless, ergo I may carry you."

The ocean swelled high enough to touch the clouds.

"Beware, the Sisters of Storm and Sea will give Their all to kill you. To Them, you will be a trespasser, a contamination. But with the stars in your hands, that is when I see you the clearest, and I will reach you. You must only promise me that you will refuse ruination."

Ares shielded his eyes from the dread of the answer he was about to give to Her. "I'll go. I'll take Luxea to the Iris."

"Promise me!" pleaded Oscerin.

"I promise," he said under his breath.

A warm breeze caressed his cheek. *"I will be with you, my child."*

Ares gasped and sprang up in his bedroll. Sweat soaked his bare back like the rain had followed him out of his dream. He folded his arms around his head and curled his talons into his hair, bracing for the revision of destiny's weave.

✗

A day later, Luxea woke up with slush in her veins. The Mooncallers would depart for Tzapodia erelong, and she feared that nothing would save her from the skyway air.

The Mooncallers ventured up the staircase to the airship landing, but Luxea's legs were betraying her. Her pulse was erratic, her vision spun, and at the fifth step, her ankles slipped. Brielle caught her.

"Don't force yourself, Starlight," she uttered.

Ruka had refused to go near Luxea since the night Cherish had attacked, but as death embraced her, he pondered how frightened *she* must be. He stooped low and nudged her weak knees.

"My brother is asking to carry you," said Brielle tenderly.

On the landing platform, the Mooncallers were captivated by *Matha ou Machina.* Navy sails scooped the high winds, hot air blasted from the propellers, and vents whistled with exhaust from the engines.

"Hithas, senase! It's a delight to see you all — and you, Your Highness. At last, on my own turf," greeted Nika, but Ares' attention was fastened onto Luxea. Nika hemmed, "Erm, Your Highness?"

Ares blinked himself out of his head. "Forgive me. Likewise."

Avari boarded the airship without batting an eyelash. Oliver took his time. Far below was a fatal drop, and all that separated him from falling was a flimsy metal sheet. Brielle idled with Ruka and Luxea, supremely unsure as she watched the ramp wobble under that skinny aestof's footsteps.

"Dirty Boy! Will the metal beast carry my brother?" called Brielle.

Nika looked both ways and realized that she was addressing him. He studied Ruka and estimated his weight. "We may be a tad over the limit, but maximum capacity is more of a suggestion than a rule."

Ruka whimpered frightfully, but Brielle thought it was best to trust those strange elves and their stranger machines.

"Walk slow, Brother. You'll make it," urged Brielle.

Ruka's nails raked the flooring as Brielle pushed him along. The ramp bent under his heaviness, and Luxea started to slip from his back halfway up. He scurried to the end with his tail tucked.

After the fact, the airship gate was terribly warped out of shape. A sky-sailor hastened to the ramp and folded it inward once everyone was on deck. The metal screeched unpleasantly, but they managed to bring it close enough to the hull to just barely latch the gate.

Oliver white-knuckled the railing. "We're gonna capsize!"

"The Lady's design has no faults," said Avari sternly.

"I'll love to hear that again when we're free-fallin' to our deaths."

Luxea opened her eyes as Ruka lay down. They hadn't even taken to the sky, but she was too cold to feel her nose. To distract herself, she watched the cogs and gears at *Matha ou Machina's* bow gyrate at slow speeds. Some were as big as placemats, and others, dining tables.

Peyamo emerged from an opening abaft. "Welcome! She's a beauty, ain't she? Got a few bolts loose, but she's bigger n' better than anyone else's ship — sky or sea."

No one responded. Flashing Luxea a pained glance, Peyamo stomped to the helm and popped open the intercom lid. Nika snapped his goggles on over his eyes and yanked a few levers into position.

Peyamo yelled into the intercom, "Sharney, let's get 'er on up!"

The airship rumbled, the crankshafts at the bow spun faster, and steam shot out of every tube. A vent by Ares' feet screamed oily-smelling air up the back of his coat.

Matha ou Machina heeled as it dislodged from the landing. The anchors *snapped* as they struck the hull, and stomachs lurched with the change in elevation. The airship rose up, up, and up. Clouds rushed through cracks and swirled around the passengers. Nika banked west over Eternity's Ocean.

By mid-afternoon the next day, *Matha ou Machina* had surpassed Anatatri's Grasp and was gliding downwind. As Ruka offered his warmth to Luxea, Brielle shot arrows over the handrail, impaling birds each time one flew by. There wasn't a point to their deaths, but Brielle was starting to believe that there never was.

Ares watched the rain bands of Sh'tarr's Iris. The center was hundreds of reaches away, yet the area of effect was so expansive that it looked as if it were right in front of him. As he stared, he tried to convince himself that the Mythics would be able to reverse Luxea's malady, but his defeatist mentality begged him not to believe it.

If there were books aboard *Matha ou Machina,* Ares would have searched all of them, but even then, there'd be no mention of the Mythics. They were meant to be forgotten, after all. He was desperate for confirmation, but he would just have to torture himself with questions as Sh'tarr's Iris laughed at him from afar.

Just then, an arrow zipped past Ares' head and stuck a seabird twenty or so feet from the handrail. He spun around. Brielle pretended like she was doing something else. Ares inhaled to admonish her, but then he was pierced by an idea; he much preferred that to an arrow.

"May I speak with you, Brielle?" he requested.

"It was nowhere close to you, Dragon. If I'd aimed for your head, it would be gone!" barked Brielle.

"I only have a question," said Ares calmly. Brielle joined him abreast. "How much do you know about forgotten legends?"

"More than you," said Brielle bumptiously.

"I don't doubt it. There were once beings born from the Crystal Spire called *'Sil'simani.'* Have you any knowledge on them?" asked Ares, lighting up a cigarette.

"*'Sacred children,'*" translated Brielle. She touched her left temple, and her lips formed words without sound. "I've harbored many a story, but some surpass even the eldest of teachings. This may be one of them. I'm sorry, Dragon, but I fail to —"

"Brie! I know of what Dragon asks!" cut in Ruka. *"What about the legend of Wynd and the Crystal Strangers?"*

Brielle's thorny gaze softened. "Good thinking, Brother."

"What's Ruka saying to you?" pestered Ares.

"You'll get no answers until you give me some first," bit Brielle. "Your aroma is different lately. Like —" she sniffed him, "— like cocoa." Ares smelled himself. "And it's out of character for you to come to me like this. Confess. Why ask me about the *Sil'simani?*"

Ares didn't want to answer. His eyes shifted to the side slyly, and he said, "If you tell me . . . I'll have a fresh fenlaig delivered to Ruka every day in Tel Ashir. He can eat them alive. Indoors."

Ruka panted hungrily. Save for Brielle, he prized fenlaig meat the most in this world. Brielle would have never denied Ruka something that he loves, even if it came from a bribe with a dragon.

"Two fresh fenlaigs," said Brielle greedily.

"Two?"

"Yes, or no legends for you."

Ares hadn't even heard of a ranch that would have sufficient fenlaigs to meet Brielle's demands, but he supposed that he would have to find one now.

"Fine. Two fenlaigs every day," he sighed.

Ruka didn't know what to do with himself, so he licked Luxea's hair. Looking smug, Brielle grabbed Ares' cigarette. He relinquished it to her and lit himself another. Brielle puffed, and her eyes ate the sky.

"The God of Stags was born with the most glorious antlers of His ilk. Every night that the Irestar shone upon them, another tine would grow. Eventually, they were a reach long."

"Humankind coveted Wynd's antlers. They could forge the finest weapons and armors from the crown of a god. To lure Him, they polished a silver platter and tucked it into a bed of flowers where the Irestar reflected upon it in the evening."

"Wynd was cunning but also too curious for His own good. He believed that moonlight had fallen as a gift to Him, but when He approached, the humans gouged the antlers from His head with their dirks and poniards."

"Wynd's head was bare. He questioned His purpose and hated His foolishness, so He gave up. He sank into the soil . . . and then He was visited by strangers of crystal light."

"The crystal strangers set their hands upon Wynd, absorbed His pain as their own, and bestowed upon Him antlers of opal. When Wynd next opened His eyes, the crystal strangers were gone. He never saw them again."

The ash of Ares' cigarette was inches long.

"They healed a god?" he breathed.

"Yes, but Wynd never thanked them. They left and didn't return again," said Brielle, marveling a bit. She traced Ares' gaze to Sh'tarr's Iris, and then something dawned on her. "Dragon, if you haven't heard the legend of Wynd and the crystal strangers . . . how did you know about them?"

Truthful, Ares said, "I saw them in a dream."

THE BUTTERFLY
27.NIGHTSPEAK.25.OSC.3

FOR HOURS, Luxea swung in a hammock. Death was becoming her, and it wasn't as kind as she'd hoped. There was no light, no warmth, and no Eletheon. It was so close that she could taste it, as sour and rich as citrus dark chocolate.

A stack of paper sat on a desk across the room. Luxea didn't know to whom it belonged, but she felt like she needed it the most. She twitched her finger. The pages, and the quill beside them, hovered toward her.

Within half an hour, Luxea had written farewell letters to Avari, Oliver, Brielle and Ruka, and Peyamo. She inked the quill to write to Ares, but she was out of paper. Ares would think she'd forgotten him.

Two stars twinkled out. Shedding enough tears to fill Eternity's Ocean, Luxea dropped the quill. Ink dyed her coat black, but she was stained anyway.

"Hasahia . . . ?" whispered the Usinnon out of the blue.

The spellbook sparkled suggestively, and Luxea remembered.

✖

Ares slumped over a table in the galley and flipped through accounts. The scent of salty wood and the sound of wind moaning made him yearn for the dry midday heat of Tel Ashir.

Peyamo cracked a flagon of malt liqueur down in front of Ares and set his paperwork aside. She hadn't heeded the pages with wet ink, and Ares thought that they must've been smeared.

"This game is: you drink when I make you smile," said Peyamo.

"Best of luck to you," said Ares bitterly.

The Lady gulped her liqueur and winced from the burn. "I had a memory today," she said casually. "You might not recall it. You were only 'bout eight I reckon. I was visitin' Tel Ashir, and your mum was feelin' green. Since she couldn't, she asked me to take you to the Fire Caves to play on the rocks with —"

"What's the point of this?" asked Ares sharply.

"Just listen," insisted Peyamo. "We explored the tide pools, built sand houses, and — oh! That's the day I taught you that tavern verse."

Ares bobbed his head. "Bring your flagon, drink your ale."

"Come in from the chillin' gale," continued Peyamo.

"Light your weeds and smoke them well . . ."

"I've got for you a tale to tell."

They both drank. Peyamo said, "Harsh the wind, warm the flame!"

"Part the legs of a pretty dame . . ."

"Glass will break, beds will bend . . ."

"Tomorrow, I will drink again," they said in sync.

"Good. You at least kept that in mind," said Peyamo warmly.

"Only because I was flogged for singing it," said Ares aloofly.

"O'course, you were," tittered Peyamo. "Anyhow, back to it. You went swimmin' even though it was frosttear. You splashed 'round for a long time while I sat ashore and drew in the sand; I never much liked the sea. Then I heard you cryin'. I thought you got bit by somethin' or skinned your knee, but you came runnin' out the water just fine."

"I asked you what was wrong, and you showed me a butterfly that you'd found floatin' in the waves. You knew it was dyin', but that didn't matter to you. You still tried to save it. I had to teach you that you can't stop death, and you were so angry at me for sayin' that. You told me, *'it was beautiful, I loved it!'* Then it died."

"You stopped cryin' when the butterfly stopped movin'. You stroked its broken wings for a long time. That's when you said to me the saddest thing I've ever heard you say. *'I should've died instead.'*"

Ares took three giant gulps.

Peyamo banged on the tabletop and raised her voice. "You know why I'm bringin' this up? It ain't for nothin'! I never wanted to hear that from you again, but lately, you've been screamin' it! I'll level with you, there's not much time left for that girl, but I can read you well enough to tell you're goin' to do somethin'. I won't let you if it results in you gettin' hurt."

"Stay out of this," said Ares waspishly.

"I knew it!" thundered Peyamo, swatting her tankard off of the table. "I get that you're feelin' responsible, Ares, but guilt is a disease, and we're *all* sick! Whatever you're thinkin', I best not see it happen. Don't you do crap that'll get you nowhere but dead!"

Ares stood over the table. "I make my choices. Not you," he spat.

He strode away with his belly hot from liqueur and fervor. Ares treasured Peyamo's friendship, but for the first time in years, he would follow the course that he'd determined for himself.

Two doorways down, he was delayed by tangled, white hair in his peripheral vision. He lifted his foot to move on but, as expedient as it was, looked past the doorpost anyway.

Luxea lay motionless with her coat stained black. The Usinnon was face-down on the floor. Ares rushed to her hammock, expecting her to be dead, but then he saw her breast swell softly, and the black fluid upon her outerwear was only ink. Ares sighed mightily enough to break the world.

"Hasihi . . . shi . . . shiashi. . . ."

The Usinnon sounded like it was weeping. Ares' claw slid down the hammock stake as he knelt. "Do you want to lie with her?"

"Haishi . . . hasiishiaishia. . . ."

"Will you let me hold you?"

The Usinnon twinkled. Ares was nervous that it would shock him, but he grabbed onto it regardless. It didn't hurt him. Ares set it upon Luxea's middle and lifted her arm around it with the softest touch.

A tattered page escaped from Luxea's fingers. Something beckoned Ares to it, but he didn't feel right taking it. Then the Usinnon sparked. Ares looked up, and the spellbook's gems glittered like the stars. Hoping that he was translating correctly, Ares picked up the page. It smelled like pine.

"Take care of her," he whispered.

The Usinnon's jewels faded out as it fell asleep.

Ares pulled off his tunic over his head and slipped into his hammock. He twisted on the gaslight on the shelf beside him and unfolded the paper halfway. It was upside down, so he flipped it over.

> *"Leaves may grow and fall away,*
> *but roots forever will remain."*
> *- Anonymous*

Ares skimmed the line once more, and then his gut coiled as he opened the last fold. Within was a scrawled note with his name at the top. He stroked the letter as he read. It felt like the butterfly's wings.

Ares,

I don't know how to begin nor end, but I pray I can say everything in-between. I hurt you, and while I meant what I said, I wish I hadn't said it. Because of me, we've been ghosts to each other, and I never wanted that.

Be at peace with the fact that Oscerin will carry me somewhere else. You told me that everything She gives you is beautiful, and I fear the end, but I would fear it more if it weren't for you.

There's more I have to say, but I would need a lot of paper. I pray someday I return as someone new and am blessed enough to meet you again. You will always be part of me. Death can't take that away.

Hilien ashta,
Luxea Siren

Ares brought his claw to his face, and every moment since he met Luxea bloomed behind his eyelids. That was when he made a decision. He wouldn't dive into Sh'tarr's Iris for Oscerin, for The Six, or for himself. He would do it for the one who needed it.

✘

Luxea opened her eyes the next day and saw Oliver slouched in a chair; he'd been monitoring her. He dashed to her hammock and chirped, "Mornin', love. Sleep good?"

"I'm shocked that I'm waking up at all," replied Luxea.

"Don't say things like that," sighed Oliver. "How 'bout I take you up on deck? My piggyback offa's still on the table."

Luxea's lips formed the word *'okay.'* Oliver squatted facing away from her and helped her to wrap her arms around his neck. On the weather deck, he carried her to the leeward side where it was the most sheltered. Avari assisted him in propping Luxea up against the railing.

Brielle sat down and started to braid Luxea's hair. "Do you know what braids represent in Blackjaw?" she asked, combing her scalp.

"No, I don't," said Luxea quietly.

Brielle's spaced out teeth showed as she crossed two tresses. "If it's braided over the left shoulder, the hunt will be bountiful. Down the back, frosttear will end sooner. But over the right shoulder, like yours, the battle will be won." She fastened the end with a blue ribbon that Luxea had around her wrist and whispered, "The mightiest warriors have the tightest plaits, so I made yours the strongest I could."

By some means, the braid did make Luxea feel strong. She pinched one of Brielle's hundreds of locks and said, "You have so many. You're the mightiest warrior of them all."

"Yes, I am. But today, *you* are the mightiest," said Brielle sweetly.

Across the main deck, Peyamo swiveled on the ratlines and strained to yank the mainsail away from the mast. It had been caught. Her metal fingers grazed it, but then the sail was snatched by the wind. She dropped off of the ratline and cursed.

"Avari, Brielle!" piped up Peyamo. "You two've got climbin' arms. Could I steal you for a minute to untangle this sail for me?"

Brielle squeezed Luxea's braid reassuringly. Avari breathed warm air onto Luxea's hands and promised, "I'll come right back."

Ares stepped out from abaft. He passed a glance at Luxea as Avari left her. Now was the perfect time for him to say what he wished to.

Luxea heard footsteps coming closer and stared upward. In front of her stood a pair of pale feet with ruffled skirts from the shins up. It was the little girl. Luxea had no strength to fight her off.

"Are you here to take me away? Do it," she slurred.

The little girl's eyes filled with tears. She sat on her knees and exposed her arms. Her hands were black too. Luxea then thought that this little girl was her cognition of death itself, a mirror image.

With a lump in her throat, Luxea trailed her eyes to her friends. She touched hands with the little girl. The child lifted her up, and Luxea felt no pain. If this was death, it wasn't so horrible.

Suddenly, the little girl yanked her hands away. Luxea's palm started to tingle. She saw something squirming and scratched it. Soon, she was clawing at herself and spattered in her own black blood. Her skin fell off of the bone like rice paper. Beneath were worms that burrowed around her muscles and pressed into her veins, lodging deeper and deeper.

Gusts snapped Ares' hair as he neared Luxea, but when he looked at her, his lungs deflated. She was standing up now, covered in blood, and thick, black fluid streamed from her eyes.

"Stop it, Luxea!" screamed Ares, capturing her wrists.

The arrant horror in his voice drew all eyes.

He observed as the stars twinkled out. There were only two left. He spoke to Luxea, but she could no longer hear him. Blood surged out of her mouth, and her legs buckled. He lunged for her and held her head upright. The Felastil slipped out of his shirt and hung between them. He eyed the jewel. Oscerin had told him that he would always be heard if he had the Felastil. He prayed She was right.

Ares' talons wove into Luxea's black fingers, and he enclosed her hand around the pendant. "You know I'm here, don't you? Please, hear me," he whispered.

His voice filled Luxea's mind. Tears streaked the black on her cheeks. She squeezed his hand, telling him 'yes.' Ares screwed his face and pulled her head under his chin.

"I'm sorry for everything. Never regret what you told me, I needed to hear it," he said shakily. "I promise you, I'll go back to Goldenrise and keep those people safe, but only if you go with me. I'll tell you the truth, I'll share with you all of my stories, and I'll teach you more about dancing because, honestly, you aren't that proficient at it."

Luxea smiled weakly. Ares tried to but couldn't.

"You'll live, and we'll go home. You promised Runa, didn't you? And Mollah, she would miss you so much. And I would. Who else is going to send me butterflies on my lifeday? Luxea, we have to go home. All of us. I won't settle for anything less."

Ares pressed a soft kiss to Luxea's forehead. She shut her eyes and held onto his shirt. He pulled away. When she opened her eyes again, Ares noticed that she looked terrified. The little girl was standing in the narrow space between them, but he couldn't see her. The girl's face melted, gurgled, and popped, and her jaw unhinged.

"ANZTHORAZ!" she screamed.

The little girl shoved Luxea. She flopped out of Ares' arms and bumped into the bent airship gate. The latch snapped, and the ramp flew open. Ares swung for her, but Luxea fell. As the airship became smaller and smaller, another star flickered out. There was one left.

Ares' heart broke, and his skin burned. He leaped over the railing.

Peyamo screeched like a stew pot filled with nails. "Ares! Shut the ship down! Shut it down! Engines off! Idle!"

Nika smacked each button and flicked off every switch, leaving only Chamber AG active to keep *Matha ou Machina* afloat. The roar of machinery lowered to a hum.

Peyamo's eye was fixed on the empty space where Ares had stood. His heat signatures were still detectable. Avari had forgotten every word she'd ever known; she could only scream. Oliver's legs shook. For a second, he was quiet, and then he cried.

For five minutes, all eyes wept alike. While Brielle petted Avari's windswept hair, Ruka's fur bristled, and he began to whine. Mortified, he tried to burrow for cover. Then the same instinct charged into Brielle. She dropped to a crouch and braced to the floor.

"Something's coming!" she rasped.

The proximity alarms at *Matha ou Machina's* command center blared. Nika bolted to the control panel and glimpsed the radar display. His sun-kissed skin went chalky. He yanked off his goggles and dropped them.

"My Lady! There's something right under us!"

Peyamo's eye expanded, realizing. She clung to the handrail and yelled, "Nika, eject the sails! Everybody, hold on!"

Nika batted the emergency release lock. All of the sails unfastened from the masts, and the flaxen fabric rippled onto the weather deck. Peyamo scanned below through an infrared lens — and then it hit.

Matha ou Machina nearly flipped upside down. The sky flashed to black. A spine coated in iridescent scales cut the air beneath them, and wings over twice the length of the airship swept away the clouds. They leveled out, and the Mooncallers peeked over the ledge.

Brielle whispered, "Dragon . . ."

Hovering not far off was the most famed beast of myth. Smoke blasted from his nostrils, four horns spiraled around his head, and razored teeth stretched from cheek to cheek. A scar rode up his back between his wings, and some of the scales were dislodged.

Ares' dashed, violet eyes flitted down. Cradled in his giant talons was the limp body of Luxea. He'd caught her just in time.

Oliver started to clap but stopped when Ares hiked up his scaly brow. Ares unfurled a talon toward Sh'tarr's Iris. Peyamo didn't have an inkling of why he had to go into that storm, but she'd been unable to stop him before, so what point was there in trying again?

Peyamo gave Ares a Tzapodian salute. Avari wiped her cheeks and did the same. Oliver tried to do it, but it looked very wrong. Brielle and Ruka howled.

In farewell, Ares screeched. The sound rattled the loose screws in the floorboards of *Matha ou Machina*. He closed his wings and free-fell backward.

The wind chilled his scales, but his blood burned. He feared his actions all the more now that he'd taken them, but with every reach closed between himself and the Iris, he had no regrets.

IRIS

Wherever Luxea was, time was a thin, white line with no beginning nor end. She wiggled her fingers. They were in water. The liquid was icy like chewing on a mint leaf and inhaling through her mouth. Beneath the surface were aura crystals untainted by dirt or shadow. Lune lilies grew on the shoreline of the pond, and far above their electric purple petals was an explosion of stars. Luxea saw Amniven in the sky.

"Then . . . I did die," she said achingly.

"Not entirely," said a heavenly voice.

Luxea spun around. Her bare feet slipped across the glassy bottom of the pool, and she plunged up to her chin. She slapped her hands over her chest when she realized that she was unclothed.

In the shallows was a woman whose black gown rested atop the water. She was so gigantic that Luxea could've been mistaken for a toddler next to her. This woman's skin was chocolate, and her long, wavy hair was powdered sugar. A beaded veil cascaded between her brows, covering her nose and mouth. Her eyes were starlight — just like Luxea's.

Luxea brought her lips above the water and asked, "Where am I?"

"You are here, but also there," she said, pointing at Amniven.

Bemused, Luxea splashed her face. "I need to wake up! I need to wake up! I don't remember going to sleep, I — !"

"But you remember this," said the woman, suspending a familiar silver necklace in front of her.

Luxea froze. "How do you — ? That's Ares' Felastil."

"No, this is its twin. They were forged together when the Irestar was born. Ares has the other because I bestowed it upon him."

Luxea's eyes burst like fireworks. "You're Oscerin?"

"Time has gifted me many names," said Oscerin calmly. Ares had been right. She spoke just as rhythmically, undulating, and steady as a heartbeat. "Your soul reached for Eletheon, but I caught you first. You believe that it will all end the same, that you will die, and life will go on. No. It does not have to end. It cannot. For if it does, light ends too."

Luxea yelled, "But I'm dead. I fell through the sky — !"

"— and Ares caught you," said Oscerin with smiling eyes.

"Caught me?"

"He is the last dragon for many reasons. This is one."

Luxea dug her fingernails into her palms. "But that will drive him mad! Is he out of his mind? Why did he do that?" she screamed.

"He did it because I asked him to — and he wanted to. He was never going to let you fall, my stars. At this very moment, he carries you to the land of renewed life," said Oscerin optimistically.

"And where is that?" asked Luxea worriedly.

Oscerin glanced at Amniven. "Within Sh'tarr's Iris," She said.

Luxea shook her head wildly. "Sh'tarr's Iris will destroy him! How could You send him into it?! Ares will die, Oscerin!"

"He will not die. In fact, he is the only one who can break the storm," said Oscerin sagaciously. "You cannot yet understand, but this war of black and white is why I chose Ares . . . and why I chose you."

"Chose me? I hardly believed in —"

"But I believed in you. There has been a purpose from the start. Not one action you have taken has been unplanned —" Oscerin paused and chuckled, "— ah, except for your apple incident."

Luxea felt more naked than she had before. "Did Ares tell You about that?" she worked out.

"He did not. I had the pleasure of experiencing it through your eyes. However, he did ask me to return that child's cat. I am happy to say that they have been reunited," purred Oscerin.

Luxea felt a smile coming, but she hid it. Oscerin saw it anyway.

Less warmly, the Moon Mother went on, "One day, you will view reality through my eyes too. Since the day you were born, I watched you until the time was right. And on that afternoon that you awoke, and the world was unfamiliar, our vision became a two-way mirror. Luxea, the river did not deliver you to my Speaker's kingdom by any coincidence, no. I sent you there."

"Do You know who I was before?" asked Luxea numbly.

"I do," confessed Oscerin.

Luxea shouted, "Please, tell me! I need to — !"

"No," denied Oscerin. "Until the time is right, you must live with a mind unbiased. I promise you, the fragments of the past will fall into place as they are meant to, but the future is what matters now. Heed these next words. Ares is the parallel, and you are the divide. I have chosen you and Ares as the bearers of the keys to fate, but I must be the one to turn them."

Oscerin's stars suddenly faded to violet. Luxea was unsettled. Her own eyes were only ever that same color when she sensed danger.

Ares felt himself losing touch. Several times, he'd forgotten who Luxea was. He prayed that his wings could carry him fast enough. Whether dragon blood rotted him, or Sh'tarr's Iris shredded him to pieces, he had to try. If he slipped, she slipped.

It was becoming harder to stay airborne. The squalls made him into an insect, swatting him away from the light. Howling gales ripped his scales, and knifelike bits of debris cut the webs of his wings.

A powerful gust pitched Ares downward to the sea. Below the black clouds, he could see the outline of Mythos. He narrowed his wings to his sides and slung westward.

"TURN BACK, AND I WILL SPARE YOUR MORTAL LIFE!"

A scream resounding like stones upon a frozen lake scored the walls of Ares' skull. His scales lifted in fear. He could place one name to such a voice: Sh'tarr. Still, he launched into the heart of the storm.

Three waterspouts materialized out of nowhere and crashed into Ares. He dove left and doubled back through the cyclones. He made a break toward Mythos, but he knew that Sh'tarr was chasing him.

"Your resolve is admirable, son of the Moon Mother."

Sh'tarr's Iris froze. Every bit of airborne debris and drop of rain halted and toppled into the sea. It was eerily silent without the play of Amniven's primordial instruments.

A face formed in the sky ahead of Ares. For the first time in his life, he stared into the eyes of a divine. Sh'tarr's misty lips alone were multiple times his size.

"You are very, very senseless! You throw yourself away for a life that is already lost? Go back now!" thundered Sh'tarr.

Mythos wasn't far, but Ares couldn't go anywhere with Sh'tarr surveying him. He looked up. The crown of the Irestar was almost overhead. If he could buy himself time, he wouldn't fail.

A tormenting heat coalesced within Ares' ribcage. It hurt, but the pain was thrilling. The Storm Goddess tipped Her cloudy head, wondering what he was doing. When his mouth opened, calamitous, purple flames sprayed out of his throat. Sh'tarr screamed as dragon-fire ripped through Her. Her face puffed out into nothingness.

Ares swooped low to the sea. Mythos was no more than a half a reach away. He started to think that he wouldn't need Oscerin's help.

Sh'tarr laughed maniacally. *"So tricky. Do you know what fire cannot break, dragon boy? Haha, hahahah . . . HAHAHAHAHAHA!"*

A foamy arm burst out of the ocean. The Sea Goddess clasped Ares' slender tail. His stomach flipped, and Luxea's body slipped through his talons. Alatos tore him out of the sky. With no other means of escape, he shed his draconic frame. It burned away, crumbling into the storm. The affliction had spread dramatically. Now scales tickled the curve of his shoulder.

Alatos had let Ares go, but he was human again and falling without wings. He reached for Luxea and grabbed onto her coat sleeve just as Eternity's Ocean seized them both.

Below the sea, Alatos' marine echolocation vibrated off of every surface. She tugged Luxea underwater by the tail of her coat, but Ares didn't let go of her.

The Sea Goddess' face was too broad to fit into Ares' field of vision. Her aqueous eyes were oversized to operate in low light, Her skin was decomposing, and marine life grew from Her serrated gills and hollow cheeks. She opened Her sawtoothed mouth and lurched playfully. Her jerking movement undulated Her kelpy hair.

Ares shook himself out of horror. He tore off Luxea's coat and swam with her to the surface. Alatos growled at Luxea's empty clothing and cast it into an abyss.

Ares turned Luxea upright at the surface. The whitecaps thrashed him as he paddled to Mythos. He'd moved ten feet before Alatos snatched his legs. His hands slid from Luxea's arm, and he took in a bit of air before he was submerged.

🦋

Ice crackled beneath Luxea's skin. It was cutting but detached like a passing thought. "It's s-so cold!" she sputtered, lips blueing.

"Your soul suffers from your environment in the mortal realm. You are in the water, and so is Ares," whispered Oscerin. Her stars faded to grey. "He was trying, but now he is giving up."

"And all You'll do is wait? Say something to him!" cried Luxea.

The Moon Mother said nothing.

Luxea lunged and grabbed onto Oscerin's Felastil. She screamed into it, "Ares, don't give up! We have to go home!"

🦋

Ares knew that it was the end. Perhaps Sh'tarr had been right. He'd chosen to throw his life away over hope. His chest convulsed, but in his final seconds, his eyes rolled back to their whites.

Ares, don't give up! We have to go home!

Ares nearly gasped. In a haze, he watched Luxea's body as it bobbed about at the ocean's surface. He was sure that he'd heard her. Wanting to survive at all costs, he clapped his hands over his mouth and trapped his breath.

That was when the Irestar came to a dead halt above Sh'tarr's Iris.

Far, far away, Oscerin stood. Lunar wind buffeted around Her, and Her stars scorched. "Sh'tarr and Alatos, Your power is more terrible than any of Your world, but I am not of Your world."

Through space, beyond the hurricane, and beneath the sea, Sh'tarr's Iris went still. Alatos felt something tickle Her feet from the fissure in which She waded. A tide.

Moonlight gravitated towards Oscerin, bending the lune lilies and raising the water inside of the pond. Oscerin rasped, "You should have cautioned the skies, Sisters. If You do not deliver my children to the shore — I will!"

Oscerin's light painted the storms and the sea in silver.

The undertow sucked Alatos into darkness. Ares was suffocating, but the currents were manipulated to lift him toward the surface. He choked out water and paddled to Luxea. In fear of blacking out, he zipped the ribbon off of her braid and fastened it around their wrists.

Ares tucked Luxea's head into the crook of his neck, trying to stay awake as he stroked. Mythos was so close that he could hear the waves lapping against the black sand.

On the Irestar, Luxea's arms and legs became transparent. If her soul was diminishing, it was returning to its host. She slid into the lunar pond, and Oscerin cradled her.

"Will you do something for me ere you go?" asked Oscerin. She dipped Her hand into the water. "Drink the Irestar's pith. Never can shadow touch you with moonlight in your veins."

The Moon Mother curved Her palm against Luxea's lips. Luxea swilled the glittering fluid to the last drop. Oscerin trailed Her long fingers down the side of Luxea's head and stopped over her heart.

"I will see you again," said Oscerin sadly.

The water's skin enveloped Luxea's pale face. Her body dissolved into a cloud of stardust. Alone again, Oscerin held onto Her Felastil.

"Well done. You may rest," She sang.

Upon Amniven, Luxea opened her mouth and breathed deeper than she had in a very long time. Ares' face was too numb to feel anything, but his muscles remembered how to smile.

Oscerin's voice pulled his eyes back into his head.

"Well done. You may rest."

Permitted to let go, Ares turned onto his back. His eyes unfocused as he whispered to Luxea, "Stay with me."

Erelong, they washed up on the black sand of Mythos. Ares held tightly but gently onto Luxea's cold hand and listened to the fizzing of foam as the tide slipped out from beneath them.

Ares suddenly felt at peace when alien ringing filled the air. Footsteps ground in the sand above their heads. Crystal strangers burrowed their transparent feet as they strode nearer. One of them unlaced the ribbon from Luxea's wrist, raised her up in its arms, and walked off. Moments later, ribbed hands slid through the sand and lifted Ares as if he was weightless.

The Mythics marched into the rainforest as daybreak shone through the night. Ares reached out for the stars and fell asleep to a crystal lullaby.

REFERENCES

Pronunciation Key

Primary Characters

Luxea Siren — Loo · shee · uh Sy · ren
Ares Lavrenthea — Ah · raze Lav · ren · thay · uh
Avari Vishera — Uh · var · ee Vish · air · uh
Oliver Kross — All · ih · verr Cross
Brielle — Bree · ell
Ruka — Roo · kuh

Members of The Six

Peyamo Nelnah — Pay · om · oh Nel · nuh
Annalais Taress — Ann · uh · lie Tarr · ess
Garamat un Gatra — Gair · uh · mott Oon Got · ruh
Ralvesh un Gatra — Ral · vesh Oon Got · ruh
Val'noren Paah — Val · no · ren Paw
Vesas Kross — Vay · sauce Cross
Levelia Kross — La · veel · ee · uh Cross

Minor Characters

Elthevir — Ell · thuh · veer
Velesari — Vell · uh · sorry
Pveather — Feather
Mollah Felloen — Mall · uh Fell · oh · enn
Lorian Demartiet — Lore · ee · en Dem · ar · tee · ay
Nika Lecava — Nick · uh Lay · caw · vuh
Gajneva — Gahj · nay · vuh
Veshra — Vesh · ruh
Rakgun — Rack · goon
Omnia — Om · nee · uh
Syervis — See · air · viss

1

Cheyale — Shay · all · ee
Reychar — Ray · shar
Kodan — Ko · don
Estalyn Faust — Ess · tuh · lin Fost
Runa Faust — Roo · nuh Fost
Naiv — Ny · v Lav · ren · thay · uh
Manalaei Lorcé — Man · uh · lay · ee Lore · say
Samsamet — Sam · suh · met
Vasna Lorreen — Vass · nuh Lore · een
Hanalea Moots — Haw · nuh · lay · uh Moots
Lilivae Alanis — Lil · ee · vay Uh · lon · iss
Pertia Voulet — Per · she · uh Voo · lay
Cherish Ven'lethe — Chair · ish Venn · leeth

REMARKABLE OBJECTS

Usinnon — You · sin · on
Felastil — Fell · ass · teel

LOCATIONS

Amniven — Am · nee · venn
L'arneth — Larr · neth
Anunaru — Ah · new · na · roo
Tel Ashir — Tell Ash · eer
Tzapodia — Zuh · po · dee · uh
Lor'thanin — Lore · thuh · neen
Selnilar — Sell · nil · arr
Solissium — Soul · iss · ee · um
Ank'tatra — Onk · ta · truh
Tarot — Tar · oh
Irestar — Eye · er · star
Tehrastar — Tair · uh · star
Drenut — Dreh · noot
Xeneda — Zen · ee · duh
Sirah — Seer · uh
Hildre — Hill · druh

Ilsemet — Ill · sem · et
Tarhelen — Tarr · ell · en
Tal Am T'Navin — Tawl Am Tuh · Nav · een
Thali ou Tirima — Thall · ee · Oo Teer · ee · muh
Matha ou Machina — Moth · uh Oo Mosh · een · uh

ETHNIC GROUPS

L'arian — Lair · ee · en
Seroden — Sair · oh · den
Draconic — Drake · on · ick
Aestof — Ay · stoff
Rishja — Rish · jhuh
Felenoe — Fell · en · oh
Sil'simani — Sill · sim · on · ee

GODDESSES

Tirih — Teer · ee
Oscerin — Oh · sair · in
Ka'ahn — Kaw · n
Anatatri — Ann · uh · taw · tree
Alatos — Al · uh · toe · s
Sh'tarr — Shuh · tarr
N'ra — Neer · uh
Asrodisia — Ass · row · dizz · ee · uh
Himhre — Him · ree
Daetri — Day · tree

GODS

Wynd — Wind
Ganra — Gonn · ruh
Sithess — Sith · ess
Nall — Naw · l
Ostriseon — Oss · triss · ee · on
Raveth — Ray · veth

Theryn — Thair · in
Mamaku — Mom · uh · koo
Ocaranth — Oh · car · anth
Rin — Rin
Varnn — Var · n
Fenne — Fen

Wildlife

Fenlaig — Fen · lie · g
Falscreamer — False · screamer
Yulacai — You · luk · eye

Unknown

Anzthoraz — Annz · thor · azz

AMNIVEN TIMELINE

Months:

1. Lightsmeet (LM)
2. Clawsguard (CG)
3. Venomsnare (VS)
4. Worldbreak (WB)
5. Duskriddle (DR)
6. Blackomen (BO)
7. Kingsreign (KR)
8. Softstep (SS)
9. Riverspell (RS)
10. Redtail (RT)
11. Nightspeak (NS)
12. Snowhowl (SH)

Centuries:

1. Tirih (TIR)
2. Oscerin (OSC)
3. Ka'ahn (KHN)
4. Anatatri (ANA)
5. Alatos (ATS)
6. Sh'tarr (SHR)
7. N'ra (NRA)
8. Asrodisia (ASR)
9. Himhre (HRE)
10. Daetri (DTR)

Each month (moon) follows Earth's breakdown. There are 365 days in Amniven's year. To understand the date, take into consideration these factors.

Day (day of the month.)

Month name (as listed above.)

Year (number of the year 1-99 in a century.)

Century name (as listed above.)

Millennium number (Era 3 = 3,000 years.)

EXAMPLE:

11.LM.1.OSC.3 = 11 January, 3201

11 (Day) . LM (Month) . 1 (Year) . OSC (Century) . 3 (Millennium)

GLOSSARY

A

Aestof - The people of The Isle of Varnn.

Akitaji - Ancient spirit tribe of Xeneda.

Alatos - The Goddess of the Sea. Second goddess born to the mortal plane.

Alucard - Hired carriage master.

Amal Luciem - Translates in l'arian to "give light."

A'maru Mountains - Mountain range in Selnilar.

Amber Wing - Royal living quarters of Castle Lavrenthea.

Amniven - The world.

Anatatri - The Goddess of Time. First goddess born to the mortal plane.

Anatatri's Reach - The largest sea in Anunaru.

Anathema - Capital of the Wraiths.

Ank'tatra - Nation in southern Anunaru. Primarily deserts. One of the six most prominent territories.

Annalais Taress - Empress of Goldenrise. Youngest member of The Six.

Anunaru - The eastern continent that makes up the Joined Hands.

Anzthoraz - (???)

Apparition - Settlement in the Wraiths.

Aptuli - The orchard on Castle Lavrenthea's property.

Arcana - The essence with which sorcerers are born.

Arcanan - Dead language used by spellbooks and magisters.

Arcanan Reservoir - Naturally occurring pool of arcana.

The Architect - (See the chapter 'The Architect' for more information.)

Ardin - Husband of Pirtha.

Ares Lavrenthea - Prince of Tzapodia. Speaker of Oscerin. Member of The Six. The last remaining cursed child of Samsamet.

Ashi Priest - Priests of Tzapodia.

Asrodisia - The Goddess of Fertility. Fifth goddess born to the mortal plane.

Avari Vishera - Seroden ranger of Tel Ashir. Mentor to Luxea Siren.

Avi Yeromin - Landlocked nation in L'arneth.

B

Battle of Mountain's Fall - The final battle between Tzapodia and Naraniv.

Bavani - Chef employed by the Lady Peyamo in Thali ou Tirima.

V1

Birtha - Hen/rooster/chicken belonging to Mirtha the locksmith.
Bizzner - Innkeeper of the Woodgate Inn.
Blackjaw Hollow - Home to the Riders of the West.
Blackomen - Sixth month of the year. Sign of Raveth.
Blackwood - Parts of a blackwood tree.
The Blightwater - The sea separating Tzapodia and the Isle of Varnn.
Blissits - A slang Varnnish phrase to express surprise.
Bloodstone - Playing piece in Dragon Stones.
Briell - (See Brielle.)
Brielle - Wolf rider of Blackjaw Hollow. Sister of Ruka.
The Brood - Widow's army.
The Brood Mother - (See Widow.)
Bulaba - Settlement in Xeneda.

C

Castle Lavrenthea - Home of the Lavrenthea family in Tel Ashir.
Cheeries - A slang Varnnish farewell.
Cherish Ven'lethe - L'arian elvish sorcerer. (See the chapter 'Death Knell' for more information.)
Cheyale - Serpent counterpart to the rider Syervis.

Chief Lorian Demartiet - Chief of Border Patrol in Tel Ashir. Member of the Mooncaller Council.
Clawsguard - Second month of the year. Sign of Ganra.
Claymore Urius - Lieutenant in the Tel Ashian army. Member of the Mooncallers Council.
Court of Light - Plaza in Tel Ashir.
Cove of Tar - Body of water in northeastern L'arneth.
The Crystal Spire - Sacred tower of crystal in Selnilar. Also called Sirah.
Crawler - Skinny, quick-moving creatures that serve the Brood.
Crystal Strangers - (See Mythics.)

Danis D'liara - One of the nine Tel Ashian soldiers sent to Lor'thanin.
Day Trail - Trail in Witchsleep designated for daytime.
Daetri - The Goddess of War. Seventh goddess born to the mortal plane.
Deathbed - Fighting ring and platform for premature burial.
Division Magick - Branch of the arcana for splitting the soul.
Doc Navia - One of the nine Tel Ashian soldiers sent to Lor'thanin.
Dolses - Rider of Blackjaw Hollow. Counterpart to the stag Tyfus.

Dracas - Horselike lizards ridden in Tzapodia.

Draconic - The language of the dragons.

Draconism - Affliction placed upon the first people of Tel Ashir.

Dragon Stones - Board game won by tossing a bloodstone into the center.

Drenut - Southernmost nation in Anunaru. Primarily rainforests.

Drishti - Shieldmaiden in the Tel Ashian military.

Dundis Angle - Forest in the Storm Plains.

Dunes of Duhar - Desert in Ank'tatra.

Duskriddle - Fifth month of the year. Sign of Ostriseon.

Dustapple - Tiny apples. You can guess what they taste like.

Eaia N'manya - One of the nine Tel Ashian soldiers sent to Lor'thanin.

Ei'mithanen - Translates in l'arian to "my lady."

Elder Meyama - Fruit merchant in the Sapphire Bazaar.

Elder's Expanse - Nation in L'arneth.

Eletheon - The realm of light where souls venture after death.

Elthevir - Dracas belonging to Avari Vishera.

Eluva'eshas - Translates in l'arian to "mirror the face."

Emerald Wing - Sect of Castle Lavrenthea for conferences and the library.

Era - Millennia. Currently Era Three.

Erannor - City in Selnilar.

Estalyn Faust - (See the chapter 'Haven de Asrodisia' for more information.)

Eternity's Ocean - Ocean between L'arneth and Anunaru.

Eternity's Refuge - Manmade island on the Great Bridge, Tarhelen.

Falscreamer - Little birds that scream like people.

The Famous Tamistier Lodge - Lodge in the city of Anathema.

Felastil - Moon-forged pendant belonging to Ares Lavrenthea.

Felenoe - Catlike inhabitants of Drenut.

Felitia - Mercenary in the Tel Ashian military.

Fenlaig - Spherical pigs who have a very, very hard time escaping predators.

Fenne - The Wolf God. Eleventh god born to Amniven.

Firelily - Curled, orange lilies.

Flame Caves - Sea caves behind Castle Lavrenthea.

Flame Gardens - Royal gardens of Castle Lavrenthea.

Frosttear - First season of the year.

G

Gajneva - Chieftain of Blackjaw Hollow. Counterpart to the bat Veshra.

Ganra - The Bear God. Second god born to Amniven.

Garamat un Gatra - Sun Chief of Ank'tatra. Longest member of The Six.

General Doryan Skythoan - War General of Tzapodia. Member of the Mooncaller Council.

General Torrin - A war general from the Isle of Varnn.

Genntric Taress - Previously Emperor of Goldenrise. Father of Annalais and Rowan Taress.

The Ghostwives - The female army of the Wraiths.

Girtha - Oldest librarian in Castle Lavrenthea library.

The Golden Spire - Sacred tower of gold in Goldenrise. Also called Hildre.

Goldenhands - The army of Goldenrise.

Goldenrise - Northernmost nation in Anunaru. Primarily moors. One of the six most prominent territories in the Joined Hands.

Graed Lavrenthea - The original King of Tzapodia. First of Samsamet's cursed children.

The Great Bridge, Tarhelen - The largest manmade structure on Amniven.

The Greatgrace - The largest continent on Amniven.

Grecory Stile - One of the nine Tel Ashian soldiers sent to Lor'thanin.

The Grey - The largest nation in L'arneth. Primarily snowy mountains.

Gut Leak - River flowing from Elder's Expanse to Storm Plains.

H

Halfbend - Settlement in Ank'tatra.

Hanalea Moots - Sage in Castle Lavrenthea's infirmary.

Harpy Pass - Capital of the Storm Plains.

Havan'ha neila - Translates in l'arian to "hold him down."

Haven de Asrodisia - The guest wing of Villa de Taress.

Heart of Haven - Den of courtesans in Haven de Asrodisia.

Heavens Devil - Informal title of Naiv Lavrenthea.

Hildre - (See the Golden Spire.)

Hilien ashta - Translates in l'arian to "good luck."

Himhre - The Goddess of Wealth. Sixth goddess born to the mortal plane.

House of Worship - Building used for prayer.

1

Ilsemet - (See the Sandstone Spire.)
The Irestar - Alternative name for the Moon.
Isabelia Taress - Previously the Empress of Goldenrise. Mother of Annalais and Rowan Taress.
The Isle of Varnn - Island beneath L'arneth. Shrouded in eternal night. One of the six most prominent territories in the Joined Hands.

J

James - Son of Mirtha the locksmith.
The Joined Hands - The united continents of L'arneth and Anunaru.

K

Ka'ahn - The Goddess of Fire who takes on the form of a child. The third goddess born to the spirit plane. One of the three greater divines.
Ka'ahn's Fire - The red dwarf star visible from Amniven once biannually.
Kalo - Unborn child of Claymore Urius and Hanalea Moots.
Keeper - Accountants in Tzapodia.
Keeper Vessias - Head keeper. Member of the Mooncaller Council.

Khabe - Translates in rishjaan to "throne."
Khabeptah - Translates in rishjaan to "throne room."
Kingscore - Flaming canyon created when Naiv Lavrenthea fell from the sky in year 14. Located in Tel Ashir beside Castle Lavrenthea.
Kingslane - Guarded road leading to Castle Lavrenthea.
Kingsreign - The seventh month of the year. Sign of Theryn.
Kirtha - Father of Mirtha the locksmith.
Kodan - The bear counterpart to the rider Reychar.
Kurloy - Chef employed by the Lady Peyamo in Thali ou Tirima.

L

Lady of Bronze - Formal title of Peyamo Nelnah.
Lali - Sage in Castle Lavrenthea's infirmary.
Landheart - Mountain range on the eastern border of Avi Yeromin.
L'arian Elf - The natives of L'arneth. Found mostly in Selnilar.
L'arneth - The western continent that makes up the Joined Hands.
Leitha'maen - Translates in l'arian to "Soul Sword." Army of Selnilar.
Lemuria - The name of the universe.
Levelia Kross - One of the Masters of the Isle of Varnn and member of

The Six. Wife to Vesas Kross. Mother of Oliver Kross.

Light Seeker - Formal title of Val'noren Paah.

Lightsmeet - The first month of the year. Sign of Wynd.

Lor'thanin - Capital of Selnilar.

Lover's Nautilus - Symbolic seashell denoting the Goddess of Fertility.

Lucanin - Translates in l'arian to "Widow."

Lune Lily - Flowers that blossom in moonlight.

Luxea Siren - L'arian woman with stars in her eyes. Cannot remember who she was prior to her awakening in Castle Lavrenthea's infirmary.

M

Madam Lilivae Alanis - Headmistress of Haven de Asrodisia.

Magelas - Arcanan tattoo of a sorcerer's birth-given name.

Magick - (See arcana.)

Mamaku - The Rabbit God. Eighth god born to Amniven.

Manalaei Lavrenthea - Previously the Queen of Tzapodia. Wife to Naiv Lavrenthea. Mother of Ares Lavrenthea.

Maolam - A Tzapodian governess.

Matha ou Machina - Translates in seroden to "Daughter of the Machine." The airship belonging to Peyamo Nelnah.

Martnir - Head manservant in the Phoenix Palace.

The Masters - Vesas and Levelia Kross of the Isle of Varnn.

Mirtha - Locksmith in Nu Dalajur.

Moal - A very rude Varnnish curse word. Too rude to define.

Mollah Felloen - Head sage in Castle Lavrenthea's infirmary.

Mooncallers - The army of Tzapodia and organization founded by the Speaker Ares Lavrenthea.

Moonpass - The main entryway to Tel Ashir.

Motherpoint - Cliff behind Castle Lavrenthea.

Mountain's Mirror Bridge - The primary crossing of Tal Am T'navin River.

Musha - Dracas gifted to Oliver Kross.

Mythics - (See the chapter 'Crystal Strangers' for more information.)

Mythos - (See the chapter 'Crystal Strangers' for more information.)

N

Naiv Lavrenthea - King of Tzapodia. Husband to Manalaei Lavrenthea. Father of Ares Lavrenthea.

Naji Komaar - One of the nine Tel Ashian soldiers sent to Lor'thanin.

Nall - The Mammoth God. Fourth god born to Amniven.

Nan Jaami - Southwestern region of mountain rishja in L'arneth.

Naraniv - Southern nation of L'arneth that was eradicated by King Naiv Lavrenthea. Has since become territory of Tzapodia.

Nav'amani Forest - Forest in Selnilar.

Nav'in ei th'luneth - Translates in l'arian to "show me my dreams."

Nerroplace - Western district in Tel Ashir.

The Nightingale - Spellbook belonging to Cherish Ven'lethe.

The Nightmare Venom - Incurable poison. Induces nightmares until death.

Nightspeak - Eleventh month of the year. Sign of Varnn.

Night Trail - Trail in Witchsleep designated for nighttime.

Nika Lecava - Head engineer and helmsman to Peyamo Nelnah.

Northreach - Northernmost nation in L'arneth. Mostly frigid coasts.

Novis - The One-Eyed Cat constellation.

N'ra - The Goddess of Nature. Fourth goddess born to the mortal plane.

Nu Dalajur - Northwestern district of Tel Ashir.

Ocaranth - The Koi God. Ninth god born into Amniven.

Oilshine Black - Seroden elvish wine that might just be oil with alcohol in it.

Oliver Kross - Son of Masters Vesas and Levelia Kross. Heir to the throne of the Isle of Varnn.

Omnia - Rider of Blackjaw Hollow. Counterpart to the raven Skye.

Oscerin - The Goddess of the Moon. Second goddess born to the spirit plane. One of the three greater divines.

Ostriseon - The Owl God. Fifth god born into Amniven.

Overseer Lovelle - Officer in Tel Ashir. Member of the Mooncaller Council.

P

Palvitae - A settlement in southern Goldenrise.

Pearl Alley - Corridor of Castle Lavrenthea.

Pertia Voulet - A headmaster in Haven de Asrodisia.

Petre Kane - One of the nine Tel Ashian soldiers sent to Lor'thanin.

Peyamo Nelnah - Leader of the nation of Tarot, member of The Six, and mentor to Ares Lavrenthea.

The Phoenix Gate - Capital of Ank'tatra.

Phoenix Sons - The army of Ank'tatra.

Pirtha - A regular architect.

Plainsberry - Sweet berries that grow in rainy climates.

Porranim Courtyard - Courtyard of Castle Lavrenthea.

Priestess Daiada - Head Ashi priestess. Member of the Mooncaller Council.

Pudd - An old but powerful mule.

Pveather - Dracas belonging to Ares Lavrenthea. Called "finger-snapper."

Q

Quaritan - City located in northern Tzapodia. Eradicated in year 99.TIR.

R

Rakgun - Translates in rishjaan to "sister."

Ralvesh un Gatra - Son of the Sun Chief Garamat un Gatra.

Raveth - The Raven God. Sixth god born into Amniven.

Redrift - Fourth season of the year.

Redtail - Tenth month of the year. Sign of Rin.

Reychar - Rider of Blackjaw Hollow. Counterpart to the bear Kodan.

Rhiari Litaan - Ank'tatraan aristocrat. Sister of Tahnos Litaan.

The Riddling Roads - Unreliable roads in the Wraiths.

Riders of the West - Tribe of riders who dwells in Blackjaw Hollow.

Rin - The Fox God. Tenth god born into Amniven.

Rishja - Half-giant descendants of Xeneda.

Riverpass - Gate in Tel Ashir for access to Tal Am T'navin River.

Riverroot - Water-dwelling root used for treating burns.

Riverspell - Ninth month of the year. Sign of Ocaranth.

Rosamie - Oliver Kross' forsaken daughter.

Roseleaf - Rare blossom often smoked or steeped for tea.

Rosenbloom Red - A red wine consumed only by those who can afford it.

Rowan Taress - Previous Emperor of Goldenrise. Brother of Annalais Taress.

Ruby Bureau - Ares Lavrenthea's office in Castle Lavrenthea.

Ruby Wing - Sect of Castle Lavrenthea used for archival purposes.

Ruka - Brother and wolf counterpart to Brielle.

Runa Faust - (See the chapter 'Haven de Asrodisia' for more information.)

Rylin O'sara - One of the nine Tzapodian soldiers sent to Lor'thanin.

S

Sage - A nurse.

Samsamet - The last dragon. Cursed the people of Tzapodia with Draconism.

Sandblood - Estuary northwest of the Phoenix Gate in Ank'tatra.

The Sandstone Spire - Sacred sandstone tower in Ank'tatra.

The Sapphire Bazaar - Shopping center in Tel Ashir.

Sayshi - Tiger belonging to Ralvesh un Gatra.

Selnilar - Eastern nation of L'arneth. Primarily forests. One of the most prominent territories in the Joined Hands.

Seroden Elf - Elves renowned for their technological advancements.

Sh'tarr - The Goddess of Storms. Third goddess born to the mortal plane.

Sh'tarr's Iris - The eternal hurricane in Eternity's Ocean.

Sheishan'in - Translates in l'arian to "shield me."

The Shifting City - Capital of Tarot. Made entirely of machines.

Sil'simani - Translates in l'arian to "Sacred children."

Sirah - (See the Crystal Spire.)

Sirah Academy - Abandoned magick academy built into the Crystal Spire.

Sirah Temple - Home to the Light Seeker. Built into the Crystal Spire.

Sithe - The realm of punished souls. Also called the In-between.

Sithess - The Serpent God. Third god born into Amniven.

The Six - Organization of the six most sovereign leaders in the Joined Hands.

Skye - The raven counterpart to the rider Omnia.

Sleepthistle - Herb steeped in tea for stress-relief. Occasionally smoked.

Slumber - Mother of Unblossomed. Courtesan in Haven de Asrodisia.

Snake's Head - Settlement in the Wraiths.

Snowhowl - Twelfth month of the year. Sign of Fenne.

Softstep - Eighth month of the year. Sign of Mamaku.

Solissium - Capital of Goldenrise.

Soulpriest - Xenedan priests who utilize arcanan reservoirs for soul-splitting.

The Speaker - (See Ares Lavrenthea.)

Spell-eater - Sorcerers who cannot be harmed by another's magick.

Spymaster Ruri Nairn - Head of the rangers of Tel Ashir. Member of the Mooncallers Council.

Starlite - Star-shaped insects.

Steps of Sevinus - Royal staircase of Castle Lavrenthea.

The Storm Plains - Nation on the eastern coast of L'arneth. Always stormy.

Sun Chief - Formal title of Garamat un Gatra.

Sunrae - Third season of the year.
Syervis - Rider of Blackjaw Hollow.
Counterpart to the serpent Cheyale.

ꚍ

Tafida Dekda - Translates in seroden to "Welcome Bakery." Avari Vishera's favorite childhood shop.
Tahnos Litaan - Ank'tatraan aristocrat. Brother of Rhiari Litaan.
Tal Am T'navin River - The longest river in L'arneth located in Selnilar.
Tani Renayo - Leader of the nation of Drenut.
Tarhelen - Capital of Northreach.
Tarot - Nation located in Anunaru. Primarily mesas and igneous rock. One of the six most prominent territories in the Joined Hands.
Tashetha'hil - Translates in l'arian to "mask us."
The Tehrastar - Alternative name for the Sun.
Tel Ashir - Capital of Tzapodia.
Tell - One of Oliver Kross' many old flames. Mother of Rosamie.
Terin - Head baker at Tafida Dekda.
Titantula - Slow, hulking creatures that serve the Brood.
Thali ou Tirima - Floating fortress belonging to the Lady Peyamo Nelnah.
Theryn - The Lion God. Seventh god born into Amniven.
Timeless Mountains - Mountain range surrounding the Golden Spire.

Tirih - The Goddess of the Sun. First goddess born in all time. One of the three greater divines.
Traplane - District in southwestern Tel Ashir. Reputed for criminal activity.
Trihells - The three realms of the damned.
Trihoul - Settlement in Tzapodia.
Tuma bread - Bread made from tuma grains.
Tyfus - The stag counterpart to the rider Dolses.
Tzapodia - Southeastern nation of L'arneth. Primarily deserts. One of the six most prominent territories in the Joined Hands.

##

Unblossomed - Courtesan in Haven de Asrodisia.
The Usinnon - Luxea Siren's spellbook companion.

ᐯ

Velous Direk - Northeastern district of Tel Ashir.
Val'noren Paah - Leader of Selnilar. Formally called the Light Seeker. Member of The Six.
Varnn - The Bat God. Eleventh god born into Amniven.
Vasna Lorreen - Era two Light Seeker responsible for the purge of magick.

Velesari - Dracas belonging to Luxea Siren.

Venomsnare - Third month of the year. Sign of Sithess.

Vesas Kross - One of the Masters of the Isle of Varnn and member of The Six. Husband to Levelia Kross. Father of Oliver Kross.

Veshra - The bat counterpart to Gajneva.

Villa de Taress - Royal home of the Taress family.

Vina - Deceased cousin of Avari Vishera.

The Western Woods - Expansive forest located in Selnilar.

Widow - Deified woman who is rallying the greatest leaders of Amniven in preparation to recreate the world.

Willem Felloen - Husband of Mollah Felloen.

Wing Regent Isaak Oelar - Placeholder of the throne of Tzapodia.

Witchsleep - Settlement in the Wraiths.

Wolfswake - Second season of the year.

Woodgate Inn - The best lodging in the Wraiths!

Worldbreak - The fourth month of the year. Sign of Nall.

Wraith House - Trees with faces. Used for burying a Ghostwife's husband.

The Wraiths - Nation in Anunaru. Primarily marshes.

Wraithwood - Wood of wraithwood trees.

Wynd - The Stag God. First god born into Amniven.

Xeneda - Oldest civilization in Amniven. Inhabits mostly giants.

Yaani Belaj - One of the nine Tel Ashian soldiers sent to Lor'thanin.

Yaemin - Previous Chieftain of Blackjaw Hollow.

Yaz Magia - Translates in rishjaan to "Sun Chief."

Yeth'lavren - Translates in l'arian to "bring fire."

Ymarana - The Smiling Blackwood constellation.

Yulacai - Horselike creature with a mane and a long snout for bug-hunting.

Yula Montier - Upper class district in Tel Ashir.

Acknowledgments

First, I'd like to thank my parents. I've been difficult — I could even say impossible — but you raised me to never let go of my imagination. When I was in elementary school and didn't want to be friends with people, only trees, elves, and faeries, you let me. Most children aren't lucky enough to say that their parents allowed the same.

Next, my best friend, Kat. You've done more for me than I could ever describe — and I know a *lot* of adjectives. You're the most vulgar, borderline-criminal human being I've ever met, and I'll love you until I no longer know the meaning of the word. Thank you for creating this book with me. I quote you: "If I'm anything, I'm the prenatal vitamin that helped Mooncallers grow."

Then to my preexisting followers. Without you, I never would have learned all that I have. Each one of you has taught me lessons that most aren't fortunate enough to cross in their lifetimes.

I'd also like to thank Losse Lorien, the one who listened to my Mooncallers rants and sat by my side when I first outlined the world of Amniven in her bedroom. Jeff Walden, who met my drunken mind in the middle. Tilly and Theodore Tryon, my favorite couple. Tilly, you were the second person in the world to read the book. I can't thank you enough for being willing. Ted, you created the cover of this book, and that is what gave me the visual I needed to finish it. To Sioux Rose, the woman who has done my astrological readings since before my birth, and then went on to teach me how to self-publish twenty-three years later. To Bree, the best rat-mom in existence. To my four cats, BMO, Xya, Panks, and Courage, my fifth half-cat, Mia, and my two puppies, Prince and Loki.

About the Author

Leda C. Muir was born in 1994 in Santa Barbara, California. Growing up, she chose isolation over socialization. Her best friends were trees in the schoolyard and faeries.

Since she was thirteen, she has been an online entertainer on websites such as YouTube and Instagram — but there was only so much that she could express on those platforms.

At age twenty-three, she became a first-time author. In the beginning, Mooncallers was never meant to be released. It was merely an outlet, but she became attached to Amniven and its inhabitants, and thus decided to show her imaginings to the world.

She doesn't know what is to come, but she plans to continue to walk the paths of Amniven — until the end of all things.